IXIXIKLIS

Jason A. Wyckoff

ISBN: 978-1-960534-34-7 (Paperback)
ISBN: B0FBKR3THF (Ebook)

Written by Jason A. Wyckoff
Edited by Kasey Kubica
Cover art by CoversthatKill.com

Published by Grendel Press LLC
www.grendelpress.com

To my father
and probably David Lynch, too

Chapter I

IN EASIER DAYS, GONE more than a year now, in the good and comfortable times before Eve's mother got sick, Zander would be leaning back in his seat on the reclining sectional at this time of night, reading (if he wasn't drinking) or watching TV (if he was). He might catch sight of the slight, abrupt change in the angle and depth of shadow at the top of the stairs, signaling that Eve, who had doubtless gone up at least a quarter hour earlier, had turned off the hall light on her way back to the bedroom from the bathroom. Sometimes he'd worried—and he knew she'd worried too—that they had settled into domestic bliss far too early in their married life. But after they moved to Eve's hometown (she had somewhat presciently worried about her mother well before the cancer was symptomatic), he had no friends nearby to disrupt his sedentary life, and she was disinclined toward staying up late. Eve was a morning person; she would go for a run or go to the gym as early as 5:30. In those distant days, she would. Worry and frustration took its toll in the interim and she had fallen out of the habit.

Now, her mother was dead, and they were camping. Camping was cheap. And Zander knew, for this trip, as the emphasis was on togetherness, they were supposed to *want* to go to bed at the same time. Not for sex, necessarily—they were sufficiently experienced campers to be past the exoticism of making love on the hard ground in a smell-trapping shell (though each, un-known to the other, was considering the act, as if the unspo-ken acknowledgment of the expiration of the novelty actually resuscitated it, supplying the spark that this reconnection trip so far had lacked). So he was surprised twice in succession, when he surreptitiously checked his phone and saw it was past eleven, as Eve had shown no inclination toward turning in, and again when she suggested they stay up a little while longer.

"Sure," he said, smiling to cover the embarrassment of having been caught checking the time. He leaned forward and grabbed the arms of his chair, green canvas over black metal tubes, and scooted it over to cover the last inch between them. He swung his arm up and over her head to squeeze her opposite shoulder. She slumped over slightly so that her head rested on his bicep. It was too awkward a pose to maintain for long, but he supposed a few minutes time should satisfy the gesture. He wondered if she delayed going to bed because she was nervous. Zander had to admit that he was.

After a minute's silence, she asked the question first, "What are you thinking about?"

Zander replied, "Bears."

Eve jerked her arm up and slugged him in the chest. "Shut up. Don't jinx us."

"We'll be alright," he said. "They all hang out up north by the reservoir."

She lifted her head to cast him a sidelong glance. He tried to stifle a smile. "You're full of shit."

"Eh," he grunted, in lieu of a shrug. "They're running scared. It's almost bow hunting season."

She let her arm drop down around his waist. "Jesus. There's a bow hunting season for bears? I can almost respect that. I mean, if you miss…"

"Next week. It's bow hunting season for elk this week. And I don't think we're gonna see any elk either."

"Well, it would be a wasted opportunity anyway," Eve said. "What with you without your bow."

"Even so. I'll protect you. You know, from elk."

She squirmed a bit, which pulled her hand back across his lap. "Oh yeah? With what?"

Zander swallowed and then lightly coughed. This was what they were here for, wasn't it? He said, "With my trusty staff."

Eyes closed, she raised her mouth to him and then confirmed the presence of the indicated weapon with her hand. They kissed deeply, as neither could remember doing for a long time. And then Eve drew back, giggling.

"Wait, are you offering to fuck an elk for me?"

Zander laughed. "I'll show you what I'm offering, little lady."

Fortunately, they were both of sufficiently high spirits by then that neither the artless pet name nor what was essentially a reaffirmation of Eve's suggestion dissuaded them, and they hurried into the tent.

There was little exploring; out of their clothes, they squeezed together against the intruding coolness of the night air. He kissed her neck as he rolled his hips, staying close as he pushed into her. He soon worried it would be over too quickly and rolled her on top of him. Only then, with the heat of work accumulating, did they open the space between them, and she sat upright. Zander's hands moved in appreciation over her curves, and he felt himself once more seeking release. But he saw that her eyes were closed and she was far away into herself. She was never loud. When she shut her lips tight to hold in the rhythmic peeps that whistled through her nose instead, he knew that she, too, was close, and he tried to delay his orgasm for as long as he could. At the last second, he made a frantic movement, pulling her forward as he pushed her to the side and slid out. She yelped in surprise. The undeniable impulse propelled him forward as he clutched her to him, and he came between their bellies.

Eve, still unsure what the intent of his maneuver was, asked, "What the—" before she felt the sticky warmth on her skin. "Oh." Zander thought there was a hint of disappointment.

"Do you need me to…" he offered, but she kissed him and eased him back, and then put her head on his shoulder, one arm and one leg draped across his body.

They laid there together in something close to contentment. Zander heard Eve lick her lips. She had something she wanted to say, but clearly she was thinking whether or not she should. The thought of what it might be worried him, but he didn't like not knowing either. He lifted a hand and drowsily ran two fingers through her hair.

"I guess this means we're not trying, huh?" she asked.

Zander swallowed. He felt a cold spot in his gut. It was hardly a welcome comment; he would have been happy to put off this conversation. But he knew he should have been expecting it. He should have been, but he was caught off guard anyway, and the only reply he could make was to ask, "Now?"

She pushed off from him, grabbed his T-shirt, and wiped herself down before throwing it at his chest.

"Honey…" he began.

She fixed him with a stare. "I know it's not the best time. I just thought we could talk about it."

He propped himself up on an elbow. "Well, yeah, of course we can talk about it." Feeling guilty for having finished while she hadn't, he tried to hide his burgeoning irritation. "You just surprised me with that. I mean, right after..."

She pulled one of his clean T-shirts over her head. As she grabbed her boots, she said, "It seemed relevant, since that's the way babies are made."

"Come on..." he protested.

She got her feet beneath her, in a crouch, and pushed open the tent flap. She grabbed an LED lantern and turned it on. Zander blinked at the bloom of pale blue light detailing her silhouette and casting her looming shadow above him. "I need to take a piss," she said without looking back.

Zander sighed exasperatedly. He quietly slapped the bedding with the back of his hand and whispered, "Fuck!" hoping she didn't hear.

Now was not a good time to have a kid because they were in a financial hole. The grocery chain that Eve's father had worked for used its employees' pensions to pay off shareholder debts when it went belly-up. His cholesterol and his blood pressure were both too high even before he saw his life savings abruptly disappear. The only thing he could do to improve his wife's financial outlook was to die, which he did less than two years later. A good payout on his life insurance policy kept her comfortable for a decade, but the medical bills quickly sapped her savings when she got sick. Though she died only a year after being diagnosed, she was broke by the end of the eighth month. The last four months of her life depleted her daughter and son-in-law's savings, and worse. Her life insurance policy was no help in recouping their losses—Eve saw no reason her mother should expend any more than she had to—and covered little more than basic funeral expenses.

"Goddammit," Zander said dispiritedly. He put on a shirt, boxers, and sweatpants. He looked at the slumped tent flap. Eve should have been back by now. It wasn't yet cold outside, but the morning low would be down near fifty degrees, and the descent was well under way. He would have to go get her. She must have been angrier at him than he had thought if she was willing to sit and wait around a nearly spent fire in only a T-shirt and boots. He slid his bare feet into his boots and took one last look at the entrance before sighing. He wasn't sure what he was going to say. He was pretty sure he was going to fuck it up, though.

Just before he was about to move, he heard her, just outside, hissing, "Zander! Zander!"

There was fear in her voice. And that made him scared too. His thoughts flared with panic: *If there really was a bear…*

He pushed out into the night. She was standing by the opening, and he had to jostle her to get out from the tent. Her laser-beam stare was directed off into the trees, in line with the front of the tent. He followed her gaze but didn't see anything. "What? What is it?" he whispered.

"Look! There!" She poked hard at the air, but by then, he'd caught sight of the figure.

He supposed he had been looking for a bear or some other dark shape on all fours near to the ground. Instead, he saw a man. Zander estimated him to be between forty and fifty yards away. The man shuffled unhurriedly but steadily down the gentle slope, heading eastward. He appeared to not be paying any mind to his footing, staring forward. He was an older man, paunchy, dressed in slacks and a button-down shirt.

"He's not dressed to be out here," confirmed Eve. "Who is he?"

"He's heading out of the forest, toward town. Looks like he knows where he's going. Maybe this is normal for him," Zander said, though he didn't believe it.

Neither did Eve. "Bullshit. We're more than two miles deep into the forest. He's got dementia. Or he's sleepwalking."

They watched him. He was moving away and made no sign of having seen or heard them. He wasn't moving quickly and would be easy to catch up to, but he would be out of sight soon, especially as the trees grew denser farther down the slope. Each wondered absently if perhaps he shouldn't have been out of sight already. They registered something odd in his appearance but couldn't identify the nature of the anomaly.

"You should go after him," she said.

Zander looked at her. She was squeezing her arms to keep warm, raising his T-shirt to where she was about to expose herself. She clearly could not go after him. The darkened lantern dangled from one hand. He understood; she hadn't wanted to attract his attention, especially dressed as she was.

"I suppose we can't just let him go," he said weakly, hoping that she might suggest otherwise, contented to let the bizarre encounter expire by itself. But of course she did no such thing. He looked at her and tried to grin nonchalantly. "In case I don't come back, never remarry."

Shivering, she returned the smile with an equal lack of conviction, then turned on the lantern and handed it to him.

It would be an easier track if he went sideways to where he first glimpsed the man and then turned after him, but the more direct route was diagonally. With the lantern, he thought he should be able to avoid any missteps—though, he wondered again how the old man was so lucky, with nothing to guide his way. He strained, trying to fix the angle of pursuit, and then switched on the lantern and set out.

Eve watched him go. She desperately wanted to cover her legs, but she was afraid to let him out of her sight. The lantern bobbed and swung; the lines of tree shadows wobbled on the ground. Zander was moving much less fluidly than the old man was. She sensed something very wrong, but still couldn't pinpoint what it was. She glanced upward. A few wispy clouds idled overhead. The moon was high, three-quarters full, bright, but not dominant.

Her attention was drawn earthward by Zander's voice. "Hey, mister!" His voice sounded profanely loud in the quiet forest, yet somehow muted by the very silence upon which it intruded. "Hey, mister!" again, then, "Hey! Hey, buddy!" and a few seconds later, "Hey, bud!" The calls were each slightly farther away, but the tone of each was the same—as if Zander was not any closer to him. The light stopped moving. Had Zander found the man? No; the light moved again for several seconds, farther off. But then it stopped again. Remotely, Eve heard, "Hey, buddy?"—a query, more unsure than a call. The light remained still. Then, in the same spot, it brightened. Zander had turned around. The path the light carved was straighter on its ascent, though it still lurched and weaved. About halfway back it suddenly swung sharply downward and went out. "Ah! Fuck!" Zander cried out.

"Zander?" Eve was alarmed at the degree of fear in her voice. She hadn't realized her nerves were drawn taut. "Zander? Zan? Are you alright?"

He grunted then said, "Yeah." He added grumpily, "Well, no."

She saw him, without the light, pulling himself from tree trunk to tree trunk and cursing. As he drew closer, she could see he was favoring one leg. She hurried down to greet him.

"Careful! Careful!" he warned. "Shit's slipperier than it looks."

She caught up and grabbed one arm to steady him. There was a hole in his sweatpants at the right knee and a slap of blood sticking the cloth to his leg. "Oh, shit," she said by way of condolence, and then asked again, "Are you okay?"

"Smashed the lamp," he replied.

They made it to the level area where their encampment sat. She helped him into one of the chairs. "You don't think it's broken?" she asked hopefully. They weren't too far off trail but getting help to him would be difficult.

"No," he assured her. "Just hurts like a bitch. And it's gonna be sore tomorrow. Goddammit!" He thought about what it might do to their plans.

"Don't worry about that. I'll get the Bactine and crack a cold pack. Or is it cut too deep?"

"It's fine. Just a scrape."

"I need to put some pants on," she said apologetically.

He smiled. "I'll survive until you return. Promise."

"Okay."

She kissed his forehead, beaded with sweat. She retrieved the supplies and hurriedly returned to tend to Zander's injury. He had torn the hole in his sweatpants larger; the flensed portion drooped, barely attached.

"I guess you know this is gonna sting a bit."

"That just means it's doing its *job*!" He yelped the last syllable as the spray hit his knee with a flash of cold.

"So… you couldn't find the old man?"

"As unlikely as it sounds, I lost him."

She peeled the wrapping from a three-inch square adhesive bandage and pressed it to his knee, evoking a hissing wince. She squeezed the cold pack until she heard the inner pack break, and then shook it before putting it next to the bandage. "Hold that there. One more thing." She reached into a webbed pocket at the back of his chair and retrieved a metal flask. She unscrewed the top and handed it to him. "Doctor's orders."

He took a swig. "I kept losing sight of him through the trees. I couldn't seem to get closer. And then I lost sight of him and he was gone. I couldn't find him again. I called out to him—you heard me—but he never replied."

She took the flask from him and took a slug for herself. "He was kind of… easy to see, wasn't he?"

Yes, he thought there was some truth to that, but he didn't know what it was. So he asked, "What do you mean?" He chuckled nervously. "It wasn't like he was *glowing* or anything." He wasn't so sure he was right.

She looked him in the eyes for a second and then took another drink. "There were no shadows on him. I kept thinking about the shadows from the tree trunks from the lantern. But it only just came to me a minute ago. Yeah, there's a moon out, and there aren't too many trees here. But he was… His image was *steady*."

Again, Zander thought she was assessing things correctly but couldn't derive a proper meaning from it. He realized he was striving to explain away her observations, and failing. He took the flask back. He needed to shore up his courage to admit the next part.

"I said I called to him and he didn't reply. That's true. But it was more than that. I stopped a couple of times and listened. Just listened. And I didn't hear *anything*. I had lost track of him by then, but unless he came to a dead stop and was hiding from me—I *guess* that's possible—I should have heard something. If he was still moving, and not breaking a single fucking twig? Uh-uh."

"So we saw a ghost," Eve stated.

Zander shrugged and laughed nervously again. "Sure, I guess." Though unprecedented in his experience, if he accepted that it was not impossible, then it seemed a logical conclusion. But for him to believe, he had to negate the momentousness of it; to incorporate it, he had to cheapen its relevance. He couldn't say yes to it and he knew he'd be a fool to say no. The only possible response left was a half-hearted "So what?"

Eve scowled. She wasn't sure which she found more insulting: that he didn't believe it or that he did and chose to react in such a blasé manner. "Sure, you guess? That's it? Nothing life-changing, nothing profound to you about seeing a ghost in the woods at night?"

He shrugged again, as though trying to dislodge any weight of meaning to the encounter. "I just don't know what to *do* about it."

When her mother began treatment, when there was still a fighting chance against the cancer, Eve would ask him, "What if she doesn't get better?" and he would reply, "We have to let the chemo do its work," which wasn't an answer to the question, and wasn't the response her worry required anyway. If something couldn't be done, then there was no outcome to fret over, only a course to be navigated; but if a decision was made and enacted, then the result needed to be seen to be judged—so how should he know how to feel about the situation when the end was unclear?

Zander knew his casual response was inappropriate, but he tried to reason it through, "Okay, if that is what we saw—a ghost," he added, seeing her look of disapproval, "then, yeah, that's crazy. But it also means there isn't a strange man wandering the woods at night who we either need to worry *about* or we need to worry *for*, and frankly I feel a bit better if I don't have to do either of those things. So, really, I'm trying quite happily to believe it was a ghost we saw because, well, okay, then." And he hated himself for shrugging yet again instead of better articulating his argument.

Eve stifled an annoyed sigh and said, "Okay," believing that was the best statement she was going to get from him on the matter. "What the hell would it be doing out *here*, though?"

"Maybe he's gotta get his steps in," Zander said. "Gotta drop a couple ell-bees of ectoplasm before his big date with the suffragette."

She pursed her lips to quash a smile and shook her head. Despite her anxiety and still-smoldering frustration, she began to relax. The hour of night came upon her suddenly and her yawn was nearly a gasp.

He touched her shoulder. "Come on, night owl. Let's get you to bed."

"There's no way," she said, but almost immediately yawned a second time. "Yeah, okay."

She rose and helped him up. He grimaced at the throb in his knee.

"What if he comes back?" she asked.

"He didn't seem to care about us at all. And, if nothing else, I think we can be pretty sure that's the last ghost we're gonna see this weekend."

CHAPTER 2

DARREN DIETZ LEFT THE gravel road, which grew like a spur from a sharp bend in US Route 219 a half mile back down the hill, and started walking up the dirt drive to the house he shared with his brother. The two-rail metal swinging gate was open. Darren had had it put in to mollify Lyle's paranoia, but it was never closed. Not when Darren was around anyway. But Darren had just spent the last thirty days in Gowanda Correctional facility courtesy of the State of New York. It concerned him that Lyle *hadn't* given free rein to his neurosis with him away so long. He might have worried less if he'd been able to get ahold of Lyle anytime in the last nine days.

He lost the moonlight under the trees, but Darren could find his way blindfolded. Lyle had wanted him to set traps around the property too. Darren had at least been able to convince his brother that they shouldn't put traps on the road they had to drive in and out on all the time. One day, Darren made a show of taking a few bear traps with him out into the back woods. He intended to bring them all back and hide them in a corner of the garage in a tub under a tarp. But, once set to the task, he thought it might be a good idea after all. His biggest worry was that Lyle might venture out to where they were set and accidentally teach himself a painful lesson about how not to deal with anxiety. There wasn't much chance of that, though; Lyle wasn't outdoorsy.

Darren was out of prison and almost home, but he was in a foul mood. His month-long stay in a medium-security lockup had been his own damn fault. Yes, as a man, he felt it was necessary to take no shit from no one, but as a criminal, he knew it was crucial to manage your anger. Getting busted was inevitable. But keeping the film of dirt on his record as thin as possible meant he couldn't add unnecessarily to the inherent jeopardy of his chosen profession, especially when the weight of each sentence was cumulative. When some spit-sheen 'new country' asshole in Salamanca got riled at Darren for watching his girlfriend dance, Darren knew it was a dumb move to bust a bottle over his head. So he didn't. He just cracked the bastard's eye with a monster left hook and watched him drop like a finely coifed rodeo clown with his strings cut. Sitting back on his stool to finish his beer was just showing off.

"Fucking stupid," he muttered, assessing the last, and spat into the brush.

Darren didn't try to make (and skip out on) bail. The last thing he wanted was for somebody to come looking to serve a warrant at his residence. That gave them probable cause. He pleaded no contest to simple assault. Maybe a public defender could have gotten him down to drunk and disorderly (if he could find anyone to testify that the other guy had started it), maybe not. It didn't seem worth bucking against the wheels of justice.

"Pick your fights," he told himself. An owl hooted tacit agreement.

Darren had Lyle come to pick up his truck so it wouldn't be impounded. He expected it to be waiting for him up at the house. He called every few days just to check on things—they couldn't discuss business on the phone, but Darren would be able to tell just from Lyle's tone about his general well-being. He worried about Lyle sampling too much of his own product (which was whatever was available: There were still mounds of OxyContin to be moved; heroin and meth were the big sellers these days), but he never sounded unduly compromised whenever Darren called. Everything seemed fine, and he expected to return home with not much changed in his world. The first time he called and Lyle didn't answer, he didn't think anything of it. The second and third times he got a bit pissed off. By the sixth time, he was getting impatient. The last few days of his sentence dragged. He did his best to avoid conversation and irritation. There was no reason to extend his stay just to express his displeasure with another inmate's opinions.

Lyle wasn't there to pick him up when he walked out the front gate. By that point, Darren wasn't expecting that he would be, but it reinforced his suspicion that something was wrong. The bus from the prison would only take him up to Buffalo—north, the opposite direction he wanted to travel. From there, without any better option, he jumped on a coal train running down the Buffalo and Pittsburgh Railroad. Two inexplicable stops, each in the middle of nowhere, added five hours to the trek.

His right ankle rolled a bit on his next step. He checked his pace and moved to the side of the path to keep from stumbling in a shallow dip. The water dried out much slower in the depression so that the ruts there never evened out. Next, the road began a wide arc right, angling up again, the last stretch leading to the house. He could make out two lights through the trees: the bright white flare of the floodlight (one of a pair, the other long burned out) and dull yellow light from inside the living room. The house was a single-level ranch with a floorplan like two squares laid half over top each other. Extending from the front of the recessed square on the left was a metal carport ending in line with the front of the house.

If Lyle had been unable to come and get Darren for some reason, he *should* still be expecting his brother to come home. But he wouldn't get to hear the familiar sound of the approaching engine. Darren couldn't call from his cell phone. He couldn't remember if it was included in his personal effects when he started his stint, but it sure wasn't among them when he got out. If it was still in the truck, the battery would be run down. There was really nothing to do except approach in the usual way and hope that his brother wasn't too fucked up to remember he was coming home—and didn't have a loaded gun at hand if he was startled by the midnight arrival.

Right before he opened the door, he called out, "Hey, Lyle, it's me! I'm coming in!"

He opened the door and took a step in. Two lamps were lit in the living room; the kitchen, to his left on the other side of the door, was dark. He called again, "Hey, Ly—*fuck!*"

There was a blur of motion in the shadowed kitchen. Darren ducked and caught the brunt of a frying pan on his forearm. Whoever was attacking him didn't have a good hold of the pan and it ricocheted free, carrying on over his head across the room, where it bounced off the far wall and knocked one of the lamps off an end table. The choice of weapon, strength of swing, and high-pitched yelp while making the strike told Darren his attacker was a woman who was not used to such measures, and so, despite his anger, he reacted with an open hand to catch her by the throat rather than a closed fist. He pinned her hard against the refrigerator, knocking the breath out of her—breath she struggled to recover through his crushing grip.

"Dar-ren… Shit… Sor… sor-ry…" she managed to squeak.

The red in his thoughts receded as his eyes adjusted in the dim light. He released her and let her slump to the floor, coughing.

"Jesus fucking Christ, Hannah," Darren said, "What the hell were you thinking?"

His brother's girlfriend sat splay-legged on the floor, one hand on her chest as though assisting the air in and out. She had on gray yoga pants and an old Avenged Sevenfold concert T-shirt Darren recognized as Lyle's, now with the collar and sleeves cut off. "Didn't realize… you were coming home… today."

Darren crossed the living room. He stooped to pick up the frying pan and to right the toppled lamp. "Didn't he tell you?" he asked over his shoulder. He stood and glanced around. The room was clean. Not immaculate; there was a full ashtray and a red plate with thumbprints in white powder on the crate-like coffee table; rumpled blankets pushed into the crevasse where the sofa cushions were sliding forward akimbo; pink Chuck Taylor high-tops sat at the foot of the recliner as though belonging to the unfamiliar cell phone perched on the seat. But otherwise, there was no mess. Darren didn't like to live like an animal, but the two brothers were far from neat freaks. It was a noticeable improvement over the usual.

He watched Hannah struggle to her feet. "What are you doing here anyway?"

She blinked at him while biting her lip. "We… Lyle and I… We were trying something while you were gone."

"Trying something?"

"Domesticity."

"Ah." Darren considered it briefly. The house looked good. Lyle could use a steadying influence. But he didn't know Hannah well enough to know if she would fill that role. She was a better class of person than they were; he had no illusion about that. Her father was an optometrist. Probably wondered where he went wrong with her. Probably tried to let her know she could always come home, no matter what. In Darren's experience, young women like her who got into drugs (and took up with drug dealers) either wised up or got bored and went back to the lives they should have been leading, or the good times got the better of them and they spiraled into addiction, burning bright and flaring out early. If there was a middle-ground option, Darren hadn't seen it.

Tears welled up in her eyes. Brave time was over. "Do you know where Lyle is?"

Darren stood stock still while the chill worked its way over his body. He hadn't expected *her* to ask *him* that. "When was the last time you saw him?"

"Eight days ago," she said, "here, at the house. I was still in bed. We ran out of smokes the night before and he was gonna go into town to get some more."

Darren grunted at the mention of the time frame that matched his. He weighed the cleanliness of the living room again, and looked at her, considering her youth. Despite knowing what Lyle did, she might still be naive enough to trust the authorities wouldn't be prejudiced against them. "Did you report him missing?"

She sputtered, as though worried the wrong response might make him angry.

"Come on, now. Did you?"

"Well, that's the thing…" she said. "The cops had him."

Darren laughed. He felt a measure of relief, though small. "He got himself arrested? What'd he do—steal the cigarettes?" He moved past her and opened the refrigerator door. "*Please* tell me there's beer in here." The interior was almost empty. Condiments lined the door racks, but the shelves held only a couple Styrofoam carryout boxes, a jar of spaghetti sauce, a carton of orange juice, and a single can of Schlitz toward the back. "Goddammit." He sighed. "Well, one's better than none, I suppose."

"Lyle got picked up for murder," Hannah said.

Darren cursed as he jerked upright and hit his head on the freezer door. *"What?"*

"B-but they let him go," Hannah added hurriedly. "I mean, that's what they told me."

"Who told you?"

"Sheriff Pearcey." Hannah scurried to the couch and snatched a pack of cigarettes from the folds of the blankets.

"*Chief* Pearcey," Darren corrected.

"Ut?" Hannah asked as she lit a cigarette.

"Nothing. What happened?"

"Lyle called me from the station. Some woman who worked at the Dollar General got killed. Dora something. I had heard about it but didn't really pay any mind to it."

"So you didn't know her."

"No. I recognized her when I saw her picture on the news, from the store. She was young and short. Glasses. I probably wouldn't have noticed her at all except I watched one of the haggard old bitches who work there lecturing her about stocking peaches face-out or some bullshit, and she was just standing there taking it. I felt sorry for her but thought she was kind of pathetic for putting up with it too. I don't think there's any way Lyle would have known her at all. She definitely didn't seem the sort to be a customer."

"You'd be surprised," Darren said. "But never mind that. Why did the cops pick up Lyle?"

"He called me from the station. He said it was just some 'usual suspects' sort of shit, 'cause murders don't happen here. So you might as well arrest the nearest criminal to see if you can pin it on him. Try to keep people from freaking out about it. Not that it helped much."

She puffed rapidly at her cigarette. She seemed like she had something else to say she hoped he would draw out of her, but Darren was fed up with digressions. "You said that *they* said they let him go."

She nodded. "They kept him all day. I was pissed. But I didn't think there was anything I could do about it. Didn't think lodging a complaint was gonna help Lyle out much. I figured they could only hold him for so long, like forty-eight hours, right? So I'd just wait. In the morning, some lady called and said they were done with his truck, so he could come and pick it up. I said, 'What the hell are you talking about? What about Lyle?' and she was all, 'What the hell are *you* talking about?' So we got in a shouting match that neither one of us understood, as far as I could tell. Finally, Sheriff—uh, *Chief* Pearcey gets on the phone, and he says they impounded Lyle's truck to search for evidence, but they released him the night before, like six o'clock. And since Lyle was pissed they were keeping his truck, the chief had a couple deputies drive him out and drop him at the bottom of Hill Road."

"Officers, not deputies," Darren corrected. "Two of them?"

She shrugged, dislodging ash that fell to the carpet. "Shit, I'm sorry." She extinguished the last half of the cigarette as though to make up for the accident. "Yeah, I guess. That's what he said. I don't know which ones."

Darren took a swig of beer and wiped his forearm across his lip. "Clay and Tuttle. Would've had to have been."

There were only four members of the Adler Borough Police Department, plus Bobbi Sturges, the city clerk, who handled dispatch when she was in. Pearcey had been trying for years to get an appropriation to bring on a fifth employee to the Borough PD, but the city council couldn't be swayed—there wasn't enough crime in Adler to warrant it, they said. Officer Grant Bundy manned the station during off hours—early evenings and Sundays. He would have been at the station by six on a normal day, sure, but Darren never saw Bundy share a cruiser with anyone. He may have been getting on in years but he was still six-foot-six and three hundred pounds of ex-NFL big Black motherfucker. Of course, it would have been all-hands-on-deck for a homicide, rare as they were for the Adler PD. The county sheriff's office would have been called in to assist. So maybe it *was* a couple of deputies who dropped off Lyle. Maybe, but probably not—would they really have been amenable to run Chief Pearcey's errands? So if it *was* two Adler PD officers, it would have been Clay and Tuttle to do it. Darren knew Barkley Clay 'professionally', from the occasional run-in or shakedown. He was the sort of cop who thought taking an oath to preserve the law placed him above it. He was no better than Darren; he took the coin-flip path that put him on the other side, that was all. John Tuttle, on the other hand, was a decent man. Darren both resented and respected him for it—a conflicting view grown from knowing John since childhood.

"Huh. Two officers to drop off one suspect released on his own recognizance," Darren mused.

"So I went down there and I brought his truck back. And I waited. I didn't know what to do. I-I called the station again two days later. All they said was, 'Well, he ain't here' and asked did I want to file a missing persons report."

Darren raised an eyebrow.

"I didn't!" Hannah exclaimed defensively.

"Probably wise." Darren wouldn't have been angry with her if she had. Whether or not she really cared about Lyle, he still wasn't sure; but she cared enough about her situation enough that, for now, it amounted to the same thing. It would have been a reasonable thing to do for someone you were concerned about. But, as always, best to keep the cops as far away as possible. "Still, he *is* missing."

With her elbows tight at her sides, Hannah raised her open hands up to the ceiling, as though trying to make a larger gesture, but suddenly feeling small and restrained. Tears again threatened to spill out."I know! But I… I didn't know what to do!"

"I'm not blaming you for anything." There was no landline at the house. She wouldn't have picked up his calls to Lyle's phone if she didn't know the number, and maybe not even then. He looked at her and understood her posture, how adrift she looked; she seemed to dangle from the ceiling more than stand on the floor. She was in the center of the room, exposed, but cramped into the space she occupied, making her body small, as though waiting for him to pluck her up, carry her to the door, and blow gently. "Look. Lyle brought you in. It's up to him to kick you out. So, don't worry about that," he said.

He meant his reassurance to settle the situation. But an unexpected shift followed. No matter the intention behind the statement, it brought the weight of complication with it: "You, young woman, live here with me, unrelated man." He could see her thinking it: "What will be expected of me?" He saw something fragile in her he wanted to violate, and he felt the draw of taboo and betrayal, and he felt thirty days in prison behind him. He was angry at himself for considering it.

"I'm gonna take this beer and go outside for a bit," he grunted. "Might have a few words with the chief in the morning."

"He—" Hannah began as he turned, but faltered.

Darren stopped. "What?"

"I've been dealing—just a bit. Oxy. Just for grocery money, you know? A teacher at the high school. He moves it through one of the kids." She glanced at him to see if any of that information made him mad.

Darren did the math: Some idiot kid was bound to land himself in trouble at some point, but high schoolers had disposable income just waiting to be tapped, and there were a couple steps of separation for cushioning. He ticked his head up; *go on.*

"Well, I've heard you say—and Lyle said it too—the sheriff—the *chief*—has been kind of falling apart since his wife died."

It was true. The last few times Darren had seen Pearcey, the chief had looked like shit: unshaven, dark circles under the eyes, shirttail falling out. Telltale signs of drinking and depression and apathy toward a diminished world.

"Yeah?"

"So—this is all secondhand, you know, from the teacher? But… last week he had some kind of breakdown. N-not like, in public or anything. But apparently he started going on about how she was back—his wife. Like, he'd seen her ghost or something?"

Darren stood with his hand on the doorknob. He wasn't sure what he was supposed to do with the new information.

"I just told you, so you'd know," Hannah said. "I guess, just to know his mindset."

Darren nodded. "Okay." She was right; any intel on the local PD was worthwhile, no matter how inconsequential—or in this case, odd—it seemed to be. "Alright then. Get some sleep," he commanded. He didn't want to see her again when he came back in. When there was too much to think about, the self-destructive urge to make things simple was at its worst, no matter how bad of a mistake it might lead to.

He stepped outside. Moths and mosquitoes smacked their heads on the floodlight. He moved away from the door and farther into the gloom.

Your brother is dead.

The thought had been with him for a couple of days now. It seemed all the more likely given the new information he had. And yet, that information was scattershot and bewildering. He couldn't make sense of it. Lyle disappeared in daylight just off of 219? They didn't have any real competition in town. Could be some junkie recognized him and didn't take no for an answer trying to get a fix? It didn't fit. Junkies can't cover up crimes. Cops can. But if Tuttle was there...? Was Tuttle there just to give the escort legitimacy? Is *that* why it took two officers to drop off Lyle? And why on the side of the road and not at the house?

"Shit." Darren finished the beer. "Double shit." He whipped the empty can off into the brush. Maybe there was some bourbon in the house somewhere. If there wasn't, then Darren would just have to do without until tomorrow. He never did anything harder than drink anymore—well, a bit of coke and smoke now and again, but none of the crap he sold junkies and meth heads.

Something Hannah said came back to him. He chewed it over. "He had some kind of breakdown, but not, like, in public? What the hell does that mean?" Then he *did* get mad about what Hannah told him earlier (*this is all secondhand*), specifically what she left out. If she got the news from the teacher, then the teacher probably got the news about this not-in-public breakdown from Chief Pearcey's daughter, just starting her senior year. *How ex-*

actly the teacher came to know this information could have a big impact on all their lives.

"Triple shit."

He looked down the dirt lane, expecting Lyle to come sauntering up, some wild cock-and-bull story of where he'd been for the last eight days ready to spill. And why shouldn't he? Darren couldn't internalize it: *Your brother is dead.* Those were just words. Senseless words.

And then he did see movement, off to his right. Someone emerged from beside the house, walking past the carport. It wasn't Lyle, whoever it was. Darren tensed and did an instant mental inventory of available weapons. The answer came back, *None, you dumbass, you're standing in the middle of the patch of dirt you call your driveway and you've got nothing on you but your two good fists.* These he squeezed, drawing the skin tight over his knuckles.

The figure seemed to pay him no mind. He didn't look his way and didn't navigate toward the dirt road, but just walked across the open space toward the woods and brush. And just as he went into them and disappeared from view (without making a sound, Darren noted), he recognized the man. It was Rocky Klute, the gregarious owner of the ice cream shoppe on Market Street he used to go to every time he could steal a little money from his mom's purse.

Rocky Klute, who showed off both rows of pearly whites beneath his bushy moustache every time he smiled, right up until the minute he died of a heart attack on the floor of his store more than a decade past.

Chapter 3

Zander was flat on his back, one elbow up by his ear, wearing his forearm like a French admiral's hat, snoring. Eve turned to face the tent wall and waited. She'd just about allowed herself to become drowsy again when the tan, nylon fabric began to lighten with the arrival of dawn. She slipped free of her sleeping bag. A memory of their duo sleeping bag flashed in her mind. It had been used once and then abandoned to the closet where it remained. They preferred to rough it, leaving their car behind and making camp after a hike far from parking lots and designated campgrounds whenever possible; the duo bag had proved ungainly and cumbersome. Some things were better separate.

She grabbed her clothes and set them on top of her boots, planning to dress outside. Even within the close confines of the tent, she wasn't especially worried about waking Zander. Careful movements and a slow crack of the zipper's teeth were enough to leave him undisturbed. There was much they agreed on regarding values and politics and entertainment, but their body clocks were on permanently different schedules.

She exhaled and hugged herself in the crisp morning air. Emerging from her comfy sleeping bag was one thing, but moving from the immobile, body-warmed climate inside to outside the tent was another thing entirely. Eve would have been happy to release a boisterous "Woot!" in playful protest of the chill, but she constrained herself for Zander's sake. *That* might wake him. She cast a glance in each direction to assert, as expected, there was no one nearby. Then she slipped his T-shirt over her head. She bent to grab her clothes but paused to welcome a mischievous impulse. "Why the hell not?" She spread her arms and threw her head back to flaunt her naked form to the sun. But the September sun was not warming, and after a few seconds, both relieved and a little disappointed not to hear a distant call of appreciation, she hastily put on her clothes.

She popped open the pocket stove and set it on a flat rock. She plopped a white solid fuel tab into the burner, poured a half liter of water into the pot, put the cover back on, and lit the tab with a match. With eight minutes or so to boil, there was no rush to fish out the instant coffee.

She stood and regarded her surroundings. The site they found was flat and round in a natural clearing. Two dry logs had been pulled into the circle and set at an obtuse angle as benches around a crude firepit. The previous tenants had even left a few sticks of deadfall stacked nearby, ready for use. They weren't going to refuse the opportunity at hand. While she and Zander preferred to be off on their own, they weren't so fanatical as to demand virgin territory. They were in the oft-visited Allegheny National Forest in northwestern Pennsylvania. Despite its size, it seemed unlikely to them any genial spot wouldn't have seen campers at one time or another, especially a site not too distant from one of many charming towns that dotted the forest like ornaments on the larger tree (in this case, the town of Adler).

Though 'uniform' would have been an unworthy word to apply to such a wild and beautiful setting, there was nonetheless a sense of consistency to the tableau before Eve. There were few low branches and little spread to any of the trees here; nature had ordered semi-arrayed columns of similar width to buttress the fluttering canopy high overhead. The reason lay in the region's history. The original, slow-growing, shade-loving forest of hemlock and beech had been logged to oblivion for charcoal; the second-growth forest of slender cherry, maple, and birch that Eve now perused dated to no further than a century before when the land had been put aside. Tickles of pink-orange limned the leaves of the sugar maples, the first to melt into the grand cascade which would soon engulf the hills for miles in every direction. And when those leaves made their descent, they would be caught by the multitudinous bowing fans of ferns waiting below. Eve walked to the edge of the clearing and touched the rock-gray bark of a black birch. She ran her finger along the neat, notch–like horizontal lenticels. They reminded her of the perforated rolls of a player piano, and she wondered what secret music the tree might hold.

She walked to the spot where she first saw the old man the night before, guessing where his path had crossed the plane of their campsite. She looked up the hill from where he must have come, and then down to where she guessed he would have to have gone. She didn't see any sign of disturbance near her position. *Perhaps there might be something farther down,* she thought, *where the ground was less level.* She held to her assessment that they had witnessed the supernatural, but she had to look—Zander would likely insist upon it for himself when he woke; it was better to stave off the inspection and disappoint herself, if she could, than to leave it to him. Green feathers brushed her shins as she moved down the slope, glancing back toward camp, again relying on her best guess for distance. She scanned the forest floor for skid marks in the leaf mulch and for broken fern branches, but saw none—from a man walking without concern for his footing. Of course, she knew if she was off by ten or even five feet in either direction, she'd likely miss any trace. And it wasn't like she was a tracker anyway. She always found it dubious how often this expertise—and the conferred title—was doled out to characters on television shows. Sure, there were people like that out there in the world somewhere, but she was an experienced outdoorsman, and she suspected the leap from one to the other was much rarer than the entertainment industry would have people believe.

She experienced some sort of validation on her way back to the camp along the diagonal Zander took. *His* track *could* be seen—nowhere more obviously than the deep rut where he slipped and left speckles of blood on a jutting rock.

She was right: It had been a ghost.

She sat on one of the log benches. Sipping her coffee in the sunlight, it was easy to dismiss the encounter to the realm of anecdote—even believing wholeheartedly her assessment of her experience, it was now a *story*, and in its very nature as such, inherently fictional to some degree. The thought brought out the bitter notes in her drink.

She heard the sheeny rustle of polyester from inside the tent. A minute later, Zander emerged. He took a few cautious steps, looking downward and limping slightly. Eve tensed forward to stand, but he seemed steady enough. He stopped, and then straightened, apparently satisfied. He smiled at her. "Mornin'."

"How's the knee?" she asked.

"Eh." He waggled his leg gingerly. "We'll see how it does with a trip to the privy." He shambled off through the ferns in the opposite direction from where they'd seen the old man.

Watching him return, Eve thought he might be hiding the hobble in his walk. "You sure you're alright?"

"Eh," he said again. "I've got a bit of a hitch in my giddy-up, but I'll make it. No need to change plans."

She offered anyway. "We could drive down to Pittsburgh instead. Go to… to the Carnegie Museum of Natural History, or something. Get some dinner." The last words dribbled out with little resignation. She knew they both were tallying the costs of every new suggestion.

"Nope!" he barked playfully, stopping her before she got to the depressing extravagance of suggesting they get a hotel room. "None of that high-falutin' book-learnin' stuff for us, dollface. We are born to be wild!"

She laughed, snorting in the middle. "My God, what did I marry?"

He grinned placidly—reassuringly, he hoped. "We'll be fine."

She smiled back. "So I won't have to listen to you bitch for hours on end?"

"Oh, I didn't say *that*. But if I can't take another step, I give you leave to, uh, leave me. Buzzards gotta eat too, don'tcha know."

"Sit down," she said, slapping the log as she stood. "Let's get you some coffee." He opted for one of the chairs they'd left set up the night before.

After the five hour drive the previous day, they set out with no particular destination from the campgrounds where they'd parked. They traced a jagged, serpentine line through the forest, enjoying the steady exertion and small challenges. After a four-hour hike, they found their campsite just as either was thinking they should be on the lookout for just such an inviting opportunity. When Eve caught an intermittent cellular signal and used her phone's GPS, they were a bit disappointed to discover their wanderings had taken them closer than expected to the next day's destination; today they were grateful for the serendipity.

There were still five miles between them and Hector Falls, where they would lunch and do a bit of sightseeing, and then another two miles to Sheffield. From there, progress would be much more relaxed, as a wetter-than-usual summer had kept Tionesta Creek navigable by canoe. They would likely have to port their craft over a few shallow spots, but they only had ten miles of drifting to get back to their car. From there, the plan was to drive into Ridgway or Kane for dinner, and then go back into the forest to an official campground. Sunday morning they would go out on the Kinzua Skywalk, built from the leftover supports of a railway bridge traversing a gorge (looking out across the hills and directly down on the wreckage of the remaining supports leftover from the tornado that felled them). One last look, a bit of breakfast, and back in the car, their marriage reinvigorated and secure.

As they broke camp, Eve wasn't so sure. Zander kept up a brave face, but he was noticeably favoring his right leg.

She asked again, "Are you sure you're okay?"

"Sure," he said, just a bit of testiness behind the bravado. To deflect the inquiry, he asked, "Say, you're not still angry at me about last night, are you?"

Her reply was more passive-aggressive than intended: "What do I have to be angry about?" Eve didn't want to start a fight, but, as they finished their work in silence, she wondered if maybe she hadn't precipitously managed to smother one in its infancy. When they were ready to leave, she gave him a peck on the cheek and said, "Love you" to right the tone.

She took the lead and decided to hew to a more northerly path to begin. She figured if Zander wasn't going to be able to make the day's trek, he would know early in the offing, and she thought it would be better to be closer to the forest's edge, and to Adler.

Eve kept from glancing back, accepting the sounds of Zander's movement as reassurance of his ability. He grunted and huffed more than the day before, most noticeably on sloping ground. At one point she stopped to take a sip from her water bottle and nodded at his knee inquiringly as she swallowed.

"Yeah," Zander said optimistically. "It's loosening up. I took a couple ibuprofen before we left. All good. Shouldn't we be turning west?"

"Yeah, 'bout now." Eve didn't mention why she'd led him that way. She looked west and surveyed the swell of the hills farther into the forest. Their path wasn't going to get easier, but Zander seemed up to it—or insisted he was. She cast a last glance eastward and felt a longing she hadn't anticipated. She was surprised to find herself almost hoping they'd forget the whole thing, just head on down to town and catch a lift back to their car. Naturally, she worried for Zander's fitness, but there was something more that made her ache for an alternative, a feeling of trepidation she couldn't account for. But canceling the remainder of their weekend would have meant admitting defeat not just on their trip but also on the reconciliation or team building or whatever ill-defined purpose it was supposed to serve. Clearly, onward and upward—fighting through—was the way to go.

"What's that?" Zander asked.

She looked at him, surprised to see him peering in the same direction she had been. She followed his gaze. Other than a rockier tumble and a few more felled trees, there was little difference from the scene surrounding the campsite they'd just left, so it was not hard to make out the anomaly in question. It was a golden-brown lump that seemed to encase the lowest five feet of a tree trunk. Facets or ridges reflected sunlight. It appeared the greater mass of the object was on the eastern side, away from them.

"I don't know." Eve avoided adding "but I don't like it," another feeling she could not credit.

They stood still, staring. A breeze rustled through the leaves and the shrill piping of a hawk sounded in the distance. It was in the wrong direction, down the slope. They meant to go the other way.

"I gotta go see what that is," Zander said as he started toward the tree.

"Zan—" Eve called after him haltingly. Why shouldn't he go see? She wanted to see too. Wasn't exploration the point of trudging through the wilderness?

He made a quarter turn to lead with his left leg as he descended, making sure of his footing among the ubiquitous ferns. Eve followed at a distance, exercising the same care, and so was still a distance away when he got to the far side of the tree and turned around—and was still a few paces back when he recoiled and cried out.

He looked back at Eve, eyes wide with horror. He raised his hands and shook splayed fingers in warning. "Stop! Don't look!"

But his exclamations drew her forward more quickly. By the time he tried to hold her back, she was already stepping around the tree, and his open hands served only to keep her from tumbling to the ground.

She turned to see what could have so alarmed him. Her first glimpse offered no clue. Before she'd started toward it, she had thought perhaps it was some gargantuan accumulation of resin (though she'd never heard of such a thing and couldn't believe any tree could bleed so much and live). At close range, the notion was unexpectedly reinforced. The material was semi-opaque; it shone with sunlight both reflected and refracted. Given the color, she thought of amber (which, after all, was fossilized tree resin).

Of course, one of the notable aspects of amber was that it could be found occasionally with something trapped inside…

Eve flinched and gasped.

The body appeared desiccated. The skin clung tight from scalp to cheekbone to jaw; the nose was pulled flat; the only creases on the face were the shriveled cheeks scored into parentheses around the howling maw. The eyes were mercifully closed, the eyelids sunken into the sockets. The head was tilted to one side, exposing the deep, black gash across the throat—beneath which the skin was *not* stained by blood. The substance covered the body entirely, several inches deep. It surrounded the tree because it followed the arms bound behind it. The corpse's legs were bent at the knee, causing the body to sag. At full extension, it would have been at least six inches taller. From its appearance, age would have been impossible to determine—as would any guess as to how long the body had been there—if not for the clothes fixed onto the crumpled body.

"Super Bowl Champions," Zander muttered, also noticing the emblem on the T-shirt, darkened but discernable, celebrating the Eagles' victory. Then he chuckled nervously. Eve was startled by the sound and scowled at him quizzically. "I mean, it's gotta be a joke, right?" he explained. "It's a prop. They're getting ready for Halloween."

Eve scanned the remote area to express her disbelief. Zander didn't believe it either, but he wasn't ready to give up on alternative explanations quite yet.

"Or it's just to fuck with people like us," he said, but his voice was already quavering. "I mean, it *can't* be…"

Eve swatted tears from her eyes. "It most definitely fucking *is* a dead body."

"Christ." Zander sighed. "What *happened*? Like, what is this shit?" He touched the brown substance above the corpse's shoulder.

"Jesus, don't touch it!"

"His throat's cut," Zander said in defense.

"Yeah, but the other stuff—a knife didn't do *that* to him!"

"Okay." Zander lowered his hand to his side and surreptitiously wiped his fingers on his pants. "It's solid. Smooth. Room temperature, as it were." He saw her tapping the screen of her smartphone. "Are you getting service out here? I thought…"

"No. One bar, in and out. I'm hoping it's good enough so I can mark our GPS."

"Ah." Zander admired her levelheaded thinking. "We're still closest to Adler, right?" He was anticipating their next move.

"Yeah," she said absently, then, "Got it—I think—yes!" She looked at her screen for a second longer and then turned off her phone. "We should be able to find our way back here. What are you doing?"

Zander was peering closely at the corpse, scanning it up and down. "Just trying to see what I can see. In case they ask us questions. I don't know."

Eve turned her back and stepped away. "I don't want to look at that anymore. I don't know how you can stand to."

"I'm sticking with pretending it's not real." Zander circled the tree, looking at the ground. "Maybe there's a pack nearby. Something to identify him."

"Let's just *go*. We're not detectives. We're *campers*. Leave it to the police."

"Okay." He nodded. "Okay." He caught up with her. "So much for kayaking."

"Jesus, Zander."

He shrugged. "I don't know. I don't know what you say in this kind of situation. What the hell *is* this situation?"

Eve glanced over her shoulder at the yawning, blank-eyed sentinel melted to the tree behind them. "It's just wrong. Eighteen kinds of *wrong*."

Chapter 4

DEATH, DEATH, DEATH. BRITT Pearcey was goddamned sick of it.

She didn't mind picking up her friend Valeria and driving her to her job, not even on a Saturday morning. She was happy to do it. But the idea that she had to do it *to keep her friend safe* was intensely annoying. Was annoying the right word? Yes, yes, it was. Valeria shouldn't have to worry about such things. Britt shouldn't have to worry about such things. Death shouldn't feature so goddamned prominently in the life of high school girls, especially one starting her senior year. And yet it had dominated Britt's life since spring. And that was as irritating as it was tragic.

Death inspired other emotions too: most especially sadness, but along with it, guilt, and now fear. The sadness began in June, the Friday night two weeks before school let out for summer. Her mother died in a car accident driving back late from the Walmart south of St. Marys. The unwitnessed crash spun both mangled vehicles off the county two-lane into the tree-bounded, grassy berm on opposite sides, so it was impossible to tell who had gone left of center. And the Vietnam War vet driving his rusted wrecker was badly concussed, so it was impossible to fault him for wandering away from the scene and not being able to remember what happened. And it took so long to find him that it was impossible to get a good reading on his blood alcohol level, despite him being a notorious drunk. And since it happened outside of his jurisdiction, her father couldn't do anything about it.

Before the accident, Britt had to keep reminding herself that she loved her mother and father; they were her parents, after all. She didn't want to be weird and not love them. She knew arguments were natural, that feeling confined and not understood was natural at her age. So she was sure there must have been something else eluding her conscious thoughts, a deeper connection she told herself might one day make more sense and bloom into a relationship not based on skirmishes and eye-rolling. Yes, she was sad when her mother died. Her world had changed, unbidden. And she felt robbed of their certain, eventual deeper understanding, no matter how unconvinced she had been that it might ever come.

In truth, half of the time she had thought she would move away and just lose touch with them. And so she felt like shit that she didn't feel worse when her mom died. She felt guilty that she felt sorry for herself, instead of just mourning her loss—and thereby acknowledging its importance. Self-hate approximated real sadness in the eyes of everyone else in her life. *They* were convinced of her sincerity, at least. But that just meant that everyone consoled her endlessly, relentlessly compounding her guilt.

It didn't help that her tragedy came on the heels of Valeria's friend's suicide. Keith Belores killed himself with an overdose of prescription pills on the eve of April Fool's Day (ensuring rampant disbelief when the news began to spread at school the next day). Britt knew Keith; Adler High wasn't big enough that she wouldn't. But she wasn't friends with him, and being a year older, she wasn't in the same class with him like Valeria was.

Britt tried to be consoling, but without the close connection, she couldn't help but share the general view of Keith's death as more of a scandal than a tragedy. She knew she wasn't being empathetic enough and wondered if she'd learned detachment from her father. In her house, death wasn't personal, it was a professional matter. Or it had been until that Friday night in June.

Under the circumstances, the last thing she expected was to become good friends with Keith's older sister, Gwen. They were in the same class and had grown up together, but Britt knew Gwen's family was hardcore Baptist Sunday *and* Wednesday night bible study churchgoers, and she didn't think they had much in common. She certainly didn't expect Gwen to smoke her out beneath the bleachers the last week of school—and with *good shit* too. Finding out who she got it from literally staggered Britt.

Britt turned onto the drive leading up to Valeria's father's farmhouse. Valeria was already hurrying toward her, having seen Britt's car approaching. Britt smiled. Valeria was trying to save her the trouble of pulling all the way up, even though she'd have to do so anyway in order to turn around. Britt saw Valeria's father out near his barn slaving over a car engine. The car was probably not his. Even without having any insight into their finances, Britt knew the farm wasn't big enough to be their sole source of income. Valeria started working weekends at Rosa's Pizza in town as soon as she turned sixteen. She wanted to go to Pitt after graduation. Britt hoped she had good grades because two school years part-time and two full-time summers working at Rosa's would barely see her through one semester.

Valeria was breathing hard when she leaped into the passenger's seat. "I'm so sorry," she panted, "I would have had my dad drive me to work, but he's *so* busy right now."

"I told you, doofus, it's not a problem." Britt pulled up the drive as she had intended and turned the car around. Valeria's father flashed a gap-toothed smile and waved a grease-blackened hand. Britt waved back. "Hola, Señor Hernandez," she said, but only Valeria could hear her with the windows shut and the air on.

Valeria laughed. "Shut up."

Britt thought Valeria might be embarrassed by her heritage, or by her father. It couldn't have been easy living in small-town White America, but she thought Valeria had every reason to be proud of both. Her father loved her. It was easy to see. It was simple, the way familial love was supposed to be. "I can get you after work too, if you need me," Britt said.

"Oh, no, I'm sure my dad can get me."

"Seriously, dude." Britt deepened her voice and bobbed her head toward Valeria with each word. "It's no bother."

She was a bit ashamed she hadn't been able to drive Valeria home from school the day before—Friday afternoon seemed a more dangerous time than Saturday morning. That judgment, so strange to make, was related to the 'fear' component of her feelings about death. A young woman who worked at the Dollar General had been killed the week before. The details were sketchy, but apparently, she had been found behind one of the field houses at the park and *something* had been done to her body (this last part was either vague or grotesquely precise depending on the teller). Homicides in Adler were almost unheard of, and when they did occur, were the sort common to any small town, involving squabbling family members or sexual jealousy or drugs. The last possibility had alarmed Britt. Sure, getting high was illegal, but despite being the daughter of the chief of police, she had never thought of it as *criminal* activity. For the first time, she had had to think about the origination point of her recreational fun and the connections between it and her. She was concerned enough that she asked Gwen about it in the most non-accusing or leading way she could think of: "Did she maybe have a drug problem?"

Gwen saw through the clumsy ruse and dismissed the question Britt was not asking. "Connor said it didn't have anything to do with drugs." Gwen didn't say how he might have known that. Britt was pretty sure someone named Dietz controlled the flow of drugs in Adler, based on conversations she'd overheard her father having on the phone. And she still thought of 'Connor' as Mr. McAuley, of course.

The crazy thing was that Tim Neuworth had been arrested for the murder (or questioned in regard to it at least) almost right away. Tim was best friends with Keith Belores, the suicide, brother to Gwen, and, again, part of that little group with Valeria that Britt didn't know too well. Gwen had mentioned to Britt before the arrest that Tim had gotten weirder after Keith killed himself (though she didn't seem to think of Tim as anything more than her brother's weird friend to begin with). Even so, Britt couldn't believe someone she knew at her high school (if only by proxy) could do something so awful. She was relieved when Tim was released the next day. Her father wouldn't tell her why the police had brought Tim in to begin with. The quick release did little to settle anyone's mind at the high school, though. Tim was already an outsider (even to his chosen metalhead subcaste) before the cloud of his best friend's suicide settled over him. The murder accusation cast him as a pariah. His attendant behavior—ambling between classes apparently unconcerned of the stigma, almost contemptuously disengaged with his surroundings—cemented the role. The administration offered repeated assurances that there was no cause for concern and emphasized no one at school was a suspect (as though not naming Tim kept his identity secret). It seemed unlikely that Bill Wollert and his jock friends were concerned about anyone's safety, but they knew a target when they saw one. After Tim's second trip to the nurse's station, the principal called Mrs. Neuworth and recommended Tim be kept home from school "for the time being". Of course, his absence reinforced the idea of his guilt in the minds of gossiping students.

It certainly had been a strange week at school. Unprecedented events might seem especially dramatic to young minds, yet those same minds were more pliable to the change when it occurs. The teens knew murder was bad but they didn't really have a sense of how often people were supposed to die. So when some country-bumpkin-type a few seniors could barely remember from when they were freshmen drowned in the reservoir, only the alarmists conjectured a parallel (pointing out that that his body had not been found, making it only a supposed drowning based on where his truck was discovered).

As far as Britt knew, since Tim's release, there had been no other suspects in the murder (though she had heard the name Dietz again, but nothing seemed to come from that either).

Britt started to ask Valeria a question, but then reconsidered and rephrased it as a statement. "I hope you weren't too nervous walking home yesterday."

"Oh!" Valeria piped. "No. It was just kind of a pain, really, with the bus out."

Valeria's bus had apparently been vandalized *during* the school day and would not be available to make the afternoon run. Rather than cram the affected students onto the other bus (dismissed because of unspecified safety reasons) or have the other bus run its route and then return to school for the rest (dismissed because of similarly vague security concerns), students were told to find other means of transport. It seemed to Britt that the principal was dubious of the decision, and she wondered if he had been instructed by a higher authority. It had crossed her mind that her father had been the one to warn them away from running the second route. She could see no reason why he would do such a thing, but the hunch seemed reinforced by his instructions to her: She was to come home directly after school where he would be waiting—precluding her dropping off Valeria. Then, as soon as she arrived home, he went back to work. The only reason she could think of for his strict directions was that he felt he had cause to worry for her safety. Assuming that was the case, Britt felt all the worse for leaving Valeria to walk home alone. As soon as her father left, she called Valeria and stayed on the phone with her until she got to the farm.

"Yeah. I never heard of that before—just *not* having a bus run." Britt's comment was meant to be leading, though she wasn't sure what response she was expecting. Valeria couldn't have any more information than she did. She supposed that, as Valeria's house was at the end of the route, perhaps her friend might ascribe some sort of racial motivation to the occurrence (even if it was unclear who was to blame).

Valeria just laughed and said, "I know, right?"

Britt didn't know if Valeria would even consider such a thing, but she should've guessed her friend wouldn't speak up about it regardless.

"Do you think Tim will be back in school on Monday?" Britt winced after asking the question. She'd inadvertently connected the fear of a murderer-at-large with Valeria's friend, who had been cleared of suspicion.

"Yeah. I don't know. I think it would be good so that people can start getting past it." Valeria looked down at her fidgety hands. "But it's hard to know what's best for Tim anymore."

"Sorry. I don't mean to be a downer. Guess it's just kind of a shitty way to start a school year."

"Well, yeah, but at least now we have homework!" Valeria said brightly.

Britt shot Valeria a wide-eyed look of disbelief.

Valeria burst into laughter. "Oh my God. You really think that way about me." She raised her hands, palms out. "It's okay. It's my fault, I know. Nerd central here."

Britt smiled. "You're not a nerd. Well, maybe you are, but that's okay."

"Hey! You're not supposed to agree with me!" Valeria leaned forward to look at the street sign. "Why are we turning this way?"

"We're picking up Gwen," Britt replied.

"But Keith—*Gwen's* family lives over on Martindale."

"They *do*, as a matter of fact," Britt said, smiling. "But Gwen came to *my* house for a sleepover last night."

"To *your* house? But…" Valeria stammered. "But… Oh! *Oh!*"

"Now you're getting it," Britt said. She slowed the car and pulled over to the berm.

Valeria didn't recognize the house. It was a nondescript brick cottage with a neat lawn and no flower beds or bushes in front. She thought it seemed small for a family. She couldn't imagine it would be easy to sneak around with your parents inside. Maybe Gwen and the boy who lived there had taken advantage of their absence. They waited in silence for a minute.

"Should you honk the horn, or do you want me to go up?" Valeria asked.

"Definitely *no* to both those options," Britt said. "I'll text her."

Before she began, Valeria said, "Here she is."

The screen door on the side of the house opened. On her way out, Gwen leaned back, presumably to give someone out of sight inside a farewell kiss. Then she strolled down the driveway. Valeria's first thought was that Gwen was not at all rumpled. If those were the same clothes she'd worn the night before—and it struck Valeria that they were not—then she wore them unashamedly. Tall, svelte, and prim in new, cropped blue jeans that flared at her calves and a pearl collar cap blouse, she radiated the sunny confidence of the devout young lady her parents still believed her to be. If she was at all surprised to see Valeria in the car, she showed no sign.

Valeria opened the car door and jumped out. "Here, I'll get in back."

Gwen swatted the suggestion away. "Don't be silly. I'll get in back. Sit, sit." The instruction was delivered with such calm authority that Valeria felt she had no choice but to do as she was told.

As soon as she got in, Gwen slid to the middle and leaned forward. "Hey, bitches," she crooned.

The young women in front responded with a unison singsong, three-syllable, "Hey-ey-ey."

"We're dropping Valeria at work."

"Cool," Gwen said. "And what are you doing *after* work, Valeria?"

Britt stiffened, unsure of the junior's reaction to this part of the conversation. Nevertheless, she prompted, "Tonight's entertainment?"

Gwen patted her clutch. "It's in the bag."

"Wait, don't tell me…" Valeria began, and Britt was afraid she was going to follow with *you guys do drugs?* Instead she asked, "You're not gonna have some random giant house party with a killer on the loose, are you? I mean, I don't watch a lot of scary movies, but that's the plot to *most* of them. And please don't justify it with some 'safety in numbers' crap."

The others laughed. "No, just a casual hang," Gwen said. "A few friends getting together for a few hours to kill the boredom of living in a small town—however temporarily un-boring it's being right now."

"It should be a nice night for a fire," Britt said.

"At *your* house?" Valeria asked. She couldn't imagine the chief of police would look the other way, even if it was only pot that Gwen had in her purse (she hoped it was only pot). Valeria blushed when the others laughed at the suggestion.

"I don't think that would go over too well with Dad," Britt said, agreeing with Valeria's unspoken assessment.

"No," Gwen agreed, "plus, I was over at your house *last* night, *cough cough*, so it has to be somewhere else."

"Somewhere we can have a fire," Britt said.

"At the home of someone with unimpeachable moral standards," added Gwen.

"At *your* house?" Valeria asked again, of the other passenger, and again, the others laughed.

And again, she caught up late, with two little hoots. "Oh. *Oh!*"

CHAPTER 5

B OBBI STURGES LOVED AUTUMN three out of every four years. Usually, this would be one of the three. Currently serving her fifth term as municipal clerk, the general sense in Adler government was that the job was hers as long as she wanted it, but Bobbi never considered her position to be secure. When the partisan pendulum swung, it could cleave off anybody. If the wrong kind of populist angst was churning, voters who didn't know one candidate from the next suddenly took an interest in the down-ballot races and voted party lines. Ten years back, the county coroner found himself out on the street despite a blameless record. If it could happen to him, it could happen to her.

This year, the end of summer inspired trepidation. Summer was tourist season. Though he was hurting over the loss of his wife, Chief Pearcey—Walt to her, but only in private conversation—stayed busy during the summer, never once shirking his duties. And though his cordial attitude toward out-of-towners might have lost some of its earnestness (a good deal of it, if Bobbi was being honest), he maintained his professional demeanor at all times. And he didn't drink *on* the job. His nights were his own. She hoped she was the only one who could see that his nights were hell. His wife's death was a terrible, sudden tragedy. A good man like him didn't deserve such ill fortune. She knew only a good man like him would suffer as he did. He deserved to be comforted and sometimes she wished there was more she could do for him. It didn't seem impossible the time might come. She was only a few years older than him, after all.

She worried. It was one of the things that made her good at her job. Walt had once called her a "levelheaded worrier" because of how she kept her cool whether dealing with the public, or handling the disparate personalities of local government, or relaying information on the radio. Bobbi's desk was in the police station. Most of the time she issued licenses or processed tickets, but she also handled dispatch for the Adler Borough Police Department. Her boys—all four of them—were happy to have her on the team. None of them knew how little she slept. She might have maintained her levelheadedness, but the concern never waned. And she didn't take the chief's "medicine" to calm her nerves.

Bobbi had been prepared to worry over the slowdown brought on by the arrival of autumn. She would never have guessed the effect it would have on the chief when things unexpectedly went the other direction. He had damn near fallen apart over the last week. Murder was terrible business, no doubt about it, but it wasn't the chief's first homicide, or second. Might've been his fifth, she guessed, counting his time as an officer. So she didn't understand why he was so *wrecked* by this one. He was distracted, confused, short with his officers, worse in the mornings than he'd been even his first week back after his wife died. She didn't think he knew Dora Givens. What had been done to the body of the young woman was disturbing, to be sure. It was by no means an ordinary homicide. Still, she would have thought *now* was the time he would respond and be his best—now, when the town needed him most.

In the very near future, he was going to learn there had been another murder. And she worried what that was going to do to him.

The woman said she called as soon as they were in range, about a half mile out from town. That explained the two earlier calls, about fifteen minutes apart. Bobbi heard a woman's voice on the other end, but it kept crumbling into digital static until the call was dropped completely. The third time through, a few details kept cracking off, but she got the general gist of things. The woman and her husband had been hiking in the forest where they'd found a body attached to a tree. She said she had a GPS marker for the site of their grim discovery. Three things flared simultaneously when Bobbi heard the report: worry for the chief, grim anticipation for the tenor of the day, and an old-fashioned fearful shiver. She hissed a string of curses through her teeth that would've shocked even the borough police familiar with her vocabulary.

Then the levelheaded worrier went to work. The first step was to gain control of the flow of information. She told the woman that she and her husband should come directly to the station. Bobbi assured them that if the marker was good, then they wouldn't lose anything by not retracing their steps immediately, and it would be better to coordinate from the station with all available intel. It sounded reasonable, and Bobbi spoke authoritatively, so the woman readily agreed. Bobbi gave them directions and then spoke soothingly at the end, sympathetic of their ordeal.

After she got off the phone, she sat rigidly, staring at the door. Officer Clay was at his desk; she could have said something to him right away. She could have sent him out to retrieve the hikers. She did neither. She wanted to give Walt more time to get to the station on his own. And she wanted him to be the one to take control of the investigation from the outset. She could have called him on the radio, but she didn't want to mention the homicide. Someone somewhere was sure to be listening on a police scanner. She'd known more than one retiree who kept a scanner going in his garage or shop or even set next to his recliner in the living room as a sort of background-noise companion. And if she called just to ask, "What's your 20?", he'd ask why—or he wouldn't, assuming she was just playing mother hen because he was tardy. She almost called him on his cell, but she was afraid he would make that same inference; if so, then calling on his cell would have been all the more embarrassing, because it would have meant she was keeping the call on the down-low because she noticed his *repeated* tardiness, which up to that point, they'd been willfully ignoring.

No, the thing to do was to wait, and hope to high heaven the chief got his shit together before the hikers made it in. She watched the clock at the corner of her monitor. One minute went by. Then another, an eternity later. And another eternity after that.

Bobbi sighed; her plank-like back slumped. Sometimes prayers were answered. Chief Pearcey's Range Rover pulled into the angled spot reserved for him in front of the station house. She sprang up from her seat and came out from behind the counter. Chief Pearcey had worked in the same building for twenty years. Only in the past week had he began trying to push the door in before remembering to pull it open. His annoyance at the digital *bing-bong* doorbell that sounded anytime anyone came in or went out had returned as well, five years after acclimating to it.

Pearcey was six foot and change, with a bit of middle-age spread in the midsection. His head seemed a bit too big for his neck, and his nose seemed a bit too big for his face, but he had coal in his eyes and cool in his voice enough to make the badge almost ornamental (even if neither carried quite the usual power in the last few months). This morning, the furnaces looked damn near spent and the ash spilled in circles underneath. Bobbi noticed and thanked God that at least he wasn't wavering; he might be worn down, but he didn't seem hungover, which was its own small victory.

"Chief—"

"Mornin', Bobbi," he muttered, then called, "Mornin', Bark!"

"Morning, Chief!" came the reply from the rear of the bullpen where Officer Clay's desk sat.

"Chief, I need to talk to you right away."

"Jesus, Bobbi. Can't a man get his coffee first?" He sidled past her to a table set with a silver airpot. A caddy with sugar and Splenda and stir straws sat next to it. Bobbi used to stock creamer in the mini fridge under the table, but nobody ever used it and it always went bad. She squeezed her hands together to subdue her impatience as the chief glanced at the bottom of a mug and frowned. Finally judging it to be satisfactory, he placed it underneath the spigot and depressed the dispenser. He flicked the stack of white sugar packets in consideration.

"Chief!"

"Alright, dammit, Bobbi, what is it?"

"In your office," she insisted, grabbing his elbow.

Chief Pearcey switched his coffee to his left hand to avoid spilling. He yelped, "Whoa!" in complaint, but followed as instructed. As she guided him into his office, Bobbi glanced back to see Officer Clay watching with ill-disguised surreptitiousness. He would have seen when she took the call. He would soon know what it was about and know that she'd waited for the chief to come in before addressing it. So what? Barkley Clay wasn't her concern.

Walt ducked forward as he went around his desk, as though cringing from the sun bleeding through the plastic slats of the blinds. The desk was almost as old as the building and cried out to be covered with loose stacks of paper and carbonless forms, but the notched and over-lacquered top was naked but for a computer and two monitors on an adjustable stand, a telephone, and a framed, upright photo of Christine, Walt's departed wife. A dry-erase board and a hanging wall calendar covered some but not all of the curious clean spots of yellow wall where recently removed filing cabinets once stood. Walt set his coffee down on his desk and then removed his duty belt and dropped it into a drawer. As he settled into his black mesh-backed chair, he asked, "Now, what's this—"

Bobbi interrupted. "I just got off the phone with a couple of hikers. They found another body. Another like Dora Givens."

She didn't know what to expect his reaction to be, but she was nonetheless surprised by how subdued it was. He lifted his head and looked at her, but then his gaze went further, far away into his own head. The tip of his tongue stuck out over his lower lip. "Why didn't you—"

"I j*ust* got off the phone with them," she lied. "They're on their way here. Should be any minute."

"Where's the body?"

"In the forest."

He nodded. Bobbi thought it strange to see something like relief in the motion.

She asked, "Should I contact the county?" meaning the sheriff.

"Fat lot of good they did last time," Walt harrumphed. "No, let's hold off until we hear what our hikers have to say." He stood and straightened his shirt. "Go ahead and bring some coffee and water into the conference room for them, would you?" She nodded and backed out into the main office ahead of him. He called to his officer. "Bark, can you get the camera set up in the conference room for an interview?"

"Sure thing, Chief," Barkley replied, hopping up from his desk. "Where's John?"

"Officer Tuttle had to take his wife her phone," Barkley jeered.

Walt scowled, confused.

"His wife. She left her phone at home. She *had* to have it, apparently."

Walt shook his head. "Ain't he a sweetheart." He turned toward the front of the station. "Well, unless I miss my guess, that's them now."

They stepped to the curb on the far side of the street and looked both ways before crossing. Walt half smirked; he'd let them off without a jaywalking ticket this time, on account of their willing participation in a homicide investigation. They were a good-looking, young-ish couple. She was a couple of inches taller than normal, all in her legs. Her hair was pulled back in a ponytail, no muss, no fuss. He had a short, unsculpted beard, not too hipster. He was trying not to show the limp in his walk, but the sheen of sweat he wiped from his brow betrayed his struggle.

They weren't out of breath, and they'd thought about what they'd say the entire way down the hillside and out through the forest, but as soon as they entered the police station, their minds went blank, as though conditioned to surrendering relievedly when given the opportunity to pass on the responsibility that burdened them. Standing on low-pile carpet under fluorescent light, they stalled, suddenly uncertain.

Walt had seen it before. He welcomed it. Passivity meant co-operation. He stepped forward and extended his hand in greeting. "Hi, I'm Adler Borough Police Chief Walt Pearcey. I take it you're the hikers I was told to expect. Thanks for coming in."

"We found a body in the woods," Zander said in between gasps. It was clear the chief already had had that information conveyed to him, but it was important to say out loud, to acknowledge that this incredible thing, like their ghost, wasn't sequestered to the mystery of the woods and a weekend getaway; it was a real thing in the real world.

"Eve and Zander—Alexander—Nowlan," Eve said, and they each shook Walt's hand in turn.

"Hell of a thing," Walt said. He shook his head. "You must be pretty shook up. You'd better come on in and sit down in the conference room and we can talk it through. Bathroom's there if you need it to wash up or whatever." He gestured, making sure to draw Zander's attention to it.

The front door opened and Officer Tuttle came through, a bright face with an apple chin under dark curls. "Sorry, Chief, I—" he started, stopping short when he saw the unfamiliar couple.

"Officer Clay told me all about it," Walt said. "Officer Tuttle, this is Eve and Zander Nowlan. They found a body out in the woods this morning." He shot the younger man a glance.

John paused, then said, "A body, huh? That's terrible you had to see such a thing."

Walt admired John's perception and restraint. The question John wanted to ask was, "Was it like the other one?" but that could prejudice the interview. Their minds might fill in things they did not see before—things that might not exist at all—if they thought this was one in a series. John was doing what he was supposed to do.

"Why don't you get a portable evidence kit and put it in my Rover. Then get yourself ready for a hike. You and Officer Clay are gonna be going up into the woods while I interview Zander and Eve here."

"Chief?" John asked, unable to check himself. If it *was* another murder like the first, he would have expected the chief to want to lead the investigation. He kicked himself mentally; it was probably completely unrelated—probably not a homicide at all. He'd reacted before he had all the information.

So when the chief growled, "You heard me," he stammered with embarrassment that yes, sir, of course, he'd get right on it.

Barkley stuck his head out from the conference room. "All set, Chief." Walt repeated his instructions for the task before the two junior officers. Barkley readily assented.

Walt led the way into the conference room. The only other holdover furniture in the station matching his desk was the thick, blond wooden table in the conference room. Eve and Zander huddled together on the far side. They accepted the proffered coffee and warmed their hands on the paper cups. Bobbi stood at a corner of the table behind a video camera on a tripod. The center pole was extended too high for her to look through the viewer, but she had her fingers up to the controls on the rear of the camera.

"Chief, do you want me to start?" she asked.

"Just a moment, Bobbi." To Eve: "Bobbi mentioned that you were able to mark the position of the body with the GPS on your phone?"

"Yes. At least I think so," Eve replied. She leaned over the arm of the chair, reached into her pack, and retrieved her phone. "The signal was weak, but it recorded a red pin that seemed to be in the right place, according to where I thought we were." She turned on her phone and toggled through the app. She zoomed in on the area on the screen. "Where the body was," she began, and then turned the phone around and handed it to the chief. "You can see it's in the green area on the screen, just barely."

"In the national forest," Zander added.

"Right. So we weren't sure who we should go to, to report it."

"Who has jurisdiction."

Eve moved her hand over and put it on Zander's wrist to let him know he was interrupting. "Right. But since the signal was so weak, and Adler was closest, we figured it was best to come here."

"You did the right thing," Walt assured them. He prompted, "You came straight down on foot?"

"We were nowhere near our car," Eve said. "We parked at the Minister Creek campgrounds."

Walt nodded. He pointed at Eve's phone. "Of course, the borders indicated here aren't exact, so we won't know whether the body is on forest grounds until we get there, but either way is okay."

Zander asked, "Does the FBI investigate if it's on federal land?"

Walt's answer was memorized and pat. It was one of the most common questions he got from out-of-towners. "The national *parks* fall under the purview of the Department of the Interior, and, yes, sometimes the FBI conducts investigations related to crimes occurring within the parks, in conjunction with the Investigative Services Branch of the National Parks Service. The national *forests* are Department of Agriculture, and if it's necessary, we'll contact the US Forest Service Law Enforcement and Investigations unit. But as your tax dollars at work are stretched pretty thin in that regard, local law enforcement assists, such as our borough PD here. Technically, we're supposed to request permission from the Forest Service to enter and enforce, but there's pretty much a standing okay for us to intercede whenever appropriate. If we're on one side of an invisible line and we see something illegal happening on the other side, we're not going to just stand there with our—uh, twiddling our thumbs." Even the concession to propriety at the end was well rehearsed.

Zander and Eve nodded. Walt knew it was unlikely they could repeat back any of what they'd just heard, but he'd established his credentials to their satisfaction, and that was all that was necessary for the time being.

Walt looked back at the phone screen, prompting Eve to ask—as intended—"Are you gonna need to keep my phone?"

"Huh? Oh, no, no. I'll give it right back to you here in a minute. Matter of fact, if you'll excuse me, I'll give these coordinates to my officers so they can go ahead and get out to the scene."

As he rose, Zander asked, "Don't you need us to go with them?"

Walt shook his head. "Nah." He held up the phone. "This should be all we need. No reason for you to have to see that again. And it looked to me like you might be better taking a load off that bum knee anyway. 'Scuse me just a minute, then we'll get started."

Bobbi studied the drawn, blank faces of the hikers as they waited. They weren't sure whether or not they were in the midst of *an ordeal*; the experience was too new to quantify, and so they weren't sure how to react. They were content to be lead. She had to admit, despite everything and contrary to her fears of his ability in the face of this new crisis, Walt was doing damn fine. He had their confidence, and he had hers, as well.

"You guys okay? Do you need anything else?" she asked.

"No, thank you," he said.

"We're fine," Eve said.

Walt reentered the conference room with a clipboard under one arm. "Okay, they know where to go." He leaned across the table and handed Eve's phone back to her. "Thank you for that." He settled in his chair and turned toward Bobbi. "Why don't you go ahead and fire that up now?" he said, in reference to the video camera.

"Recording," Bobbi said. "Would you like me to take notes?"

"No, I'd better fill in the report myself, by the book." He brought the pen in his hand up to his mouth and froze as though thinking. "Actually, this might take a while—and I apologize for that," he said to Eve and Zander, "but you understand, the seriousness of the crime, we need to make sure we have every detail right."

The couple murmured their assent, though their shoulders slunk with disappointment at the mention of the vague time frame.

Back to Bobbi, Walt continued, "Why don't you go ahead and get back on the front desk in case the boys call in?"

"Sure. Will do." She almost stopped and asked on the way out, *do you want me to call the county sheriff now?* but she held back. He would ask her to do so if that's what he saw fit to do. It was his show, and he was being the reliable, sober, and prudent lawman she always admired. He'd need all those qualities in the coming days. Maybe sooner than later. On top of everything else, it was damn sure not a good sign that Darren Dietz was outside the front door talking with Officer Tuttle.

Chapter 6

I T HAD BEEN A shitty trek back home, his brother was missing, he was pretty sure—no, he was certain—he'd seen a ghost, and he had a new housemate he didn't know whether or not he wanted there, but god*damn* if it didn't make a man feel good to wake up in his own bed after a month in the pokey. There were things he needed to do, conversations that needed to be had, but Darren luxuriated in the Darren-sized indentation in his mattress. His sheets and pillowcases were both musty and musky, needing a wash. He counted this as a positive in Hannah's favor. He appreciated that she'd kept the house neater than the bachelor brothers managed for themselves, but it demonstrated a proper respect for boundaries that she'd kept out of his room. It was a theory anyway. He sat up on the edge of the bed, rubbed his scalp, leaned forward, and pulled out the middle drawer of his bureau. He fumbled blindly beneath a cluster of unfolded underwear. His fingers touched the cool, hash-textured grip of a snub-nose .38, which he left in place. He drew out a roll of bills. He didn't bother counting it. It looked how twenty-five twenties wrapped in a red rubber band was supposed to look. Unlike the gun, the roll of bills was right at the front of the drawer, on display with no fishing required. So the theory seemed validated. But that was just a roll and a popper to grab if he had to jump out the window. That wasn't the Dietz Brothers' stash. He'd check on that in a minute. First, there was railway funk to scrape off in the shower.

He toweled off, tucked a plain black tee into a pair of blue jeans, and went into the kitchen to make coffee. The house was quiet. Hannah was still sleeping. It would take a few weeks for Darren to ease away from his prison-life regulated six a.m. wake up. Even when he was back on civilian time, he would be up before eight most days, no matter how hard he partied the night before. He usually woke up angry, as though he had a tiny rage-powered alarm clock that grew testy with each new dawning day. He wouldn't be mad about anything in particular, and wouldn't bother searching his thoughts to guess what might be pissing him off. Usually, he'd just let the anger simmer for a bit and then settle. He figured it was just who he was. He didn't worry about caging the wild in him; he just tried to keep it in control enough to keep from being caged himself.

As the first drops of coffee fell and sizzled at the bottom of the glass carafe, Darren drifted into the living room. He stood in front of the entertainment center, a basic arrangement of open shelves made from particle board with black veneer, dominated by the fifty-inch television. He felt along the inside of one of the smaller shelving units beside the component shelves in the center, and pressed a button. A wide, shallow panel that appeared to be part of the base the TV sat on popped forward an inch. Darren pulled it out and down, where it clicked into place at a thirty-degree angle. Nestled in charcoal foam were an AR-15 rifle and two Glock 10mm pistols with extra clips for each. He slid the hidden panel back into place. He crossed to a bookcase set against the wall opposite the front door, separating the living room from the sunroom. Lyle had wanted to fill it with books, but Darren thought that was too obviously out of character for the duo. So it took up what it naturally might: yes, a few books, but comics and magazines were more prevalent, with CD and DVD cases more dominant still. Loose mail, menus, a steak knife, a flashlight, a game controller from a system long absent, and other forgotten debris littered the shelves. Darren examined a small, green-white, maple-veined block of onyx carved in relief into a stylized lion or dragon he'd never seen before. He guessed it was Hannah's. He recognized Lyle's phone attached to a cord charging from the wall socket next to the bookshelf. He unplugged the phone. The screen lit up, revealing a keypad. Darren entered 3595 and was granted access. It spelled 'Lyle' backward—his brother was paranoid, but not overly creative. He checked the call history and saw the number of the correctional facility and a few anonymous numbers—customers, probably. He pocketed the phone. He reached up to the top back right corner of the bookcase and released a latch. He slid out a rack, confirmed the presence of a shotgun and two rifles, and secured the hidden rack once more. He almost didn't think it was worth it to move the coffee table and rug beneath it to get into the floorboards to inventory the really illegal guns (unregistered automatic rifles, sawed-off shotgun), but he did this too, just in case he could deduce something about his brother's disappearance if anything was missing—which nothing was. Unless he had his own bedroom gun on him, or the Luger in the panel box in the carport, then he was unarmed when he went missing. Maybe he really didn't ever make it back from the police station.

He pulled out the drawer under the coffee table. It was almost empty, just a quart-size zip lock bag half full of Oxy, a few dime bags of pot ready to sell, and a tin with that much again for personal use. This was the kid's stuff Hannah must have been getting her grocery money from. Darren wasn't worried about that. He went back into the kitchen. Beneath where the counters met was a lazy Susan cabinet. It could go a quarter turn one way or the other to display cans of chili and beans and soup, bottles of olive oil, hot sauce, and ketchup. But again, a special touch was necessary to get to the hidden quarter. Darren flipped the latch and spun the tray column around.

The hidden space was empty. No meth. No heroin. No cash.

"Hmm. Did you make coffee?"

Darren had almost a hundred pounds on the drowsy twenty-year-old in sweatpants and one of his brother's flannel shirts, half buttoned. She didn't constitute a physical threat. But Darren's shock at the sight of the empty cache space and the immediate resulting anger spurned his instincts to force submission. He spun around, stepping to the side. He grabbed her wrist and pulled the arm straight back behind her. She shrieked at the pain and at the sudden downward motion when he swiped her legs out from under her; the sound was cut short when her chest hit the floor. She heard something crack but didn't know if it was a bone breaking or just her head bouncing off the tile. Then she felt the hard weight of his knee in the small of her back. He jerked her head from the floor with his other fist, full of her hair. He made her face the intersecting angle of the cabinets, forcing her gaze upon two empty shelves on the hidden lazy Susan. She felt the half hiss, half growl hot on her ear.

"Where is it?"

She wanted desperately to answer, but she couldn't. She gulped inefficiently.

"Where is it?" he yelled.

He tugged her head back, and that provoked a squeak, a small vocalization she used to find her voice.

"What?" she cried. "Where… What?"

"Right *there*," Darren said, shaking her head to indicate the void. "Right there, I should be looking at cash and hard drugs worth a quarter mil all together. But instead the only thing I see is a problem. A very big problem. So, I'll ask you again: Where… is… my… *shit?*"

He leaned on his knee, increasing the crushing pressure on her back; worse, he torqued her arm just a little bit farther, and the terribly wrong ache in her arm threatening impending trauma sent Hannah into a panic. "I don't know!" she sobbed. "I didn't know there was anything there! Please—I don't know anything about it!"

"Well, if my shit ain't there, then tell me, poodle—where did it get to?"

Hannah bugged out her eyes and stared, looking for something that might give her an idea of what she could say to placate him. All she saw was the corpse of a grape and two strands of hair in a glinting spot of red stickiness under the counter edge where she thought she'd swept clean only the day before.

"I don't know," she said again, tugging her hair at the roots as she tried to shake her head. "I never saw the hard stuff. Only when Lyle was divvying a little up into the foil packets. I never saw the cash. Just what he gave me. I swear. I swear."

To Darren, his next move was obvious: Yell, "Bullshit!" in her ear, smack her head against the tile, and twist the arm until she screamed, just to be sure she was telling the truth. But he was already sure. He was already sure because his brother was his brother. No matter what Lyle felt for the young woman, he'd been partnered with his paranoia for much longer. If he even suspected Hannah had seen the secret hiding place—and of course he would at least suspect—then he would have moved it. And that same refined sense of distrust meant he probably moved it somewhere even Darren would never guess. He'd have to pry every board of the house apart—to begin with.

Darren released Hannah and stood. She rolled onto her back and hugged the strained arm across her chest. She clutched the collar of Lyle's shirt and pulled it up to wipe her eyes and nose. She saw Darren watching her.

"I'm sorry… about his shirt," she said.

Darren exhaled loudly, trying to release his anger. He cursed himself. It wasn't the first time he'd seen a victim apologizing for getting beaten up. Maybe she'd been abused. Or maybe he was her first monster. She pushed herself into a sitting position and leaned against a cabinet door. She started trying to do up the remaining buttons on the rumpled shirt but her trembling hands failed her. Darren could see she wasn't wearing anything underneath.

Scared as she was now, if he was gentle and soothing, he could take her defenselessly; double walloped by the alternating cruelty and kindness, she might see it as him reaching out in reconciliation, or she might be too afraid to deny him and feel grateful that at least he wasn't hurting her any more. It would be awful of him to take advantage of her that way. But not awful enough. The urge to make a bad situation worse surged inside him. *Your brother is dead,* the thought came again to him, cajoling him to do whatever he wanted with this girl. And what he wanted was to tear the shirt off of her. Pin her down on the kitchen floor. His fingers tingled with the feel of her hair and he thought of biting it like a rutting beast would latch onto scruff. As these thoughts careened, the deepest part of him watched as if from outside at a distance, and the spectator was alarmed. Because Darren wasn't going to play nice with the world, not with the pressures of this sour homecoming. He was going to fuck up badly, and soon, if he didn't get his mind right.

"Clean yourself up," he grunted, "I'll get my coffee in town." Then he asked, "What was the name of that teacher you've been selling to?"

Chapter 7

CONNOR MCAULEY KNEW THE pretense of having Gwen leave through the kitchen instead of the front door was ridiculous. He'd been a fool to let her talk him into staying the night. He'd taught teenagers for more than a decade and seen a hundred flimsy cover stories crumble under the lightest scrutiny. Even the best liars among them were incautious. It came with the youthful sense of immortality—or at least *inconsequentiality*. Connor faced real consequences if he was caught. Losing his job was a minimal worry—losing his career was more likely. Prison was a real possibility too. He was careful never to house, carry, or sell too much product at any one time, to minimize physical evidence, with the vain hope that he could plead down if the DA had to rely on the weight of testimony. But, considering that the source of that testimony was high school children, he doubted any prosecutor would be inclined to go easy on him.

He benefited from a certain amount of anonymity in appearance. Mr. Beecher, the English teacher, was the hottie most often swooned over and tittered about. Of course, he was chastely unavailable, as he was recently married to a gorgeous environmental scientist who those same young ladies either hated or admired. Connor looked and played the part of the semi-dour history nerd—with just a dash of John Lennon to up his game. He wore wire-rimmed glasses and his auburn hair was one side-part away from a bowl cut. Each year he picked a senior, preferably already eighteen (for obvious reasons), and preferably college bound (to insure subsequent departure). He never approached them romantically. He "elevated" them to adulthood by complimenting their maturity. He let them know he thought of them as equals by casually mentioning past recreational drug use. He would encourage them to try new things. Then he would tie it all together. It hadn't always gone further into a sexual relationship. Sometimes it didn't work out at all—Beth Whitley freaked out after sharing one joint with him and never looked him in the eye again.

It was a delicate process, from tutelage to friendship to drugs to sex to dealing. If any step faltered, he dropped the pursuit. But more often, he didn't have to push at all, and the final two steps were initiated by the young woman (after a few vague prompts).

He would have never gone after Gwen. He knew her family was devoutly religious. That by itself was by no means a disqualification—he'd lived in small towns all his life, and he knew that the sanctimonious were often the most likely to sin. Assured of forgiveness, they didn't wrestle with temptation; they fell without qualm, believing the muck did not cling. Still, that sort had a tendency toward finger-pointing when it suited them. Why admit fault in oneself when you can identify an exterior source of corruption? But Gwen had fallen into his lap, so to speak. He'd been "passed on to her" by Ada Howard, who'd been a bit of a disappointment as both a lover and a dealer, but who was at least disinterested enough to be discrete.

That meant Connor was involved with Gwen earlier than he'd hoped, and would be bound to her longer than anyone before. He broke his rules for her. He slept with her at age seventeen and had started her selling dime bags by the spring of her junior year.

He was worried when he found out her brother killed himself, thinking she would be entering dangerous emotional territory. Unfortunately, that meant he couldn't just break it off, lest he suffer the brunt of any misdirected hostility. When he saw how she actually dealt with the loss, he wasn't sure whether to be relieved or frightened. He could see she was affected by the suicide, but she wasn't communicative about it. She developed an icy coyness. He didn't like not knowing what she was thinking; he couldn't control her. Worse, he was discovering that he couldn't control himself. He'd never agreed to a sleepover with anyone else.

"Watch out, bucko," he muttered. He pulled the carafe out from beneath the drip and filled his mug. Just as he finished, there was a light tapping on the side door. "Christ, did you forget something?" He pulled back the beige lace curtain covering the window.

No, Gwen had not returned for some forgotten item. Connor recognized the cord-muscled man with the crop cut mullet and goatee in a black T-shirt leaning a forearm on his doorframe. Darren didn't say a word or twitch a muscle. He didn't have to ask to be invited inside. He just waited for the door to open. Connor froze with fear for an instant, but then lurched toward the door to open it; a lick of coffee slopped over the rim of his mug and fell to the floor. As much as he didn't want Darren Dietz in his house, he wanted him leaning against his door even less. At least he hoped that was the equation—not knowing what Darren wanted muddied the math. But it wasn't like he had a choice either way. He opened the door and stepped back.

Darren took a step up and let his body fill the doorframe as he looked around. "Nice place you got here, teach."

Connor took another step back, hoping and dreading Darren would come all the way inside. "Thanks," he murmured.

Darren cocked his head and smiled. "Bit modest for a man with two incomes, though, don't you think?"

Connor swallowed. He knew this day might come. He had to find his courage. Be respectful but be respectable too. He said, "I don't need much."

"Sure. Simple pleasures, right? I suppose you know who I am." Darren's eyes lit up. "Oh, fuck yes! Do you mind?" He picked up a dirty mug next to the sink and scanned the inside.

"Go right ahead," Connor said as Darren poured coffee into the mug.

Darren took a big sip, smiled in appreciation, and then grimaced as he swallowed. "What is this shit, teach?"

"I–it's Sumatran, single source. I like earthy tones." Rather than being embarrassed by the highbrow terms, Connor was proud of himself for not shying away from being who he was.

"Earthy, huh?" Darren took another long sip, swallowed, and frowned again. He set the mug down. "So that's 'earthy.' I admit, I don't have a very refined palate, you know? In prison, you can only get instant. No earthy coffee there, teach."

"Do you—" Connor's courage faltered as he tried to broach their connection. "Is this about—"

Darren put his hands up. "Whoa, now. This isn't really about anything, is it? There's nothing that ties the two of us together. I just wanted to make sure you *understood* that fact."

"Of course." Connor nodded enthusiastically and emphasized, "I understand."

"Well, alright, then!" Darren whooped, slapping Connor on his shoulder. Coffee fell once more, this time on Conner's naked feet, but it seemed to have cooled unusually fast, as though assimilating to the atmosphere of the room. Darren wagged a finger. "I should have known a teacher such as yourself would be *astute*," he said, enunciating the last word. "I wonder, though." He scratched at his goatee. "I wonder just how astute you are. That means perceptive, right?"

Connor shrugged nervously. "It can mean that."

"In this case, let's assume it does mean perceptive. Because perception is very important in our mutual—though entirely separate—line of business. Being *astute* can keep you safe. The details are of great importance. For example: Did you happen to notice when your girlfriend left just a minute ago, she got picked up right out there on the street in front of your house by none other than the daughter of the chief of police?"

Connor shivered. He grasped his coffee mug with both hands in a futile attempt to keep it steady. His mouth was suddenly dry. He was scared of what Darren might do—was he going to punish Connor for his indiscretion? But he was worried too, because he knew Darren was right to point out the problem. Connor *was* being incautious. He rasped, "I didn't know that, no."

"The details…" Darren prompted.

"The details are important," Connor said. Darren stared at him. "The details are of *great* importance." Connor turned and set his coffee down on the counter. "Do you want me to stop selling?"

"Oh, now *that* would be a damn shame, don't you think? Seems to me this two-income setup you've got going is a very good thing, overall. No, I would never tell you what to do, Mr. Teacher. It wouldn't be my place, as we have nothing to do with each other. I just want you to make your own decisions mindful of the consequences, that's all. It's what an *astute* man would do."

Connor tried to read Darren, tried to discern what he wanted, tried to understand what he was supposed to *perceive*. Lacking a better answer, he simply said, "Okay."

Darren smiled. "Alright then." He picked up the mug he'd set down earlier. "One more thing: You know my brother, Lyle?"

"I know who he is. I've never had the pleasure... I've never spoken to him at all."

"Never once, huh? You seen him in the last week, eight days?"

Connor scanned his memory. "I don't know. Yes. But it was probably two weeks ago. I was getting gas. Not since then."

Darren seemed to consider the answer and nodded. He took a sip of coffee and then set the mug back down. As he turned to leave, he said, "You know what, teach? I'm really starting to come around on those earthy tones."

Chapter 8

Roads crisscrossed the Allegheny National Forest. Some were paved and some were little more than dirt tracks, but you were never far from a car-width trail. The best Chief Pearcey could do was to select a dead spot about a mile equidistant from anywhere his officers could drive to. If they took the most direct route from town, then their resultant hike from the roadside would take them over usual brushy forest hills and through one small gulley, nothing too complicated to traverse. When they arrived at the location he'd identified and they didn't find anything there, they would spiral out to continue their search. Walt guessed they might extend their search radius a quarter mile before calling it in. Tuttle would want to go farther. If he searched a full half mile out, he might actually come to the spot where the hikers had discovered the dead body. But Clay would unquestionably protest. Walt hoped Barkley's pessimism proved stronger than John's sense of duty.

Walt estimated that gave him a good ninety minutes to waste with the Eve and Zander Nowlan. He wanted to delay them as long as possible, but still make sure they were out of the station by the time Bobbi heard back from his officers. He took down their personal information, adding any irrelevant question that came to mind that didn't seem *too* invasive: "How long have you lived in your current residence?" "Have you ever visited

Allegheny National Forest in the past?" He took their statements in excruciating detail ("I'm sorry, but you understand, if this is a homicide investigation, we have to make sure to get everything right, or a murderer could go free."). His pen ran out of ink; he had to use the bathroom; he'd better check to see right quick if his officers had reported in yet. When he had Bobbi run their licenses, he left them alone for as long as he thought permissible before they went from feeling antsy to antagonistic. He got his ninety minutes, and wrapped things up right about the point where he thought the husband was going to ask him if *they* were suspects.

Funny thing was, he could tell they were hiding something. Maybe he'd find half an ounce in one of those zippered pockets on their backpacks. Or maybe they'd seen a ghost. He hoped they had.

That meant the process was working, and he would see his wife again.

Walt set his clipboard flat on the conference room table and patted it like a good dog. "I don't want to detain you two any longer here at the station," he said. He stood and extended his hand. As they rose stiffly (Zander pushed up with a grunt) and shook, he said, "Now, I'm going to ask you to hang out here in town for just a bit longer."

Zander and Eve looked at him in surprise.

He put his palms up reassuringly. "Not long. Just in case there's something my officers discover that needs clarification. Couple of hours, tops, then we'll get you on your way." He ushered them out the door and into the bullpen. "Though, you really can't go wrong checking out our little slice of heaven. I know this hasn't been the best introduction, but take a walk and you'll see. I expect you folks are probably pretty hungry for some breakfast by now."

He glanced at the wall clock. "Oops, I guess we're already into lunch territory. Stop down at Rosa's Pizza. They'll treat you right. They got salads and pastas too. I sure do want to thank you both for coming in today and doing your civic duty. I know it's a real inconvenience."

He extended his hand again and they were obliged to shake again. Eve said, "It's no trouble." Framed in terms of being an inconvenience, they had to measure their experience against that of the poor soul they'd discovered in the woods.

Not sure what else to say, Zander replied, "Thank *you*."

As they walked past the reception counter, Walt said, "I'm gonna have Bobbi reserve you a room at the Forest Hotel, just down Main two blocks to your right on your way out, same direction as Rosa's." Zander and Eve blinked with wide-eyed surprise. Walt reassured them, "No, I don't anticipate you'll need to stay overnight—I'm *sure* you won't. But just in case it suits your plans. And it will come out of the borough's discretionary fund, so you don't have to worry about that. It's all paid for." Again, they began to protest, this time out of courtesy. Walt shook his head. "It's not an issue at all. That's what it's there for. Look, I've got your cell numbers in the report, so why don't I just give you a call when we're done with you, okay? Until then, just try to relax and enjoy yourselves as best you can under the circumstances."

That was key, he thought: suggest not just what they should do, but how they should think about it. Make them feel resolved about not having any options. He watched as they exited the station and turned right, as expected, as instructed. Lumbering under their packs, him with a limp—after a big meal, they would more than likely welcome the opportunity for a nap in a comfortable bed.

"I'll call the hotel right away, Chief," Bobbi said. "I think that's a great idea. I hope they stay and have a good time."

"Thanks. Anything from the boys yet?"

"Officer Tuttle called in when they left their vehicle where Stubble Creek Road peters out. But that was more than an hour ago. They must be on scene by now, don't you think?"

Walt shrugged. "Maybe the going is a bit slick with all that rain we've been having. Maybe they're having trouble finding the place."

"Is it… Did they say it was like it was with the Givens girl?"

"Now, Bobbi. Let's not get ahead of ourselves. Gotta keep a level head, right?"

"Of course," Bobbi said. The disposition of the body Eve described to her over the phone, if only briefly, sounded exactly like that of Dora Givens upon discovery of her corpse. But of course, the chief was right. Police had to go by the evidence.

"We don't even have a body yet," Walt went on. "I mean, they seem like a nice couple, but you never know—it *was* in the news, after all. I didn't take them to be the sort to play a prank, but maybe they misconstrued what they think they saw." Steadfast as she was, Bobbi couldn't quite suppress her expression of dubiousness. "My point is: We don't know yet. Let's let John and Barkley do their jobs."

"Of course," Bobbi said again, more sheepishly this time.

"I'd better go grab that report and tape," Walt said.

As he turned to go back to the conference room, Bobbi piped up. "Oh! Chief! There was something else I wanted to tell you. When Officer Tuttle went out front to pack up the Rover, he was approached by Darren Dietz."

Walt froze. He'd been expecting to hear from Darren for more than a week now. He'd almost begun to hope he wouldn't be an issue, at least not until after it was over. Unlike Dora Givens and the body the hikers discovered in the woods, Lyle was unlikely to be found. His body was sequestered away inside a shuttered metal fabricator factory building. On the off chance curious teens went on the property looking for somewhere to party, there was a sort of guard dog to scare them off. Walt had been sure to patrol the site every night around dusk to be prominently visible to dissuade anyone considering the idea. He'd have to lay off that now, so as to *not* be seen by Darren in the vicinity.

"Dietz, huh?"

"Yes. It was only for a minute or so, until Officer Clay went out. I-I didn't think it was *heated*, exactly, but you can never tell with Darren. It could have been anything, I guess…"

"No," Walt said, "I'm sure it had something to do with us bringing in Lyle."

"You don't think… Well, you remember how that girlfriend of Lyle's was saying how he didn't come home even after you released him."

"Lyle's skittish. Drugs have screwed up his brain. He probably ran off or hunkered down somewhere without telling her. Might not have even told Darren. Who knows? I guess if Darren wants to talk to *me*, he'll talk to me." Walt guessed the interview with Tuttle was to confirm that the trustworthy cop was there when Lyle was let out on the side of Route 219. Which was the exact reason Walt sent John and Barkley out there together to drop Lyle off right where he told them to.

Because his mind was centered on Darren, Walt started when the front door flew open. *Bing-bong!* When he saw it wasn't Darren, he wasn't much relieved, because he guessed why the visitor was there. The commotion of her entry was outsized to her frame: Elba Wilson barely conquered five feet before age began to shrink her, but she was wiry and moved quickly with a jerky quarter-goose-step gait. With her mammoth sunglasses, floral blouse, and neon fanny pack, Elba Wilson looked every bit the part of Floridian snowbird late for her flight home.

"It's the end times!" she declared. "Oh, Sheriff, I don't want to believe it to be true, but I know it is. The dead are rising out of the grave and the living are being pulled up to heaven! I saw my dear Earl, gone twenty years, not two days ago. And now, Joe Underwood is gone, taken right out from his home. The Rapture has begun, and the thousand years is near to start. Jesus, take me now! I do not want to be left behind."

Elba stormed past the counter right up to him, crown-to-sternum, to deliver her proclamation. Walt put a hand on her shoulder and steered her toward Bobbi's chair.

"Slow down, now, Mrs. Wilson. Let's-let's not worry about Earl just yet. What is this about Joe Underwood?" In a town of a few thousand souls, Walt couldn't know everybody by name, but Elba was a vocal contributor at town hall meetings, and because he often had to endure further haranguing if she were left unsatisfied, he knew about Joe Underwood, an old friend (maybe) who graduated from recluse to shut-in sometime during Walt's service on the borough PD. She checked on him from time to time (whether he wanted her to or not, Walt didn't know). Not too often, he had hoped. Not so often that it didn't make him a good target for sacrifice, given his near-perfect location and the logistics and time constraints involved.

"Well, he ain't there, is what!" Elba shouted. "Now you know Joe doesn't leave his property. He barely walks outside his house except to spray weed killer on that little patch of earth between the back of his house and the woods. I don't even know why he bothers with *that*, to be honest. I thought I might stop by and check on him, as I do. He said the post office had lost his heart pills last month, and I wanted to make sure it hadn't happened again. I knocked on his door for I don't know how long. And then I went around back, and I knocked on his back door. And I banged on his windows too, even if I couldn't see inside all of them. I saw inside his living room, and his kitchen, and, yes, I could see in his bedroom window too—it's just one story, you know. He wasn't anywhere. No sign of him! And then I thought back to seeing my Earl—sitting on the park bench outside of city hall one minute, gone the next. Well, then I put two and two together and I got four. It's the end times, Sheriff, and what I want to know is, what do you plan to do about it?"

"Mrs. Wilson, I'm sure if it was the end times, we'd see something on the news about it," Walt said.

She scowled at him. "Don't you be glib with me!"

"I'm not being glib," he said. "I was brought up the same way as you: 'No one knows the hour or the day.'" The quotation slackened her scowl. "But it would have to be a world-wide event, wouldn't it? Now, this doesn't mean that I'm not taking seriously what you've told me here today. A shut-in with a heart condition getting on in years—that's someone we need to look in on. I promise you that I, myself, will stop out to check on Joe this afternoon, soon as I get the chance. Will that be alright?"

Elba worked her lips and jaw as though she were more than figuratively chewing it over. "That'll be fine, Sheriff. I'd appreciate that."

"Of course. And it's *Chief* Pearcey."

"Come again?"

"Never mind." He gestured at the door. "May I walk you out, Mrs. Wilson?"

On the sidewalk outside the station, she turned and said, "You promised you'll go out and see him today. God holds us to our promises."

"And if you want to give Him a laugh, tell Him your plans," Walt replied.

"You're being glib again!"

"I'm not, Mrs. Wilson, I promise. Just like I promised to go check on Joe Underwood. Don't you worry."

He watched her march off. Just as he was about to go back inside the station, his attention was drawn by the blare of a horn and the squeal of tires. He turned in time to see a parcel delivery truck knock a man to the blacktop. With a twenty-five mile per hour speed limit on Main Street, even allowing for the imaginary five mile per hour grace rule that most drivers availed themselves, accidents were rare in town. The street was wide with clear visibility; parking spots angled for easy pull-in pointed at curbs on either side of the street, in front of two- and three-story buildings abutting each other in clumps, from red brick to yellow siding to dark wood panels, all with glass storefronts. The spots were never all filled, and traffic was never busy off-season, barring a town festival or home football game. The young man pushing himself up on his elbows clearly had not been paying attention.

As Walt hustled over, the driver of the truck bent at the waist, extending and then retracting his arms, as though unsure whether he should move the injured man. When he saw Walt approaching, he gestured wildly, mouth and eyes wide open. "He walked right out in front of me! I barely tapped him!"

"I saw it," Walt lied. "Not your fault. Let's just see how our boy's doing here."

The young man, in jeans and a cloth windbreaker, was sitting upright now. He seemed familiar to Walt, so he was probably a local, though he didn't know the man's name. He looked stunned but didn't reach for any part of his body to check for injury. He just stared across at the empty sidewalk on the other side. Walt picked up a Pirates ball cap and waved it in front of the man's face to get his attention.

"You alright there?"

The man accepted the cap with both hands absently. "I could have sworn…" he muttered.

Walt touched his shoulder. "You got knocked down. Are you hurt? Do you know where you are?"

The man looked up at Walt, and his faraway stare focused in. He seemed to understand his situation, and moved to get back on his feet. Walt helped him up. "Steady there, buddy. Give it a second."

"I'm sorry," the man said. "I thought I saw… I thought I saw…"

"Nothing broken?"

"No…" The young man cast his gaze back across the street again.

"You weren't playing one of those augmented reality apps on your phone, were you? Those things'll get you in trouble if you're not careful. Whatever it was you were hunting, that's no excuse for walking out in the street without looking both ways first."

"No. No, sir. I'm sorry." Then he and the driver apologized to each other several times, until Walt dispersed the group ("as long as there's no harm done, you'd better both just go ahead and be on your way") to everyone's visible relief.

As he walked back to the station, Walt thought, *It's spreading. They're starting to show up in daytime. Good.*

He cringed at the doorbell when he reentered the station. Bobbi popped up from her seat behind the reception counter.

"Officer Tuttle just radioed in," she said. "He reported he and Officer Clay didn't find anything at the GPS coordinates you provided. So they searched the area up to almost a half mile around in every direction."

Almost, Walt thought.

Bobbi finished, "Still nothing. They're back at the original location. Officer Tuttle wanted to confirm the coordinates with you."

"What I gave him was right off of Mrs. Nowlan's phone. Could be the phone marked the location wrong, but it seemed correct based on how she described their approach to town. If there's nothing there, then there's nothing there. Go ahead and call them back to the station."

"Call them back?"

Walt went into his office. He shouted into the bullpen, "No point in them traipsing around the woods all day, looking in the wrong place." He retrieved his duty belt from his desk and put it on. He grabbed his gray Stetson from its peg and punched it from underneath as he went back into the main room. He told Bobbi, "Real quick, I'm gonna go out to Joe Underwood's place and check on him to set Mrs. Wilson's mind at ease. Could be he really is in a bad way. Guess it's a good idea to look. Soon as I'm done there, I'll catch up with the Nowlans at Rosa's and try to get this straightened out. If need be, I'll take them with me back into the forest. I didn't think that was gonna be necessary, but there you go. Until then…"

"Oh, Walt. You know I know: not a word to anyone." Bobbi was still anxious about the gravity of the situation, but Walt was acting with confidence and making firm decisions, so her sense of trust in him was restored. No matter what else happened, *he* was going to be okay.

"Thanks, Bobbi," he said. "We didn't know today was going to be like this when it started. There's no point in jumping to conclusions as to how it's gonna end."

Walt took the cruiser, and just as he said he would, drove out to Joe Underwood's property. He got out of the car and walked around. Joe's place was a bit secluded, planted just after a turn on a lane that dead-ended only two staggered residences farther on. Still, it wouldn't hurt to be seen if anybody was looking. He didn't bother putting much effort into the pantomime of looking into the house, a small affair with dingy white siding. He was afraid one of the rattling windows would shatter if he rapped too loud. Instead, he went around to the back and made a phone call to Eldon Landry. He needed a favor—one that could not be questioned or refused. Walt needed a car towed, and the bright-red wrecker Eldon got after he killed Walt's wife with the old one was just the thing for the job.

The first time Walt saw Christine—three months after her funeral—was the night before Dora Givens's corpse was discovered.

He was home, alone; Britt was at church for choir rehearsal. He was proud of his daughter for continuing on with her activities at school and church. If anything, she'd taken on more after-school activities with the beginning of her senior year. It occurred to him that she was avoiding being at home as much as possible. He could hardly blame her for not wanting to linger in a house haunted by memories, especially with the poster boy for the dangers of being overcome by grief in residence. Walt had loved his wife. He'd worked in law enforcement long enough to know such sentiment wasn't always present—hell, it might've been rarer than the opposite—but he never thought of his depth of feeling as being *special*. If he'd been asked before she died how he thought he might react to such a tragedy, after he'd been properly indignant at even considering such a possibility, he would have honestly assessed his great sadness at the loss. But he would never have guessed that he would be *devastated* by it. It didn't fit his character. He was supposed to endure. He was supposed to look out for Britt, and to provide for her.

And he did those things—but only barely. He knew he wasn't coping. The loss yawned every morning just as wide as it had that first, when he'd watched the unrepentant sun come up as though nothing had changed irrevocably during the night. What had gone from his life? He trusted Christine and could rely on her for anything, but he'd never thought of her as his rock or anchor. He would never have guessed her presence was so integral to his appraisal of the virtue and purpose of life. He felt the past and the future were negated. He felt his marriage had been tallied, year upon year, the ascending number bearing witness to the accumulating value. The suddenly final, static number nullified the point; it broke the equation, as though if no new addition was possible, then the sum was zero. If they'd grown old together, then one of them—her, probably—could have looked back wistfully on the truth of those years counted together. But she was taken from him in an instant, too soon. Walt no longer knew how to tally the value of life. He knew he was barely hanging on by a thread. And maybe even that slim filament might have proved strong enough—if he hadn't seen her again.

He finished washing the dishes and set them in the rack to dry. With just him and Britt eating, and more often than not eating separately or getting takeout when they were together, they had fallen out of the habit of running the dishwasher. That evening, Britt had tossed a salad and made a pasta bake (she usually made casserole dishes that guaranteed leftovers whenever she cooked). Britt never complained about taking up some of the slack in the housekeeping. Walt helped too, though again, with just the both of them, there often seemed depressingly little that needed doing. Sometimes he would run the sweeper, vacuuming patches of rug no one had trod since the previous sweeping, for the comfort of the noise (he missed talking to his wife, even if those conversations ran a distant second in word count to the often combative chatter between mother and daughter). It seemed as good as any activity to kill some time; he was sure he dropped a crumb from a roll under the dining room table.

He pulled the sweeper out from its narrow nook next to the pantry, levered it up on two wheels, and rolled it from tile to hardwood to the wide rug, gold chrysanthemums on leafy vines over red, bordered by scrollwork and diamonds in midnight blue. He set the sweeper flat and bent to unwind the power cord. Past the partition with its always open French doors, motion in the living room caught his eye.

A chill of fear snapped him upright and rigid. All life knows the frontier. Despite every hope looking beyond it and every prayer for application toward that goal which humanity might muster, the threshold is regarded as assuredly one-way. The phenomenon of return *must be* apprehended as unnatural—as *wrong*. Walt had wished away the circumstance of their separation a hundred times or more since that night in June when his wife was killed, but he knew every earnest entreaty to whoever might be listening was just fury against the irreversible. No matter what he might have wished, the certainty of the situation—no matter how normal she appeared—was that she should *not* be there. And so, at first, he was afraid, stricken like a bird lamenting the moon-swallowed sun.

After the initial flash of instinctive terror, his reasoning mind and his perception attempted rapprochement. He did the sensible thing: He waited for her to disappear. If she couldn't possibly be there, in their soft-lit, earth-toned living room, standing in front of the fireplace, staring at the pictures on the mantle, then it stood to reason that she *wasn't* there. To the best of his knowledge, Walt had never hallucinated before. If he thought about it, yes, the experience would be upsetting. Despair was tricking him in a moment he let his guard down, resurrecting the domestic life of a year past as he performed a very normal, domestic task; that's all.

So why was she still there, why were the details so *sure* (strawberry blonde, shoulder-length curls, faded denim high-waist mom jeans, that oversized cream blouse with the flouncy collar that she loved to relax in)? If she was just a hallucination, why did she behave so strangely when she turned to face him? She appeared to look into the dining room as though she didn't see Walt—but then, she seemed almost startled, as though realizing for the first time *he* was there. And then she looked puzzled, as though she lost sight of him again. She advanced with her elbow bent, one hand raised before her, fingers gently expectant.

At last, Walt moved, daring to ease forward a single step. Christine continued toward him tentatively. She did not appear to see him. When she was right in front of him, she mouthed his name, but no sound came out. Walt noted then that she made no sound as she walked; even in soft-soled shoes, the floorboards should have creaked at least a little. She stopped and flattened her hand perpendicular to the floor, as though against a wall. Her eyes widened, perplexed but delighted. She wasn't touching Walt—not quite. Her palm was an inch from his chest. And yet, he felt a sensation in the imminence of touch, as though his nerves were agitated by a sort of magnetism he'd never before experienced. He leaned forward.

At the instance of contact, the room itself seemed to gasp—Walt felt suddenly *dislocated*. Yet it was Christine who moved. She blinked out of existence before him, but instantly reappeared ascending the stairs to the second floor. The first six steps were visible before the wall obscured the rest. She disappeared from view, going up. Walt leaped across the room. He grabbed the banister post; he heard wood crack and felt something shift as he swung around. He looked up the stairs but his wife wasn't there. He scrambled up clumsily, falling and using his hands like an overexcited child. He got to the top of the stairs and looked down the hall. And then he looked in every room. And then he ran back downstairs, and down into the basement, and outside in a full circuit of the house. But she was gone.

Chapter 9

"Hold it. My hair is falling out."

"You too, huh?" Zander quipped.

"Charming." Eve stopped and shrugged off her pack. She dragged the elastic hair tie down the length of her ponytail. She shook her head, bent forward, and flipped upright again while pulling her hair back. As she resecured the tie, she looked at the lost dog flyer taped to the inside of the shop window. Norris was a brown-and-white collie-shepherd mix with a red collar, very friendly. Please call Ada. Then she noticed the barber on the other side. He stood between the window and two waiting chairs, clad in a classic white short-sleeved barber's jacket buttoned at the neck, with his hands behind his back. She couldn't imagine his hostile grimace incentivized much business.

"Sweeney Todd special, only five bucks," Zander whispered behind her.

Eve glanced back as she re-shouldered her pack. The barber continued to watch them as they continued down the sidewalk. "Yeah, I thought so too," she said. "What's up with that?"

"Should we check in before lunch?" Zander asked.

"Let's plan on the hotel room never happening," Eve said with less conviction than she'd hoped. She felt discombobulated by the day's events and she wanted to reassert her control over her life—though she worried that opportunity was not yet within reach.

He made a small sound that was meant to communicate, *Well, it's free, so why not?* Realizing he'd broached the subject of money talk, and anxious to avoid that still-sore topic, he quickly added, "Lunch, then. Where's this pizza joint?"

"Across the street," Eve said with surprising urgency.

Beyond the quiet two-lane street and near-empty slant parking, Zander saw a florist, a frozen yogurt shop, and an outdoor supply store. "Huh?"

"No, the pizza place is farther up. But *look*."

Zander lowered his gaze from the signs and saw the people. A mother hurriedly ushered her daughter into the sliding door of her minivan while the little girl whined about being pushed. A bearded man with two large, beige plastic bags drooping heavily at his ankles shifted his gaze between mother and daughter and Eve and Zander until the mother climbed into the driver's seat; then he held his gaze on the young out-of-towners.

"Jesus." Zander said. "Maybe they have something against the disabled."

"Is your knee still hurting bad?" Eve asked.

"Yeah, but I like to think my limp is improving with practice." A car horn drew Zander's attention back the way they came. Something was happening down by the station. On the sidewalk between him and there, Zander spotted a muscular, goateed man in a black T-shirt leering at them as he muttered into the cell phone at his ear. He touched Eve on the elbow to urge her forward. "Don't they make money from tourism here?"

"Have you ever read *The Summer People* by Shirley Jackson?"

"Oh, honey, you know I can't read," Zander said.

She patted him on the back. "I'm so lucky I married a hobbled, balding illiterate. The gist of it is, there's this vacation spot where everyone's welcome in-season, but woe to those who tarry o'er-long."

"*Whoa* is right!" Zander hooted. "That's crazy. Terry O'erlong is my porn name."

Eve laughed and squeezed nearer to him. "Thank you," she said.

He stopped, lifted her chin with a finger, and kissed her. "So, last night and this morning—this shit is crazy, right?"

"Yup."

"But whatever the fuck it was we saw, our part in it is over."

"Yup. Except for the nightmares—over. Now we get some 'za."

They crossed to the large, tinted window with Rosa's painted in diagonal gold script. A bar ran along the right side as they entered, facing one row of booths upholstered with red vinyl, which abutted another row on the other side of a divider. Long tables ran the space between there and another row of booths on the left wall. Real walnut paneling both warmed and dimmed the room. Framed prints accented with red and white and green played up *Italian!* in the expected manner. Two laminated sheets with a plan of the booths and tables lay atop a podium near the door.

A shortish Latina bounded over to greet them. "Hi! Welcome to Rosa's. My name is Valeria. Doing some hiking, huh?" She bent and extracted two trifold menus from behind the podium. "Booth okay, or did you want to sit at the bar?"

"Booth is fine," Zander said.

"Great!" Valeria seemed genuinely happy at the choice. She made a mark on one of the laminated sheets with a black crayon, though, given the scarce clientele and absence of other visible servers, Zander wondered if the notation was necessary. "Right this way."

They watched the faces of the people at the only other two occupied tables turn their way as they walked to their seats—one family of four, one young couple. They seemed inquisitive, but too invested in their food to be hostile. "Not too bad in here," Eve murmured, "so far."

Valeria led them to a booth in the middle of the row on the far side of the divider from the bar. "This okay?"

Zander got stuck in the consideration, caught with slap-happy thoughts about asking how difficult it would be to change the crayon mark at the greeter's station, so it was Eve who smiled and said, "This is fine."

They unburdened and sat. Zander glanced at one of the televisions hung in the corners over the bar.

"Please tell me you're not going to watch football the whole time," Eve chastised him.

"Huh? No." Zander shook his head as though confused. "I just thought—I don't know why I thought there would be something on the news about it already. I mean, that would be impossible. It's just weird to think that *we* know about it and the world doesn't."

"No. I get it," Eve said.

A middle-aged woman with billowing waves of black hair emerged from the kitchen and went behind the bar. She looked at Eve and Zander with eyes harrowed by sleeplessness and muttered to herself. Then she slid an empty pint glass off the bar and dropped it into the bleach-water sink and muttered again at the thirty-five-cent tip, disparaging a two-syllable name that Eve didn't catch.

Zander scanned the menu. "Sea scallops? That seems a bit optimistic."

Eve spotted the item and noted the price. "Get whatever you want," she said. "I might just get a salad." She hadn't meant to use a tone, but she knew Zander caught it. She cursed herself mentally. Too often, they still circled each other on eggshells.

"That's all you want?" Zander asked meekly. It was the wrong thing to ask, but he had to ask *something*. Every uncomfortable second obscured the exit.

Eve shrugged noncommittally.

"I wonder if they serve pizza here," Zander said.

"I think they might," Eve replied, and she felt the lightening tug as they pulled each other up.

"Breath death?" Zander asked, in reference to their favorite combination of salty and pungent toppings: banana peppers, green olives, and anchovies.

"Sure," Eve said, closing her menu. The decision to share a food few else could appreciate engendered a delicate détente.

Valeria returned. They placed their drink order, both opting for beer, almost sighing with relief to even say the word. Zander picked his up immediately upon delivery and took a large swallow as Eve ordered the pizza.

They sat for a minute in grateful silence. Then Eve leaned forward and said, "The bartender keeps wiping down the same spot on the bar. All the better to stare at us."

Zander shifted his eyes but didn't turn to see. "Maybe we're celebrities and don't know it. Too incognito even for ourselves. They were nice enough at the station."

"Yeah," Eve said. She chewed her bottom lip, thinking. "Although..."

Zander raised an eyebrow. "Seriously?"

Eve cocked her head and asked, "Did you think it was kind of strange that the chief didn't start recording the interview until after he handed me my phone back?"

"No, not really," Zander said. "Why would that be a problem?"

"I don't know…" Eve considered. "But it's almost like he deliberately left it undocumented that I gave him that marked coordinate."

Zander chuckled. "That's a bit of a leap. And why would he?"

Their attention was drawn to the front of the building, as a gray pickup truck pulled into a spot faster than warranted and then stopped abruptly, causing the body to lurch over the tires and rock back again. A svelte, young woman with tangled, mouse-brown hair clad in a pale gray sweatshirt and jeans climbed out hurriedly and burst into the restaurant. Then she incongruously took a quick breath and slouched, affecting a relaxed posture. She scanned the dining room as though picking out an empty table, though her gaze seemed to stop on the one occupied by Zander and Eve. Before Valeria could make her way to the front to greet her, the woman strode forward and slinked into the booth on the other side of the partition from them. Eve noticed the intensity of the bartender's expression at the newcomer's arrival. The young woman glanced over at Eve, as though noticing her for the first time.

"Howdy," she said, and the word sounded unnatural. She pulled a lock of hair down over her forehead to cover a bruise.

Eve blazed her eyes across at Zander, who pursed his lips to keep from laughing. "Howdy," he tossed back. He and Eve looked around the room at nothing, suddenly self-conscious about saying anything.

Valeria stopped by the other booth. "Oh, hey—Hannah, is it?" she asked. This time it was Zander who noticed the fire in the bartender's eyes at the mention of the young woman's name.

"Yeah," Hannah said. "Do I know you?"

Valeria shook her head and tittered nervously. "No, I just remember you from school. I was a freshman when you were a senior."

"Oh," Hannah grunted. She didn't like being reminded of school.

"Well, i-it's good to see you again—I guess!" Valeria laughed again. "Um, what can I get you?"

Hannah seemed perplexed at the question momentarily, as though she'd forgotten she was in a restaurant. "Coke," she said, and then amended her choice to something more grown-up. "No, *coffee.*"

Zander and Eve were relieved they did not have to wait long under the ocular scrutiny of the bartender and Hannah's presumed eavesdropping before their pizza arrived. Both thought, by the size of it, that they'd be forced to make a decision about leftovers before long, but the pizza was good, and they were more ravenous then they'd imagined. If Hannah was listening, then the only intel she was picking up from them were bleats of approval and appreciation. The one thing they were certain she was doing was using her hair to try to hide her face from the bartender.

They collapsed into their seat with the last bites they could manage still in their mouths and fresh beers set down in front of them when the bartender suddenly crashed into the neighboring booth, facing Hannah.

"You're Lyle's girl, ain't you?" she hissed.

Hannah had not wanted to come to Rosa's, but Darren had said it might have something to do with Lyle. She didn't want to come to Rosa's because of Lita The kids in high school were already calling her Psycho Lita before Hannah enrolled. It was only after she got involved with Lyle that she found out Lita really had had a breakdown, and what precipitated it: She had lost her beloved son when he turned three years old. The poor kid choked to death on a balloon. How did Lyle know that? Because his brother Darren had been the father.

"You are, ain't you?" Lita pressed.

"Yeah." She hadn't meant to, but she surprised herself by asking, "Have you seen him? Have you seen Lyle?"

Lita ignored the question. "You see Darren, you tell him…" Breath shuddered in and out as her shoulders trembled. "You tell him Tommy's back."

Hannah failed to hide her shock at Lita mentioning her son's name.

"And no, I ain't *psycho*," Lita stressed. "I know what you young bitches say about me. You tell Darren that I have seen Tommy and that I have seen him for *true*."

"Um, Lita?" Valeria stood beside the booth, tentatively reaching toward her shoulder.

Lita drew back and spat at Valeria, "Don't you touch me! I don't even know why I hired one of your lazy type."

Valeria folded her hands over her chest, embarrassed but worried.

Lita pushed out of the booth, leaned back toward Hannah to say, "You tell him. You tell him to come see his boy." Then she marched past Valeria and slammed open the doors to the kitchen.

"Jesus," Hannah muttered.

"She should not have said that to you," Eve said to Valeria.

"I'm okay," Valeria replied. She'd learned not to say, "it's okay," because whenever someone followed up by pointing out it's really wasn't, it sounded like an accusation of cowardice on her part for not fighting back. "I'm sorry about that," she said to both tables.

"Don't take this the wrong way," Zander prefaced, "but is this town insane?"

Valeria let out another little, nervous laugh. "Everyone is just on edge. Maybe I really shouldn't say, but I wouldn't want you to think we're usually like this. It's because this local girl… She got killed."

Eve and Zander locked eyes. Hannah noticed.

"I heard about that," Hannah said. "Wasn't there something weird about the body?"

Hannah watched as Eve reached to grab Zander's hand.

"There's a bunch of rumors, that's all," Valeria said, trying to downplay it. "I mean some of them are pretty crazy, like she was zipped up in a cocoon…" She laughed; Zander squeezed Eve's hand. "They even arrested a kid I know from the high school."

"What?" Hannah asked, her attention suddenly drawn back to Valeria. "Who was that?"

"Oh, it was…" She stopped herself from saying "my friend." "It was this kid, Tim Neuworth." Then added hastily, "But they let him out again, like, right away! I mean, there's no way Tim could've hurt anybody, I'm *sure.*"

"They just let him go right away, huh?" Hannah asked, thinking about Lyle's experience.

"Yeah—I mean, they kept him overnight, but, like, they always do that, right?"

"Sure," Hannah said. "That's what they do."

"Hey, Valeria!"

None of them had even noticed three young men come in. They were all six feet tall or better, athletic in build, hair buzzed short.

"So, I hear we're coming over to your place tonight," Bill Wollert said.

Stammering, Valeria reluctantly drifted toward the boys.

Hannah squeezed up against the divider. Darren had wanted her to follow them because there was something going on at the police station and he wanted to know if it had anything to do with Lyle. She took a wild stab. "I wouldn't worry about it," she said, "I'm sure Sheriff—uh, Chief Pearcey has got everything under control."

Eve became animated. "We were hiking in the forest…"

"Eve," Zander cautioned.

"No! I think it's weird that he didn't mention there'd been another one."

"Another one!" Hannah exclaimed.

"Maybe he didn't want to, I don't know, prejudice the investigation or something," Zander said.

"Prejudice the investigation! What the fuck does that even mean?"

Zander huddled down. "Well, if people weren't looking at us before, they sure as shit are now," he grumbled.

Eve saw that the other patrons were staring, and she felt a flash of anger. On top of everything else she'd been through in the last fifteen hours or so, the crumbling support from her significant other was just too much.

She turned to Hannah. "We were hiking in the forest and we found a dead body. The body was desiccated, and it was encased in something like amber. There. Now you know everything we know. And now, if you'll excuse us, *if* my husband is willing,

I think we're going to get the fuck out of your charming little town."

Chapter 10

D ARREN FELT LIKE HE might have stripped the gear on the seat adjustment mechanism trying to make room for his legs in Hannah's electric blue two-door compact coupe. The car was older than she was. It made more noise than he cared for, like an old man hocking morning phlegm on a loop, especially as the whole point of driving her little crumble-at-a-touch import was to be inconspicuous. Chief Pearcey knew Darren's truck; he had no doubt of that. But he regretted his choice. At least if he'd been spotted trailing the chief in his own ride, he'd only have to suffer the failure of being caught, and not have to worry about compounding it with the humiliation of driving the automotive equivalent of a petulant basset hound.

He didn't know why he felt compelled to take Hannah's car. He didn't trust his instincts—they'd let him down countless times before—but he didn't see any point in wasting time arguing with himself when there was plenty enough arguing to be done with the rest of the world. He was sure that something stank to high heaven in his brother's disappearance, and as much as he was determined to find out what—and as much as his core nature bristled against subtlety in such endeavors—operating with a low profile seemed a smart idea at the onset. The conviction wore thinner with every minute spent cursing at his cramping calves and at the sickly growl of the engine. It didn't help his mood that, so far, he'd learned little of use.

The teacher had been no help. He'd been pretty much as expected—a nice predator, manipulating his way into teenagers' panties by telling them how grown up they were. Darren gave him the alpha bully-to-bookworm scare with his quick visit just to say, "I know where you live." There was no point in going further at that point, especially if he really was moving product effectively. But Darren made a mental note to beat the shit out of him sometime in the future. That carelessness of being one step removed from the chief's daughter was a matter of concern. And there was a hint of condescension in how the teacher talked to him that he wanted to address.

When he approached Tuttle outside of the police station, he could just about watch the process as his old friend froze the muscles in his face and tacked the skin down tight. John might not give anything away, but he betrayed the effort right from the start.

"Darren," John acknowledged. "Haven't seen you around for a bit."

"Been vacationing in New York," Darren replied. "They got some great state-sponsored resorts up there."

"Uh-huh," John said. He shut the back lift of the rover and leaned against it, arms crossed.

"While I was gone, it seems my brother went missing."

John kicked at the blacktop. "Still hasn't shown up?"

"No," Darren said, then added more sternly, "He hasn't."

"We had him in," he said. "But the next day we dropped him…"

"Off of 219," Darren finished. "Yeah. You and Clay together. So I hear." They stood in silence. Darren didn't lean to the side or shift his eyes to look at the Rover when he said, "Looks like you're planning to do a bit of hiking. That have anything to do with Lyle?"

John swallowed, then said, "I can't comment on police business."

Darren nodded. "Ongoing investigations and such?"

"Something like that." The voice was sharper. Officer Clay had joined the conversation. His left hand was on his hip. His right hand was on the grip of his holstered sidearm.

"Well, if it isn't Deputy Clay," Darren said with mock cordiality.

Barkley knew that to take the bait and correct him with "*Officer Clay*" would be to let him get the upper hand. "What did you do with that brother of yours?" He asked.

Darren chuckled. "You'll get whiplash turning around that fast," he said. "Seems to me you're the ones who lost him."

From there, things went nowhere. He and Clay did a bit of posturing until Darren got bored. By the time Clay had interrupted, he already knew that something was going on—but he also knew that the officers weren't entirely sure themselves what it was. If it did have something to do with Lyle, Darren would have to wait to find out. He wouldn't be able to follow them into the forest; there was no way he would be able to avoid detection. They'd just stop and tell him to get lost, or maybe just go ahead and arrest him for impeding an investigation or whatever other bullshit they could come up with. He decided to move out of sight of the station front and keep watch for a while longer. Chief Pearcey was the real target—though, between Tuttle's ignorance and Clay's antipathy, Darren thought it unlikely the chief would be any more forthcoming about his brother's disappearance. At best, Darren might provoke a subconscious facial tic or other tell. It wouldn't provide any new information, but it would strengthen his suspicion that the cops were involved somehow, and he wasn't barking up the wrong tree.

Then the backpacking strangers came out of the station. They had the look of out-of-towners, and seemed frazzled, besides. They turned right out of the building. Darren started following them. It was an obvious thread: officers going up into the woods, anxious hikers coming out of the station—the cops may not know anything (yet), but they were likely responding to whatever this couple came in to report, and he wanted to know what that might be. Even so, Darren's instincts—those damn things, again—were telling him to stay on Chief Pearcey. Darren called up Hannah. The phone rang several times. For a second, he almost thought she had had the good sense to pack up and go after he'd thrown her on the kitchen floor earlier. She answered excitedly, "Hello? Lyle?"

Darren winced. "No. Lyle's phone." He hadn't mentioned to her he'd taken it. "Listen. I need you to get in my truck and come into town, right away."

"Wha-? Why?"

"No time for questions, okay? We might find out something about my brother." He said it encouragingly, like they were aligned together on the same team, like he was really relying on her to come through for him.

"Sure. Yeah. Yeah, of course." The last two words were almost bright. He'd been forgiven without apologizing by letting her back into his good graces. "Where should I meet you?" Her voice sounded different, she was already outside.

"We're not meeting up. There's this couple—shit!" A car horn sounded behind him and the man turned and looked right at him. Darren exhaled exasperatedly, but then remembered that he wouldn't be the one following them anyway, so it didn't matter if he was spotted. "There's this couple of hikers in town. I need you to follow them and find out anything you can about why they went to the police station this morning. You got that?"

"Um…okay, I guess I can." He recognized the sound of his truck door slamming shut.

"Looks like they're going into Rosa's. Fucking of course they're going to Rosa's. Get on down here quick as you can, okay? I've got something else I need to do."

He hung up as she said something over the sound of the truck engine starting.

Five minutes later, Chief Pearcey left the station in the cruiser parked out front, and Darren followed as discretely as he could in Hannah's bright blue gargle-rod. The first part was easy, going down Main and turning onto State (which became 219 outside of city limits). But then the cruiser turned right onto a side street. Darren saw an opportunity and whipped the sports coupe into a formless gravel lot on the other side of the "T". He turned the car around just in time to see the cruiser turn left, two short-side blocks down at the end of the lane. He spurred the car out of the lot and straight across two lanes to the side street, slipping neatly through the flow of traffic. Darren knew the town well. He was pretty sure the road Pearcey took dead-ended after a right turn. Darren turned left down the first street slotted between 219 and the other.

This road dead-ended as well, only four large plots farther, in a tight, circular turnaround. Darren eased in, wheeled the car around to face back down the road, and turned off the engine. He got out of the car. As he gently pressed the door shut, he heard Pearcey's voice—but not close by, and not addressing him.

Woods surrounded the turnaround. Darren had parked in deep shadow. He scanned in the direction of Pearcey's voice. He crept from tree to tree; fortunately, the canopy was thick enough to discourage much undergrowth, and he was able to make his way stealthily. He ducked behind a thick trunk as the chief strolled into view, pacing in someone's backyard. He was giving instructions to someone over the phone and finished his call by demanding the task be done right away. The chief pocketed his phone and marched around the side of the house to where he'd parked the cruiser. Darren tingled, trying to decide what to do. The cruiser's engine started up. If he wanted to keep after Pearcey, he'd have to bolt back through the woods to Hannah's car. But he stayed rooted to the spot.

Why did the chief stop to make a call from someone's backyard? Why *this* backyard?

Darren watched the cruiser drive off and then emerged into the sunlight. He didn't know the house. It didn't look like much. Dingy, wide, white siding on a square box. There was one wood-slat recliner painted dark green set next to a giant spindle used as a table on a small deck rimmed with half-empty planters. This was the house of a single person who did just enough to relax and probably couldn't hurt anyone if they tried. So again: Why here?

No one had come out to talk to the chief. Probably no one was home.

Darren sighed. "You ready to add on a B and E?" he asked himself. Coming off a month-long stay that he'd earned by not hewing to his fragile rule of avoiding unnecessary crime, it seemed like a bad idea. But if it had to do with Lyle... and if Lyle was really dead...

He resolved himself to the idea that several possible felonies lay in his near future. He'd have to change his focus to avoiding incarceration by doing crime the *right* way. And the right way, once the decision had been made, was to go hard, hit quick, and clean up before anyone knew the deed was even done.

On the ground beside one corner of the deck was a grill with a moldering cover. The disintegrating black vinyl shed tufts of felt lining as Darren pulled it free. He swatted off spiders as he folded it over. He climbed the deck and pressed the cover against the glass pane nearest the doorknob. He loved doors like this with a nine-square of small panels on top. Less effort, less mess, less noise. He punched the cover and heard the muted tinkle of shattered glass dropping to the floor. He tapped around the edge of the frame to knock free any jutting shards and then tossed the grill cover into the grass. He waited for a minute in case there actually was someone at home, or in case one of the neighbors called out to another, "Did you hear that?" Birds chirped, but that was all. He slipped his hand through the door, unlatched the lock, and pushed his way inside.

Fragments of glass scraped across linoleum with a yellow tile pattern. Dark-stained cupboards soaked up the meager light let in through angled venetian blinds. Narrow counters beneath were cluttered with cereal boxes, sealed tins, and appliances spanning decades of manufacture. The air reeked of plug-in air freshener. Kitchen and dining area were undivided. Darren had to navigate around an oval table elongated with its leaf but set with only two chairs on the same side. Cascading stacks of magazines encroached on a nearly finished jigsaw puzzle of a snowy country road. The living room opened to his left: couch and recliner, navy blue shag carpeting, four remote controls on a coffee table pocked by blond water rings. To his right was a narrow hallway with four doors.

Darren flinched and staggered backward, his hands raised in defense. Adrenaline flared in his nerves, drawing the heat from his suddenly numb teeth and knuckles. The hall was dim, but his eyes weren't playing tricks. There was a large shape at the end, between the two shut doors. It was the size of a man, but not quite the shape of one—too wide.

Darren kept his pose, spring-loaded, ready to move. He held his breath and listened. There was something terribly wrong about the shape at the end of the hallway, but whatever it was, it wasn't moving. There was a pair of light switches on the wall around the corner from the kitchen. Darren leaned forward and stretched, watching. He flipped the lights on.

A recessed bulb in the middle of the hallway ceiling came on. It was a low-wattage bulb, sufficient only to light the way. Darren squinted. His mind worked to unscramble the jumble. There were two dark spots where he expected eyes to be, but the rest of the head was too wide, the shoulders too slim. He stepped closer and a second shot of fire pushed through his veins. The two dark spots weren't eyes. They were the blood-rimmed wounds where nails had been driven through the ankles and into the walls. The body was inverted; the wrists were tied with cords, one to each doorknob. It was the body of a flabby older man, though the skin hung loose in folded crags beneath the strange, brownish epoxy resin, which Darren guessed must have been poured over him. He couldn't see the man's face. The head had been tipped back; the forehead touched the floor. A wide, deep gash ran from ear to ear across the exposed neck. But there was no dried, dark spread on the carpet—not even beneath the hardened brown gum. Darren guessed he must have been the lonely bachelor of residence. Whoever it was, it wasn't Lyle. Lyle was an inch taller than Darren and bore his nervous nature in a rail-thin physique. Still, it was not an encouraging scene. The appearance of a murder victim in Adler—especially in this strange disposition—raised a thousand questions, and none of the answers were likely to lead to Darren finding his brother alive.

He nearly jumped out of his skin at the vibration in his pocket. He unleashed a string of profanities as he dug Lyle's phone out and answered the call.

"Jesus!" he hissed. "Yeah?"

"Darren? Sorry, you… you wanted me to call," Hannah stammered.

"S'okay." He exhaled. "You able to find out anything?"

"I talked to them—those hikers? Holy shit, Darren, they said they found a *body* in the woods." She was talking low. She was in public somewhere, still at Rosa's or outside on the sidewalk. "Which is wild, right—after that girl from the Dollar General? But there was something else."

Darren waited. She seemed to need prompting, like whatever she needed to say came with a "hey, you asked for it" afterward. "What?"

"They said—this is the woman's exact word—she said the body was desiccated. And that it was like it was stuck in amber."

Darren looked back at the body at the end of the hall. Darkness roiled inside him. When he wasn't sure what to do, he usually resorted with violence, that tried-and-true constant companion in lockstep with his shadow.

"But it wasn't Lyle!" Hannah added hurriedly. "When they got up to leave, I showed them a picture of Lyle to see if it was him. They said they couldn't say for sure because of how messed up the body was, but they said they didn't think it was tall enough for it to be him. And they said the body was wearing a Eagles jersey! And you know Lyle would never…"

Darren chuckled and finished the thought. "Lyle wouldn't be caught dead in a Eagles jersey." It was gallows humor, but it held some comfort.

"And, uh, Darren…"

He sighed. "Yeah?"

"I mean, it's crazy, but I have to tell you. Lita came over to my table and she insisted I tell you that… that she's seen Tommy. That she's seen your guys' son." When Darren didn't say anything, she said, "I'm sorry, I promised I would tell you. I know you probably don't wanna hear it."

Darren didn't like being reminded about his son. He was never much of a father, and he suspected he'd never get any better at it, but he resented that he'd never have the chance to surprise himself somewhere down the line. If he'd been told a week ago Lita had seen Tommy, he would've just cursed her for being a nutjob, or a manipulative bitch. But she wasn't the only one seeing ghosts. And now this other shit. These murders. There was no way they weren't connected.

He could hear the worry in Hannah's silence. "Okay," he said. "Don't worry about it."

"Oh! And one more thing."

Christ, Darren thought.

"So, Lyle got pulled in for that dollar store chick's murder, right? But he wasn't the only one. The server at Rosa's told me this other guy got pulled in too, but was released just like Lyle."

Just like Lyle.

"Who was it?"

"Some kid named Tim Neuworth."

"Who the fuck is he?"

"I don't know. Some high school kid. I guess his sister is friends with the chief's daughter."

Darren was going to have to break something soon. There was no getting around it.

"Stay with them," he growled. "I want to know—"

Hannah interrupted him. "Oh, they went into the Forest Hotel just a minute ago. I followed them."

Darren grunted acknowledgment. "Okay. Let me know if they go anywhere." He hung up before she could reply. He went down to the end of the hall and froze. There was someone in the living room. A bald, older man sagged into his jowls, sank into the sofa in boxers and a dirty undershirt. He paid no attention to Darren. He seemed to be glumly watching television, though the apparatus was powered off. Darren would have sworn the man on the couch was the same entombed in hard tar at the end of the hallway if only the inverted body wasn't so—what was it?—*desiccated*.

"It's wild what he can do."

The voice was the nasally tenor of a ripening adolescent. He stood in the kitchen, just inside the door. Brown roots bled into his shitty black dye job; the greasy tips blended into the sagging collar of his Slipknot T-shirt. Dark-rimmed eyes drooped at the corners and his top lip was fixed into a gummy snarl. It was the kind of face that asked you to punch it on principle. And even if it turned out he was more wiry than willowy underneath his ill-fitting clothes, Darren could still drop his hundred-fifty-pound ass with one shot. But the punk kid stood there almost casually slack. He pulled his hand from behind his back and showed why he wasn't concerned. The luster of recent whetting shone on the keen edge of the ten-inch hunting knife.

The thing could cut, for sure. And there was ample evidence on hand that the kid could use it. But his cool confidence was a failing; he relied on the weapon to give him strength, while Darren knew that his strength was no more secure than his grip on the handle.

"He told me someone was here." Tim tapped the flat of the blade against his crown. "He can talk to me *direct*."

Oh great, Darren thought, *A fucking nutjob. He'd have to be, wouldn't he?*

"Hearing voices?" Darren hissed.

"Hearing *truth*," Tim spat. "Hearing *power*."

"Who the hell are you?"

"I'm Tim fucking Neuworth." He paused to sniff, as though to give Darren time to acknowledge the revelation. "So what?"

Darren bared his fangs in a smile. "That's funny. I was just about to come looking for you." He saw a fracture in Tim's confidence, a twitch beneath the lethargic non-expression. "Did you kill my brother?"

Tim's grip tightened. His eyes flashed to the side in response to an unbidden consideration of how quickly he could go back out the door. He shifted his weight and squared his feet. Darren tracked every movement.

"Why don't you ask him?" Tim said.

He lunged forward, using his empty arm as a buckler, cocking the other elbow back to attack. It was a good move. If he had led with the knife, Darren would have just pivoted and grabbed the wrist. This way, he wouldn't be able to get to the knife without the knife getting to him. Instead, Darren went on defense; he dropped back and sideways to the "off" side, kicking his right shin into the side of Tim's knee. Tim cried out as he fell, trying to swing the blade around. But the uncontrolled arc swept skyward and Darren grabbed the back of his shirt to make sure he landed facing away. From there, he had a safe vantage to grab the wrist and bring it down to the floor. Tim tried to push himself up, but Darren barred his forearm across the bony shoulders. Then he leaned the heel of his palm onto the back of Tim's hand until he heard a pop and the kid screamed. Pain reflectively caused Tim to try to free his trapped fingers; Darren eased the pressure enough to let him and then snatched the knife away. He spun the handle like it had been his for years, snapped his fingers closed, and slammed the point into the floor with the blade facing Tim's nose an inch away. Tim yelped and tried to jerk backward, but Darren held his head in place. Then he eased it forward a fraction.

He leaned close and breathed in Tim's ear. "Now that I have your attention, let's try this again: Did you kill my brother?" He pushed Tim farther forward, to a half inch from edge to bridge.

Tim's sense of self-preservation kept him from replying, "Yes." Instead, he stammered, "T-the important t-thing is that he d-doesn't have to *stay* dead." His face bounced on the linoleum and he cried out.

Darren seethed. "No fucking games."

"No! No, I swear!" Tim cried. He sniffed; snot and tears trickled sideways over his face. He tasted blood inside his cheek and spritzed the floor in front of his mouth. "I can take you to him. You'll see! If you see, you'll understand. You'll *believe.*"

Any other day, Darren would have figured Tim's pleading as a delay tactic, spewing the first desperate, dumb bullshit that came into his head. Any other day, Darren would have pushed forward and seen just how keen the kid kept his blade. But suddenly, his sleepy little hometown of native hicks and seasonal hipsters went and got itself a plague of ghosts.

Darren snatched the blade out from the floor and sprang to his feet. He grabbed Tim's hair and hauled him up. Tim whined, reaching for his head. Darren pushed him into the table to keep him from collapsing when he let go. A stack of magazines tumbled over the side.

"Don't go thinking it's your lucky day," Darren said. "I'll still probably kill you before it's over."

CHAPTER II

BOBBI LOOKED UP AS the Range Rover pulled into the station. She blinked, wondering who was in the passenger's seat before she remembered Walt had switched out with John and Barkley. After they got out, body language communicated their attitudes regarding their fruitless search: Barkley took off his hat, stretched his arms out to the side, and smiled up at the sky, chewing on a toothpick. He was content to have wasted his time. John was looking at the sidewalk and not seeing it, roaming miles away in his own troubled thoughts. As John moved to the door, Barkley called him back, jutting a thumb toward the back of the rover. John made a dismissive gesture meaning, "leave it." He clearly thought it was too soon to stow the mobile evidence kit and hiking gear. Barkley shrugged, happy to leave the task until later. The electronic chime sounded *bing-bong*, generically cheery and incongruous with the cloud John brought with him.

"Chief out on a call?" John asked.

"Well, that was a whole lot of nothing!" Barkley proclaimed. "Nice enough day for it if you're the outdoorsy type. Better with beer, though." He dropped down onto a vinyl-cushioned metal chair in the waiting area, and then spun and lay back across the row.

"Elba Wilson came by and asked the chief to look in on a shut-in for her," Bobbi said. To Barkley, "Get your dirty boots off of those seats!" Back to John, "After that, he was going to catch up with that couple, the Nowlans. I guess since you couldn't find the body, he was going to take them back out to the scene."

"The scene!" scoffed Barkley. "That ought to suit our John here just fine. He was all fired up to keep on rooting through the forest like a skunk after a wasp's nest." Barkley covered his face with his hat. "Have fun."

"Seems pretty damn serious to me, Bark," John said testily. "We got a murderer on the loose."

Barkley pulled his hat off and sat up. "We did the work on Dora Givens. State, county, local: all-hands-on-deck. We aren't any more to blame than anybody else that we got nothin' to go on."

"But now—!"

"*Now* we got another body," Barkley interrupted. "Except we *don't*. So *now* Chief goes and picks up our witnesses and we go back out to the woods. We got nothin' to investigate until we got somethin' to investigate. That break it down enough for ya, John?"

John didn't want to broach the subject, but he felt he had an obligation to do so. For better or worse, this was the team, him and Bark and Bobbi and Grant and the chief. "You don't think…" He swallowed and started again. "You can't tell me you haven't been a bit concerned since Christine died."

The statement let the air out of the room. Bobbi felt a sense of relief that John had said it out loud, that she wasn't alone in her anxiety. But the sound of it scared her too, as though naming the problem brought too much attention to it for it to go away on its own. She spoke first, quietly. "Hush about that, John. Of course we're concerned…"

"Concerned?" Barkley cocked his head and raised his eyebrows. "Concerned about the chief or about his police work, Johnny-boy?"

John took in a long breath through his nose. "We took an oath…"

Barkley burst out laughing and then jumped to his feet. "You're just the best, you know that, Johnny? Just the goddamn best!"

"Boys…" Bobbi cautioned.

Barkley pointed to the chief's office. "You think that chair is comfortable? It ain't. You just keep that in mind before you make plans to sit in it, Johnny!" He put his hat on to let it be known he wasn't going to listen to any protest. Leaning in to glare at John, he said, "Bobbi, I'm going out." Then he stomped to the door and threw it open. *Bing-bong!* "So much for my beautiful day!"

John sighed. "Bobbi, you can tell me to go to hell too, if you want. I'm just worried, is all."

Bobbi crossed around behind the service desk and sat. She pulled on the countertop to wheel her chair in close. She picked up a stack of papers and tapped the pile flush. "You know I think the world of Walt," she said flatly.

T HE WOMAN AT CHECK-IN for the Forest Hotel—the proprietor, they both thought—with a pyramid of hard, blonde curls propped on broad shoulders, made an effort at small-town congeniality, but her nervous frittering betrayed her unease.

"Well, at least we know *why* now," Zander said, flopping backward onto the king-size bed. "Small town done got itself a murder." He ran his hand over the billowy, white comforter. "Jesus, that's appreciated."

Eve glanced to see what he meant as she sat on one of the chairs at the small, round table by the window.

Zander lifted his head and explained, "Just getting off my feet." He propped himself up on his elbows. "Look, I didn't mean to be argumentative earlier."

"We were arguing?" Eve challenged.

"I'm sorry if I didn't back you up," he said, then caught himself. *Leave off the "if," dumbass. You should know better by now.* "I'm sorry I didn't back you up," he corrected. "I don't know what to make of this. I don't. I wish this wasn't our weekend."

Eve leaned back. She sighed as she looked out the crack in the curtains to the unbusy street beyond. "You really don't think there's anything suspicious about the sheriff not telling us about the other murder?"

Zander sat up, pulling his ankle in gingerly, feeling the creak in his swollen knee. "I would say weird, I guess. And I don't know what I mean by that." He cocked his head in the direction of the front entrance. "God knows what *she* thought with the cops setting us up here. No wonder she kept dropping the keys."

Eve smirked. She got up from the chair and crossed to sit on the edge of the bed. She grasped his hand and squeezed. "I think we should leave. They have our statements. What else are we supposed to do?"

Zander twirled his loose hand. "And give up all this? How often do you get the chance to watch oddly chaste porn on Cinemax after dark and charge it to the cops?"

"Maybe next murder, darling," Eve said. "I'll call a cab and we'll go get the car. And just to be… whatever… *civically minded*, we'll leave our packs here, come back and get them, and check to see the sheriff didn't call before we take off. Alright?"

"Okay if I jump in the shower first? We can at least take advantage of *that*."

"Well, I definitely wouldn't jump, in your condition. But go ahead. I'll make the call."

Even if he wasn't washing off the full funk of a camping weekend, the shower was a welcome relief. It seemed much longer ago they'd parked their car and began yesterday's hike into the forest, where the only expected spectacle came courtesy of Mother Nature. Eve was right; there was no attraction to the mystery, not now. Zander might obsess over the events that marred their little reconciliation getaway from the security of his own home, but he felt no compulsion to divine any deeper meaning until then.

When he emerged from the bathroom with a towel wrapped around his waist, Zander was surprised to see Eve hurriedly removing items from her pack and setting them on the table.

"What are you doing?" he asked.

"I have to go," she said. "The cab will be here in a minute."

"Well, wait for me!" Zander lumbered to grab his pack beside the bed.

"No," Eve said. "I have to go by myself, right now. Apparently, there's, like, exactly one taxi in the county. And he can take me now, but it has to be right now, and he can only take me to where 666 splits off of 948. Then he's got another appointment already scheduled."

"What? That's crazy!" Zander tore the towel off and sat on the bed. They had studied a map of the area conscientiously when they planned their trip. He recalled the picture. "That's almost to

Sheffield. That's gotta be ten miles to the campsite!" He tore into his pack, snatching his clothes out in clumps.

"It's ten miles from Sheffield on the *creek*," Eve corrected. "Look." She moved her phone into his line of sight. If I get off at 666 and go straight across, it's more like five miles."

"Five?" Zander asked dubiously. "And alone?"

Eve shrugged. "Half of it's on the road. It's daytime. Hour and a half, tops. Maybe close to two. Plus driving, I'm back here in less than three hours, easy. And I've got my phone."

"With spotty service! I can't let you go by yourself." He struggled to pull on a pair of cargo shorts.

"Babe, I say this with love: You're no good to me right now. I know you think I'm being all wiggy paranoid about this." She held up a hand as he started to object. "If I am, then great. No worries. But it feels like this is our get-out moment, and I think we should take it."

"Are you sure this isn't our don't-split-up moment? Sure as shit seems more like *that* to me. The whole point of this fubar situation is that there's a killer on the loose, remember?"

Eve looked him in the eyes and hesitated for just a moment. Then she glanced at her phone and said, "He's here. I have to go." She leaned in and kissed him. "If I have to, I'll run. And you know I can fucking run."

She left him sputtering with his shorts half on as she hustled out of their room. She hurried out the front of the hotel, ignoring the proprietor's wide-eyed stare. When she got to the sidewalk, she acted as though she saw the cab waiting up the street and started west.

"**F**UCKING DUMBASS." GWEN HUNG up her phone and slapped it down on her lap.

"What's up?" asked Britt. She stopped at the sign, signaled, and turned onto Martindale Avenue.

Gwen slurped the dregs of her mochaccino through a red straw until air gurgled in the bottom of the large plastic cup. She examined the ice as she shook it and then jammed the cup in the center console. "Bill stopped into Rosa's with Dave and Chris. Probably freaked out Valeria. You might have to do some damage control and make sure we're still on for tonight, okay?"

Britt pictured it: Valeria being her regular cheerful self and scrambling to get her work done at the perpetually understaffed pizzeria when in walks three leering Aryans. Yeah, she probably would be flustered about now.

"*Okay?*" Gwen insisted.

"What? Yeah. Yeah, I'll call her."

"Good. Three guys, three girls. Equal pairings, *should* the need arise." Gwen's tone implied the situation ought to be expected.

"Ugh. I'm not sure I want any of those three touching Valeria."

"Maybe it's about time she got *touched*. Someone has to pop her piñata."

Britt frowned. "Why do you even bother with high school boys if you're… getting it from Mr. McAuley?"

Gwen laughed. She leaned toward Britt to drip the euphemism. "I must remember to call him that the next time I'm *getting it* from him." She leaned back and looked out the window. "Connor is forever *seducing* me. He is determined to be fascinating. It's like he's trying to prove to himself that he has these powers of manipulation."

It wasn't exactly an answer, but time was up. Britt pulled off onto a driveway of hexagonal cobblestones. Gwen's house was pale blue with a deep porch and three tall dormers jutting from the gabled roof. It had been more than adequate for a family of four and was now tragically spacious for their diminished three. Big enough for Keith's parents to leave their dead son's room just like it was, as long as it suited them. "What are you doing?"

Gwen slapped the glove compartment closed. "I'm leaving the night's entertainment with you. No reason to take it into chez goody-goody. You're driving, right?"

"My dad's a cop. You remember that, right?"

"A cop with his very own cop car," Gwen responded, "who trusts his daughter implicitly."

Britt was sure that wasn't true, but she didn't think it likely he would ever go through her glove compartment either.

"Come in for a minute, my alibi," Gwen said as she opened the car door. "You know the routine."

Mrs. Belores was vacuuming the living room carpet. She made a little start to indicate delighted surprise when she saw them and shut off the sweeper.

"Hi, girls! Did you have fun?"

"Yes, Mrs. Belores," Britt said. "Thanks for letting Gwen come over."

Mrs. Belores winked at Gwen. "I hope you stayed out of trouble."

Gwen put a hand on her stomach and wilted. "We put M&M's in the popcorn. And it was a *big* bag. Does that constitute trouble?"

Mrs. Belores gave her daughter a sideways hug. "Well, if it is, it looks like you're paying for it now."

Britt made a little sound as she looked at the blank screen of her phone.

"What is it?" Gwen asked.

"It's Valeria. She wants me to come over tonight to hang out for a bit." She explained to Mrs. Belores, "She's been a little freaked out with what happened to that Dora girl and everything, with living so far out on the edge of town."

"Valeria?" Mrs. Belores asked. "Is she the one with… with the father?"

"He's Catholic, but he's very religious," Gwen reassured her. "Just the two of you?"

"Jenna Lister too, I guess," Britt said.

Gwen shot her a sharp look. "Is that right?"

Britt held her gaze. "Yeah, but she's staying the night. I have to drive back later."

"On your own?" Mrs. Belores asked concernedly.

Britt shrugged. "I'm sure it will be fine."

Mrs. Belores let out a small gasp. "Oh, I don't know, Britt." She had an idea. "Gwennie, why don't you go with her? Just don't stay out too late. You don't want to fall asleep in church tomorrow."

BRITT HUNG HER KEYS on the rack by the door. She sat on the sofa and listened to the quiet of the house. After a minute, the dehumidifier in the basement signaled that its bucket was full with a series of five beeps and the fan turned off. Sometimes Britt's father was home on Saturdays, sometimes he wasn't. Britt preferred to be alone. When she was home by herself, it was just that, just a circumstance of who happened to be in at the time. But when she was alone with her father, her mother's absence became a palpable thing, a *presence of absence*. The too-quiet house resounded with smothering emptiness. The contradictions, confined, strained against each other, as opposing like charges. She remembered what she thought about the Belores's house. What right did she have to judge them? Her situation was no better. She wasn't sure it mattered if they truly persevered or only maintained a devout facade; whatever they had to do to deal with their loss was the right thing to do if it brought them comfort.

Britt's problem was that she wasn't looking for comfort. It was the *situation* of her dead mother that vexed her, the dull turmoil of her mother not being there to serve her function and take her place. She didn't want her there to argue with her; she didn't miss that. As arguing had become the near total of their communication, it was disheartening but honest for Britt to confess to herself that she didn't miss *her*—and it irritated Britt both to feel that way and to have to reproach herself for it. She had wanted to grow up and shake the dust of her hometown in the prescribed manner of a million young women who wanted something more for themselves. Her leaving was never more inevitable than now, but the joyful empowerment of the act—the *accomplishment* of it—had been taken away and could never be reclaimed.

Britt had thought her friendship with Gwen might act as a panacea for the various symptoms (or anxiety over lack thereof) of her grief. Here was someone else in her class who had lost a family member and who seemed to be doing a better job of handling it than Britt was. Of course, Britt knew that Gwen might similarly be hiding an internal struggle, but though she watched for it, she never saw her give anything away. Perhaps Gwen was more adept at hypocrisy, navigating as she did the expectations of her devout family along with the indulgent reality of her "sinful ways." But the longer Britt knew her, the more she thought Gwen was simply not as affected as she should have been, and the recognition *she* might be like Gwen frightened her. Partly because Gwen was trouble. She skated her dual existence effortlessly, though that meant *carelessly* as well. *You can't fuck your teacher and deal drugs for him too without it coming to a head eventually,* Britt thought. And when it all blew up, it would blow up big. Anyone in her orbit was going to get scorched. A scandal like that might even lead to calls for Britt's dad to resign. She thought she should care more about that too.

Why didn't Gwen seem bothered by her brother's suicide? Britt didn't know him well and didn't know their lives together. Maybe Gwen hated her little brother. "You're supposed to love your family," she murmured to herself.

Maybe she shouldn't have told Gwen about her father's breakdown. But she had to tell someone; he had scared the hell out of her. She came home from choir practice and found him rushing around the house from room to room, throwing open every door, and yelling her mother's name as tears streamed down his face. He had been disconsolate since Christine died, but this was something else entirely. Britt thought for a second that he had tried too hard to keep up appearances despite the fraying edges showing through, and now he'd broken with reality and forgotten entirely that her mother was dead. If that was true, was this something he could ever come back from, or had she just lost a second parent to his own dark recesses? He went out the back door and rushed onto the deck, again calling, "Christine?!" She leaped after him. Someone would hear; someone would see. She grabbed him. She didn't realize until then that she was weeping too; only then did she hear her own sobs and cries of, "Daddy! Daddy!"—cries that finally hushed him. His eyes refocused and he saw her, saw her tears and distress. He swallowed her in his arms to comfort her, possibly the only automatic, unashamed embrace he'd given her since childhood.

After they had gone back inside, he explained. He had seen Christine. She was right there in the living room, right where they were now. He had watched her *see* him and come near. And then suddenly she was going up the stairs and she disappeared. And then he looked for her. No, honey, he knows that she's gone. But she was *here* too. He was sure she had come to see him. To see *them*.

No one said the word "ghost." To him, it was insufficient. To her, it was tacky. She was comforted (slightly) that that was what he thought he saw, even if she believed it was only his grief-stricken mind playing tricks. As scary as it was, maybe this wasn't a step back, but instead a messy breakthrough. Then again, maybe she would soon have to take care of herself. Regardless, it was too big of a thing not to unburden.

She wondered if Gwen was peeved about the last-second inclusion of Jenna Lister in their plans for the night. Britt was proud of herself for the sudden inspiration. Jenna was nice, and cute, with a couple of big handfuls up front—all qualities that endeared her to boys. But she was embarrassed of her short, thick legs, so she was always surprised and flattered when a boy wanted to touch her. Add to that a naive conflation of physical and romantic love, and Jenna never developed the neck muscles to resist when someone pushed down on the top of her head. Hopefully it wouldn't come to that. Hopefully they'd just get high and hang out and go home. But Britt figured it might save Valeria from getting into a situation she didn't want to. And hey, if it *was* what Valeria wanted, then Britt was only too happy to avoid giving a rushed handjob around the corner of the Hernandez family barn. Gwen said that Dave Pruitt bragged about tasting his own jizz because he came a *lot* and it shot up into his face, and Britt had no desire to have to deal with that kind of mess.

"Shit!" Britt laughed at herself as she pulled out her phone. Jenna definitely wasn't coming if she didn't remember to invite her.

After she sent the text, Britt got up and turned to go into the kitchen to grab a Coke out of the refrigerator. Her mother stood looking out the back window over the sink. Britt dropped her phone and heard it crack on the floor.

"Mom?" she asked. But there was no question. Of course it was her. Knowing someone so well, you didn't need to see their face. Every brushstroke of shape and posture from every angle told Britt who was there—who could not possibly be there.

Her mother straightened as though remembering something. She half turned and cocked an ear to listen with a playful look on her face, before turning back to face the sink.

"Mom?!"

This time, her mother did not seem to hear. Her father wasn't crazy. God, how she wished her father was crazy. Britt shuffled forward through the dining room, her hands splayed before her waist-high to feel for the chairbacks, not wanting to take her eyes off her mother for a fraction of a second. Achingly slow-ly, she made her way into the kitchen. Her half steps became quarter-steps. "Mom?" she tried again, but with no response. She stretched a trembling hand to touch her shoulder.

And then her hand was at her mother's shoulder, but only overlaid in perspective, as her mother suddenly moved in a shift between moments to the back of the yard. She turned once more, now wearily, and her expression spoke something of futility.

Then she passed through the unopen gate and was gone.

CHAPTER 12

THE KID HADN'T SHOWERED in days. He stank with that vine-gar-sharp hormonal BO only teenagers could produce. Darren rolled the window down to let in fresh air. The guttural roar of the sports coupe's engine filled his ears. He glanced down at the hilt of the knife sticking up from the door pocket. It might've been safer just to make the kid drive. It didn't seem likely he would steer them into oncoming traffic. But Darren wasn't one for giving up control. If things were going to hell, he sure as shit wanted to be at the steering wheel on the way down.

He cut speed and turned off from the main road. He drove past a power station half hidden behind huddling, shaggy arborvitae. The drive split, straight and right, to go around the blocky, metal-sided behemoth in both directions.

"Which way?" he asked.

Tim shook a finger forward. "Straight on around back."

Darren had had customers who used to work at the sintered metals fabricating plant, but he'd never driven into the parking lot or loading zone to do business there—too exposed, too many prying eyes. He had been disappointed to hear about the plant shutting down. Steady income meant reliable, discrete customers who didn't try to haggle over price.

Gravel kicked over from the berm by countless semi tires crackled on the faded blacktop as Darren slowly drove the length of the building. The sun warmed the smell of diesel and pennies from the industrial husk. Darren noticed that the siding didn't sport any tags and figured it was probably too far back from the road for any notoriety-seeking teens to find the effort worthwhile.

"Wonder what they made in this shithole," Tim murmured.

"Fittings," said Darren.

"What the hell does that mean?"

"It means fittings," Darren growled. Rubber creaked as he rolled his knuckles over the steering wheel again.

Tim chuckled nervously, trying to regain his cocksureness. "You'd probably better let me show you where your brother is before you strangle me."

They circled around the back of the building. Loading bays faced a broad lot. A pair of long, rusted dumpsters bookended a stack of mangled conveyer belts at the far corner. Across from them was a storage building with six corrugated roll-up doors. Darren stopped the car halfway between the buildings. He thought there probably wasn't too much looking around to do at this point. "You sure I still need you?"

Tim swallowed. "Yeah, you do. You need me to explain the why. And you need me to tell you the how—how you get your brother back." He opened the car door and got out. "The two go together," he called back over the car's roof as Darren emerged.

"Fine," Darren said. "Get to it, then."

Tim stayed put, elbows propped one each on door and roof. "Now, you're not gonna like this. I can't help that. But I need you to remember *all* that I said: Your brother doesn't have to *stay* dead."

"So you've said. And I think you want me to believe your bullshit long enough for you to figure out how to get away." He slammed the door; Tim flinched. "You can give up on that idea."

"Which part? That I could get away? I know I can't. But the part about believing me? You already do, at least a little bit. Because you've seen what you've seen. And I'm willing to bet the old man on the sofa wasn't your first." Darren stared at him, working his jaw back and forth. "Yeah, I suspected as much," Tim said. "They're just ghosts now, but we can bring them back for real—all the way alive. But it requires some killing first to get back the one... the ones who're already gone. You need death to make life, like rotting plants go back to fertilize the soil. You wanna know who Chief Pearcy saw?"

Darren's eyes narrowed. "What?"

"Yeah, I thought you might find this part interesting." Tim chuckled, whistling through his top teeth, his confidence returning. "The first one was this girl who worked at the dollar store. She was just so meek. I knew I might fuck it up, so I needed someone easy. It's fucked up, isn't it? I almost felt bad because she was, like, totally innocent, right? But I had to start somewhere."

Darren spat. "You proud of yourself? I've bunked with killers. You're nothing special."

"Me? No, *I'm* not special." He shut the car door and stepped around front. "I'm a total fuckup. I left her somewhere too easy to find. I mean, they have to be fixed in a certain general area to form the hexagram, so my choices were limited. Funny thing is, now that it's a crime scene, it's a *good* place to stow one of the bodies until the work is done. Especially with the chief in on it."

Tim was enjoying the superiority of his knowledge. Darren wanted to be rid of him, but he was playing catch-up, and he didn't know the way. For the moment, Tim had the advantage.

"I barely even remember getting fingerprinted for the missing children database," Tim said. "It was just something we did one day at school. Didn't know a criminal search would dip into juvenile records either. Doesn't seem legal, does it? But you know better'n anyone, it's the cops who say what's legal. Anyway, that's how dumb I was: didn't even wear gloves to do the deed. So, I get pulled in. A bloody fingerprint at the scene, for shit's sake! Open-and-shut. But the chief is rattled, and I know why, because *he* told me." Tim looked toward the factory on the emphasized word. "*He* knew that the chief had seen his wife right before he got the call about the girl I killed, and *he* knew if I told Pearcey all about it, if I told him what *he* could do, then the chief would let me go so I could finish my work. Pearcey even came up with my story, that I came upon the crime scene after the fact but was too scared to report it. That was a big help. But I definitely didn't expect him to call me up the next day and volunteer the next victim."

"Lyle," Darren muttered. "You'd have needed help."

"Yeah."

Darren bent his neck to pop the vertebrae and release the tension. It was that or kill the kid. "What's this *he* shit? He, who?"

Tim shook his head. "Won't do any good to tell you." He pointed at the main building. "Number four." The number was stenciled on the loading dock door in paint that used to be bright orange, large enough that the points reached near to the edges. Doors three and four shared a bay; a short ramp with a handrail leading up to a standard door divided four from the next higher two numbers.

Darren motioned with the knife. "After you."

Tim went straight toward the door. He planted his palms on the narrow platform lip jutting from the side of the building and swung his legs up. Darren scowled and mounted the ramp. When he got to the top, he straddled the handrail and stepped over.

"Why not just use the door with the handle?" he asked.

"Door's chained," Tim replied. "You gonna trust me with this?"

Darren saw the curved claw of a flat pry bar sticking out from underneath the dock door. He held the blade out in front of him meaningfully, and then jerked it upward to signal "lift."

"Open it," he said, and bit down to keep from saying anything more.

Tim levered the door up three inches with the pry bar; Darren heard the bar clank back against the cement as Tim curled his fingers underneath the lip. From his squat position, Tim groaned with effort to lift the heavy door. Darren made no move to help him. Tim stood. With the bottom of the door at his chest, he threw it upward with a final heave and then ducked and swung his right hand inside the building. Darren tensed. Tim rotated open again with a broom handle in his hand, which he jammed into the track. The door shimmied down and stopped, blocked open just short of five feet up.

Tim smiled, pink-white gums glistening. "Come on in."

Darren followed inside. The copper and oil smells wafted more strongly, accompanied by a layered stench that made him recoil—that of moldering straw and rotten eggs and dead animal. As he dipped under the door, he heard something shift in the darkened empty space—or felt something disturb the air, he wasn't sure. He rushed up behind Tim, grabbed his right wrist, and pinned it behind his back as he brought the blade up to his throat. "Who else is in here?" he hissed.

Tim trembled in his grasp. "Please, there's... I promise you, we are the only *people* in here."

Darren slipped the blade to the side and shoved Tim forward. He looked around. Sunlight sneaked through long, narrow windows high up along the broad side wall. The far corners were deeply shadowed. Trackways painted in yellow on the floor lead along empty spaces where machines once sat, their absence indicated only in a few lighter square footprints of unsullied cement. Girders stuck up at regular intervals to support the frame. The track lighting on the peaked roof high overhead was predictably shut off. A few small piles of refuse orphaned by a hasty exit lined the walls. Three brute hulks were left dead: a long, covered conveyance split in levels with numerous hoods leading skyward, and two shuttle bus-sized drums with teardrop-shaped spindle arms, set on four squat legs, the whole painted green.

Tim tracked his eyes. "Yeah, fuck if I know what they do. Look expensive, though."

Darren glared at him. "I don't much care. You said you were taking me to my brother. Time's up."

Tim nodded and then pointed. "Yup. Round the other side of that first one, there," he said, indicating the nearer of the bug-like machines.

Darren kept one eye on Tim as he took a wide arc around the metal husk. The smell of dead animal grew stronger. Nearer the far machine, there was a slack lump on the floor in the middle of a roughly painted circle bordered by strange symbols. The body was decayed, but the two-tone fur and long legs identified it as a dog. When Darren turned to face the machine closer to the bay door, he saw the glint of sloping facets on amber glass he recognized from the old man's house. The constricted sunlight made it hard to see the figure entombed therein, but familiarity made it recognizable, even drained and sunken, even dark and indistinct. He had told himself what he knew to be true the night before: *My brother is dead.* But here was the reality. He stepped closer. Lyle was upright, not like the old man. His eyes were closed. But his mouth was open, anguished and pleading—frozen with final desperation. It wasn't bad enough to have to see his brother dead, here was his *death* on display. It was an offense that would not be left unpunished.

He was almost surprised to see Tim come around the side of the machine, albeit haltingly.

"You and Pearcey did… *this*?" he accused.

Tim's lip quivered and red swam over Darren's eyes as he realized it was an attempt to suppress a smile.

"We had help," Tim said.

Darren scoured the word from his throat. "Who?"

"Not so much a *who*." He motioned with his eyes to direct Darren's sight above his brother's petrified corpse.

For the first time in his life, Darren was paralyzed with fear. And the kid *wasn't* afraid, which meant he was somehow familiar with the loathsome creature perched atop the machine. It was black; crouched, it was as big as a boar; leathery wings rippled and stalk legs clicked, folded in on a sable black fur body shifting in agitation, making its full form and size impossible to guess in the dim room. And Darren did not want to see its full form; he did not want it to stretch out; he did not want to see what was wing or leg or mouth or claw. Its eyes were horror enough. Two shining clusters of opals blinked at him in rhythm, like fingers tapping on a table.

Darren staggered backward by little steps on leaden feet. He was cold, but there was sweat on his forehead. The paroxysm of fear was so foreign to his body that it was trying to throw him into shock. His hand wobbled and the knife began to slip. He commanded his fingers closed even though he could not feel the hilt. Even though he knew the knife was a joke. The kid's renewed confidence showed him that.

"I call it Bat-with-ten-eyes, which I guess is near enough to what his name really means," Tim said, gazing up at the creature admiringly. "My master told me its real name, but I couldn't pronounce it. *His* name is complicated enough."

"Your master?" Darren asked, little more than a squeak, the question expressing confusion that the dark thing that could likely tear the two of them apart in seconds was not the one in charge.

Tim laughed. "Bat-with-ten-eyes is just a servant, like me!"

"Then—who...?"

The voice was a hungry, burrowing swarm attacking his ears, like the flurry in the heart of a pitiless dust storm; yet the feeling in his head was of the *after* of such scouring violence, the emptiness and neglect of tombs and ruins.

Ixixiklis, it said.

Chapter 13

EVE POPPED THE CAP on the insulated plastic bottle and threw her head back. She pulsed cool water into her mouth, swished it around once, and swallowed. The day was warmer than she'd expected, and direct sun was beating back up from the blacktop. She'd been walking for more than an hour. She didn't think she was going to have to go this far on foot. She hadn't tried to ask for a ride in town; the cold reception and general strangeness of her and Zander's encounters with the townsfolk had been off-putting. Hell, as she was headed back down Main toward the forest, she was near certain the young woman from the restaurant had driven by in her gray pickup and then circled back toward the hotel. She thought about calling Zander, but she wasn't *certain* it was her, and besides, what would she say—"Hey, watch out for that nosy chick"?

She reasoned it made more sense to get onto the forest road and hitch a ride there. She would be sure that at least the driver would be headed in the right direction, and the chances that someone on the road would be a fellow outdoors enthusiast from out of town seemed much better. She was keenly aware that being a woman showing fit, long legs walking alone by the side of the road was a double-edged sword. Even without sticking out her thumb, the offer of a ride seemed likely, but she had to hope chivalry was the impetus and the only desire in play was to help her get to her destination. So far, most of the few vehicles that had passed her were going the wrong direction, and the only one to slow down was a wrecker hauling a silver crossover that looked just like hers. The driver was a slack-jawed older man with a long face and unkempt gray hair. She looked forward determinedly while he leered at her on his way past.

Every hundred yards or so, the thought crossed her mind again, what *am* I doing out here? They'd started their day by finding a dead body in the woods, for Christ's sake, and since then she'd come to know there was a potential serial murderer on the loose. Zander's every objection to her setting off on her own seemed more and more prescient the deeper she went into the forest. Of course, Zander had issued those warnings when he thought she was going to be driven in a cab for the first fifteen miles of her trek. If he'd known what she really planned, he would have found some way to stop her.

Yes, she had found a cabbie. And yes, he had told her that his was the only available cab in the area. Though he was willing to take her all the way to her car, he was starting from forty-five minutes away, and he would have to charge her the entire fare to come pick her up as well as the trip from hotel to campground. When she pushed back, he told her she could take it or leave it. Frustrated, she hung up. She checked two ride-share apps, but there was no one in range. Swallowing her pride and calling the cabbie back was never an option; she wasn't going to pay the exorbitant fair. Not while her legs still worked.

She hated the fact that money was still such a source of anxiety to her and in her marriage. She didn't know why she and Zander had such a hard time talking about it without arguing. The idea that they had to be frugal had never been a source of contention; it was an obvious mandate. And he had never complained that *their* money went to helping *her* mom. Nevertheless, the imbalance creaked in every conversation, and if she was the only one to hear it, then didn't that mean he was insensitive to the problem—or simply dismissive of her feelings? Or maybe there was more to it than that. Maybe all the other little problems had latched on, remoras on the circling shark. Maybe the worst aspect of their money troubles had been the way it had exacerbated trifles they could have worked through with minimal effort otherwise. He had mentioned an old friend from Boston had invited him to come for a weekend sometime. She had said that was fine, he should go. But maybe she hadn't said it with enough encouragement. He assured her that no, he didn't think he'd be able to do it this year. A few weeks later, they decided to go on a weekend camping trip. It seemed like a good idea, a return to form, but even landing on that idea was delicate. They agreed on it and walked away before either could tie it back to that trip to Boston he wouldn't be taking on his own. Everything was like that. Everything referenced something else it shouldn't have, because they'd spent a year with every decision glommed together by that one, overriding concern, and they'd forgotten how to wrest the bits apart again into manageable pieces. They found themselves left with a new anxiety in the form of a question that should not have been so impenetrable, that gnawed with every asking: When does it get *easier*? The question was especially vexing because, during those easy times when they seemed to huddle together away from the looming, dark cloud, the zippy repartee still flowed, and she remembered every reason she fell in love with him in the first place.

She took her phone out and checked the signal. She was getting one bar steadily and a flicker of two on and off. She guessed she might be out of range in another half mile. She smiled at the thought of calling him, of the reassurance of hearing his voice, but then she remembered the ruse she'd perpetrated. She could pretend she'd already been dropped by the cabbie and that was why she was calling while walking along the road, but that was doubling down on a plan that no longer held her confidence. She figured, to be back in three hours, so that he wouldn't worry, she was going to have to turn around in no more than twenty minutes. He would be angry she lied to him and set off on her own, but with her safely returned to the hotel, he couldn't be too mad. She was tempted to give up and turn around right away. What was the point of walking another twenty minutes, only to have to retrace those same steps? But there was still the matter of getting to the car one way or another, and there was the still pressing matter of getting the hell away from Adler.

Eve heard the rumble of an engine approaching from behind. She stepped sideways off from the pavement and half turned to look. It was an innocuous motion that could have meant she was being cautious about oncoming traffic or that she might be interested in getting a lift. A white, extended cab truck with a green stripe slowed as it approached, and she could see there was an emblem on the side of the vehicle and a flat bank of signal lights on top. The man behind the wheel wore a broad-brimmed, tan hat. The passenger's-side window rolled down as the truck slowed to a stop. The shield on the side of the car indicated he was with the Forest Service Department of Enforcement and Investigations. The man was young, with cheeks that swelled up into tight plums under his eyes when he smiled.

"Afternoon, miss," he said. "Doing alright?"

Eve bent and laid a hand on the car door. "Well, actually, if you're offering, I sure could use a ride up to the Minister Creek campgrounds."

"Sure, why not?" He twirled his wrist. "Hop in."

As they pulled away, he asked, "Minister Creek, huh? You weren't planning to walk the whole way, were you?"

Eve smiled and relaxed her shoulders to show her relief. "I was sure hoping I wasn't going to. I'm glad you came along."

"Happy to help," he said. He pivoted his right arm open at the elbow to offer his hand. "Allan Andrews, Forestry Service, by the way."

She shook and introduced herself. "We left our car at the campgrounds and I was on my way to pick it up. I was hiking with my husband, but he hurt his knee." She glanced at him.

"Oh, I'm sorry to hear that," Allan replied. "He okay?"

The concern was slight, but seemed genuine, and his face didn't twitch when she mentioned she was married, which was a good sign. "He'll be fine," Eve said. She weighed whether to mention the body they'd discovered that morning, but couldn't decide, so she thought she'd probe first. "I saw on the side of your car, it said Department of Enforcement. So, you're a… forest cop?" She giggled. "Sorry, I didn't mean it to sound like that." She watched his face again, scanning for offense taken.

He laughed. "That's alright, ma'am. Forest cop it is." He waved at a family traveling the other direction. "Somebody's gotta keep those bears from stealing all the pic-a-nic baskets."

She laughed and played along. "Catch any bears today?"

"Nope, nothing today."

Nothing today, she thought. No dead bodies glued to trees or nothin'. "Do you live in Adler?"

"Oh, no," Allan said. "My wife and I have a small farm off of state route 6 near Smethport." Eve felt encouraged by both the distance and the mention of a spouse—encouragement tempered when he added, "But we go into Adler all the time. We love it.

We have dinner there every Friday night, and go to the football games during the season."

"Huh." Eve adjusted her feet around her pack on the floor. "Do you ever work with cops outside the forest?"

Allan's smile drooped. "Sometimes," he said. And it was his turn to glance sideways.

Eve didn't know where the body of the other victim was found, the one she'd learned about at the pizzeria. But even if Allan wasn't involved in the investigation, his familiarity with the town would mean he was certain to know about the murder. Her other questions might have seemed innocent enough, but the last one must have raised his suspicions. Rather than press on his curt answer, she shrugged it off and gazed along the side of the road—casually, she hoped.

"I didn't catch where you're from," Allan said.

"Columbus," Eve replied. "We just came out for the weekend. Do some hiking."

"And then…" Allan prompted, and gave her a look under eyebrows scrunched in sympathy.

Eve sighed showily. "If you want to give God a laugh, tell Her your plans."

Allan laughed. "That's just about the way I heard it." He slowed, signaled, and then turned onto route 666.

They drove on (more slowly on the two-lane-and-nothing-to-spare road), talking in generalities about the weather, which led to Allan speaking at length about the recreational possibilities in the forest should they ever get a chance to come back. There was a pleasant banality to the conversation that placated each's concern. Eve thought again about telling him about the dead body, but the ease of situation and the impending relief of getting to her car, made her doubt her lack of confidence in the local police force. Maybe she was just being paranoid, and besides, soon enough it wouldn't matter if she wasn't.

Allan followed the curve of a silver guardrail bending away from the road onto a squarish lot tucked among the yellowing trees. About ten vehicles were parked in varying accordance with faded lines on the asphalt.

But Eve and Zander's car was not among them.

Chapter 14

Connor McAuley knew seducing high school girls and using them to sell drugs at his workplace was dangerous. And he was well aware the practice had a limited shelf life. In a few short years, the idea would go from excitingly taboo to objectionably creepy in even the most easily influenced young mind. He might be able to continue to reap the benefits along that path for a while, but there would be no seduction. They would take what they wanted and laugh behind his back; there would be no loyalty and little discretion.

His relationship with Gwen had precipitated just such a scenario sooner than anticipated, and he didn't like it at all. It was bad enough they'd started having sex before she was eighteen, but worse still that she'd initiated it. She had all the control but wasn't in control of herself. He'd been expecting some sort of interaction with Darren Dietz at some point, and really, it had gone about the way he thought it would. But the circumstances inflamed his anxiety. Darren came to his home in broad daylight; again, bad enough, but again, worse still because Gwen was the person she was. Connor knew what he wanted and he knew it involved risk. But he knew the best way to continue getting what he wanted for as long as he could was to mitigate that risk. Inaction was preferable; a change in balance would likely be literally upsetting to someone. But Connor felt, this time, action was needed. Somehow or other, even if increased his exposure, he needed to reassert control. After he watched Darren leave (in what he knew to be Hannah's car), he sat with a fresh cup of coffee (he wasn't going to let the unwelcome visit spoil his routine) and analyzed the situation.

There wasn't much to be done about Gwen. He'd have to wait until after graduation. Hopefully she would get bored or move away or both. If he tried to cut her out, she'd probably take him down out of spite. It would ruin her good-girl bullshit reputation, but she would probably be happy to be done with it, and besides, she could claim victimhood and hang her moral descent on him, as well. If he kept selling her drugs, either to sell or just recreationally, she might be fine with that; he didn't really think she cared that much about having sex with him. But for all the trouble she presented, and regardless of whether she enjoyed it, he didn't want to give up the physical relationship. That was the whole point to the exercise (in contrast to Gwen, he didn't care much about getting high). And damned if she didn't make it all worth it during those few ecstatic minutes. And if he *could* give that up to get more distance, then he'd have to find someone else to fulfill that need, which would mean both starting over again and adding another element to the already dangerous mix. It was best to keep things with her as they were for the time being—at least as far as *direct* interaction went.

The one aspect of Darren's surprise visit Connor had not been expecting was to be asked if he'd seen Darren's brother, Lyle. Connor's supply line was Hannah, Lyle's girlfriend. It was easy enough to guess where she was getting it. But now Lyle was missing. Darren had been trying to be casual, asking if he'd seen Lyle around, but he asked specifically about the last "week, eight days". That span of time—and the fact Darren would ask *him* of all people—indicated Lyle wasn't just off doing his own thing. Darren was casting about, more desperate than he let on.

Connor thought there might be something there to work with.

With Lyle out of the way, if he could get rid of Darren… it likely would mean a disruption to his supply line, but he thought it might not be too bad. Maybe Hannah already knew the players further up. And he'd dealt with other people before he started in with Hannah anyway. There was always somebody selling. Sin abhors a vacuum. All the casual users who considered themselves law-abiding citizens would probably be shocked to find out just how ubiquitous drug use was in every small town everywhere.

Of course, violence was out of the question. He had no desire to commit such an offense, and he would be toast in any encounter with Darren, even if he was armed and Darren was buck naked and hog-tied. He would have to use the law against him, that much was clear. But if he went after Darren for being a drug dealer, he involved himself in the equation, which he wanted to avoid at all costs. If he raised suspicion against Darren, the question of *how would he know* was sure to come up. And he feared an anonymous complaint would be toothless.

But now this business about Lyle might present an opportunity. There was a weapon hidden in the murk; Connor just had to feel it out. A benefit of going after Darren this way was that it obscured the drug connection while still leaving "possession with intent to sell" viable as an angle of attack. Obviously, he couldn't produce a body. But he didn't need to; all he needed to do was to arouse suspicion enough to produce a warrant. Connor had no doubt whatever drugs and guns the cops found in Darren's house would be enough to send him away for a while—hell, he might be on parole even now. This reduced all of Connor's concerns to the single logistical problem of how to get the cops into Darren's house, which made him happy. It all came back around. Logistics were his forte.

What else did he have to work with? Well, there was that other dead girl, the one from the dollar store. Dora something. He wondered briefly if he should ask Gwen if she was dealing to her. It might tie in nicely somehow, but he decided it was better off he didn't know for sure one way or the other, even if plausible deniability wasn't applicable to his situation.

It was *almost* enough. The cops might know Lyle was missing too, or they might be otherwise suspicious of his absence, if they were keeping an eye on him. They sure as shit were desperate to solve the dollar store girl's murder. A plan started to germinate in Connor's mind. He took his time with it, letting it bloom; he finished his coffee, went for a short run, took a shower. He ate some leftover Chinese carryout, straight from the oyster pail with chopsticks as every metropolitan-set TV show had taught him to do. By the time he'd finished, everything was planned, with one variable that he felt he had no choice but to settle on when the moment came.

He drove out to Selby Run Park to confirm some details of the topography and layout of the various structures. He thought everything looked good. He strained to curb his enthusiasm. He knew he was feeling drunk on the success of a venture not yet begun, and he worried he might become incautious. He wandered around the park to give himself time to review the set up.

The park's main attraction was two fenced-in baseball diamonds (the North Diamond and the South Diamond), each with home and away dugouts. Between the two was the North Shelter House, a playground, and a covered picnic area. There was a second covered picnic area near the South Diamond, and then farther away, abutting the woods and nearby two marked trailheads, was the less impressive and less often used South Shelter House, where Dora's body had been discovered. Word had it the body was attached to the back somehow. As might be expected, news of the body's discovery spread fast in the small town and dominated the local newscast. Connor remembered the scene behind the field reporter; he remembered thinking how provincial it was for all the lookie-loos to linger near the crime scene. The authorities (there were several agencies represented on-site) had closed the park and blocked access to the park road, but people had pulled off along the roadway and lined up to lean on the left field fence of the North Diamond to gawk. There would be little to see other than flashing lights and officers standing around or suddenly rushing from one spot to another, but it would have been novel to the community.

Connor crossed the road that curved around the park and went up a fat-tire rutted, short incline to a plateau where piles of gravel were situated in anticipation of use by the construction company doing work on the Selby Run overpass a bit farther down. It wasn't much of a rise, but it did give a full view of the park. Getting up against the left field fence would put someone much closer to the action but utilizing the advantage of the elevated viewpoint of the gravel-storage area would be sensible for someone eschewing the crowd. Connor didn't know if anyone had done so, but it wouldn't be unreasonable—though probably few did, which meant no one would dispute his story. Also, the park and every structure therein were sure to be searched thoroughly by the authorities, but the surrounding area would probably not receive as strict scrutiny. Evidence there might have been missed.

He had decided to go up on the rise, he would say, because he wanted to stay out of the way (though yes, he had to admit he was curious). While he was up there, he heard two men arguing on the other side of one of the gravel piles, the one closest to where the dirt path looped back down to the roadway. He edged around to see them but stayed out of sight because he didn't want to get involved. It was a heated argument, but he didn't know what it was about. He heard them talk about "the girl" but he didn't know what it had to do with the murder. He thought it was none of his business anyway, and figured they were probably just part of the road crew. (Connor thought that was a nice, believable touch, a tip of the hat to the perceived elitism of educators, that he couldn't tell the difference between construction workers and criminals.) He heard car doors slam and then saw them drive off in a late-model, electric-blue sports coupe with a loud engine. He didn't think anything of it until he ran into one of his old students in town getting into the same car. He told her he saw two men driving around in the exact same kind of car and she told him it must have been her boyfriend, Lyle Dietz, and his brother Darren. Now that doesn't mean anything necessarily, but when he found out the men *weren't* construction workers, then he thought again about their heated argument, and about them talking about the girl, and well... he knew it wasn't much to go on, but the police *were* asking for *any* leads...

That left the one variable. He dropped a half-smoked joint in the area he described. That would help. But he needed something that would confirm his story, something that would tie the brothers directly to the scene, something specifically theirs that he could leave there before he filed the report. He didn't know yet what he needed, but if he could just get a few minutes in their house, he would be sure to find something. He just needed to know he would have the time.

Gwen had moved most of his stash through the week, and he given her part of the leftovers that morning, so he had a legitimate need to make another buy from Hannah. And if he did so today—and if it was bigger than usual—then maybe Darren would be curious and either come along in person to the deal or observe from a distance. If things went according to plan, he needn't worry about Darren's anger at him for missing the buy. He texted Hannah requesting a meet.

She texted back, "Not today busy."

He decided to take a chance. "Met D. Should I go direct to him at the house around 4?"

"NO," then a few seconds later, "No one there. D is with me."

And just like that, Connor had his open window—open right away, from the looks of things. He checked satellite imagery to consider his approach. He thought about going straight up the drive but reconsidered. It was a long drive, one vehicle wide; it would be bad if they returned while he was there. The long drive might give him some notice of their approach, though; he could scamper out the back. There were open woods behind their cabin abutting a dirt road turnoff a half mile north. That was the way in.

He had dressed with foresight, up to and including a romp through the forest, so he didn't need to waste time stopping at home. He drove through and then up out of town to the north. He slowed suddenly as he neared the dirt road, pissing off the driver behind him. He turned and drove a hundred yards up, then pulled off to the side under a tree. He checked his phone again. Nothing new. He could text Hannah again, but he thought asking again where they were might be suspicious. He marched into the woods toward the Dietz cabin. He was more worried about ticks than anything else, which led him to direct his eyes at the ferns and underbrush instead of watching his footing directly beneath him. But even if he had been concentrating on where he put his feet, he still might have missed the well-hidden bear trap that snapped shut, tearing through his calf muscles and cracking his tibia.

Chapter 15

ELDON LANDRY HAD BEEN sorely tempted to stop and ask the long-legged hiker if she needed a ride. Not that he expected gratitude to lead to gratification. That was a nice fantasy he could hold on to for later, but he knew he was old and he looked like shit. Hell, she would have been out of his league back when he was tight-bellied and rod-backed hopping off one of the last troop carriers out of 'Nam. Now, decades on—*"Fuck!"* he muttered at the thought of the span of time—after the drink had taken its toll, he was nothing but a leering creep. If that was his role, so be it. Besides, even if it might have been good to do something nice for someone one time, he had his orders. He was at the beck and call of the man whose wife he had killed. Even if Chief Pearcey couldn't nail him for vehicular manslaughter ("It weren't that! It was an accident!"), he could make his life hell a million other ways—he'd said as much, unambiguously. Eldon knew he would never be released. And if he couldn't get free from his mistakes, couldn't even take a minute to help a pretty lady, then he saw no reason to break off the only reliable relationship he'd ever had. He kept to beer these days. Most days anyway. Sure, he kept a flask in the glove compartment, but that was just for emergencies. It had sat in there for weeks now, full and untouched. Because he was disciplined. "That's right," he agreed with himself. He ruffled open the crumpled brown bag on the seat beside him and slid it down over the sixteen ounce can beaded with condensation. He raised the parcel to his lips and took in a mouthful, and then put the can back down and pulled the bag up over the lip once more. "Discipline is key." It was what got you through the trying times. He'd have to be vigilant. He'd felt himself sliding toward a full-on bender since Tuesday when he opened up his work shed and saw his dead father sitting on a stool, staring down at an empty workbench, flipping pages of an invisible magazine while he rubbed his crotch. Eldon had staggered back into his house (the one he'd grown up in, and inherited) and sworn off drink. A few minutes later he went back out and found the shed empty and decided to crack open a cold one to steady his nerves.

Eldon passed the station, and then turned on the side street, and again into the alley parallel to Main. There was a lot next to the station used primarily by a steakhouse on the corner. A section near the alley formed the short part of an L, with spots on either side of concrete parking blocks. On rare occasions, the police used the spots for civilian vehicles. There was no impound lot, you had to go to county lockup for that, but they could boot a car if they felt the need. Usually, confiscating the keys sufficed. Eldon maneuvered the silver crossover into the spot nearest the station, facing the alley. He got out of his wrecker and was about to lower the boom when he saw Bobbi Sturges marching toward him. Eldon groaned. If that wasn't enough, a cruiser approaching the front parking must have seen her go around the corner looking hot, because it pulled in after her.

"What the hell are you doing?" Bobbi demanded. "I can't believe you have the gall to show your face around here!"

Eldon gestured at his truck. "What does it look like I'm doing? Here's your car, as requested. You're *welcome.*"

The cruiser stopped. Big Grant Bundy climbed out. The driver's side of the car raised up as the suspension sighed relief.

"Nobody called you," Bobbi said with conviction. She would have heard over the radio if someone had requested a tow. And nobody in the station would have called Eldon, regardless.

Grant lumbered over. His smoky baritone rumbled, "What's going on, Bobbi?"

She folded her arms and tilted her head, boring holes into the back of Eldon's skull. "That's what I'd like to know."

Eldon had hoped he would have been able to drop off the car and get away unseen. He hesitated, not sure how to answer, then decided to tell the abridged version, pleading innocent of the details. "I was instructed to pick up this vehicle from the Minister Creek campground lot and to bring it back here. Which I have done!"

"Minister Creek—" Bobbi wondered aloud as she realized who the likely owners were. "Who was it that called you and asked you to bring it here? You get their name?" She was hoping there was a mix-up; maybe the young couple was expecting it to be delivered to the Forest Hotel.

Eldon took a step closer and folded his arms in imitation of his interrogator and reiterated, "I was instructed to pick up this vehicle and bring it to the station!" Grant was standing next to her, but Eldon refused to be intimidated, even if he had six inches and more than a hundred pounds on him. But getting closer and becoming more vociferous had been a mistake.

"Is that beer I smell on your breath, Eldon?" Grant asked.

Bobbi gasped. "I don't believe that you would get behind the wheel—"

"I'm sober as a church mouse!" Eldon protested, but his defiant expression wavered as he doubted the saying—was it *quiet* as a church mouse?

Grant rested a hand on his belt just over the pepper spray. The other hand he reached out and clapped on Eldon's shoulder. If it came to it, Eldon thought he'd prefer the spray.

"Tell you what, Eldon," Grant said. "Why don't we go inside and see if a breathalyzer can tell us just how sober a church mouse really is?"

THERE WAS A KNOCK at the door. Zander was groggy. He'd put on a shirt after Eve left and didn't remember anything after that. How long had he been asleep? His hair was dry. An hour? The knock repeated, soft but urgent.

Zander got up and crossed the hotel room. He didn't bother looking through the peephole, as he expected to see the pyramid-head owner. Instead, the mousy-haired heavy waif from the pizzeria was there, shifting her feet nervously.

Zander blinked and tousled his hair. "Um, hello?"

"Hi. You remember me? I mean, of course you do—I'm Hannah. I don't remember if I introduced myself."

"That waitress said it. I'm Zander. What can I do for you?"

She looked up and down the hallway as though she was afraid someone might be listening. "You're gonna think I'm crazy..."

"Okay," Zander said, and smiled to put her at ease (though his agreement held some expectation of truth).

"It's just that... my boyfriend is missing."

"Lyle," Zander said, amazed that he'd remembered that bit of minutiae.

Hannah was frazzled by his alertness. "Wow, yeah, that's right. So, I'm worried about him, okay? And you guys… you guys seemed like you might know something somehow, so I… I followed you."

Zander frowned.

"I said you were gonna think I was crazy," Hannah added hurriedly, "but I'm just worried. Anyway, that's not why I came up here. I came here because I saw your wife leave the hotel, right?"

"Okay, sure. And then she got in a cab to go get our car."

Hannah shook her head. "No, she didn't. She just started walking. I was wondering where she was going, so I followed *her*."

"Wait, no." Zander waved his hand, not believing her narrative. "Eve called for a cab. She left when she said the cab was here."

Hannah shrugged nervously. She actually had seen Eve walked away and had no idea of their arrangement, so she didn't know what it meant that she'd lied to him. "I can only tell you what I saw. Did you watch to see if she got in the cab?"

Zander twisted his mouth. "No," he murmured. "I just assumed…"

Hannah didn't give him time to dwell on it. "So, she starts walking west, and I figure maybe she's going back to the station. But then she just keeps on going like she's going outta town straight back into the forest. So, I think, 'maybe I should give her a ride,' but right then this cop car pulls over and this officer gets out. And I don't know what it is they're talking about, but your wife looked kind of upset, and she pointed back toward the hotel here. And then the officer opens the door and waves her in the back seat. So, I think he's gonna bring her back to the hotel and have a talk with you two for some reason. Instead, he takes her farther west, and so I think *he's* giving her a ride. But then they turn south on Selby Run, which must've surprised your wife 'cause it seemed like she was leaning forward and yelling at him from the back seat. It sure surprised me, 'cause there really isn't much out that way."

Zander felt a sudden swell of hate for everything to do with Adler and the decision to go hiking in the Allegheny Forest. He didn't trust this girl's ridiculous story, yet it jibed with their experience so far, and especially with Eve's suspicions. He was mad at himself for not aligning more closely with her viewpoint. "Where is my wife?" he hissed.

Hannah stammered. "Okay. Okay, so I keep following him, all the way out to Selby Run Park."

"What?" Zander exclaimed incredulously. "A park?"

"It's where they found the first girl who got murdered. As a matter of fact, that's where they went, to the shelter house where her body was found. And there's another cop car there waiting outside. So, this cop stops and lets your wife out, and she's pissed as hell. But he's all trying to calm her down and motions her into the shelter house. All I can think is maybe they think she could answer some questions they had."

Zander shook his head, scowling.

"Hey—I don't know. I don't. That's just what I saw. I figure they're coming back out again soon enough anyway, right? But they don't. Not your wife or the cop, or any other cop. I'm sitting there—what?—half hour, forty minutes, just getting confused and scared for her. After all, what can I do? I can't exactly call the cops, right? So, I'm just sitting there and finally the only thing I can think to do is to come and tell you." She opened her hands as though dropping a weight at his feet.

"Why don't I just go ahead and call her?" Zander suggested.

"They probably won't let her answer," Hannah said.

Zander shot her a look of doubt and turned back toward the bed.

"But of course, yeah, that's the right way to go," she added. "Call her up. It would set both our minds at ease."

Zander called Eve. The fifth ring cut short and the call transferred to voicemail. He tried her again, with the same result. He realized that if she had gone into the woods as planned, then she might be out of range. But what if she hadn't? It's true he had not seen her get into the cab. Was that why she was determined to leave before he was dressed and ready to come with her? He had been confused by her rush to go. But then, she had mentioned it was motivated by her desire to leave town as soon as possible, and now, more than ever, he understood that desire.

"Did you get through?" Hannah asked. He glared at her, as it was obvious he hadn't. "Sorry, stupid question." She looked up and down the hallway again. "Look, I just thought you should know. Probably they left there right after I did. If you walk down to the station, I'm sure you can get the whole thing sorted out pretty quick. I don't wanna get involved. The truth is, Lyle and the cops ain't exactly friends, and he wouldn't want me talking to them. Besides, I have to live here. So, you'll have to go there on your own. I'd better take off." She turned, then stopped to wave, and started down the hall.

Zander didn't know what to do. Everything about her was so awkward. Her surveillance at the pizzeria had been a joke that blew up in her face as soon as she sat. Did he really think she could craft such an elaborate ruse? The one thing he was sure of is that he didn't want to leave Eve alone and vulnerable, no matter what was going on. Hiking through the woods alone in daylight was bad enough, but this—what the hell *was* this?

He lurched out into the hall. "Wait!" he called after Hannah. "Can you take me to her?"

Variations on "It's not far," were just about the only thing she said on the drive to the park. Zander wondered how she could afford the truck they rode in. It didn't help to think the truck was her missing boyfriend's; someone her age should be driving a beater. Which meant either he was older or he made a lot of money young; neither consideration was encouraging. He tried to reassure himself he was making the right move. She was a small thing, no match for him, and besides, the window was open and the door unlocked; he could get away any time he wanted.

They turned onto the park road. They passed a jogger on his way out. Zander didn't see anybody else.

"Nice day," he said. "You'd think there'd be more people here."

"People are scared," Hannah replied.

They curled around the South Diamond and passed the covered picnic area.

Hannah sighed. "Shit."

They pulled up in front of the boxy, brown shelter house. A cordon of police tape was draped from stakes around the building. A sash of tape drooped down the doorframe. "Well, I was right," she said. "They must've left right after me." She put the truck in reverse and began a two-maneuver pivot. "I'll drop you at the station. Heck, maybe they took her back to the hotel." She shifted into drive and turned the wheel to start their way back out of the park.

"Wait," Zander said.

She paused. "What's up?"

He stared at the tape on the doorframe, attached at one point and not barring the door.

Hannah waited, holding her breath.

"I want to check," Zander said.

"If… if you want to," Hannah said uncertainly, but Zander was already out the door. She followed him.

His knee creaked painfully on the first step up and he slouched into the handrail. Hannah leaped to keep him upright. She felt a sudden strange pang when she felt the warmth of his arm under her hand.

"Thanks," he said.

"I'm sure there's nothing to see." She kept her hand on him.

He looked down at it, which made her instinctively drop the hand away. "It won't hurt to look," Zander said.

He climbed the next step up to the door and tried the handle. It wasn't locked. "Alright, then." He pushed the door open.

The interior was dim. He saw folding tables stacked against the far wall next to a rack full of metal folding chairs. He turned to his left. He saw movement but couldn't duck in time. His vision flashed white as the fist clipped his temple. The door slammed shut as he sprawled onto the floor.

"Darren!" Hannah screeched.

Darren? Zander wondered as he struggled upright. *Not Lyle?*

Darren grabbed a fistful of hair. Before Darren spun him around, Zander glimpsed the man's blazing eyes and bared teeth.

"Why are you doing this?" Zander cried. "I don't know you!"

Darren pulled his head back and hissed in his ear, "That *is* why."

Zander felt the slice across his neck. He was amazed at the smallness of the pain, then immediately overwhelmed by the awfulness of it as air found the open wound. He was shocked by the everything of the moment—the blank, arbitrary knowledge that he'd just been murdered, the disappointment at having been duped, the queer detail of Hannah's scream as though she hadn't thought it would go this far, the terrible sadness of abandoning Eve and of having to leave his own life.

And the cruel surprise of finding out he was hellbound, for what else could explain the black monster in the rafters, the unfurling horror slavering as it descended into his dimming light. How strange it was that Hannah's redoubled screams should follow him down.

CHAPTER 16

HAVING PERFORMED THE PRETENSE of checking up on Joe Underwood at Elba Wilson's request, and having dispatched Eldon to retrieve the Nowlans' vehicle, effectively freezing them for at least a few hours longer, Chief Pearcey drove around for a little while, but he couldn't concentrate. He stopped in the parking lot of the VFW, but castigated himself almost immediately for not anticipating that the old gossips who congregated there would want to come out and talk to him about Dora Givens's murder, or to ask when it would be safe to go back to the park, or, in the case of Sloop Hutchinson, to tell about his trip to the doctor's office. It turned out he didn't have a stroke or "nothing else wrong, neither," despite seeing his high school sweetheart on the porch of her father's house, looking just as she did in the last picture she sent him at the base in West Berlin just before "the train got her."

He pretended to get a call and drove away. There was nothing for it but to go home and hope Britt wasn't there. Not that she was likely to ask him any questions anyway. There would be a lot to talk about soon enough, if what Tim Neuworth said was true, if he could get her back, in the flesh. No, not if, *when*. He had to believe it was true. He'd seen the proof, hadn't he? And not five minutes ago Sloop Hutchinson backed it up with his own experience. And besides, if it wasn't true, after he'd let Tim do the things he'd done, after he'd *helped* Tim do those things—that alternative was too terrible to contemplate. He told himself he was just a good man making tough choices. He was righting an imbalance in the universe. Christine shouldn't have been taken from him like that.

He knew he needed to wrap things up quickly. The pace of events was accelerating, and if the work wasn't completed quickly, the plan was likely to fall apart, with dire consequences. Tim's grand scheme of sabotaging one of the school buses hadn't produce any results. Walt would never have agreed to go after high school kids if the plan hadn't been in motion by the time he'd been informed of his part in it. Of course, he'd done so much already he never thought he would agree to, even if his selections thus far—Lyle Dietz and Joe Underwood, the criminal and the decrepit shut-in—weighed less heavily on his conscience. He was relieved when Tim told him that he'd followed "a girl," but that she'd stayed on her phone the entire way home, and he was afraid she'd say his name before he could subdue her. Still, that left vacancies to fill. And it was time to start looking at who was available instead of who was justifiable.

Perhaps it was the wrong play to keep the Nowlans around. Maybe he should have taken their statements and driven them to their car and escorted them straight out of the county. But they needed two more sacrifices to appease that grotesque beast in the abandoned factory. He had hoped to even the scales by making Eldon the sixth sacrifice, but he wasn't going to handicap his one shot at success by obsessing over revenge. There was time enough for that afterward. And it seemed almost like a gift to have a couple of out-of-towners thrown into the mix, involved enough to expect he might interact with them further, but whose absence was easily accounted for. What explanation rang truer than they left? He brought their car in to keep them from striking out on their own. Why did Eldon bring it to the station and not the hotel? Oh, that damn old drunk; he couldn't do anything right. Or, if need be, it *had* been impounded—for reasons Walt hoped to think of before the question came up.

He pulled into his driveway and parked beside Britt's car (formerly the family car). He sighed. It was fine. It wasn't unusual for him to be home on a Saturday afternoon, and it *would* be unusual for her to want to interact with him. He just needed a little time to formulate a plan. The first thing he needed was up-to-the-minute information. He pushed the angled monitor flat against the dashboard and leaned across the center console. He popped open the glove compartment and pulled out the burner phone he'd bought in St. Marys on Monday night. Even knowing he would destroy the phone as soon as the ordeal was over, he hadn't been foolish enough to program the one number he would ever call on it (and deleted the call history after every use). He dialed Tim's cell phone number from memory.

After five rings, Tim answered, "Hey, Chief."

Walt swallowed a snarl. There was no point fighting with the kid about how he answered the phone. The greeting was overloud, as though compensating. Walt heard a constant noise in the background like an engine and the space of wind. Tim was driving somewhere.

"Two hikers found the body in the woods this morning," Walt said. "I sent my deputies just far enough away to miss it, but there'll be more questions about it soon."

"Yeah," Tim drawled, "probably sooner rather than later. The guy's dead."

"Guy? What guy?"

"The hiker guy who found the body this morning. He took the place of that girl from the dollar store."

"What?!" Walt scanned the windows of his house frantically to make sure Britt wasn't watching from the row of three looking out from the living room. He glanced at the second story as well, though he thought it unlikely to see her there, as her bedroom was at the back of the house. "You killed him?"

"I told you: He's dead."

Walt's face reddened with fire. He was both angry and fearful the plan had progressed without his knowledge. It had been his intention to possibly make use of the hikers—but Tim hadn't known that. As calmly as possible, he asked, "Where is he?"

Tim snorted. "I told you that too. He took the place of that Dora girl. Like, literally. Or just about. He's *inside* the shelter house this time."

"Jesus! Are you fucking kidding me? He's in the same place?"

"Hey, Mon Capitan, it's all good. Numeral one, he *has* to be somewhere near that spot. We're building the hexagram—you know, the one you screwed up when you dug little Dora out of her cocoon. The sacrifices mark the points." Walt knew that. Tim had explained it when he had enlisted his aid: The start of the hexagram generated the power to begin the resurrection, by gathering the town's ghosts. That was how his wife had appeared to him… and why she would not again if they failed to protect the points and complete the ritual. "Numbero two," Tim went on, "there's police tape everywhere to keep anyone from finding him. Though you might want to stretch a few fresh pieces across the door."

Walt grumbled wordlessly. He had to admit, it wasn't the worst place to stash a body. But with the man dead, that meant there

was no getting rid of the woman unless they *got rid of her.*
"What about the woman?"

Walt heard a rustle and thought, *The idiot is shrugging on the phone again.*

"Do you know where she is?" he pressed.

"Wandered off into the forest for some reason," he said. "The guy had a gimpy knee, so she left him behind. That's love for you."

Walt had been right in thinking they might go to retrieve their car. Impounding it might have been a good move—or it might prove disastrous given the new development. He threw off his hat and rubbed his head to ease the throbbing. His hair was greasy. He wondered how long it had been since he showered. He heard a crunch: wheels on gravel.

"Look, I gotta go," Tim said. "I'll call later about number six."

"Wait," Walt pleaded. "One more thing: Do the bodies stay where they are?"

"Huh?"

"The bodies of the sacrifices. Do they get 'used up' somehow at the end of the ritual? Or do they stay where we put them?"

Tim rephrased it. "Are you gonna have to clean up after me?" He inhaled noisily through his teeth. "Hadn't really thought of that." Walt heard a door open and then shut. "I guess corpses just stay corpses, don't they? All but one anyway."

Then Walt heard another door open and shut.

"Are you alone?" he asked in a panic. "Is there someone else there with you?"

"Later, tater," Tim said, and the connection went dead.

"Goddammit!" Walt shouted as he punched the steering wheel. Then he scanned the front of his house again. Behavior like this

Britt would have to ask about. He was relieved he didn't see her watching.

Was there someone else with Tim? If there was, they undoubtedly heard him call Walt "Chief"—and Tim undoubtedly *wanted* them to. Walt had always assumed Tim was working alone. Did he have help the entire time? He hadn't thought it occurred to Tim that Walt would have to deal with him when the work was done. Maybe Tim was smarter than he gave him credit for and had planned ahead. Walt tipped his crown back on the headrest. Things were going to keep getting messier. But it was too late to stop, even if he wanted to.

And he didn't want to. The goal—the inviolate *necessity*—hadn't changed.

The woman—Eve—would come to him. She'd have to. Her car was gone and now her husband had disappeared. He could use that. Maybe he could tie the two things together. He would drive by the shelter house. If more tape really did need putting up, he would do that, but he wouldn't do anything to draw unnecessary attention to the crime scene. Tim said he would call later. There was nothing else he could do until then. Maybe he could still finagle it so Eldon was the sixth victim, or maybe it had to be Eve. It would depend on how things shook out. He caught his scent in the warming car. Maybe a shower would be a good idea. If he needed to rely on the support of the department later, it would be best to avoid raising questions about his fitness to perform his duties. He got out of the cruiser and went up the walk.

Britt eased away from her parents' (*her father's*) bedroom window and then hurried down the hall to the stairs when she heard her father opening the front door. She scampered softly halfway down by the time he stepped into the living room. He looked shocked to see her, as though caught doing something wrong—in addition to looking more haggard and overwhelmed than usual. And after the performance she'd just watched through the window (where the trauma of seeing her mother's ghost had driven her), she was worried about him, and about herself, and about her world falling apart even further than it had since June.

"Dad? Are you okay?" She tried to sound innocently concerned, but her voice shook, and she was certain he heard it.

"Hmnh? Oh, yeah, I'm fine, peanut. Just work stuff." He gestured to brush away the invisible trifles.

Britt couldn't remember him ever calling her "peanut" in her life. "Is it about Dora Givens?"

Walt scowled and nodded after a pause.

"If-if it's okay… I don't want you to worry, but I'm supposed to go over to Valeria's tonight for a few hours. I'll be driving there with Gwen and we'll be right there on her dad's farm the whole time."

"Oh. Oh, sure. That's fine, honey, I trust you." He realized after he said it that he was supposed to be worried about her safety in light of recent events, but having already agreed, and thankful that she would be safely out of the way for the evening, he couldn't think how to append the right sentiment of concern.

She came the rest of the way down the stairs and lingered with her hand on the small globe atop the newel post. "Dad, I just wanted to say… I want to tell you that I believe you."

He stared at her uncomprehendingly. "You believe me?"

"About Mom," Britt said. She sniffed. "I believe you about seeing Mom. I want you to know it's okay with me. That you saw her."

"Oh, honey," he said. For the first time in half her life, he felt a fatherly instinct that he obeyed without question, and he went toward her with open arms. She rushed into them, sobbing and smiling. He wondered what had caused the change and realized with chagrin what might have transpired. "You didn't—honey, did you see anything?"

"Me?" She snuffled into his shoulder. "No. No, I didn't see anything." She pulled back and wiped her eyes. "Dad, you're, um… stinky."

He laughed. "I know. I was just about to wash up." He passed her and started up the stairs. Halfway up, he turned back. The moment with his daughter confirmed for him he was doing the right thing. He felt suddenly reinvigorated, almost jubilant. Beneath his tussled hair, his bloodshot eyes were wide with joy. "Thank you for telling me that," he said. "I want you to know that you don't have to worry, not about anything. I'm gonna put it all right! I'm working on it right now and you're gonna be so happy when it's done. You'll see. We're gonna get back everything we lost. We'll be a family again!"

Then Walt bounded the rest of the way up the stairs, unmindful of the fear in his daughter's eyes after his manic rant.

CHAPTER 17

D ARREN WAS GLAD TO be back in his truck after folding up inside Hannah's sports coupe, which had proved to be the least-inconspicuous decoy imaginable anyway. He took comfort from the solid performer; it steadied him. Perhaps that was why he left his hand on the hood as he crossed in front of it, to draw from that constancy and keep from punching Tim's teeth through the back of his skull. Once more he faced the loading bay doors of the abandoned factory.

"You told Pearcey what we did."

"I didn't tell the chief *we* did anything at all," Tim replied. He fished a rumpled pack of Marlboros from his jeans pocket and shook one to his lips. "Besides, he has to know," he muttered as he lit the crooked cigarette, then exhaled. "It's hard to go on a murder spree in a small town without the aid of local law enforcement."

The scent of tobacco wafted under Darren's nose and he scowled. The dizzy rush of a nicotine buzz might work wonders for his head right now, but he be damned if he was going to share a friendly moment with his brother's killer. "What did he say about the woman?"

"Not much," Tim said. "I figure that's his problem. I don't think *she's* the chick we need to worry about. Your girl freaked the fuck out back there. You sure she's on board?"

It was true; Hannah hadn't reacted well. What should he have expected? Crime was all good fun until harsh reality stumbled bleeding out from the abstract. He hadn't told her he was going to kill the guy—and right in front of her too. He didn't tell her because he didn't think she *was* on board, not with murder. And there was no way she would be convincing if she suspected that was the case. But he didn't tell her otherwise. He just told her what he needed to have done and relied on her natural disinclination to believe the life she'd adopted could ever go that far to keep her from extrapolating the outcome. And in the aftermath, he would rely on her self-recrimination at facilitating something that she only pretended wouldn't end badly to bring her in line. Her guilt would have made her manageable.

But any fear- or guilt-born loyalty was smothered in the crib by the appearance of Bat-with-ten-eyes. A blood-guzzling, amber-guano-weaving, jumbled-up monster would do that. He turned away; he had no desire to see the creature at work. But horror held Hannah's gaze fast, and unbidden, she stretched her neck to watch even as he tried to obscure her view. He had to haul her up from the corner and take her out of the shelter house to stop her from screaming despite the danger of discovery. Fortunately, the park was still empty, and he kept his hand firmly over her mouth until he could shove her in the cab of his truck and shut the windows. He would've given just about anything not to have Brad Paisley's "Ticks" be the song he pumped up to cover her terror-fueled meltdown.

"Not something you can do much to prepare for," he responded to his own thoughts. Then, he clarified to Tim, "She's not my girl."

He scoffed. "Great. So, no loyalty, then? Just some rando along for the ride? Brilliant."

"She's my brother's girl," Darren growled. "You remember him, don't you?"

Tim affected an unconcerned attitude, but his hand shook as he dragged on his cigarette. "Well, that's fine then, I suppose. Now that you've explained to her that you cut that guy's throat open so that Ixixiklis will bring her boyfriend back after he gets his sixth sacrifice."

No, of course he hadn't explained that to her. He hadn't mentioned Ixixiklis or identified Bat-with-ten-eyes or the human hexagram. She was already overwhelmed. The specifics would've sounded as meaningless as if he'd sat her down and started from nothing. In the end, after she'd calmed enough, he told her only that he was in control and that that was all she needed to know. And then he sent her home. Told her to smoke a joint and lie down. He'd take care of everything. He'd almost fooled himself into believing it had worked.

"Don't forget who's holding the knife," he scolded Tim. "Why are we back here anyway?"

"To keep the master up-to-date," Tim said.

They crossed the lot and climbed up to loading bay four.

"He can tell you things, but you can't talk back?" Darren asked.

Tim smiled. "Okay, so maybe I lied." He squatted and jimmied open the door with the flat bar. "This is for your benefit. There's something you need to hear direct from the master."

They went in. The competing scents of industrial stain and barnyard rot once again assailed Darren's nostrils. He heard fluttering and a pinging, skittering sound overhead. The ever-indistinct black-winged spider-thing moved through the rafters.

"How did he get here before us?"

"Motherfucker is fast, that's how. Bat-with-ten-eyes jumps from shadow to shadow when it tries not to be seen. But it's even faster when it takes to the air."

They passed the green beetle-like bulk of the first machine. Darren didn't turn to look at his brother in his faceted tomb. He'd see him again soon enough. He'd see him put right. As they walked deeper into the gloom, something large shifted in the angle farthest from the twilight seeping through the high windows.

A shape rose from the dense nest of refuse gathered in the corner. Darren couldn't see it as well as he could earlier in the day, and he was thankful. As terrifying as Bat-with-ten-eyes was, there were aspects to its appearance that registered easily: It was a beast, a predator—it killed with tooth and claw; the horror of its inscrutable form was still recognizable from the inexpertly-realized nightmares of a hundred special effects artists; warnings screamed from the unevolved root of the cerebellum that this thing was alien and adversarial. But Ixixiklis was so much worse somehow. There was no comfort of a primal ideal of evil. He was a thing that should have been a joke, but could only have been a demon, for only a scion of blasphemy could be so grotesquely bizarre. After one glance of the fiend, Darren had understood he would never be prey to it. He did not rate as prey. "Plaything" was the best he could hope for.

Ixixiklis was well over twice as tall as Darren, strangely lean, yet with a bulbous stomach under which a long, red penis drooped, occasionally twitching like a wounded snake. His arms reached to his knees, tapering to slender, pointed fingers. His neck was crane-like, almost too reedy; its head wobbled atop. The head was birdlike as well, but the wide, sloped, shoebill beak was broken halfway back. A pale, pink tongue swelled and retracted from the open fissure of a maw like a slowly beating heart. The eyes—those atop the head—were hidden under an ever-shifting crown of flies swarming over each other. The other eyes—the bloodshot, fist-size eyes in the face of the distended belly—rolled with dumb hate, like those of an intractable dog whose only sin was to see instinctively the usurping threat of a newborn human parasite. A puckering, star-seamed mouth took the place of a belly button. Ixixiklis was oddly brightly colored: oily stone-blue feathers covered his back and limbs; his chest and neck shimmered with absinthian scales; the abdomen and terrible face thereon were ochre. And midnight-purple wings hung like a cloak, lizard wings rent with tears, useless and impotent with disuse.

Ixixiklis and his emissary may have been the first things Darren was truly scared of since his father, but the same deep-rooted resilience that enabled him to leave dear old Dad in the trunk of a burning car held firm even in the face of this most awful potentate. He rejected God when he was a teenager; what greater authority was there to defy? Darren stood his ground and spoke first.

"I did it," he squawked. He cleared his throat and started again. "I made the sacrifice."

"We know of the fifth." Neither mouth spoke, though the tongue-crop rolled and the belly-maw quivered. It occurred to Darren that it was the cloud of flies speaking the itchy words. *"A stranger to you."*

Was it a compliment? Darren responded as though it might be. "Yes. Untraceable."

"The final sacrifice… must be known to you… must have mean-ing… to fulfill the pact."

Darren shook the scratching echoes from his ears as he chuck-led. "Not a problem," he said. "I've got just the man in mind.

And believe me, killing him will have great meaning to me." He resisted the urge to glance at Lyle's corpse. "Been building to it for a long time even before he decided to offer up my brother."

Ixixiklis raised its arms at the elbows and waved them over its belly, crossing and uncrossing. The eyes there ricocheted with excitement, watching the lithe hands move. Darren interpreted the gesture as a sign of approval or assent.

"One thing I gotta ask, though," Darren said. Tim cackled behind him at his impertinence, but it only steeled his determination. "What do you get out of it?"

"We feed," was the reply.

"Feed on the sacrifices?" Darren asked. "But Lyle is one of them. So how can you bring him back if you feed on him?"

"We will feed," Ixixiklis reaffirmed. *"The pact… is ever honored. He who offers… the final sacrifice… is rewarded."*

The statement was clear, declarative, and unsatisfactory. Darren had heard lies that said too much and lies that said too little.

"We do not lie."

Could it read his mind? Darren jumped as Tim slapped him on the back, laughing.

"I, for one, believe him *completely*," Tim said.

CHAPTER 18

ALLAN ANDREWS SHOUTED, "MYSTERY solved!" to the far end of the parking lot where Eve had wandered in the vain hope that when she turned around her silver crossover would be sitting there, waiting. Allan explained that he'd radioed the Adler Police Department and found out that the Nowlans' vehicle had been towed there, though he couldn't explain why exactly. "Bobbi Sturges—she's the county recorder, she does dispatch for the department—she said she didn't know it was going to be brought in, but she guessed maybe Chief Pearcey had had it done to save you the trouble of having to go get it."

Eve thought Allan's interpretation overly optimistic; to her, the mystery was only deepened, and the motivations of the local authorities made only more inscrutable. Feeling exposed and alone out in the woods, she was reticent to accept Allan's offer to drive her to the police station but saw no other option. As they emerged (safely) from the forest, she considered telling Allan about the body she and Zander had discovered that morning. She needn't say anything about her concerns as to the chief; she could let him find his own discomfort, wondering why the Forestry Service hadn't been notified. But she was still nervous about how simpatico the two agencies might be, and instead asked to be dropped at the hotel. Her best strength would be found in the company of her husband. No matter what else had troubled them, and no matter what they might squabble about privately, they were a team of two against the world. She was sure that was the truth at the core of their relationship, and having realized it, she was more anxious than ever to be home—not merely to be out of and away from that damned town, but to be home *with* Zander, starting the rest of their lives together.

Upon discovering his absence, she rapidly vacillated between panic and anger, cursing him for his nonchalance in going out on his own and not even leaving a note. But she soon settled on panic. She could be mad later, if that was what was called for. If she found him safe and sound strolling down the sidewalk with two scoops of moose tracks in a waffle cone, the northeastern United States could rest assured they would hear her give him a piece of her mind. She looked forward to it. She prayed she would soon be bawling him out. Soon. Maybe. But now—now he wasn't there. Now she had no idea where he might be.

Could he have gone to the police station by himself? Yes, that made sense, if they'd called the hotel to let him know their car had been towed—though why they hadn't just brought it to the hotel, she couldn't guess. Or maybe they had, and Allan got the details wrong. Had Zander drove out trying to find her on the forest road? She checked her phone: no messages.

She went down to the reception desk and asked the pyramidical blonde woman if she'd seen Zander.

The woman took on a disapproving look and said, "Well, certainly I saw him. He left about an hour or so after you did, in the company of a young woman."

"What?" Eve had not been expecting that information. "Who was she?"

"Honey, the town's not *that* small. I don't know *everybody*."

Eve coaxed a description and recognized the nosy, mousy-haired girl from the pizzeria. Why would Zander leave the hotel with her? And what the hell did that girl want anyway, spying on them?

"Get me out of here!" Eve yelled as she banged through the hotel doors, and she did not care if the judgmental blonde heard her.

She could have gone back to the room and waited, but she knew that would have driven her crazy. There was only one possible destination. She hoped Zander would be there; regardless, reuniting the two of them with their vehicle required gathering all three pieces, and so Eve decided to start with the one she knew where to find.

Bobbi raised her head at the *bing-bong* toll. Usually, she caught sight of anyone approaching before they got in the door, but Bobbi was tired. It was far past time for her to leave; there were no Saturday hours for the county recorder's office (officially), and she rarely saw Grant on duty at all. But the report of the dead body, and the inexplicable silence of the nonevent it seemed to have precipitated, had stressed her out the entire day. She'd been waiting for the other shoe to drop. And the other shoe looked to be a leggy, pissed-off hiker.

"I understand my car is here for some goddamn reason, which I did not consent to," Eve barked.

Bobbi raised her palms and pushed them down gently in an "easy" motion. "Yes, that's right, Mrs…"

"Nowlan. Is my husband here? Has he been here?"

Bobbi hesitated, not sure where to start. She hadn't expected to be asked about the husband. It worried her further.

"Do you or does anyone here have any idea what is going on?!"

Bobbi's position had taught her toughness and patience. It was rare anyone flustered her, but she found herself on guard for the chief and not herself, and she sputtered.

Eve looked past Bobbi to the conference room she had occupied that morning (was it only that morning?), out of which emerged an enormous African-American man in an officer's uniform.

"Everything okay out here, Bobbi?" The question was honest and not directed confrontationally at Eve. Grant had been wondering for the last few hours why Bobbi was still there. She'd told him about the report of the body in the woods. He'd thought it odd the way Bobbi had downplayed it, but as nothing seemed to develop from it, he trusted her assessment.

"Officer Bundy, this is Mrs. Nowlan. She was the one, with her husband, who reported the body in the woods."

"Reported—" Eve was aghast. "Discovered! Are you telling me they didn't find it?"

"The sheriff sent Deputies Tuttle and Clay out to the location you provided—you saw," Bobbi said, though she couldn't remember if the deputies had left before the young couple. "Well, they didn't find anything, so…"

"Didn't find anything!" Eve interrupted. "They didn't find a fucking dead body stuck to a tree?"

Grant advanced toward the desk partition. "Miss, we can see that you're upset, but I'm gonna have to ask you to calm down."

A jolt shot through Bobbi and she leaped to intervene before Eve could respond to that most-hated instruction. "When we heard back that the deputies had not been able to find the body, they were recalled to base, and Chief Pearcey said—he said he'd go and find you and your husband to try to sort it out." The last part faltered. Bobbi knew it didn't sound good. She heard

Grant take in a deep breath behind her, as he, too, put together the timeline.

"How long ago was that?" Eve cried. "Here's a clue: We weren't in our car!"

"No, of course not. That was… separate," Bobbi muttered.

"When was the last time you spoke to the chief?" Eve demanded.

"Well, here you go," Grant said and gestured at the front of the station. "Here's the chief now."

Bing-bong!

Bobbi smiled through her fatigue. Walt was shaven and clean; he even seemed to have a spring in his step as he bounded up to the station entry. His face hardened at the sight of Mrs. Nowlan, but Bobbi had confidence Walt would soon put things right.

"Mrs. Nowlan," he greeted her sternly.

"I barely know where to start," Eve said. "You have my car. Do you have my husband too? As for the body, I really don't give a damn anymore. That's your problem now."

Walt crossed his arms. "Your husband is missing?"

"Yes! He was at the hotel when I left to go get my car where it was supposed to be!"

"I'm sorry to hear that, Mrs. Nowlan," Walt said. "I'm really sorry to hear that because I sure would like a word with the both of you. Your little prank—"

"Prank!"

Walt reared up, puffing out his chest. "We aren't a big department here, Mrs. Nowlan, and we don't have a lot of extra resources we can waste on a fool's errand when we have a real homicide that needs investigating. And seeing as we don't yet have a suspect for that homicide, and seeing as your husband is now missing, the circumstances being what they are, I'm going to ask my officer here to find you accommodation until we can sort this out to *my* satisfaction."

The declaration reverberated in the dead pause that followed. It was delivered with authority on a two-thirds friendly crowd who were used to jumping at the smallest request from its author. But Grant and Bobbi were stunned silent and immobile. It was Eve who found her voice in the interlude.

"You've got to be fucking kidding me!" Eve whirled around, hoping, somehow, for sympathy from the people she'd been arguing with moments before.

The best she got was Grant's dubious hesitation. "Uh, Chief?"

"Do I have to spell it out for you, Officer Bundy?" Walt shouted. "Throw her in lockup! I've had enough of this shit for one day. If a hotel's not good enough for her, then she can have a hard cot for the night."

Eve repeated, "You've got to be fucking kidding me!"

Bobbi wanted to say something, but she withered. Walt saw her plaintive expression and said, "We're overworked and we've got homes to get to. Bobbi, you're worn out. Go on now."

"Chief, it's just that, well, Eldon Landry is in lockup already."

The wheels spun hurtfully in Walt's mind. There was nothing to be done about it.

He said, "That's fine, then. She can't say we're not neighborly."

CHAPTER 19

Everything looked different on the day Tommy was born. Darren wasn't at the hospital. He'd already sloughed off Lita before she knew she was pregnant, and much as she might have wished it otherwise, the news didn't change the situation much. Darren knew he wasn't going to be deeply involved in his son's upbringing. Lita might have been a wildcat in the sack, but he counted that quality as the one agreeable expression of her too-turbulent personality. Besides, considering his experience with his own father, he thought he might be doing the kid a favor by staying away. Still: a son. Might get some fishing in. Teach him to take no shit and how to bloody a nose. Laugh like hell at his first hangover. He remembered looking at all the cars in the Walmart parking lot, looking at all the people coming out of the store, looking at the trees and the clouds—and everything was more brightly tinted, yet curiously appeared more fake. All these distractions were reduced to two dimensions because he had found a deeper connection to a hidden truth behind them. It didn't last, and he was glad of it. He didn't want to go waltzing around high on his own serotonin when life was waiting to bite his junk at the first opportunity.

He pulled up to his house and he didn't recognize it. Not because of any greater truth, but because the lie of ownership—of *any* connection—had been exposed. How could he make a claim on any part of this earth now that he had seen the things that really held the deed? He'd always been wary of threats of bodily harm, but he'd thought his vigilance and the greater danger *he* posed would see him through just fine—until they didn't, and who cared after that, right? He had not before seen menace in both shadow and light. Every plank of his house was kindling. The dirt it stood on was a place to dig a grave. To pretend otherwise was to buy into the deception. He wasn't even sure anymore whether it mattered if he brought Lyle back or not, but he would continue; he would see it through because he had started it. The rebel in his head was dazed and dumb and proposed no alternatives. He wondered if this was what other people felt like all the time—people who listened to other people and believed them, people who accepted authority, people who had faith. Was that what this was? Had he accepted a higher power—or was it a joke to think he even had the option whether to accept it?

"Fuck it," he said, and tried to pretend it was Darren the badass talking and not a disconnected passenger playing at being Darren the badass. He scowled at his doubts and squeezed his fists. He charged through the front door in reclamation of his domain; tinder and tomb it may be, but it was *his*.

Darren's uninvited housemate yelped at his sudden entrance. She stood by the bookcase at the far end of the living room. It took a second for Darren to recognize the small object she cradled as the onyx figurine he'd first seen that morning. She'd changed clothes; Darren couldn't remember if she had had blood splatter on her. She wore jeans and a tight purple top. She had on black boots. He noticed that the pink Chuck Taylors weren't on the floor in front of the recliner.

"Going somewhere?" he accused.

Hannah wrapped her hands more tightly around the onyx dragon. "I think… maybe I should give you some space, you know, until Lyle comes back."

He flashed a smile as he took a step toward her. "You don't think Lyle is coming back," he said. "But you're wrong. Oh, he's dead. There's no doubt about that. I've seen his body. He looks a mess, let me tell you. Not real sexy right now." He took another step forward. "But I'm gonna get him back anyway. Got a pretty sweet deal going with a demon. You go ahead and laugh at that if you want."

Hannah sniffled. "I'm not laughing."

"No, you aren't, baby doll, are you? Could be you're not in a laughing mood on account of what you saw me do a little while ago."

"I didn't know you were going to… to do that," she said. "I didn't know…"

"Oh, you knew. You knew damn well what me and my brother do, what this life is. Did you think you could be a tourist, just peek in for a bit, then go back home, same as you left?" He took another step, and another.

"Please," she started, and then pivoted. "That—that *thing*."

"That was the demon's apprentice. It's helping to build a hexagram out of the bodies, whatever that is." Hannah stared uncomprehendingly. "You poor thing," Darren mocked her. He stepped within arm's reach and raised his right hand to brush the streak of tears from her cheek. "You don't know which of us you're more afraid of." He pushed up against her and she shuffled backward into bookcase. "I know it's early yet, but you've had a rough day. Why don't you go get ready for bed?" He slid his knuckles down from her cheek and along her neck, and then turned his hand over to grab her breast hard. "Then we can *really* talk about rough."

Darren thought she might acquiesce out of fear. That would have been disappointing; he hoped she would resist. He was ready for a tumble. He didn't think Hannah had it in her to whip the onyx block up from her hip faster than he could react and crack his eye socket.

Hannah hadn't thought she'd had it in her either. She'd hoped to be gone before he got back, partly as a general life adjustment brought on by seeing a man murdered in front of her and partly because every encounter she'd had with Darren since he got back had involved violence in one way or another. The sight of the dark monster in the shelter house had filled her cup of fear beyond its tipping point. She reacted on instinct; her body processed the threat to its well-being without the filters of doubt or judgment. It continued in service, as she twisted, ducked, and leaped to the side in a singular motion, almost dodging Darren's wild swing. The clip on her cheekbone didn't slow her. She sprang toward the front door, wild with hope. A hand on her ankle toppled her. She fell, smacking her left arm on the coffee table, turning her over on her back. The onyx dragon clattered across the floor into the kitchen. Darren grabbed at her legs, climbing from ankle to knee to thigh, forcing one leg between hers. She screamed and clawed at his face as he pushed his bulk up on to her torso. He gripped her left wrist and brought it across her body, preparing to turn her over. Then he froze.

Hannah saw he was looking toward the kitchen. She tried to angle her head to see what he saw. His grip slacked slightly as he said, "Lyle?" Hannah crunched her abdomen down and snapped her legs up in one desperate flex. Darren groaned as her knee smashed into his groin. She squeezed out like a shot from beneath him and staggered to her feet, hurtling into the sunroom. With Darren still on the floor, Hannah glanced toward the front of the house.

Lyle stood inside the closed door. He looked the same as the day she'd last seen him, droop-eyed and lanky in his faded Dickies work shirt, with that slight stoop from a lifetime of adjusting to being taller than everyone else in the room. He just stood there, staring at Darren or staring at her, or both, somehow, as though two faces were projected atop each other. There was something strange about him, almost as though he wasn't there at all. Hannah thought it was the surprise at seeing him, suddenly, after so long, that made it seem that way. If she ran to him and grabbed hold, then she would know he was real, and maybe she could even rely on him to protect her. But perhaps that was why it seemed he wasn't there—because she knew he wouldn't choose her over his brother. And she suddenly realized that she didn't care. He didn't seem real because it didn't matter if he was there or not. She understood this was not where she was supposed to be, and she needed no one's approval to leave. And that door swinging shut in her heart nudged her to move while Darren was still recovering. She thought briefly about hitting him again hard across the back of the head, but decided her best course was the one she had intended from before he stepped through the door, which was to get away as fast as possible.

She careened through the sunroom and burst out the back door. Rather than run around the house to the front, she charged into the woods. The low, three-quarter moon helped, though the trees still held most of their leaves. She wished she had her cell phone flashlight to guide her, but she felt she could find her way without it. She knew the woods better than either of the Dietz brothers might have expected. She hadn't been in the house long, but she liked to walk there when she was alone (or when she needed to be alone). It was simple for her to find the C tree—so named because it looked like a person forming the letter while performing the chorus of the Village People's "YMCA." Five feet beyond she dropped to her knees. She moved aside two crossed branches and then scraped away an inch of dirt, revealing a buried popcorn tin. She pried the top away. She grabbed the rolls of cash set on top and then replaced the lid, dirt, and branches. She didn't want to take the drugs with her. It wasn't Lyle who'd moved the stash when Darren went to prison, it was she who did it after Lyle went missing. She didn't want to be busted with all of that in the house and no one else to take the fall for it. She wasn't sure why she'd lied to Darren when he'd attacked her. Some instinct of self-preservation guided her to do it. Or maybe she just didn't like getting slammed to the floor.

Lyle had warned her Darren had set traps in the woods (at his behest), but she'd seen on her first walk they weren't well hidden and guessed Darren had only set them to placate his brother, and she'd memorized their locations. As she steered clear of a bear trap she knew to lay ten yards to her left, she heard a weak voice call out, "Hello? Help! Is someone there?"

She glanced back the way she'd came to make sure the Dietz brothers weren't in pursuit. Whoever needed her help, alive or dead (nothing would surprise her at that point), she wasn't stopping if they were coming after her. But she didn't hear anyone crashing through the underbrush. The voice called again, louder, dry throated, "Please! Is someone there?"

"Shhh!" she cautioned. She crept nearer to the sound, guessing correctly that it came from the vicinity of the sprung trap. She was not expecting to find the person caught therein. "What the hell are you doing out here?" she hissed.

"Oh, thank God!" Connor exclaimed. "I'm stuck in this thing. I think my leg's broken. It hurts!" He groaned in emphasis as he tried to sit upright. "I passed out from the pain and I can't get the damn thing off!"

"Hold on!" Hannah said as she knelt beside him. Lyle had shown her how to work the bear traps. It took her only a second to find the release and trip it. Then she pulled the jaws apart, inhaling through a sympathetic grimace as the teeth slid free from Connor's flesh and out from his blood-soaked pantleg. He cried out as she did, and she again admonished him, "Shhh! Or do you want them to hear you?"

She cupped the back of his knee to ease his leg clear from the trap. He muffled another groan as she set the trap aside.

"I need to get to the hospital," he urged.

"You sure as hell do," she replied. "Where's your car?"

He pointed. "A hundred yards or so that way, off the dirt road."

Hannah sighed exasperatedly. "This is gonna suck for the both of us."

He nodded. "I know. I appreciate your help," he said. "Though I don't care for the situation, all things considered, it's good to see you, Hannah."

DARREN COULDN'T READ LYLE'S expression. Other than constant anxiety, Lyle never gave too much away. Was he angry at him for going after Hannah? Did he even see Darren attack her at all? What did it matter, really? Darren knew this was just a shade, a massless placeholder wandering dumb and, well, dead to the world. If he did see, would he even remember when Darren brought him back? There would be other things on his mind at that point, undoubtedly. Half bent from the throbbing ache in his balls, Darren steadied himself against the entertainment center. He pulled himself fully upright, hoping that if he could look Lyle directly in the eyes, he could better understand what his presence there meant—or if it meant anything at all.

But just as he got his feet under him, the door opened, and Lyle disappeared as if it wiped him from existence. In his place stood feral-haired Lita, her body heaving with deep breaths, her eyes ablaze.

"I saw everything, and I heard some of it," she said. "Now I need you to explain to me exactly what is happening."

Chapter 20

V ALERIA GLANCED TOWARD HER house and twisted down a little smile she didn't want anyone to see. She appreciated her father for maintaining the conceit of the party—that she and her friends were on their own, away from prying eyes. They were drinking beer and smoking weed, right? What else should they think? But she knew he was keeping an eye on them—not excessively; not watching but still watching out, and she was thankful. She was happy to be included with these popular girls (even if she had been pressed into hosting), but she felt out of her depth and didn't know what was expected. When she apologized to him for the short notice in asking to have friends over that night, he teased her, "I always felt I missed out on one of the great joys of being a parent with you: I spent your entire youth getting a good night's sleep *not* having to put together projects for school at the last minute. You were always too well-prepared!" Not only had he consented to the gathering, he had helped to set up.

He fashioned a shallow firepit, forming a four-level circle with loose bricks from an old outdoor oven he'd dismantled. He moved the two wooden chairs from the porch and sprayed down the two plastic chairs from the garage. Then assembled a pair of simple benches from milk crates and twelve-foot planks. He left a space around the circle where he told her she could enlist a friend to bring over the outdoor swing if she wanted; he said if he brought it over then they'd known he had done it, winking.

"It's not gonna be that many people," Valeria said.

He shrugged and replied, "Sometimes more people show up." He hugged her shoulder and added, "You might not believe this, but your father used to go to parties long, long ago when he was your age."

She giggled and chided him. "Dad!"

"No, it's true!" he went on. "Me and my friends, we liked a good fire, sure. And we might have a few beers, and you know, maybe even smoke a little something… but that was *it*. Oh, and stay on *this* side of the barn."

Valeria blushed and shrank, but she was grateful that, not only did he understand, but he laid out the parameters. She felt emboldened to be able to say what was allowed and not allowed if it came to that.

Despite that, she was also relieved to see that it might not be an issue at all. Gwen had flashed a crumpled baggie of cocaine before the boys arrived, but when Valeria said she didn't want anything heavier than beer and weed at the party, Britt had backed her right away. Gwen pouted for a second and rolled her eyes to say "lame," but she put the coke away and didn't bring it up again. The boys brought the usual domestic cans.

Dave Pruitt had a flask, but it was small, and as soon as he'd passed it to Jenna to take her first sip, she shook it and complained, "There's nothing in here!"

Dave nodded and smiled as he pocketed the flask, proud of himself, "Damn! Killed it already." Despite his bravado, Valeria didn't think there could have been too much in it to begin with, as the boys seemed sober.

And rather than finagling to get their hands under the girl's shirts, the boys were consumed with fondling Chris's latest toy. He'd just bought the drone that morning and done one successful test flight with his dad around the school parking lot.

The other two taunted Bill Wollert's use of the anachronistic phrase, "She's a beaut!" which led to a quick round of shoulder punches.

Chris cautioned, "Watch out for the drone!" and that stopped the tussle abruptly, out of respect for the awe-inspiring gadget.

"Christ, were they geeks this whole time and no one knew?" Gwen sneered.

Bill was nearer her than the others and overheard. Sensitive after his earlier mocking, he rebutted, "Ain't no geek shit, babe, this shit is cool! You can fly this up and see everything on the control screen, real-time. We can fly right over the whole town if we want."

Britt thought, *And what are you going to do with the* next *five minutes?* But she kept it to herself. She wanted Valeria to feel good about her party; matching Gwen's cynicism would only spoil things. Besides, Bill's pitiable identification with the object (*"We can fly"*) made the swipe too cruel to inflict.

Jenna straddled the gender divide, popping up from the bench and expanding the cluster around the drone, blurting, "Really? Let me see!"

Chris squeezed next to her and showed her the glowing screen angled up from the controller he held in two hands. "Hang on, I've got to turn on the night vision, then I'll take her up."

The four splayed rotors whined and the small circle bloomed open. The shiny pearl finish gleamed yellow from the fire as it shuddered and rose. Valeria, too, was excited, and she got up to stand underneath as the drone ascended to twenty feet. The group all moved together following in baby steps in the direction of the drone, as though drawn after it. "What are we doing?" Dave laughed, and they all remembered the purpose of the view screen.

"This is not happening," Gwen said. She brought her phone out and turned it on. "I might have to make contingency plans so this whole fucking night isn't a waste," she said to Britt. She called Connor by pressing the number saved as "Fellowship."

A woman's voice answered. "Hello?"

Gwen was struck dumb. She couldn't have misdialed; the number was programmed.

"Hello?" the voice repeated.

"Who the fuck is this?" Gwen demanded.

The connection went dead.

Gwen redialed the number, again using the preset. It rang six times and then went to Connor's voicemail. Gwen hung up and stared hard into the fire.

"Everything alright?" Britt asked. She could read it was not.

"I think I'm going to be very pissed off," Gwen said. "Some fucking bitch just answered Connor's phone."

"Oh," Britt said. "Well, I mean—he's a perv, isn't he? Do you really care?"

Gwen turned to glare at her. "I care to not be fucking *usurped*." She grabbed her red velveteen clutch and stood. "Come on. I need you to drive me to Connor's."

Britt arched her eyebrows. "You can't be serious." Gwen tilted her head and opened her eyes wide to signal her expectation of compliance. "I'm not leaving. Not yet. It would be rude. And certainly not to drive you to Mr. McAuley's house so you can—what? Confront him for sleeping with *another* high school girl?"

"Wow." Gwen seethed. "Wow. I didn't know you cared so *little*."

"I do care," Britt protested. "That's why I don't like seeing you throwing your life away—"

Gwen laughed. "Jesus! Overdramatic much? 'Throwing my life away?' I'm getting fucked by my dealer because it suits me. I get mine. You think *he's* in control? I want to protect my investment—you know, instead of *throwing my life away* at this lame-shit excuse for a party where everyone is playing with a remote-control airplane!"

"Gwen, come on," Britt said. She picked up the pack of cigarettes beside her and pulled one out. "Look, I'm sorry I've been lousy company tonight. I've got a lot on my mind. This afternoon—"

"So, just to be clear, you are *not* gonna help me?"

Britt looked at her, the cigarette dangling from her lips. She couldn't think of any reason she should help Gwen. Or be her friend. "No," she said, "I'm not ready to leave just yet."

Gwen huffed exasperatedly and spun on her heel. She marched to the group ooh-ing and aah-ing around Chris as he controlled the drone's flight. She grabbed Jenna by the arm and yanked her away over Jenna's protestation. Britt watched them. Gwen outlined her demands. Jenna made a limp gesture indicating Britt. Gwen spared a dagger-shot glance at Britt and then quashed Jenna's objections. Jenna slumped dejectedly and straggled over to the fire. As she picked up her purse and phone she said, "Thanks a lot," to Britt.

"Sorry," Britt replied. And she was sorry for it; sorry especially that Jenna would have to leave with an angry Gwen in tow, even if Jenna was at the party only because she'd wanted a decoy for Valeria to begin with.

The boys were upset that Gwen and Jenna were leaving, but Jenna promised she'd be back just as soon as she dropped off Gwen. Whether it was that reassurance or their otherwise-occupied attention, their show of disappointment was short-lived.

Britt sighed and stood as they left. The night was getting cooler and she was sad to stray from the fire. She meandered toward the group, taking several long drags on her cigarette.

"What is that?" Bill asked.

"It used to be a metal factory," Valeria said. "It's off of Wilburville, almost straight across those fields on the other side of the street. It's closed now."

"Cool," Chris replied with a lilt of giddiness in his tone, as though its status as abandoned made it worthy of further investigation. "Let's go down and get a little closer."

"Who's that?" Dave asked.

"Who?"

"Where?"

"There," he said, pointing at the screen. "Out near the road, there's someone standing there."

Britt maneuvered into the cluster and got a look at the green-hazed screen. Dave was right, there was someone there, and he appeared to be looking up at the approaching drone. As the drone lowered, the face grew larger and more clearly defined, until all present could make out a recognizable smirk.

"Tim fucking Neuworth," Bill snarled.

Tim had his hands in his pockets. He tipped his head, as though in greeting. Then the image shook violently and went blank in a squall of static.

"What the hell?" Chris exclaimed.

"What happened?"

"What did he do?" Bill asked.

"Are you sure it was—" Britt began.

"That shitbag!" Bill interrupted. "Of course it was him!"

"Come on!" Dave said. "Get your keys. Let's go get him!"

"Let's just run across," Chris suggested.

"Wait, guys, no!" Valeria yelled, but they were already hurrying down the driveway toward the road. She started after them, calling, "Please don't hurt him!"

Her father's voice stopped her. "Valeria? *¿Qué pasa?*"

"**I** KNOW WHY YOU'RE here," Barkley called out into the dark from his front porch. John Tuttle, off duty and out of uniform, stepped up onto the sidewalk from the street, into the diffuse border of the porch light's glow. Barkley swept his arm across his body and pointed at the driveway. "Use the walk. One of my goddamn neighbors' dogs keeps shitting on my lawn. If I find out who, I'll come shit on your lawn!" he informed the neighborhood.

John walked over to the driveway and then followed the arc of the walk up to the porch. Barkley sat on one of two metal chairs with floral vinyl cushions tied to the back and seat. On a stand beside him was an ash tray with a smoldering cigar and a small radio with an announcer giving the play-by-play of a football game. On the floor to his right was an open twelve pack of beer. Barkley reached into the torn opening and pulled one out to offer wordlessly to John.

"No, thanks," John dismissed with a wave. "I'll just be a minute."

"Probably just as well," Barkley said. He popped open the beer for himself and set it next to the ashtray. "Buffalo," he said. "Non-conference against Troy, I think, or some other Sun Belt joke."

John leaned against the end post of the balustrade. "You said you knew why I was here."

Barkley laughed. "You might've saved yourself a trip. You know damn well Bobbi called me too, just like she did you. She wants us all to be one happy family."

"I think she wants peace because she wants us all on the same page."

"I *get* it, okay?" Barkley picked up the cigar and chomped down on it, muffling his words. "Bobbi loves the chief; you love the chief." He opened his arms. "We all love the chief."

"She told you who's in lockup?"

"Yes, she did indeed." He took the cigar out of his mouth and blew steely smoke at the crackling bug zapper. "Both of 'em. Should be a fun night for Grant, babysitting."

"Now, I don't want you thinking I'm questioning the chief's call—"

"Do tell."

"I understand we have an unsolved murder," John said. "So, if he wants to hold Mrs. Nowlan, then okay. But I'm thinking that won't lead to anything. And I'm thinking the best way to get the chief to drop that line is to come up with something else."

"We ain't got anything else," Barkley replied.

"No, we don't," John said. "So, we start looking again. I want to pay Darren Dietz a visit in the morning, try to find out some more about Lyle's disappearance, see if there's any connection there." Barkley chuckled. "I know it ain't much, and it likely won't be too pleasant. Which is why I need my partner with me."

Barkley guffawed. "Ain't you a goddamn peach? Oh, man, Bobbi works her magic well." He set the cigar back down and appraised John, who waited patiently. "Maybe you haven't met me and my sparkling personality, but I think you're better off taking that meeting by yourself. But I'll tell you what: I'll come in and catch up with you at the station afterward and we'll go from there, okay? Now get home to your family, for God's sake. What the hell are you doing wasting your Saturday night hanging out with a coworker?"

John smiled. "Alright then. See you tomorrow." He straightened, left the porch, followed the path back to the driveway, and continued to his car waiting on the dark street.

After John drove away, a man with a buzz cut passed in front of Barkley and sat noiselessly on the other chair.

Barkley chuckled. "You should've come out a minute ago, that would have been something." He picked up his beer and took a sip. "I'd offer you one, but…" He set the beer on his lap and they sat in silence for a minute. Then Barkley said, "I know I shouldn't be so hard on him. But it ain't the same. He ain't a friend. He ain't the guy that I grew up with and chased girls with and signed on with. Don't get me wrong, I'm damn glad to see you, but it makes it harder, thinking about how things should've been. Hell, we might not be in this mess at all if you'd've just come home from Afghanistan in one piece."

The man in the chair turned his half head as though distracted by a noise.

"COME ON, MAN! WE don't want him to get away!" Bill called over his shoulder.

"I'm coming!" Dave replied, thirty yards back. "Goddamn flip-flops!"

"Do you see him?" Chris asked.

"Watch out for the ditch!" Bill cautioned.

There was a ruffle of brush at the edge of the field of prickly fescue. Between it and the road lay a shallow rut for rainwater runoff glinting in the blue moonlight, just wide and deep enough to twist an ankle in. Bill and Chris jumped over easily and continued across the empty road.

"There it is!" cried Chris, spotting the wreck of his new prized possession.

"There he is!" said Bill, pointing to Tim, who was leaning his rear and hands on the cement company sign of the plant's former occupant.

"Hey, guys!" he shouted. "Missed you since I haven't been at school. I haven't been able to keep up with my daily beatings. I've tried to get my mom to do it, but you know what a useless lump she is."

"You're a sick fuck!" Bill shouted as he approached, fists up. "You want a beating, freak? You're about to get one you ain't gonna get up from!"

"What did you do to my drone?" Chris held the shattered implement in his hands, trying to will the broken pieces back together over the mangled wire sinew connecting them.

"Oh, I didn't do anything to your precious drone," Tim said. "He did." He pointed to the top of a utility pole behind him, causing Bill to stay the punch he was about to unleash and look up.

Bill was still inhaling for his scream when it was cut short still-born. The black mass flashed wide as it fell on him: enshrouding wings; obsidian spike legs; an opening under the soulless marble eyes—which must have been a mouth, its shape and interior too dark to make out before it clamped over his head entirely. Bill was smothered deaf and blind, but in the second before his head was ripped from his shoulders, he had time at least to feel scimitars stab into his chest and torso. And in the torturous eternity of blackness after he'd been disembodied, he suffered the heat and pressure of the crushing maw on his cracking skull.

Chris staggered backward. His legs trembled; the machinery of them suddenly foreign to his brain. The thing looked up. Eyes blinked in succession, a foul flirtation. It scampered forward and then leaped. Chris hurled the broken drone at it and spun to the side, smacking face-first into the utility pole by the road. But instead of tumbling over his useless legs, he remained upright; how, he didn't know. Then he realized he couldn't move at all. In fact, he couldn't feel anything below his waist. The pain in his midsection arrived simultaneously with the understanding that he was speared to the pole by one of the monster's spikelike legs.

Dave whimpered, face down in the rut, putrid rot assailing his nose. He tried to hold his breath; gurgling sobs leaked through his snot-strewn face.

"Now where did bozo number three go?" Tim wondered above him. "I suppose he must've run off, real quick like in his flip-flops."

Dave heard spattering on his back, then warmth. Tim was pissing on him. Tim knew where he was. Tim was going to have his pet abomination kill him and eat him.

"Flippity-floppity all the way home, scared little rabbit."

The stream trailed off and stopped. Dave heard an engine in the distance.

"Uh-oh. Company's coming to dinner."

Dave waited. He couldn't move. He listened. The engine got closer. It was a truck, for sure. He had to get up. He had to get help. He just had to *move*.

CHAPTER 21

"Hey! Hey, goddammit!" Eldon grabbed hold of the cell door bars and shook them so hard that his whole body rocked. But the door was securely locked and affixed; the clanking he produced was little better than knocking a pair of cans together. Realizing the futility of the endeavor—temporarily, because he was sure to try it again—he resumed shouting, "Hey, goddammit, I ain't even drunk! You gotta let me out!"

It was his second outburst in the hour since he woke up, and it was worse than the first. Eve didn't know if the reason Eldon was becoming more adamant was because he was telling the truth: He was sober, and he was pissed off because of it. Nighttime was prime drinking time; no responsibilities and no limits, so long as he stayed home. For Eve, Eldon's tantrum was just the icing on the crap cake. She had bigger worries. Shouldn't Zander have bailed her out by now—even if he couldn't manage that, if he'd been to the station at all, shouldn't they have let him talk to her? And if he hadn't been to the station, then what did that mean? She was worried for her husband's safety, and her own. She heard Zander's voice in her head and it brought her fleeting comfort to imagine the exchange:

Her, "Well, the next time we find a dead body, we're going to keep it to ourselves."

Him, "Sure, but where would we put it?"

At least she didn't have to look at the noisy SOB. The two cells in the holding area were side by side with a solid wall between them. Still, if he was going to rant all night, there would be no getting away from it. The holding area was small and the sound bounced off the hard surfaces of cement floor and metal cot and toilet. A shape blotted the light through the small window, and then the heavy secure door swung inward.

Grant glanced at her, giving nothing away, as he sauntered past to Eldon's cell.

"Eldon, on any other occasion, I'd let you just shout your lungs out. But we're full up, and I'm gonna have to ask you to be respectful of your neighbor here. She don't need to hear you going on all night."

"Well, then, why don't you just go ahead and let me out of here so I can get out of your hair, *Deputy* Bundy?" Eldon hissed. "Did you tell the chief you had me in lockup?"

"Did I tell the—now why in the heck would you think Chief Pearcey would be sympathetic to your plight? If it was up to him, we would lose the key. And yes, as a matter of fact, he *is* aware that you are spending the evening with us, and he's just fine with it."

"He... but..." Eldon stammered. "Look, Bundy, even if I was drunk when you brought me in—which I was not, no sir—obviously I'm stone-cold sober now, and you got no reason to keep me. *Legally* speaking."

Grant's booming laugh careened off the walls. "Go on and tell me about the law, Eldon. Tell me all about the injustice you're suffering."

"Aren't you standing a bit close to the bars, Bundy?"

Eve slinked up from her cot in the tense silence and peeked around the wall. Bundy stood with his arms folded, as big a man as she'd ever seen up close.

"You gonna entertain me, Eldon?" he asked flatly.

Grant's phone rang in his trouser pocket. He stood stock-still and held his grave stare through the bars at Eldon. He let the phone buzz four times before backing away to retrieve it. He answered as he left through the holding area door, "Adler Police Department, Officer Bundy speaking."

"Big man," Eldon spat.

"Well… *yeah*," Eve said.

"It ain't right. They got no cause to hold me."

"There's a lot of that going around."

"What they got you in for anyway?" he asked. "Shoplifting tampons?"

"Wow. You're a real charmer, aren't you?"

"Eh." Eldon grunted. "I was doing police business too! Chief asks me to tow a car from the forest to the station, I tow a car from the forest to the station! Ain't like I can say no, not if I don't want to catch hell."

"That was you!" Eve exclaimed. "I saw you when I was walking on the forest road, heading out to the campground. I thought that car looked just like mine. That was you towing it!"

"Oh yeah," Eldon replied. "I saw you. You're the one with the… with the legs."

"Well, yes. Two of them, as a matter of fact."

"I was just trying to pay you a compliment. Damn."

"You might need more practice," Eve said. "I was on my way to get our car so that my *husband* and I could get the hell out of this town. I don't know what beef you've got with the Adler

PD, but they've been nothing but unhelpful since we came in this morning to report that body we found in the woods."

"Say what again?"

"Only *they* said they couldn't find the body where I marked it with my GPS. And now my husband is missing and—and I'm in *here*." It all caught up with her, and a sob wracked her throat.

"Damn." Eldon sighed hoarsely. "I'm sorry I towed you in—for both our sakes. I don't know what's going on. I ain't the man I want to be," he admitted, mostly to himself, "but I don't like what I'm being asked to do. I don't want to be turned into something *worse*."

"What? What are you talking about?"

"Eh?" Eldon was roused from his reverie. "Nothing. Shit, I don't know. Best to get some sleep. Nothing else to do about it."

The door burst open. "I don't like leaving the station with anyone in lockup, but I have to go out on a call," Grant announced. "Eldon, I'm asking you nicely—be decent."

"A call? What's happening?" Eve asked. A cold feeling crept over her.

If Officer Bundy heard, he chose not to respond, and the door swung shut and latched.

"**I** HOPE THEY DON'T hurt him," Valeria said. She picked up a pack of cigarettes Dave had left on the bench and took one out.

"You smoke?" Britt asked incredulously.

"Not regularly," Valeria admitted, laughing. "But sometimes, yeah. Everyone thinks I'm this total virgin." She lit the cigarette and sucked in. Britt noticed she didn't inhale afterward to draw the smoke into her lungs. She raised her eyebrows quizzically at Valeria, who blushed. "Okay, I'm a virgin, but not a *total* virgin."

"Usually it's an either-or sort of thing." She smiled warmly to let her friend know her secret was safe. "I'm sure your dad got there in time."

Valeria looked out across the field to where she knew the abandoned factory sat beyond. "He should've just driven his truck across the field, instead of going the long way," she said. "They've all been gone a while."

"You really care about Tim? I mean, he *is* a freak," Britt said. When Valeria frowned, she added, "I guess we all know what it's like to feel like a freak sometimes."

Valeria grinned. "Touching moment much?"

"Shut up, bitch." Britt laughed.

Valeria said, "I… I don't want to be mean, but the truth is I don't think I ever liked Tim that much even before… all this. But he was Keith's friend, and I was Keith's friend. I guess I'm not sure why Keith liked him, really."

"You never found out why he…" Britt trailed off, not finishing with "killed himself."

Valeria shook her head. "I think maybe he felt constrained. Small town, right? I guess maybe that's how we all feel. But… you're getting out, aren't you? You don't… you don't want to stay." The last was not a question.

Britt gestured. "Whole wide world and whatnot." She flicked the butt of her cigarette into the fire. "You're going to college for sure, though. You're getting out."

"Yeah," Valeria said. "But I'll miss it. Adler will always be home. And I'll miss my dad. I know I complain about him and I get embarrassed by him…"

"That's what you're supposed to do," Britt reassured her. "That's the way dads are supposed to be." She stood. "What the hell?"

Valeria stood and followed her gaze. Red and blue lights flashed far in the distance. She heard an ambulance siren approaching the spot on the far road. Her phone played a pop jingle and she answered. "Dad?"

Britt could hear Mr. Hernandez shouting through the speaker. "Valeria, I want you to go inside and lock the door, right away!"

Another set of lights approached from town, arriving concurrently with the ambulance.

"Dad? What's happening?"

"Please, mija, go inside, okay? I just want to make sure you're safe. Everything is—it will be okay. Britt's father is here now."

"My dad is there?"

"Britt?" Mr. Hernandez asked. Valeria turned her phone so Britt could hear better. "You should go inside with Valeria, okay, Britt? Until we get this… oh, God!" They heard him moan. "There's some kind of animal loose! It did something terrible! Please, hurry inside and lock the door."

"Okay, okay, Daddy! We're going in right now!"

Valeria stopped after a few steps and looked back. "Britt!"

Britt opened her car door. "Go inside, Valeria, like he said. I have to see what's happening. My dad might—he might need me."

Valeria didn't know what that could mean. Britt wasn't sure either, but she shut the car door and turned on the ignition before she could be dissuaded.

CHAPTER 22

"GET DOWN!" GWEN URGED Jenna. She grabbed her T-shirt at the shoulder, accidentally snagging a lock of her hair, and yanked her toward the dashboard.

"Ow!" Jenna complained.

Gwen shushed her while focusing on the familiar copper sedan as it pulled into Connor's driveway (bought new less than a year ago, too rich for a history teacher to afford—rather nondescript given his side hustle, Gwen thought, but the coy flaunting of wealth was part of the seduction. When one of the other teachers asked how he could afford it, he shrugged and said, "No pets, no kids," as if that was all that was required). She kept her hand on Jenna, unwilling to trust her not to give them away as she peeked over the front corner of the open passenger's-side window, past the end of the hedge dividing Connor's property from his neighbor's. A woman got out of the driver's-side door of the sedan. Gwen didn't recognize her. She looked to be a few years older, definitely not in high school—not his type, Gwen thought ruefully, though uncertainly. Was she feeling an actual twinge of jealousy about a man she didn't even care that much about? No, she scolded herself. She was protecting her investment of time and flesh. Connor was *hers*. Her motivation for being there wasn't anything so petty as jealousy (Connor would be ashamed to be involved with someone who acted out of *pettiness*); she was there to make sure the arrangement was understood by all parties. But there was something in the way the other woman carried herself as she circled the car and opened the passenger door that wounded Gwen; even though her gait was hitched with pain, her face taut with tension, she moved with a sort of well-earned assuredness that Gwen only aspired to or affected, and she hated her for it. She craved to have the effect of experience conferred open her without the cost and hassle of living it.

The woman helped Connor out of the passenger's seat, stooping to get under his shoulder to lift him upright. Connor's pant leg was split to above the knee. There was a seafoam-green plastic apparatus on his lower right leg; she thought she saw bandages swelling beneath it. The woman retrieved a pair of crutches from the back seat while Connor leaned on the open door. Gwen felt the briefest pang of empathy at the sight of the injury, but it disappeared as she wondered why *this* unknown person was the one to assist him. Gwen had no interest in playing nurturer to an injured sugar daddy, but she resented that anyone else should be willing to do so.

The night was quiet. She could just make out what they were saying.

"Are you sure this is a good idea? They sure weren't keen on you leaving," the woman said.

"They wanted to know about the bear trap," Connor replied. (*Bear trap!* Gwen thought.) "I think they were waiting on someone from fish and game. The trap is illegal. But then they'd want to know where I was—whose property. And one question leads to others. You know I don't like questions."

"Yeah, I know," she said. "Let's get you inside."

Gwen fumed, pressing her lips together to keep from screaming. This bitch knew. This bitch knew *everything*.

"Was that Mr. McAuley?" Jenna asked. "What happened to him?"

Gwen jumped; she'd forgotten Jenna was in the car with her. Reminded of her presence, she at last let go of Jenna's shirt, now hopelessly wrinkled from her angry grip. "I don't know," she muttered.

"Gwen, can we go back to the party now? I mean, what are we even doing here?" Jenna asked. She made a connection and gasped. "Are you stalking Mr. McAuley?"

Gwen glared at her. "I'm not stalking anyone. I don't have to stalk. I'm not *desperate*, like some people."

"I'm sorry—it's just…" Jenna stammered. "Who was that with Mr. McAuley?"

"I—don't—know—!" Gwen growled.

"You're pretty," Jenna said, desperately trying to be supportive. When Gwen turned her head and knotted her brow as though trying to understand why someone would say something so inscrutably stupid, she asked again, "Can we *please* go back to the party?"

"You are going to stay right here," Gwen commanded her. "You are going to wait for me while I go have a closer look."

"Let's put you on the couch in the living room," Hannah said, navigating the path she knew quite well. She chuckled as she removed a coffee table, topped with koi in a pond in a swirl of tile. "New car, same couch." She took the crutches from him and lowered him down. "Oh, if this couch could talk, what naughty things it would say."

Connor winced as she helped him elevate his leg. "I have my lifestyle. I know what I want. I don't equivocate about it."

Hannah laughed. "Is that your daily affirmation? Believing strongly in your choices doesn't make them right. That's not how that works." After Connor grumbled something indistinct in disagreement, Hannah said, "Look, I'm not gonna judge you. I'd be the last, not with how things turned out for me. What the hell were you doing going up to Darren and Lyle's for anyway?"

Connor shifted to get comfortable and groaned. "Darren came to see me this morning—threatened me, if not in so many words. No surprise, really, but—I guess it pissed me off. I thought maybe I could frame him somehow, get him in trouble for the murder of that girl from the dollar store. Eliminate the threat. Figured the cops would be happy enough to believe it if I could just arrange a couple of pieces of evidence to back it up."

"You don't need to frame him," Hannah said. "He's a monster." The trials of the day swept over her and tears streamed down her face. She crumpled to the floor beside the couch.

Connor stroked her hair. "What's the matter? You never said why you were running through the woods. Did he hurt you?"

Hannah sniffled. "He tried. But it's more than that. He—he killed someone today, right in front of me. And there was this—this *thing*… I don't want to try to describe it. I'll just sound crazy. But, back at the house, he was trying to explain it to me—whatever crazy shit is going through his head. He said he killed that guy as a sacrifice."

Connor sat up. "What?"

Hannah nodded. "He said Lyle was dead, but he could get him back if he built this hexagon for a demon."

"Wow." Connor shook his head. "I didn't think I would ever say this, but—maybe we need to get the cops involved—without *us* getting involved, of course. If he's hearing voices and playing at devil worship—which it sounds like he even isn't getting *that* right."

"Huh?"

"A hexagon?" Connor wondered. "Usually it's a pentagram in devil worship."

"A hexag*ram*," Hannah corrected herself. "Yeah, that's what he said."

"A hexagram?" Connor repeated. "That's even weirder. Hexagram's a six-pointed figure. The Star of David is a hexagram, and I'm sure it wouldn't be that. Well, presuming he has any idea what he's doing." He thought of something and carefully sat up straighter. "Hand me that pen and paper off the counter."

Hannah got up and retrieved the items for him.

"There's another kind of hexagram," he said, beginning to draw.

"Of *course* you would know about this stuff," Hannah said.

"Idle hands and curious minds. Look." He showed her the finished symbol.

"It's called a unicursal hexagram. Unicursal, meaning continuous—drawn with a single line. That one *is* used in, you know, magic." He made a face to show his skepticism of the practice. "It's different in that, though it's a six-pointed star, there's really a seventh point—in the middle, where the line crosses itself."

"So, like… seven… people?"

"Jesus." Connor exhaled at the thought. "I don't know. Where was the guy he killed tonight?"

"At the park, in the shelter house. The same place where they found that girl."

"So there *has* to be one there," Connor said. "It's a fixed point in the hexagram. If we knew where one or two of the other points is, we could—"

"Figure out where the center point is? We already know. The center is gonna be dead center downtown Adler. How could it be anything else?" She bent her head back to look at him.

"What the hell have you gotten yourself into?"

"Just trouble. Same as ever." She sniffled. "Only now, I have nowhere to go."

He touched her cheek. "So stay."

S OMEONE WAS DEAD, THAT much was certain; the only question was who. It wasn't the presence of the four police vehicles (two Adler, one county, one forest) and the ambulance (with another one approaching, from Kane most likely) that told Britt that; a bad accident that blocked the road would merit as much response. No, she was sure someone was dead because that was what happened in Adler. Her souring town wouldn't be a death trap without fulfilling both conditions of the label.

She rumbled over a dirt service road most often used for recreational four-wheeling. She pulled halfway off the path near where it met the main road, staggered to the shuttered plant entrance. Officer Bundy was surprised to see her approaching the scene on foot.

"Britt? Where the hell did you come from? You shouldn't be here right now."

"Is my dad here?" she asked.

"Yeah, but honey…"

Sirens crested in clashing waves as the second ambulance arrived on scene, passing the first on its way out. Dave sprung up from his seat on the tailgate of the county PD's Rover, red-faced and screaming, "It wasn't a fucking bear! It wasn't a fucking bear!"

An agent from the Forestry Service asked, "What else could it have been?"

"Britt, you can't be here," Grant repeated.

She pointed with her thumb back across the field. "I was at the Hernandez farm when Mr. Hernandez called over and told Valeria she had to go inside. I need to get a ride with my dad."

"You walked—" Grant began. "Why didn't you go inside with her?"

"He said my dad was here," Britt said guilelessly.

"Jesus," he huffed. "You girls." He shook his head and then scanned the area. Everyone looked his way when he raised his arm and bellowed, "Chief!"

Walt saw Britt and disentangled from the group around Dave. He hurried over, his face blank with surprise.

"Britt! You shouldn't be here!"

"I was at Valeria's, remember?" she asked, sure that he didn't, counting on shame at that failure to cripple any objection to her presence. "What happened? The boys all ran over here because their drone crashed, and then we saw the lights, and Mr. Hernandez called." Something cautioned her from mentioning Tim Neuworth for the moment.

He put his hands on her shoulders as though preparing her for awful news. "We don't have all the details yet," he said. "We think there was a bear attack." Britt didn't bring up Dave's loud objection to the assessment. "Two of the boys were hurt." His cheek twitched when he said "hurt," telling Britt she was right; at least one of them was dead, or soon would be. "I can't say anything more about it right now. But we're getting them the help—we're doing what we need to do."

The young man from the Forestry Service joined them, pausing to nod at Britt. "Um, Chief Pearcey?" He looked from him to Britt questioningly.

"It's okay, Agent Andrews," Walt said. "Go ahead."

"We're going to put an alert out on the bear," Allan said. "We've got a copter on the way to do aerial surveillance—thermal—in case it's still in the area."

Grant said, "Might be a good idea to check the factory doors, make sure it can't get in there."

"I'll do it!" Walt shouted. He scanned the startled faces of the others. "And then I'll get Britt home. Nothing much else I can do here, but I can do that much. I'll check back in after. And I'll…" He lowered his voice, but Britt could still clearly hear him. "I'll make notification."

"Okay, Chief," Grant said, trying to hide his bewilderment. "If you say so."

Walt grabbed Britt's wrist so hard she gasped. "You come with me, little lady," he said, and allowed the last part to drift back to the others, "so that I can keep you safe."

He dragged her after him toward the abandoned factory. Britt struggled to keep up. She waited until they were past the tree-shrouded power station and out of sight of the others before she said, "Dad! Let me go!"

"Huh? Oh!" He released his grip, seemingly surprised he had still been holding on to her. Then he got an excited look. "This is good!" Britt shied away, wondering how he could say such a thing under the circumstances. "You remember, I told you earlier, you'd soon see—we'd get our lives back. *All* our lives." He waved her onward. "Come on! You're here now. It was meant to be, I'm sure of it. Because now you can see for yourself!"

She followed him warily up the drive to the main building. He continued straight along the near-featureless side abutting the main drive.

"Dad?" Britt asked, sparing a last look at the front entrance before chasing after him. "Aren't you gonna check the doors?"

"No need!" he said breathlessly. "I check them every day. I already know there's only one way in."

Britt caught the gist. "We *want* to go in?"

He stopped and turned. Breath wheezed through his smile. "I told you: You can see for yourself." He grew pensive as she caught up with him. "Now, I don't want you to worry. It *will* be a bit scary at first, but it will all make sense, I promise."

Britt didn't like the conviction in his statement. No "it *might* be scary" or "you don't have to be afraid, though."

"Come on!" he urged again and hustled around the corner to the back of the building. He led her to the loading docks situated in the middle. One of the bay doors was propped. Walt drew up short. Britt came up beside him and saw someone in ill-fitting dark clothes hop down from the ledge of the open bay. Tim sauntered toward them.

Britt did not expect her dad to say to him, "You can't be here."

Tim's gum-exposing snarl-grin was his only reply as he looked from Walt to Britt—and lingered on her.

"They're saying it's a bear," Walt said. "You need to go before anyone thinks anything differently. Take the train tracks back into town. Shit." He wiped his brow. "There's a copter coming. Watch out for it."

"Dad?"

"You're friends with Gwen now," Tim said to Britt. "I guess death makes… strange bedfellows."

"Don't talk to her like that," Walt cautioned Tim, who sneered. "Just get outta here," he said in a more conciliatory tone. "I'm gonna show her. She needs to know."

Tim chuckled. "Oh, man. But I'd love to stay and watch."

Walt drew on his reserves and puffed up into an authoritative stance. Even if he wasn't in charge here, he was still in charge of the town.

"Fine. Laters. I'd love to stay, but I've got a train to catch." As he passed Britt he said, "If you see Gwen… Actually, you probably won't see her again." He continued to a small track passing next to the smaller storage building and then disappeared between the trees.

"Dad? You're letting him go?!" Britt asked. "Did you hear what he just said?"

"He didn't mean anything," Walt said unconvincingly.

"But after you arrested him? Everybody knows about that," Britt said. "And he was here tonight—the boys saw him just before the drone went down. He was involved, I'm sure of it. And you were talking to him like you knew!"

Walt exhaled slowly, as though suggesting she do the same. "And now I'm gonna show you."

"Who was it?" Britt cried. "They weren't just hurt! Who was it, Daddy? Who got killed tonight?"

"Just come with me and you'll understand, I promise." He extended his hand.

She slapped it away. "No! I don't want to understand! I don't want anything to do with this! There's too much death!"

"We can *reverse* it," Walt said. "We can bring your mother back."

Britt's eyes opened wide in disbelief. She feared for her father's sanity. "No," she whispered. She thought about the ghost she saw. She wondered if it really was possible. But her answer was the same. "No. No, not even if you *could*. Not even then. It isn't right."

Walt scowled. "Of course you would say that. I should have expected as much." He shook his head and began to stamp around in a circle. "You know, it was always *me* and *her*, and *then* you."

Hot tears streamed down Britt's cheeks. She didn't care if there was a killer bear on the loose. She didn't care if the dead walked the earth. The only thing she wanted was to be away from her father. And so she ran.

CHAPTER 23

Someone horse-collared him by the shoulder pads and spun him around. Coach yelled at the rook to get his ass in there and pushed him onto the field. He was dressed in visitor whites, but it wasn't his Bills uniform, and he didn't recognize any of his teammates in the huddle. Their numbers all looked like hazy double eights, which he knew couldn't be right. Someone called out the defensive set but he didn't know the codes and half the words were nonsense. He got down in a three-point stance in the "B" gap and hoped that was right. Someone slapped his hip and he slid over to line up opposite the right guard. At first, he thought the other team was dressed head to toe in black, but then he saw that their arms were covered in coarse fur. And their necks. He looked up at the face of his opponent.

A merciful *bing-bong!* roused Grant from his impending nightmare. He blinked the blur of sleep from his eyes and realized he was spread out across the waiting area seats. Bobbi crossed from the door to the counter.

"Morning, Bobbi," he mumbled and sat up.

"Oh!" Bobbi jumped. "I didn't see you there, Grant."

He chuckled. "First time anyone's ever said that."

"Why are you still here?" she asked, and then put the pieces together. She gestured toward the back of the station. "Oh, of course."

Grant nodded. "Yup. Both of 'em are still back there. Waiting on the chief to tell me what to do... mostly because I couldn't begin to guess, myself. So, what are *you* doing here? It's Sunday."

Bobbi sighed. "The same, I guess. And other stuff too." Her unspoken concern for Walt lingered in the pause that followed. "There's just so much going on, isn't there? *Too* much."

"I'll get some fresh coffee going," Grant offered, but instead he remained in place and sighed heavily. "Bobbi, it's even worse than you think. Shit's gettin' crazy in this town."

"Oh, no," she said in anticipation of bad news. She frowned as she looked at the phone and the sprawl of notes on the counter. "What is all this?"

"There was a bear attack last night. Least, that's the best anyone can figure."

"A bear attack?" Bobbi asked dubiously. She didn't bother to point out the unlikelihood of the event; they both knew black bears almost never ventured near town and tended to hurry away from humans under most circumstances.

"Some high school boys, out by that empty metal fabricator north of town. Boy named Bill Wollert got killed. Another is critical at St. Marys, waiting to get airlifted."

Bobbi gasped. "That's Harlan Wollert's boy! He used to be on the board of the Chamber of Commerce. God, that's awful!"

Grant stepped up to the counter and pointed to the mess of sticky notes. "And then *this* started around midnight and has been going on and off ever since. When I said this town was going crazy, I wasn't exaggerating."

Bobbi picked up one of the notes. "1:18 a.m. Mary Davenport, 565 Peoria Lane. Saw..." She peered through the scratch lines to read "intruder," and then continued with the correction. "Saw mother in her upstairs hall—dead." She looked up at Grant. "Her mother died?"

"Sure," he answered. "Eight years back, according to Mrs. Davenport."

Bobbi scowled in confusion. She snatched up another note. "12:55 a.m. Charlie George, 124 Walnut Street. Woman walking in middle of street. Went to ask if she was OK—disappeared." Another. "2:22 a.m.—I didn't realize anyone stayed up so late in this town—Ester Tyler—son on roof of garage—dead 1977."

"I started writing down the year," Grant explained. "Ghosts. Or maybe gas. LSD in the drinking water. I don't know." He ambled past the counter and grabbed the near-empty coffee decanter from the side table. "I came here for the quiet, Bobbi," he said dejectedly.

Bobbi set down the notes in her hands with the rest. She wasn't sure if there was any point in reading through them all, but she knew she would. But first, she thought she should check on the guests in back. Officially, she wasn't allowed back there on her own, but she knew where the keys were, and she knew Grant wouldn't say anything. She unlocked and opened the holding area door as quietly as possible. It would be best, really, if Mrs. Nowlan and Eldon were both asleep. She was not surprised to find that neither was.

Eve sat bolt upright and then leaped to her feet. "When are you gonna let me out?" she demanded. "I have rights," she added limply—she suspected her rights weren't much on anybody's mind.

"I'm sorry, darling, I can't let you out—"

"Hey!" Eldon grabbed the cell door bars and shook them. "Goddammit, let me out of here! You got no right to keep me locked up!"

Eve worried Eldon's mutual but more vociferous complaint compromised hers by unwanted association.

"Eldon, shut up now, and I'll tell you," Bobbi said. "I'm going to call the chief as soon as I get back out front and see if I can get the okay on that or see what else he might be thinking. But until he says so, there isn't anything I or anyone else can do about it, so there isn't any point raising a ruckus."

"I want to report my husband as missing," Eve said. She drew close to the cell door, holding Bobbi with her stare. "He would have been here by now if he could have. Maybe you don't want to let me out—fine. But this is still a police station and I want to file a police report. And I know damn well I don't have to wait for the fucking chief to get here to do *that*."

Bobbi was flustered. She was right. "I'll see—I'll check with Officer Bundy. I'll let him know what you want to do."

"That would be swell," Eve dripped.

When she came back into the main area, Grant said, "Thanks, Bobbi. I had about all I can take of Eldon Landry for one lifetime."

"You and me both," Bobbi agreed. "I can understand why Walt would want him locked up, but I'd just as soon see him gone."

"Mm-hmm. Another minute on the coffee."

"Oh, shit."

"Huh?" Grant followed her gaze to the front windows.

Bing-bong!

Barkley threw open the front door and barreled in, clutching his hat in his hand. "Grant!" He paused, asked, "Bobbi?" and then decided her presence was inconsequential to the emergency that hurried him in. "Grant, I just saw it on the way in—there was an accident up at Main and Market." He waved his hat toward the intersection two blocks east as he paused for breath.

"Why didn't you—" Grant began.

Barkley interrupted, "There's a butane tanker on its side!"

Chapter 24

Britt avoided her father that morning. She thought he might apologize for the hurtful things he said the night before, and she had no interest in his apologies. She was galled at the thought he might *not* apologize, as well—that he would feel justified in his behavior or clueless as to why she was upset. The last seemed the most likely. She heard him puttering around, talking to himself distractedly, almost in opposition, seeming to alternate between anticipatory elation and mournful recrimination. Britt thought he was losing his shit. That was bad enough, but his ability to do harm as the chief of police concerned her. And she worried that that concern was overdue.

When she heard him banging about in the kitchen, she crept down the stairs. She peered over the rail toward the back of the house and saw him by the sink. It reminded her of seeing her mother there the day before and she felt a pang of sympathy for him. But she didn't let it stop her. She rushed to the door, grabbed her keys, and hurtled onto the drive. If he called after her, she didn't hear. She started her car and peeled out without looking back.

Gwen wasn't answering her texts or calls. Britt wasn't inclined to speak to her friend just then, but she thought Gwen needed to be warned. With the omnipresent specter of death looming over Adler, Britt took Tim's vague warning seriously. Though why he would want to hurt the sister of his dead best friend, Britt had no idea. She had driven by the Belores's house on her way home from the horrific scene at the factory entrance, but the lights were out. She then briefly considered driving by Mr. McAuley's house, but weariness smothered her and she was desperate to go home. As she pulled into the Belores's drive and noticed the absence of their long, blue Buick, Britt remembered it was Sunday morning. Gwen and her parents were sure to be at church. She sighed exasperatedly and cursed herself. She was about to pull back out from the drive when she noticed movement through one of the ground floor windows. She didn't see who it was, but someone was definitely inside. She went to the front door and knocked twice. She thought she heard a muffled voice, but no one answered.

Britt remembered the fake rock key holder by the back door that wouldn't have fooled the dumbest burglar. As she walked along the side of the house, she thought again about how much her quiet little town had changed and how the Belores family might want to reassess their home security. At the back door, she saw the rock turned over on its side with its little sliding hatch open. The key was in the lock and the door was slightly ajar.

She reached inside her purse and retrieved the compact vial of pepper spray her father gave her. She pushed the door inward a few inches with her shoulder and listened. Not hearing anything, she stepped inside the house. The back door opened into a sunken mud room. Three steps led up to the kitchen on one side and a hall to the dining and living rooms straight forward. Britt opted for the kitchen, thinking she might grab a second weapon there. She bobbed her head in. Mrs. Belores was fiercely proud of the new oak floors; the walls were matte white, as were the slatted cupboard doors above the marble-patterned Formica counter. An island under three hanging pendant lights dominated the room. A knife block and cutting board sat on the matching marble counter beside the sink, opposite the chrome-finish oven. Britt made her way to the knife block on the island.

"Drop the mace."

Britt whirled to face the dining room entrance. As Tim was barely as tall as Gwen, it seemed almost comically awkward the way he had to hold his elbow out to keep the blade at her neck—his arm blocked half his face, obscuring any menace he hoped to convey with his expression.

"The *one* fucking time I skip church," Gwen said, laboring to keep her voice steady.

Britt knew she should run and get help. Her father had taught her that to get away from the situation was always the first priority. But Britt had every reason to believe the threat to Gwen was real. She thought if she left, Gwen would be dead by the time the cops arrived. She worried her father wouldn't be much help anyway.

It flashed in her mind to go ahead and spray him. Gwen would be hit, but Britt could lead her out, while he would be stumbling, blind. But he was too far away for an effective blast, and just one wrong—or right—move of his knife would slice Gwen's throat open.

"Put it down," he reiterated, as though guessing her gambit.

She set the pepper spray on the wooden countertop of the island and stepped away. "Tim, you don't have to do this," she said. It was trite, but what other argument did she have to make?

"I really do," Tim replied. "Move," he instructed Gwen and they shuffled in tandem into the kitchen. "That direction," he told Britt, not indicating but clearly intending her to move toward the entrance they had just vacated.

She complied, and then asked, "Why are you doing this?"

He sneered. "You couldn't begin to understand."

Gwen laughed, a sound cut short by a chirp of pain and fear as the blade nicked her skin. "I think she can understand it just fine," she said. "It's really not that difficult to wrap your head around. The reason he wants to kill me is the same reason my brother killed himself. I fucked him. I fucked this little piece of shit."

Britt's mouth fell open. "What?"

"Shut up, you bitch," Tim snarled.

As promiscuous and mischievous as Gwen could be, Britt couldn't believe she would ever willingly fool around with a greasy outcast—much less an underclassman. "Why?"

Unable to wipe them away, Gwen tried to roll her tears out from her eyes. "I fucked Tim to show my brother that Tim would never fuck *him*."

"Keith was gay?" Britt asked.

"Keith was a *fag*." Gwen leaned into the vulgarity to emphasize her disparagement.

"Jesus, Gwen," Britt objected.

"*Jesus, Gwen*," Gwen mocked her. "If my parents ever found out, they would have disowned him."

"I thought I told you to shut *up*!"

Gwen tried to laugh. "Or what? Look," she said to Britt, "my tagalong little brother annoyed me from the time my parents brought him home from the hospital. But he was still my little brother and I looked out for him. And I didn't understand why the hell he cared so much about *this* useless shit."

"He was my friend!" Tim cried.

"He was your *only* friend, you freak. And you knew *why* he hung out with you, and you strung him along so that you wouldn't be alone. Don't even try to say you didn't. I saw it. I saw it all the time. I don't know why Keith liked you—maybe just as one freak to another—but I thought if I could clear that one thing up for him, he would drop your ass. I would have preferred he get his head on *straight*. But failing that, at least maybe I could show him that he could do better than *you*."

"Jesus." Britt shook her head. "You know what's truly fucked up? You two users were made for each other."

Gwen smiled and fluttered her eyelids. "Oh, Britt. You see everything so clearly. We've all got our little freak friends to follow us around, don't we?" She cackled. "Do you know what he did when it was over? He *told* Keith. I didn't even have to. He went right to him and told him, like it was just the perfect little setup. You can be my clingy friend while I fuck your hot sister. We'll be one big, happy family."

"I am genuinely excited to kill you," Tim seethed. "I've been really looking forward to it, but you've gone and made it just so much better than I could have dreamed."

"Well, then fucking do it already!" Gwen wailed. "Then maybe Keith will leave me alone!"

Gwen's sobs and sniffles puttered through the tense silence. Britt knew what she meant right away, as did Tim. But neither had anticipated the revelation.

"You've seen him?" Britt asked.

Gwen's nods were constrained by the knife at her throat. "Every night for the past week," she whispered. "At the foot of my bed. I try to talk to him, but I don't know if he hears me. I don't know if he sees me."

"I told you, you didn't understand, not really," Tim said. "I'm not gonna kill you just because I want to. I mean, *yeah*—but that's the icing on the cake. I have to sacrifice somebody who means something to me."

"Sacrifice?" Gwen asked.

"To bring Keith back. To bring him *all* the way back from the dead. He can do it. Ixixiklis can do it. He's shown you—he's shown you by sending the ghosts."

"Ix—"

"Ixixiklis," he finished for her. "He has the power. He'll bring one dead person back to life. The one who gives him the final sacrifice gets to choose who."

Another pause quavered. Britt wasn't sure who was or wasn't crazy anymore. It might as well have been her, for all she knew. This wasn't reality; it couldn't be. But she knew it was. So, she must be crazy.

"Okay," Gwen said.

"What?" the other two asked simultaneously.

"Okay," she repeated. "I'm on board."

Britt was incredulous. The Gwen she knew would never give up her life for another. "You're gonna let him—"

"No, of course not. I don't want to die. But I want my brother back."

A chill coursed through Britt's veins.

"You do?" Tim asked.

"Of course. Who else would I want to bring back more than him? So, I'll help—I'll be the one to give Ixawhatsis the last sacrifice. I'll do it and I'll choose my brother. It's win–win. I live and we both get my brother back."

Tim sniggered derisively. "Yeah, like I'm gonna trust you."

"You have to. How do you think my brother will feel if he comes back and finds out you had to kill his sister to make it happen?"

"I wouldn't tell him."

"Are you sure he won't just *know*?"

Tim fell silent. He motioned with the knife at Britt. "Her?"

Gwen looked at Britt with mock dolefulness. "Oh, no. Not little Brittney. She doesn't fill me with homicidal rage just because we're having a little tiff. But I can think of someone *meaningful* to me that I'd be very happy to cut into right about now, after watching some skank-ass whore riding his cock last night."

"Mr. McAuley!" Britt exclaimed. "Gwen, you can't!" She recalled her father's admonition about getting out of a bad situation—and this one was spiraling. She lunged to grab the pepper spray. Her frenzied snatch missed and she pushed the vial farther away. She reached again, splaying her fingers, one of which was abruptly shortened as the knife blade bit through to the countertop between the first and second knuckle.

CHAPTER 25

V ALERIA CUPPED HER HANDS around her eyes to cut the glare on the tinted glass and peered into the darkened restaurant. The dining room lights were off, but one over the bar and one outside the kitchen were on. She didn't see any movement, so she pulled back and knocked on the door a second time. Despite the steady (and often racist) verbal abuse her employer hurled at her, most days she was happy to go to work. Regulars and strangers alike appreciated her and tipped well, and while she was unwaveringly motivated by her college aspirations, she genuinely enjoyed interacting with people. Today, she would have preferred to stay home. The terror and tragedy of the night before—fortunately out of sight, yet so near her father's farm—kept her awake until almost dawn. She cried because one of the boys was dead, even if it was a boy she didn't know well, and even if she was yet to learn *which* boy it was. She cried for his nameless family, because she put herself in their stead. She couldn't imagine how bad it would be for her to lose her father, or for her father to lose her. And she cried because she knew she would have to leave him sooner than either would have liked, a departure made even more certain by the stain of the awful occurrence across the field.

She went to work because she wanted to keep her job, and Lita had intimated her employment was at stake if she didn't come in, telling her, "I just don't know how useful you are to me if I can't rely on you." Valeria had had every intention of working her shift as usual; her hesitancy in the face of the heavy-handed "request" to come in early had prompted Lita's remark. Valeria hadn't heard anything about it, but apparently Lita had taken a late catering order for the local artisan's collective. Sylvie, originally scheduled to open, had called off sick, Lita said. Valeria never opened or closed, so she didn't have a key. She decided she should go around back—if Lita was loading up her van, she might be waiting for Valeria there. Just as she turned to go, a shadow blocked the light at the back of the restaurant, and then she saw Lita approaching the front door. Lita snapped the lock open and turned back in without pushing the door open.

Valeria followed her inside. "Good morning, Miss Fiore!"

"Lock it behind you!" Lita commanded. "We're going out the back."

"Oh—okay," Valeria said, and did as instructed.

"Good of you to show up, finally," Lita barked over her shoulder. "The van's already loaded."

"Am I late?" Valeria asked, knowing full well she'd arrived five minutes before she'd been asked to. "I'm sorry, I thought... Do you still need me?"

Lita grunted as she went behind the door to shut off the overhead light. "Trying to get out of doing a little work, are you? No surprise." She slapped the bar flap shut and turned down the narrow hall dimly lit by three recessed bulbs that led past the bathrooms and then out the back. "I still need you to help set up, don't I?"

"Yes, of course," Valeria replied. "Happy to help!" She laughed nervously.

Lita stopped abruptly halfway down the hall and leaned a hand on the top of the grease-tacky wainscoting as her shoulders drooped.

"Miss Fiore?" Valeria hesitantly reached a hand toward her boss.

"Yeah, you'll help me," Lita said with a weariness Valeria didn't understand. Then she cleared her throat and her spine whipped back into alignment. "Let's get on with it."

As Lita locked up, Valeria walked around the front of a white van; red letters in a green circle near the rear doors identified the business. She climbed into the passenger's side and bounced on the stiff vinyl cushion. She glanced into the back to try to get a sense of the size of the order. There were two small stacks of something, both covered with blankets, with chafing trays and paper bags between them. She didn't smell anything, and there was no warmth emanating up to the front.

"Are we doing all the prep there?" she asked as Lita climbed behind the wheel.

Lita guessed what she meant and glanced toward the rear before catching and holding Valeria's gaze. "Yes," she said, "it has to be done on site."

D ARREN DIDN'T OWE LITA anything, no matter what she saw or heard. Still, Hannah's knee-strike hadn't left him in the mood for further fighting, so he didn't throw her out right away. And with Lyle gone—if only temporarily—and now Hannah, having fled into the night, he didn't have anyone to talk to. Normally, that was just fine with him. But he was trying to make sense of what had happened to him, trying to explain to himself all he'd seen and to justify what he'd done, and talking through it with an audience was the best way to scrutinize everything. Lita listened intently and asked questions only for clarification. She seemed to buy into the basic premise immediately on his word alone, which struck Darren as insane as anything else he'd experienced. But he was used to craziness from Lita. Maybe that was the other reason he let her stay and told her everything. As expected, when talking time was over, she climbed on top of him. He didn't want to encourage her, didn't even want to look at her, but the pressure of his time solely among men rose with him. He didn't push her off, just down, and found relief in her mouth. *Then* he kicked her out, almost surprised she didn't fuss about it, as though her thoughts were still on what he'd said or on something else entirely.

He slept lightly. He'd had a few bad cellmates in his day and had learned the habit of treading the surface of sleep. His eyes popped open every time the freezer kicked on, but otherwise nothing disturbed him, not even his plans for the coming day. He woke with the sun, showered, and ate breakfast, and thought about how he might lure Pearcey to his death. He mulled and rejected a few schemes. The only reasonable course was to play out to the end their common interest, with the advantage of knowing something that Tim assured him Walt did not: that the killer of the final victim was the one to make the choice who came back. It wouldn't be easy, because Walt would never let him out of his sight or turn his back. He geared up. The hunting knife in the ankle scabbard didn't bulge his jeans' cuff. (He had given Tim's knife back to him. The stick needed it more than he did, now that they were on the same side.) He wore an unbuttoned gray work shirt over a white tank top to hide a SIG Sauer micro-compact 9mm tucked into his belt in back. It wasn't much more than a popgun, but it would do the job at close range. He was about to grab something heavier to stick in his glove box when he heard a car pull up the drive. He couldn't believe his luck to see the chief's Rover turning sideways to park. Maybe getting the two of them to the sixth site was going to be easier than anticipated.

"Shit," Darren said when he realized it wasn't Walt behind the wheel.

Tuttle got out of the vehicle and adjusted his duty belt before cautiously approaching the front door. "Darren?" he called out. "Hey, Darren, it's me, John."

"Yeah, I see ya!" Darren shouted back. "I'm coming out." He opened the front door slowly. "Don't shoot me or nothin'."

John chuckled. "I'm not gonna shoot you."

"You can't be too careful." Darren swaggered out, showily recoiling from the sun peeking through the hole in the canopy around his drive. "You shot me with a BB gun that one time when we went out gigging frogs at Selby Run."

John said, "What are you talking about? *You* shot *me*!"

Darren affected confusion. "Is *that* what happened? Huh. Well, bygones, right?"

"Sure. Sure thing, Darren." John eased backward and leaned against the Rover's passenger door. "I thought we might talk a bit more about Lyle."

"Oh, you've found him, then?"

John grew serious. "I think you know that we haven't."

"Huh." Darren shrugged. "Probably not too much to talk about, then."

John took off his hat and lay it on the hood and then tousled his hair. "The forest is big, but this town isn't. We might have... different roles, but we all have to live together. Something's going wrong, and you know it. I figure, anything else we got going on, that's between us. Right now, we need to pull together. I'm asking for your help, Darren. Maybe nobody else thinks you'll come through, but I think you will."

A taste like warm vinegar rose in the back of Darren's throat and he scowled. What right did this *cop* have to appeal to his goddamn sense of decency? Sure, they might have grown up together. So what? His little speech about roles to play—that was just one man looking down on another and trying to make pity sound palatable. He looked at John with new scorn. What was so good about being good? He was a fool *not* to be a dirty cop—to have that power and holster it just so his ass didn't itch in a church pew. Everything about him was contemptible. If it was beneficial to keep him on good terms, then, sure—because he was a tool to be used, nothing more.

"I got nothing to say," Darren said.

John looked at him for a few seconds in silence and then sighed. "Alright then, I guess." He stood up straight and put his hat back on.

John's *disappointment* with him was the final, galling straw. Darren suddenly remembered why he'd shot John with the BB gun—because he *wanted* to. John gigged one frog and got sad about it, without having the courage to say so. He'd chase the rest away if they got close, splashing too loud or hollering suddenly, without being willing to admit he was doing it on purpose. Darren picked up his BB gun from the bank and shot John in the back on the way home, and he didn't really care if he did it because John had spoiled the fun or if he was a hypocrite or if it was just fun to shoot him. The why didn't really matter.

He was right: John was a tool, nothing more.

"Hold on, now," he called as John opened the door of the Rover. "I got nothing to say because telling you wouldn't do any good. You have to see for yourself, John." He leaned into the familiarity of the Christian name, imbuing it with trust, proffering an olive branch. "The truth is…" He hitched his shoulders up, then let them drop with a heavy breath, as though he was making a hard decision, but relieved to be sharing the burden by doing so. "The truth is, I know where Lyle is. I can take you to him, if you like." He kicked at the dirt and then raised his gaze to meet his friend's. "Do you wanna follow me, or should I ride with you?"

ELBA SLAMMED THE CREAKY, heavy door of her long sedan, and then marched her half-bent, goose-step march up the drive to Joe Underwood's porch. Chief Pearcey hadn't gotten back to her about Joe's sudden silence or disappearance or whatever, and when she'd tried to call the station, Bobbi had been downright short with her.

She announced her father's oft-repeated mantra as she pounded on the aluminum frame of Joe's door, "If you need something done right, you have to do it yourself!"

There was no answer. She crossed her arms and made a sound indicating the result was both expected and frustrating. She went back down the small porch and strode around to the back of the house. As she ascended the top stair of Joe's patio, she saw the broken pane in the door and stopped short.

"What in the world…" she murmured.

She felt a sense of foreboding, and for the briefest moment, even suffered the awareness of her age and fragility (at least as it related to armed, young criminals). But the moment passed and the instinct was quashed. She was careful to be quiet crossing the deck and turned the unlocked door handle slowly, just in case, but the air inside was still in a somnolent way, not a crouching one. Broken glass tinkled as she pressed the door inward. The kitchen table and chairs were jostled out of alignment, and one of the stacks of magazines had spilled onto the floor. There was a splatter of blood on the linoleum. It was clear a struggle had occurred. Why hadn't Chief Pearcey said anything to her? Maybe it was the end times, after all, and he was too busy. Elba snorted derisively. Maybe she was being too charitable.

She dared to call, "Joe?", ready to dash out the back door as quickly as her stringy limbs would allow. But only silence greeted her. She could hear the air running and thanked God her ears were still good. Since one call didn't bring out an attacker, she tried a second to bring out the resident. "Joe? It's me, Elba. Well, you know that, of course." Still no reply.

She fretted that maybe she shouldn't be in his house uninvited and alone. But then, Joe hadn't been answering the door—and him a shut-in. Then there was the scene in the kitchen. What could she do? Notify the police *again*?

"Joe, I'm coming in." She was in already, of course, but with a few more steps, she'd have view of the living room and the hallway to the bathroom and his bedroom, so she thought the warning was warranted. And with no reply forthcoming, she took those few steps farther.

She didn't know what the shape down at the end of the hall was, but she was sure it didn't belong there. And even the briefest glance told her it was *wrong* too. Her lips and tongue felt suddenly dry and she smacked them against each other. The dark sense returned, but less to do with danger than with the imminence of sad discovery. She tried to say his name again as she approached but could not. She tried again when she saw it was him, saw the withered flesh and the degradation of his inversion, and this time she cried out full and loud. Then, more quietly, touching the smooth, soapstone-like glass, "Oh, Joe. Look what they did to you."

Here he was, left like this; his property violated and unsecured. The law was nowhere to be found. Elba would not let it stand.

"If you want something done right…" she echoed.

She went into the living room and retrieved the dusty wrought-iron poker from beside the fireplace. She hefted it in one hand, considered its weight, felt the strength of her own grip. Then she strode back down the hall and went to work like John Henry on a mountain.

CHAPTER 26

"**J**ESUS, DO YOU SHOWER?" Gwen pinched her nostrils shut. The open window was supposed to provide fresh air, but it only served to agitate the scent.

"Yes, I shower," Tim responded defensively. "I just forgot to put on deodorant this morning. At least I can fucking drive."

"My parents don't want me to drive yet," Gwen said. "Nice car, by the way."

They sat in a gray minivan that reeked of cigarette smoke competing with Tim's adolescent armpits in the same spot where Jenna had parked the night before. "It's my mom's," Tim snapped back, as if the haloed angel in silhouette with three dangling chimes on the rearview mirror was not indication enough.

"Jesus," Gwen spat again. The talk of parents felt degrading. It made her feel small, reminding her she was the jewel in the light of her parents' proud gaze. To be put in a place of esteem was to be coddled. Coddling was smothering, limiting—controlling. No one owned her. Not her parents and their beliefs, not God with his omnipresent disapproval, not even the heresy of sex and drugs, not the expectation of innocence and not the repudiation of it. She would show them all. Her whole town. She would show the whole town and they wouldn't even know she'd done it, because she could keep every secret to herself for just as long as it pleased her. She smiled. She savored the impending satisfaction.

She immersed her soul in the assurance that she could do whatever she wanted.

Tim broke the spell. "You wanna fuck?"

She looked over to see him pulling at the crotch of his jeans. Her jaw dropped open. "Are you fucking serious?"

He tried to laugh casually. "Hey, why not? Get back at him, right? We've got the van, and it isn't like we nev—"

"We're on a bit of a time crunch," Gwen barked. "So maybe let's circle back on that later, okay? Maybe let's kill my boyfriend and resurrect my brother first."

"You don't have to be so sarcastic," Tim said. "Do you really think we can do all we need to do and get back to let your friend out of the bathroom before your parents get home from church?"

"I'm not worried about *her*. If this works, my parents won't give *that* situation a second fucking thought." She caught his scent again and grimaced. Every second spent in the minivan felt more demeaning than the last. "Let's go." She opened her door.

"Hey, we need a plan," Tim cautioned.

"You have the knife. We go in and wave it around. Pretty good plan, I think."

"Shit! Close the door! Get down!"

Gwen reacted to the urgent instruction and slammed the door shut before seeing what had prompted it. Hannah stood in the driveway at the driver's-side door of Connor's car. Her head popped up at the bang of the car door closing; she squinted through the sunshine gleaming off the copper finish. She glanced around in a half circle, unsure where the sound came from, but then seemed to dismiss it as inconsequential and got into the car. Several seconds later, she pulled out of the driveway and drove off, while Tim and Gwen watched, peering over the dashboard.

"Where's she going?" Tim asked.

"If I know Connor, he just sent her to get some fucking scones." She tut-tutted disappointedly. "Too bad, really. I wouldn't have minded cutting her up a bit, but there you go. Our job just got easier. Pull into the drive."

"People will see us."

"His leg is hurt, remember? You wanna drag him to the curb?" Gwen asked. "Besides, people don't see anything."

Connor heard the side door open and called to the kitchen, "Hannah? Did you forget something?"

Gwen sashayed into the living room.

"Hannah—was that your friend's name?" she asked coyly. "She's cute. I have a friend too." Tim came out from behind her and brandished his knife, turning the blade to catch the light. "He's not cute," Gwen said, "but he's gonna help me get my brother back. And so are you!" She hopped and clapped.

Connor lunged up from the couch with the intent of barreling past them through the kitchen. But the first step he took on his injured leg sent him crashing to the floor with a howl of pain.

Gwen laughed. "Oh, come on—where were you gonna go, Connor? See—that's for *us* to know and you to find out."

"I'M SURE THERE'S A perfectly good reason," Charlie Belores said over his shoulder as he unlocked the front door.

"Better than the one Gwen gave us for skipping church?" his wife retorted.

"She can't help it if she's sick, Kate." He swung the door open and entered his home. "Maybe Britt stopped by to make sure she's okay."

Kate Belores didn't argue. She was beginning to suspect—along with thinking she was quite *late* to suspect—that daddy's little angel wasn't really living up to the final criterion, but she knew there was no telling him that. She glided around him into the living room and called out, "Gwennie, are you upstairs? You sure did pick the right day to skip church. We had to evacuate! Can you imagine?" Without waiting for a reply to the first question, and already knowing the answer to the next one, she asked, "Britt, honey, is that your car in the drive?"

She heard a muffled scream accompanied by metallic rattling coming from the half bath off the hallway leading to the back of the house. Her husband asked, "What the hell..." from the key rack by the door; Kate was already moving.

She yelped when she opened the door. Britt was on the floor of the bathroom with her wrists crossed inside the elbow of the sink drainpipe, bound together with black duct tape. One of her hands was covered with a white hand towel soaked red with blood. More tape, wet with snot and tears, encircled her head, holding fast a washcloth stuffed in her mouth. Kate cried, "Britt! Oh, my God! Are you okay? What happened?"

"What's going on?" Charlie demanded from the door, and then gasped at the sight.

"Call the police!" Kate shouted.

Charlie was frozen with confusion. "Britt? Where's Gwen?"

"Get the scissors from the kitchen drawer!" Kate demanded.

The second instruction roused Charlie and he rushed down the hallway.

"Oh, honey, oh, honey," Kate cooed, trying at first to peel the tape from Britt's cheek, and failing that, patting her hair.

"Here. The scissors. There's blood on the kitchen counter."

Kate snatched them from him. She deftly slid the narrow, bottom scissor blade behind Britt's ear and carefully cut the tape around her head. She pulled the tape away from her cheek and removed the gag, wiping Britt's nose and mouth as she did. Britt gasped for breath. Trying to speak, she coughed.

"Call the police," Kate directed her husband a second time.

"Right. Yes. Of course." He scampered back to the living room.

Kate cut the tape binding Britt's wrists to the pipe. "My God, Britt. What happened to your hand? Are you okay? Where's Gwennie?" She hadn't realized she was crying until she instinctively raised her arm to wipe the tears away. "Where's my Gwennie, Britt?"

"I'm getting a busy signal!" Charlie called desperately.

Kate helped Britt to her feet. "Britt, honey—your hand. I'll drive you to the hospital."

"He took it with him," Britt exclaimed, which further confused Kate. Britt shook her head. "I'm sorry, Mrs. Belores, but I need to go." She shook loose of her grasp and pushed past her out of the bathroom.

"Britt! Wait! What about the police? What about Gwen?"

"No need to call them. I'm going straight to the station to see my dad," Britt said as she passed the baffled Mr. Belores.

They followed her out the front door onto the porch. Kate called after her. "But, honey, your hand! And—and Gwennie!"

When she got to her car, Britt looked back at them, suddenly sad for the anxious parents. "Mrs. Belores, you don't have to worry about Gwen. I promise you, she can take care of herself."

S HERIFF PEARCEY CHECKED HIS phone as he strolled out to the cruiser. Distractedly, he noticed Britt's car was absent, and he remembered her rushing out of the house while he was in the kitchen. He felt bad. He shouldn't have said what he said to her the night before, even if it was true. He was still her father, and for the time being, sole parent, and he had a responsibility to nurture her, at least until she left home. But he didn't have time to be concerned about her just then. Better to let her go blow off some steam and be mad at him for a while; she would be out of the way. He was surprised to see eight missed calls from the station logged on his phone.

He settled into the driver's seat and turned on the radio. Sure enough, not more than ten seconds elapsed before Bobbi asked if he was listening; the frantic edge in her voice was tempered by the bland frustration of not expecting an answer. Walt wondered why she was at the station. There were multiple possibilities—things were happening, after all—but there was also the danger, especially after that black creature bit off Bill Wollert's head last night, that the situation was spiraling out of control.

He picked up the microphone and pressed the talk button. "Hey, Bobbi, it's Walt. I just got in the cruiser. Sorry, I didn't realize the ringer was off on my cell phone." Both aspects of the statement were true, which troubled him. He never turned off the ringer on his phone. Adler was under his stewardship; he was always available day or night. That he might have subconsciously decided to leave the town to its own affairs so that he could check out for a while ran contrary to two decades of service. He was no fool—they might try to hide it to spare his feelings, but he knew Bobbi and his officers were worried about him falling apart. Well, they were right to do so. But Walt knew how to fix the problem. And he was going to make sure it was done that very day. Then no one would have to worry about his performance, his well-being, or his future. Everything would be back to normal once Christine returned. He would never again have to break the laws he swore to uphold. Just as soon as he evened the scales in one fell swoop: kill Eldon Landry; bring back Christine Pearcey.

"Walt? Oh, thank God!" Bobbi's voice burst with distortion. A brief pause followed, where she *didn't* ask "Where have you been?" and Walt was grateful for her discretion. Bobbi alerted him. "Chief, we've got a dangerous situation downtown. There's a butane tanker on its side at the intersection of Main and Market."

Walt mapped it mentally: two blocks from the station. "How big?" he asked.

"Officer Clay said it was a 5,300-gallon-tank."

Too close, he thought.

Bobbi continued, "Barkley and Grant are there, going door-to-door, getting everybody out. County PD should be there by now to help."

"The church?"—meaning First Baptist, only two doors down from the intersection in question.

"Mm-hmm. Yes, first place they went. Fortunately, since it's Sunday, and offseason, there's a lot less people downtown. Still…" She got to the heart of the matter. "Chief, Eldon and that hiker woman are still in lockup! Do you want me to—I think they need to be evacuated."

Walt turned on the engine, put the cruiser in gear, and peeled around to face the street. He put it in drive and stomped on the pedal.

"Bobbi, I'm on my way to the station right now. You go ahead and get out of there. Get yourself safe. Better get at least a half mile away to be sure. I'll be there in just a couple of minutes and I'll take care of last night's guests."

"Walt..."

Tires screamed as he turned a corner, reminding him to turn on the lights and siren.

"It'll be fine, Bobbi, don't you worry. What about Officer Tuttle? Where is he?"

Traffic shuddered to a quick stop, barely in time to allow Walt clear entry onto route 219.

"I haven't been able to get ahold of him!" Bobbi yelled back, increasing volume to cut through the sirens she heard on his end. "Officer Clay said he was going to go talk to Darren Dietz. Chief—I've been trying to contact John all morning."

Walt's jaw tightened. He drove down the center line, whizzing past cars pulled to the side of the road. He stared straight forward, straight forward, and then—he glanced at himself in the rearview mirror, just long enough to look himself in the eye. He slowed down. As he turned off onto a gravel road that grew like a spur from the elbow of route 219, he said, "Bobbi, I'll be there soon," and then shut off the radio, telling himself he couldn't lose an argument he wasn't in.

He turned off onto a rutted dirt road and passed an open metal gate. Darren's truck and a late-model blue coupe were parked in the carport. There was no indication Tuttle was present. Walt got out of the cruiser, marched to the front door, and announced himself. He pounded on the doorframe. "Adler PD! Open up! Anyone in there?"

After repeating the sequence, he tried the handle and found the door unlocked. No one was inside. No one living anyway. Just Lyle. Other than that brief flicker of recognition when he first saw Christine, most reports indicated the ghosts didn't seem aware of the presence of the living. But it was clear right away that Lyle saw Chief Pearcey just fine. His tall, lanky frame coiled in on itself, his hands curled into clutching talons. His shout was soundless, but the hate burning in his eyes was clear.

Walt staggered back outside. Lyle came after him. Instinctively, Walt drew his service weapon. He shot center mass three times to no effect. Lyle dove at him; Walt threw his arms across his face. Freezing cold pushed through his chest. The smell of wet stone filled his nostrils.

Walt wheeled around. He was alone. He was shaking. He steadied his right hand with his left to put his gun back in its holster.

"Fuck." He felt terribly alone, and weak, and ashamed. He tried to shout "Fuck!", tried to exorcise the doubts and reenergize his body and convictions, but he could barely muster breath.

He stood in the drive, breathing hard, steadying himself for several moments before he remembered why he was there. Darren knew what was happening. Darren knew what to do. Darren knew where to go. Darren needed someone meaningful to him to kill. Darren was going to hurt his boyhood friend, to make his wife a widow and leave his children fatherless. He was going to kill an officer of the Adler Borough PD.

"Like hell," Walt growled.

No one was going to steal his one chance.

Chapter 27

Lita took her foot off the accelerator as she passed a stand of trees and then braked to turn under a lattice of power lines bannering the lot to County Craft Funzone. Off to the right, diagonal parking spaces flanked a long building that housed the business offices and the commercial market selling the wares of local artisans. Lita continued around back, turning away from a menagerie of brutish animals carved from wood shaded under a metal awning. Valeria smiled. Columnar bears loomed over stumpy woodchucks under the watchful gaze of shingle-feathered owls as other inchoate beasts awaited saw and chisel in a mat of shavings out in the sun.

Two other buildings behind the market ran parallel to the main road. The first was smaller and low, with beige siding. "CLAY" was painted freehand in purple letters near the door. Valeria recalled the feeling of the cool, slippery clay rolling under her hands on the wheel. The wobbly result still sat in the cabinet by the kitchen table, even if she wished her father wasn't quite so proud of it. The second building was longer, taller, and white. It was split into two spaces. A smaller room painted all white, meant to be used as a gallery, though usually only staged for single-night openings four times a year to showcase the classes offered by the business. The second, larger room had a furnace for glassblowing, shelves for storage along two walls, and three end-to-end pairs of long tables to accommodate larger classes, usually field trips from the local elementary schools.

Valeria yelped as she lurched forward against her seat belt. The van's tires slid in the gravel. Lita caught herself before she came to a full stop and let out the brake—remembering that it shouldn't be a problem that there was a police cruiser outside the large building, at least as far as Valeria was concerned.

"Oh, wow," Valeria said, "Britt's dad must be here."

"Britt's dad?"

"Sure, Chief Pearcey."

That cinched it; she was committed. Darren had told her the chief was in on it—though, she couldn't imagine them working together. Her eyes flashed wide and she made a quick sound behind her lips as it occurred to her that he meant to double-cross and kill the chief of police. That seemed far too reckless. But she hadn't told him she was bringing Valeria, so somebody else had to be meant to be the sacrifice. Perhaps each intended to double-cross the other—unless the two had brought somebody else with them.

"That's weird he's here," Valeria said. "I mean, it doesn't look like there's anybody else."

"Doesn't need to be." Lita shifted the van into park and turned off the engine. She turned and looked at Valeria. She scowled, resignedly at first, her expression almost tempered with pity, and then she mustered the necessary appraisal of the girl beside her that would make it easy, almost satisfying, to do what needed to be done. She fixed it in her head that the ungrateful "immigrant" in the passenger's seat was trying to keep her from her son.

Valeria thought she was expected to say something. "What do you want me to unload first?"

Lita opened the van door and spilled out. "Let's go inside first to see what the setup's gonna be like."

Valeria glanced back at the blanket-shrouded, scentless food and smallish collection of supplies. She looked at Lita, her boss who hated her, impatiently glaring at her, and then at the unexpected police vehicle. She was tired from being up too much of the night and overwrought from the stress of it, so she dismissed the uneasy feeling that roiled in her stomach. She got out of the van.

The main entrance led into the gallery space. The walls were empty, white but for occasional scratch marks left by a previous hanging. There was nothing in the room but a vacuum cleaner next to a blue, fifty-five-gallon trash can in one corner, and two three-feet wide rolls of brown craft paper against the interior wall.

Lita noted Valeria's confusion, and said, "We're in the big room," gesturing at the open doorway toward the back of the building. Valeria heard men's voices as she approached the portal. The first said something about "drag me out here" and the second, lower voice added, "sorry it had to be this way." She turned the corner to go into the second room—and shrieked as she flinched at the near-simultaneous shout of, "Look out!" and a burst of four gunshots. She didn't know what she saw; there was a blur of motion, something big and black dropping from the ceiling. She backed away instinctively but was shoved hard from behind. Off-balance, she spilled forward onto the concrete floor. She pushed up on her hands, bending backward to see.

The black thing straddled between two sets of tables; the sharp points of its segmented legs scratched and clacked on the tabletops. Valeria heard a whoosh of air as one of its wings whipped across its body, striking the cop (not the chief, not Britt's dad). He flew back into the stools between the tables, scattering them like tenpins before skidding to a stop, limp on the powder-blue floor. His gun skittered across the floor and ricocheted off a table leg in her direction.

A big man with a short beard in a gray work shirt and white tank top yelled, "No, don't! I need him!" The terrible beast rocked forward and back, eager to pounce. Finding breath she'd forgotten, Valeria wailed in fear as she twisted and then frantically kicked backward.

The man turned to see her, and the monster rotated to face her as well; sets of different-sized eyes aligned in parallel on both sides of a sleek, diamond-shaped head measured the morsel before them. Lita lunged past her, diving to the floor. She grabbed the officer's gun. From the depths of her terror, Valeria felt a flash of admiration for Lita's bravery and wherewithal, and for her willingness to protect her younger charge. Then Lita staggered to her feet and pointed the gun at Valeria.

"Lita! What the fuck are you doing here?" Darren yelled.

"What does it look like I'm doing? I'm doing what you told me had to be done! I brought someone for the sixth sacrifice. She's an employee. Worked for me for two years now. That has to be significant enough, doesn't it?"

"Lita?" Valeria whimpered.

"Shut up!" Lita lurched at her and shook the barrel of the gun in Valeria's face. "Shut your damn mongrel mouth! I finally found something you're good for."

The small stab of admiration died with the hope it brought and Valeria wept. She stared into the face of someone she'd always known to be a hateful person, and saw the person no more, but only the hate, the composite tormentor of a multitude of devils who'd seen her as inferior or subhuman. In her fright, somehow the gun lost all meaning and she forgot the threat it held. She wobbled upright and tried to run for the door, only to stop short as the black thing swooped in front of her. It blocked the exit, legs and wings spread wide to fill the space. A pair of lamprey-suckered stalks emerged from beneath the tufted fur of its back and reached toward her. Beholding the full horror of the thing, she screamed once more as hot urine streamed down her leg.

"That's right," Lita hissed behind her. "You ain't going any-where, girl."

Valeria staggered away from the two threats and rammed into the shelves against the back wall. She felt hopeless and thought of her father. How horrible it would be for him to lose his daughter to such a nightmare. How gutted he would feel to not have been there to protect her. How he would never experience the poignant pride of having to watch her leave on her own.

Darren spun Lita around to face him. "I didn't tell you to come here! You screwed up—now there's someone else we have to account for."

"I had to make sure. After you told me what we could do—that we could bring our son back to life!"

"What? I never said anything about that!"

Lita beamed, enraptured by her coalescing dream. She squeezed near him. "Of course you did! You told me how we can resurrect our beautiful Tommy-boy and reunite our family, so that everything will finally be right again and we can all be happy together forever!"

Darren shook his head in disbelief. "You wanna bring back Tommy. You wanna bring back the son you let die because you were too fucked up on *his* birthday to pay attention, slobbering on the phone, calling me up and begging me back." Lita's smile melted. "That's right. I ain't forgot about it. I ain't forgot about how it happened. You think you deserve a second chance with *our* son? You think he would even grow up if he came back? Did you even consider that—or did you just want him to be three years old forever and stay a chain on me until you withered and died of old age?" Darren saw that his words had hurt her but noticed her grip curl tight on the gun. He might have stunned her, but she would rebound quickly. "I guess, no matter what else, you are the mother of my child—that has to be *significant* enough, doesn't it?"

Darren shoved the blade of his hunting knife up under her sternum. And because he knew her, he knew that she wouldn't sink with surprise at being betrayed, and she would not succumb from something as simple as a single mortal wound. He grabbed her wrist and held her hand pointed away as she emptied the clip into the ceiling while he continued stabbing her in her heart until the knife was too slick with blood to hold onto any longer.

Chapter 28

BING-BONG!

The urgent inquiries about the upended propane tanker in the center of town had overtaken the sightings of the risen deceased, but suddenly the untallied calls on the waiting, blinking lines no longer mattered because Bobbi just watched a girl she'd known since infancy stumble into the station cinching a blood-soaked towel over her right hand.

Bobbi dropped the phone, shouted, "Britt!" and scrambled from behind the counter. She reached to steady the teetering young woman and nearly toppled backward herself. "Your hand!"

"It's too late for that," Britt gasped. "The finger's gone."

Bobbi stared, awed with worry. "What happened?"

There was no time to explain twice. Britt shook her head. "Is my father here? I can't get him on the phone."

"No, honey—here, sit in my chair—he's not here. He… he called in and said he was on his way, but…" Bobbi paused to swallow, trying to keep her words steady. The poor girl didn't need anything more to worry her. "We were talking on the radio but then we got cut off. I would have thought he would be here by now." She'd weakened the statement to be less alarming. He should've arrived at the station if he'd continued on his way. And that's where he said he was coming—not to the site of the accident—before she'd told him about John going to see Darren. Had something gone wrong there?

Britt nodded, almost as though she'd expected to be disappointed. "I'm not sure what to do." Bobbi began to respond, but Britt cut her off. "Where is everyone else?"

"Well, that's just it, honey. Didn't you see? There's an overturned propane tanker two blocks from here. Officers Bundy and Clay are there now organizing an evacuation."

Britt gave her a quizzical look. "Two blocks away? Is that far enough?"

"No, it isn't," Bobbi said. "You've got to get out of here, Britt."

"What about you? You're not staying just to answer the phones!"

"No. No, I have to stay because we have two people in lockup, and… and I was waiting for your father to get here to know what to do."

"What?"

The women were both startled by the male voice. Neither had heard the chime as the lanky man in khaki shirt and hunter green pants entered.

"You were there last night," Britt said. "Outside the factory."

Agent Andrews nodded. "That's right. I remember you too. I came here to follow up with the sheriff, but it seems like you've got more pressing concerns than a bear attack. If you've got people in lockup, we've gotta release them or transport them elsewhere. What have the men been charged with?"

"A man and a woman," Bobbi corrected him. She stammered, "They—they haven't been charged."

"What? Jesus—if they're not dangerous, why haven't they been released?"

"I was waiting," Bobbi said. All her confidence in the chief suddenly drained out of her in a sigh. He was getting worse. It wasn't just him coming into work a bit rough in the mornings. Something else was going on—something darker than negligence. She hated to think he was compromising his morals and violating his oath. Not that great man. Maybe there was still time to help, time to pull him back from the brink, but she wouldn't be able to do it if she didn't admit it needed doing. "I was waiting on Walt."

"Bobbi," Britt urged her.

She nodded. "I'll go get them out."

Allan went with her. Not knowing what else to do, Britt followed.

"About goddamned time!" Eldon howled as soon as the door opened.

"Eldon Landry, you quiet down," Bobbi scolded him. "I'm going to let you out on your own recognizance."

Eve sat up quickly from the hard bunk, flaring every ache in her body. "What about me?"

"You too."

"*You're* letting me out?" Eldon asked, recognizing the irregularity. "And who the hell is he?"

Allan was surprised at the identity of the second detainee. "Mrs. Nowlan?"

She echoed his bewilderment. "Agent Andrews?"

"Oh, goody, we're all friends." Eldon sneered.

"Listen up," Bobbi commanded him. "I'm letting you out because the officers are dealing with an overturned propane tanker truck over on Main and Market, so we have to evacuate. I'm gonna need you to move calmly but quickly out of the station and west from here." She unlocked Eldon's cell and threw the door open. He leaned on his elbow against the cell wall. Bobbi demanded, "What the hell are you doing?"

"This is me being calm," he replied. "Ain't I just a model citizen?"

"Well, if you're feeling all civic-minded, maybe you can take that wrecker parked out back and help out with the tanker situation," Bobbi drawled.

"Sorry, darlin', that's about twenty tons outside my weight class. Reckon I'll head any other direction." Eldon slinked away from the wall. He tipped an invisible hat as he passed by Bobbi. "But you all have yourself a hell of a day without me, now, y'hear?"

She turned and went to Eve's cell, calling back, "Fine. Go on, then, if you're gonna."

"Why are you here?" Eve asked Allan. "Have you heard any-thing about my husband?"

"Your husband?" He looked from her to Bobbi and back. "I'm afraid I don't know anything about that. I'm here to follow up on a bear attack that occurred last night."

Eldon stopped short, halfway out the holding area door. "Bear attack? Bullshit. In town?"

"North of town," Britt piped in, which drew everyone's atten-tion to her injury. "Outside of the shutdown metal factory off Wilburville. A boy from my school was killed."

"Jesus," Eldon muttered. Still incredulous, he asked, "By a *bear*?"

Everyone looked to the Forestry Service agent for the answer. "Yeah," Allan said. "Maybe."

"Maybe?" Eve asked. "Agent Andrews, my husband would have come looking for me here if he could have, and I don't know what could have kept him from it. So, if there's something going on, please—I need to know about it."

Allan sighed. "I mean—it had to have been a bear, or maybe an unidentified escaped exotic. Something large leaped down from a utility pole and attacked three boys. I-it doesn't fit with bear behavior, but there's nothing else indigenous to the area it could have been. No matter what they said they saw."

"What did they see?" Eldon asked. Allan vacillated, so he repeated his request, "*What* did they *see*?"

Allan held up his hands. "Alright. But listen—this is them talking. I don't believe it for a minute. They say they saw… this thing that was like a giant bat mixed with… mixed with a spider."

He expected a laugh, but no one had one in them. Eldon, least of all. His face drew taut and the color drained out of it in an instant. He asked tersely, "You said it was out by that old factory?"

"I'm sure the bear—or whatever it was—isn't there anymore," Allan said. He gestured toward Britt. "Anyway, her dad searched the factory."

"But he didn't!" she protested. "We went back there and then… we stopped because Tim Neuworth came out from inside. And my dad just let him go. No, he didn't just let him go—he told him to follow the train tracks back to town and to stay out of sight."

Bobbi groaned.

Eve asked, "Wasn't that the kid they thought might've killed that girl? Someone told us about it at that pizzeria Chief Pearcey sent us to yesterday. And he just let him go? No questions?"

"Jesus, Valeria," Britt whispered to herself, remembering how close her friend's house was to last night's scene. She took a deep breath. "There's something in that factory. I didn't go in. I didn't see. But my dad wanted to show me something." She turned toward Eve. "If your husband really is missing, then I think that's the place to look."

"Well, I guess I'm good to go since he towed my car here." He pointed with her thumb to where Eldon had been standing. Only then did they realize he'd left.

"I'll drive. I've got lights. There's no way in hell I'm letting you go alone," Allan said. "And I'm not going in without my rifle." He regarded Britt's injury. "But you…"

"No. No way," Britt insisted. "My dad wanted me to see what was inside of there, so that's what I'm gonna do."

"Britt, wait!" Bobbi pleaded as they crossed the lobby. She ran after her with a small, plastic pouch in her hands. She squeezed the bag until she heard a popping sound, and then handed it to Britt. "Cold pack for the pain. *Please* get to the hospital as soon as you can. You never said what happened."

Britt paused, momentarily overwhelmed by all the angles in play. Then she blinked and said, "Oh! Bobbi, I almost forgot—Tim Neuworth and Gwen Belores are gonna kill Connor McAuley."

Bobbi watched them go. She stood in the center of the station house waiting area for long seconds after, trying to understand what was happening.

Then she saw a man on the sidewalk with an aquiline profile in a smart, bright blue suit with cuffs cut high, sporting a fedora. He appeared to be in a sort of torpor and took small steps. Several paces behind him followed a hunched woman with white curls in a patterned red dress under an apron, drifting with the same passivity. Then came Frank Hoster, a second cousin, who lost a foot to diabetes ten years before his fatal aneurism, still fat, but steady on two feet, if unhurried.

Bobbi rushed out to the street. "Frank?" she called. He did not turn, but closer now, she was certain it was him. As the reports came in, she was swayed from irritation to doubt to frazzled curiosity, but she didn't believe it until she saw it for herself. The dead were walking. There were more across the street, in the street; she backed against the glass door to let another pass. They were all headed in the same direction.

"Rose! Rosie, please! It's me, Evan! Please, talk to me!"

A bearded man pleaded with a wandering shade. He reached to touch her shoulder and she blinked on and off, but did not disappear.

"Well, you can imagine, Doris was upset with him. After all, he'd said he'd invested well. He said it wasn't his fault, but you know how much he spent on those cars of his."

The woman nattered to her oblivious companion, taller than her, with gold hair in fierce defiance to the creases in her cheeks and the waddle beneath her chin.

They were all going in the same direction. The dead were walking, and the living were following them. Straight to the center of town.

Chapter 29

"I've never pretended to be a good person," Darren said. "Never pretended anything at all. I figured good and bad was all bullshit. It's just you and yours against everybody else, and you can stand up straight or you can bend over." He smiled with vicious delight and shook his head in admiration. "But this—*this* is something else. I'm coming around to think that real, full-on evil is where it's at."

Valeria struggled for breath and the corners of her vision blurred as she looked out from the tightening collar of Darren's bicep and forearm. He didn't mean to choke her—not yet anyway. He was enjoying making her watch. But his muscles tensed with excitement, and only when she began to sputter and wheeze did he notice her reddening, swollen face and her fluttering eyelids as she teetered on the brink of fainting. He relaxed the vise slightly and she gasped.

"Don't tune out on me now, girl! This show is prime-time material!"

Bat-with-ten-eyes, sated on the blood offering from Valeria's former employer, crawled delicately over the length of Lita's corpse, laid out on her back on one of the tables. With all its appendages drawn in and its focus on the body below it, the creature looked like little more than an enormous hunk of wet obsidian and soft shadow dangling from a string, its facets shiny or dull in alternation as it spun slowly in its labor. Valeria couldn't see from what foul orifice the cloudy orange syrup emerged, but it looked as though the demon worked the sickening fluid with alacrity, smoothing it on the corpse as though with putty knives before it became waxy and hardened. The sculpture developing before her was a grotesque frozen waterfall, seeming to flow from the feet and over the top of the table and the angled step of Lita's half-severed neck, down onto the floor.

The beast kept to its work, undistracted by the sudden rattle of the metal shelves against the wall that drew the attention of the other two. Tuttle was woozy. He tried to move his hand away from the shelves before realizing he was handcuffed to them. If he'd been more alert, he might have tried to better assess the situation before announcing his return to consciousness. Instead, he looked at the horror before him and once again acted without thinking, kicking at the floor and trying to raise himself to his feet; with his hand bound, he was able only to noisily huddle up into a ball turned awkwardly sideways.

"'Bout goddamn time, Johnny-boy," roared Darren. "Didn't anybody ever tell you you can sleep when you're dead?"

John flailed his left arm across his body and slapped at his right hip.

Darren laughed. "Come on, buddy. What kind of chump you take me for?" He held up his free hand and let John's gun dangle from the trigger guard on his pinky.

John tried to pull his hand away from the shelving again; two tubs of acrylic paint slapped the floor and rolled away. "Let her go!" he shouted.

Darren bent close to Valeria's ear. "Noble, ain't he?" He moved his arm from beneath her chin and in a continuous circle pivoting from the elbow, brought his palm back behind her. He pushed her hard, down to the floor, in John's direction. "Here ya go, sport. Truth is, I don't need either of you now. So, I don't really need to hurt you either. It's true, *old friend*, I brought you here for—well, that." He motioned with the gun at Lita's corpse, grimacing playfully at Bat-with-ten-eyes' ongoing efforts. "Guess I just got tired of thinking you meant anything to me. Turns out, being *un*holier-than-thou suits *me* just fine. But now the deed is done. All I need to do is go see the big bird boss to get my brother back. And my cash and stash—I mean, sure, he's my brother." Darren shrugged and arched his eyebrows. "But, really, let's not lose track of what set this whole fuckeree-doo into motion. The paranoid son of a bitch hid my *stuff*, and I want what's mine."

John stared uncomprehendingly as he put his free arm around the cowering Valeria. "What the hell are you talking about?"

Darren laughed. "Oh, man, I almost forgot who's up to speed and who's not!"

"I'm caught up just fine."

Darren wheeled at the sound of Walt's voice coming from the open doorway to the gallery room. He began to bring his shooting hand up, but Walt froze him with an, "Ut! Ut!" The chief instructed him, "Drop it!" He complied, casually setting the pistol down on one of the tables next to the blood-covered crescent blade of his hunting knife.

"Sorry, Chief," Darren said, "but you're too late." He motioned with an open hand to indicate the tableau on the next table over. Bat-with-ten-eyes, having finished its work, rose slowly, extending its many legs. A wet clicking sound came from its mouth.

Walt looked at John. "I thought I was," Walt said. "But I'm not."

"Excuse me, Chief, but, uh—that's my kill, *my* wish," Darren protested.

Walt took a deep breath and let it out again. "Maybe, maybe not. I'm half curious to see what would happen if I put you down right now. But that's not what I'm talking about." He kept his gun trained on Darren as he reached his left hand to his service belt. He pulled free the handcuff keys, stooped low, and slid them toward John without looking.

Bat-with-ten-eyes ticked backward along the table and then lowered to the floor.

Darren chuckled. "You think that .45 is enough to take down a demon? It's two against one, Chief, and I'm goddamned superfluous."

"You sure you got your count right?" Walt asked.

Bat-with-ten-eyes crawled up the front wall to the seam between metal panels where ceiling became eave. It slid three legs into the crease. Suddenly the metal screamed and screws popped like champagne corks as it rent the panels asunder. The others raised their arms against the sudden influx of sunlight, and the demon twisted with a spasm of pain. Then it spread the fissure wide, crawled through, unfolded its black wings, and shot into the air. Darren stumbled after it, confused by the beast's sudden departure.

"Get her out of here!" Walt commanded John.

John, still bleary-eyed and wobbly, asked for confirmation, "Chief?"

"First priority: Get the civilian out of harm's way."

John looked at Valeria and realized she was helping to support him from under his arm. Still, his sense of loyalty was dominant. "Chief, I can't leave you alone with Darren."

Walt didn't dare tell him he was no good to him in his half-focused condition. It would only make John double down in his determination to help Walt. He knew people with concussions felt compelled to complete their tasks. He had to make sure John knew what his task was. He snatched up John's service weapon from the table and handed it to him. "You've got her safety and the safety of the town to consider, John. Get her home and track that monster. Those are your orders. We can't have that thing running loose. It already killed one kid last night. I'm counting on you to do your duty. I'll take care of Darren."

Up on his feet, the fog in John's head was beginning to clear. He hated to leave the chief alone, but the logic of his instructions—no, his *orders*—seemed right-minded. Whatever doubts he had about Walt's recent performance, whatever confusion he had about what he'd just seen (and about why it didn't seem to faze the chief), he felt the return of his confidence in the chief's assuredness, and he led Valeria—or she led him—through the open door and out of the building.

"Now what, Chief?" Darren asked. He moved away from the tables into the open area nearer the interior wall, taking slow, broad steps to reestablish his swagger. "You gonna pick up your ball and run crying home just because you didn't win the game? Maybe you ought to consider for a minute just how deep your involvement goes before you decide you wanna bring me in and put me on the stand."

"I know my sins," Walt replied. "Whoever else knows them or doesn't, that won't change. Even so, all things considered, maybe the best thing to do would be to just not bring you in."

Darren chuckled as he came to a stop and put his hands on his hips. "Now, there's two ways to interpret that, Chief. One way is, you're just gonna let me go to do what I need to do."

Walt shook his head. "I'm afraid that's the wrong interpretation, Dietz."

"Man!" Darren exclaimed. "You really can't lose, can you? Even if you don't get your mushed-up wife back, you still managed to get rid of both Dietz brothers in a week. That's good police work, Sheriff. You want me to give you a hand—pick up the knife? It wouldn't do to have you shoot an unarmed man." He shuffled sideways and leaned meaningfully toward the blood-slick knife on the table. He froze with his reaching hand just above the outer arc of the stool next to the table and turned his head toward Walt. "Or did you just want to plant it on me afterward?"

Walt swallowed. He motioned with the barrel of the gun for Walt to move away from the table. "I think—"

Darren suddenly dipped his right shoulder, scooped up the stool, and flung it at Walt. Walt fired wildly twice, moving to his right and trying to block the stool with his left. Darren hurled himself backward onto the tabletop and tucked his legs up to roll off the other side. He crashed into the stools, scattering them. Walt fired twice more, guessing Darren's location. Darren got his legs under him and sprang straight up, knocking the table into the air. Three more shots perforated the table as it landed on one corner and tumbled toward Walt, backing up as he fired. And as the table dropped out of the line of sight between them, he took aim again, too late—his last shot went skyward as he recoiled from the impacts of a 9mm slug in his right shoulder. He tried to swing around to aim again and took a second shot dead center in his chest.

IT WAS AS PREDICTABLE as rain. You took one step away from the shitstorm your life has spiraled into, and you're reminded of the sanctimonious attitudes that pushed you that direction in the first place. Hannah knew the look: The woman at the bakery took one glance at how she was dressed, her mussed hair, and the darkening rose on her cheekbone, and aligned her against the nice folks she'd been boxing up baker's dozens of donuts and muffins for, the deacons and ushers and other early arriving church volunteers. Doubtless the news over the radio about how some of her customers had to evacuate and leave the product of her honest labor behind irked her further, and she resented having instead to wait on this waif, probably out to fuel up for extramarital iniquity, round two. Hannah's thank you meant *fuck you* and they both knew it. Her money was as good as anybody else's and there wasn't anything the judgy cunt could do about it. Hannah was happy to have parked right in front of the bakery window, so the woman could have a good look at the expensive copper sedan she eased into languidly.

She had two muffins, two Danish, and two donuts in a bag. She couldn't remember exactly what Connor liked, but she figured it didn't matter much. He was in no position to complain, and besides, she was *famished*, and her sweet tooth was aching. Even if he didn't like the selection, nothing was going to go to waste. She grabbed the bag and carefully lifted up the cardboard drink carrier and two coffees from the passenger's seat. When she pulled open the storm door on the side entry, the interior door moved with the suction. She frowned. Had she not closed the door on her way out?

She stepped inside the kitchen and put down the bag and carrier. Something seemed off. "Connor?"

Connor wasn't on the couch in the living room. The paper he'd drawn the unicursal hexagram on as well as several of his books from the coffee table were strewn on the floor. A potted plant on a windowsill was on its side with dirt spilled below it. The scene wasn't indicative of a great struggle, but in his condition, Connor wouldn't have been able to put up much of a fight. Besides, he would have known how outclassed he was by the man who'd come for him, even on his best day.

"Darren," Hannah huffed.

It had to be. Hannah thought of what she'd seen Darren do to that stranger in the field house the day before. She shuddered and felt instantly nauseous. Did he have the same fate planned for Connor? How did he know that Hannah had come there with him? Perhaps he had no idea and it didn't have anything to do with her. But even if it didn't—it did. Because she couldn't leave Connor to the untender mercies of such a man, not after leading an innocent man to his death the day before. Maybe Connor was right and it was time to call the cops. She didn't have any evidence that Darren had abducted Connor, but there was other evidence—the corpse in the field house. Maybe it was time to call the cops even if they got caught up in it. She thought that even Connor would agree it was better to be disgraced than dead.

She called 911. The phone rang eight times, then there was a pause, and a click, followed by another pause, then the phone began to ring again. Someone answered, "911, Pennsylvania State Highway Patrol. What's your emergency?"

Hannah hung up. Why didn't the Adler PD answer? Of course—the evacuation downtown. Everyone was busy. Might not even be anybody at the station house. Hannah yelped as her phone rang.

She answered, "Hello?"

"This is the Pennsylvania State Highway Patrol. Someone di-aled 911 from this number. Is there an emergency?"

"Oh!" Hannah sniffed and affected a laugh. "Sorry. Just a mis-dial. I should have stayed on the line. Sorry."

"That's alright. Take care now."

Hannah wasn't sure why she didn't ask for help from the state highway patrol. It just seemed too *real* talking to state cops instead of the local PD. It stoked her natural aversion to the law. But it was stupid. She needed help. There wasn't anything else she could do. There was no way Darren would have been foolish enough to take Connor back to his house, and it wasn't like she had any way of knowing where he'd gone.

But she did, she remembered. Lyle's paranoia. His need to keep *track* of things, including her. But it went both ways. He made it so he could track her phone from his phone, but (accidently, Hannah was sure; Lyle was no tech wizard) it also meant that she could track his—the phone that Darren was currently in possession of.

She turned on the locator app. A red pin popped up and the screen zoomed in automatically. Hannah wondered what he was doing at County Craft Funzone. And then, as the little pin shifted ever so slightly northward, she wondered where he was going next.

CHAPTER 30

"T HERE," BRITT SAID, THOUGH the destination was obvious. The door to loading bay four was still propped up by the broom handle stuck in the track. Having been sent away, Tim hadn't closed the door, and her father had neglected to do so after the young killer left.

Allan pulled up to the brink of the shallow decline leading to the dock and stopped his truck. He leaned his chest against the steering wheel to peer into the gloom. Seeing no farther than a few feet into the warehouse, he leaned back again and shut off the engine. He glanced left and right, then to all three rear view mirrors, as though taking stock of the exceptional normality of the sun and green grass and gold-flecked leaves behind and the tedium of industrial decay spread before him. Then he turned to Britt.

"You stay here, okay?"

"Like hell," she replied. "My father's involved in this mess, whatever it is. I don't know how but I mean to find out."

"Okay, fine, but—ah!" Allan jumped at the knock on his window.

"Are you coming with me or what?" Eve asked. "If not, give me your gun."

Allan opened the door and stepped out. "Yeah. We're going in. *All* of us, despite my feeble efforts." He went around to the back and opened the hatch. He unzipped a long bag and pulled out a bolt-action rifle with a sight attached. He slapped the detachable box magazine into place and then slid the bolt back and in again. He turned and looked at the others. "There might not be anything in there at all. Even if there was, it's likely to be gone by now. That said, a young man lost his life last night in the most gruesome animal attack I've ever seen. So, we might have a bear."

"Or we might have something else," Eve added. She nodded toward the open hatch. "You got anything else in there?"

Allan looked at her for a second and then sighed. He busied himself in the back of the truck for a minute and then turned around again. He presented her with a pistol. The pink feathers of a tranquilizer dart peeked out from the back of barrel.

"You're kidding, right?" Eve asked.

"I don't roll with an armory in my back seat," Allan said. "You only get one shot with that thing. Please don't shoot me in my butt. It's not nearly as comical as you might think."

Eve held the tranquilizer gun next to her face. "Shall we?"

They proceeded up the ramp. They caught the smells emanating from inside and gagged. They checked each other's faces to stiffen their resolve and then proceeded through the dock bay door. A few steps inside the warehouse, Allan stopped them with a gesture. "Give your eyes a chance to adjust," he murmured. They stood still, listening, as the farther shapes took on depth and definition. They ticked their heads in unison at a rustling sound, like the shifting of leaves.

"Is there somebody there?" Allan called.

"What are you doing?" Britt hissed.

"If it *is* a bear, we don't wanna surprise it," Allan replied.

"You don't still believe it's a bear, do you?" Eve asked.

Allan grunted. He wanted to proceed as if he still knew how to deal with whatever was waiting in the shadows.

"Shall we speak first?"

Allan raised the gun level to take aim and swung it around in a wild arc in front of him, seeking the source of the voice. Britt yelped and swatted her hair, as though trying to dislodge clinging cobwebs. Eve crossed her arms to calm the sudden shiver running up the length of her body.

"Wh-where is—" Eve stammered.

"We are... Ixixiklis."

"It's in my head," Britt said, not just of the voice, but of the speaker.

"Our appearance... will alarm you. We offer fair warning... to avoid unseemly violence."

"I think it's behind that machine," Allan said, motioning with the rifle toward the green, barrel-shaped mammoth.

"No," Eve corrected him, almost absently. "It's in the far corner."

"My God," Britt said to herself. Though she could not yet see the thing whose words scratched at her mind, she was struck by anticipatory dread, and by the correlative thought, *This is what my father wanted to show me.*

They went around the side of the bulky machine nearer the door and looked behind it.

"What the hell..." Allan wondered. He heard Eve gasp, and only then thought to warn them. "Stay back!"

But they were huddled together and they all saw the amber-crusted spindly form stuck in its silent howl. Horrified as she was, Britt peered closer, trying to see if she could place a name to the corpse-husk, but decided that she wouldn't be able to make an identification of the withered body even if she had known it in life.

"Like the one in the forest," Eve said.

"What?" the other two prompted.

"My husband and I found a body in the forest, desiccated and covered in this… this *stuff*. That's why we came to town… to report it."

"To my father," Britt concluded. He hadn't said anything about it. Of course, he didn't tell her everything that went on in Adler, but he told her to stay inside and to be careful the night they found that girl from the dollar store dead in the park. And he hadn't said anything at all when she went out last night. Either he didn't care—no. Not if he wanted to bring her here. He cared because he *knew*. "Three," she said.

Allan asked, "What?" again, but Eve nodded her head.

"Here, in the forest, and that girl we heard about at the pizzeria yesterday," she said. She explained to Allan, "This is the third victim like this. At least."

"*Six are needed. Strangely… seven are dead… but it is still not enough.*"

"Seven!" Allan exclaimed. "Jesus!" He looked at Britt questioningly.

"I don't know," she said. "There was a guy, they found his car by the lake. Everyone just thought he drowned. But—*seven*. I don't know how you could keep that hidden, e-even if the cops were covering it up."

"You couldn't, not for long," Eve said. She stepped closer to the dark corner, nearer the tall shape that she began to parse from the clutter and gloom. "You'd have to hurry."

The thing rose to its full height and scattered dead branches and crumpled cardboard and scraps of mangled, perforated metal as it emerged into the wary light leaking through the high windows. Eve heard Britt scream, and her mind willed her to join, but her body was slack, overcome by instinctual, awe-inspired fear; she knew the moment of shutdown when the rabbit's lightning prayer for miraculous deliverance goes out between jackhammer heartbeats because it is too late for anything else. Yet in her petrified wonderment, there was recognition of sorts, images recalled from old books—this is what the artists of medieval plague years and cloistered monks waging the battle between sin and redemption *recorded* as best they could; this is what demons *must* look like, bizarre chimeras depicted more accurately than could be believed by modern man. This tattered-winged man-bird with its second idiot face and its red, drooping dick and its crown of vermin, this resplendent perversity of nature—a demon had to be this alien, this foul.

The sight in her peripheral vision of the rifle barrel lifting into alignment shook Eve from her frightened reverie. "No!" she shouted, as her left hand shot out and smacked the gun sideways. Allan's shot went awry, its impact registering only a meek *ping* as it exited the warehouse.

Allan was too alarmed to continue his assault. "Mrs. Nowlan?"

"For fuck's sake, call me Eve!" she barked. "'It is still not enough.' That's what it said. It's not done. It needs more." She didn't say, "then there's still hope." She was afraid to believe it. Nevertheless, she asked, "Where is my husband? Did you kill him?"

"*We do not kill. It is . . . done for us.*"

"My father," Britt said, too quiet for anyone else to hear, too loud for herself to ignore.

"'Not enough!'" Eve quoted again. "For what? Do you have a quota to meet?"

"Six offerings ... are required."

"Offerings?" Eve pointed at Lyle's corpse. "You *eat* people?"

"We eat ... the stains you leave behind."

"What the hell does that mean?" Allan asked. Eve saw him shifting his feet, saw the sweat on his brow. He wanted to shoot again, to shoot until the clip was empty, and to reload and to shoot again.

"Ghosts," Britt said.

Eve recalled the old man in the forest and knew immediately she was right.

"You said, it is done for you!" Britt cried. "Why? Why would anyone help you to do these awful things?"

"We give one ... in return. All the dead ... for one to live."

"Tim Neuworth," Britt said.

Eve recalled the name. "That was the kid who got arrested and released, right?"

"Yeah. And he was here last night too, and my father let him go."

"Ah, yes. Last night. We forgot. Eight dead. That was ... not in service to us. Just fun ... for our companion."

Britt frowned. Her fear was slowly dissipating. Her anger at this thing, and at what it made her father do, was ascendant. "Tim wants to bring his friend Keith back," she said, believing that was who the demon meant. "Keith killed himself a few months back. But you said, *one* to live. My father... I don't know what he's done. But he hasn't done it for fucking Keith Belores, that much I know. He wants to bring my mom back."

Eve picked up the thread. "So, who gets to decide?"

"The one to offer ... the final sacrifice."

"The sixth," Eve said.

Allan asked, "But t-that thing said there are eight people dead already—or seven, at least. I don't understand entirely."

"It is farcical… to watch you run… hither and to. But it is… frustrating. And it… is happening again. A sacrifice… has been removed… and must be replaced. You shall do it."

Ixixiklis hadn't pointed or looked at her, but Eve knew she was the one he meant. "I'm not going to kill anybody! Why would I—" she began, but then pivoted and stumbled sideways as the demon lurched forward. Allan aimed the rifle again as it continued past them but couldn't guide his trembling finger under the trigger guard. A putrid odor like sewage gas wafted in the wake of the huge, crippled wings dragging across the floor. A loathsome moan emerged from the middle mouth. In only a few quick strides Ixixiklis reached Lyle's corpse. The demon's arm shot out and smashed into the hard resin, shattering it with ease. It struck thrice more in rapid succession; chips and chunks fell away and skittered across the cement. Then the beast turned back to face the others.

There was a chunk of rough amber in each of the demon's hands. The larger one in its right palm held aloft the silently screaming head, severed at the neck. The contents of the left hand were inferred by the gaping cavity in the mummy's chest.

"Kill no one… as you will. You need only take… the head and heart. The point… must be… once more affixed."

Eve backed away, shaking her head. "Why the fuck would I even do that?" And then a tear rolled down her cheek, as her body told her something her mind still rejected. A sob squeaked from her mouth and she screamed, "Why would I ever want to help you!" And the answer came as she knew it must.

"To bring… your husband back."

CHAPTER 31

"Is this… part of the plan?" Gwen asked.

"I think so," Tim said. Then, more confidently, "Yeah," so that she wouldn't have any doubts about what they were committed to do. The plan, for him, was working just fine so far: send the other assholes out of the way to kill each other for the sixth sacrifice, each believing that he would be the one granted the prize, while he completed the unicursal hexagram at its *seventh* point and became the real victor. Yes, of course, he understood: This unexpected development was just further proof of Ixixiklis's power, and it served to confirm the importance of the center point. That was why the spirits of Adler's dead were congregating downtown—them, and the dumb living sheep falling in step as they tried to communicate with the somnambulant throng.

They watched from a sunken walkway running alongside the Baptist church, crouching behind a trimmed hedge at the base of the steps leading up to the front lawn. Connor wanted to shout for help—or moan for help, as was the case—through the drool-soaked sham in his mouth (which, he realized bitterly, still smelled of Gwen's peony-scented shampoo), but the knifepoint in his ribs provided strong disincentive. And even if he could make himself heard from that distance, he doubted anyone would listen, as the distractions were too great. Officers Bundy and Clay were focused on quixotic efforts at crowd dispersal. Behind them, county deputies were working with technicians dispatched by the Pennsylvania Department of Transportation in a cordoned area in the middle. The trucker had been driving through Adler just after dawn ("a bit fast, maybe, but there weren't nobody on the road") when he had to swerve to avoid a man "who was there all of a sudden, then weren't there" crossing against the light in the intersection. He ran the tanker truck up onto the corner, banged off a streetlight, and skipped one tire up onto a planter, knocking over an old-fashioned clock that got wedged under the right side of the front axle, causing it to act like a ramp. The cab ended up at a forty-five-degree angle; a bent drawbar left the trailer balanced on the side of the rear tire. Miraculously, the tank saddle anchors held the mounted cylinder in place and the hoses stayed fastened, otherwise there wouldn't have been a downtown left to save. The DOT workers, having attached the boom winch from an anchored heavy-duty wrecker to stabilize the truck so the contents could be transferred to a second tank, wondered why the hell all the crazy townsfolk of Adler were gathering at the potential epicenter of a disastrous explosion.

Connor recognized Bill Konak, the recently retired PE teacher. He was whirling among the shades, bumping into them and causing them to shudder or skip forward, but frustrated in his search. Whoever he was looking for, he hadn't found them yet. There was a Black family in Depression-era garb, parents and a boy and a girl. He'd never heard of an Adler family dying all together, but it would have happened long before he'd been born, much less moved to town. There was a tall man with a grand mustache and long hair wearing a mint-green three-piece suit. Those were only the ones to stand out among the more modern and normal in appearance. For most of them, the only noticeable difference between living and dead was the divide in expression between resolved and bewildered.

"How the hell did you ever learn to summon a freaking demon anyway?" Gwen asked.

Tim's voice took on an awed tone. "I discovered an old book hidden in a crumbling wall of an old farmhouse."

"Really?"

Tim laughed loud and snorted. "No! On the internet, dingus."

Gwen scoffed. "You discovered how to summon a demon on the internet?"

"Yeah, I did," Tim said proudly. "It wasn't what I was looking for—I was really just looking for ways to communicate with the dead so I could talk to Keith again. But, you know, internet rabbit hole."

Gwen articulated the same doubt in Connor's mind. "Wait—but if this shit is on the internet, then why isn't everyone doing it?"

Tim shrugged. "Maybe one day they will. That's the thing—all these universities everywhere are doing this digital archiving, but the jag-offs working to pay down their student loans aren't paying much attention to *what* their scanning. So, yeah, maybe it's just a matter of the information not being out there *yet*. Guess I'm a pioneer! I was just searching 'occult' blindly when I found this old book handwritten in, like, Latin. I was just up for the gnarly pictures. Wouldn't have been able to read a line of it if it weren't for the AI translation that popped up automatically! Right around that time I was pissed off at all the knuckle-draggers smiling and laughing when there I am in the corner with my best friend dead. So, I tried to summon a demon to kill everyone at prom."

"Wasn't that an episode of *Buffy the Vampire Slayer?*"

"I don't know. So, fuck me, I'm not original. Whatever!"

"Jesus, I'm just saying."

Tim curled his lip up and scrunched his nose to show his pique. "Well, it didn't happen, so never mind. But I think I almost succeeded. *Something* happened, I could *feel* it—and it scared the shit outta me, big time." He laughed. "I was such a chickenshit feeb! Fuck all boring as summer was without Keith, I was too scared to try anything again for a long time. And then I didn't get it *right* until a couple of weeks ago. Killed a dog at the abandoned factory north on Wilburville and summoned Ixixiklis."

As he rhapsodized, Tim's grip loosened, and he let the knife point fall away from Connor's ribs. Seeing his chance, Connor lurched forward, breaking free from Tim's grip on his arm. But his balance was off and he misjudged his footing, so he pitched and fell face-first onto the sidewalk at the top of the steps. He tried to roll on his side and kick forward as he wailed through the gag in the direction of the police surrounding the wreck. He felt two sets of hands grab his ankles. He kicked again and got one leg free, but the second grip clamped tight and dragged him backward over the cement. He continued to flail and moan as hands grabbed the back of his belt. He was yanked back down the stairs, smacking his cheek on one step and then his temple on the next. He tumbled to a heap at the bottom. Tim turned him on his back and squatted with a knee on his chest, raising the blade to Connor's throat.

"Not smart, Mr. Teacher Perv," he growled.

"We've got to get out of sight!" Gwen urged.

"We have to wait for Bat-with-ten-eyes before we kill him," Tim said.

Connor's eyes widened in horror and he wailed again. Though the intention had seemed clear, no one yet had mentioned the conclusion outright.

"Do we have to wait out here?" Gwen asked.

"Where are we gonna go?" Tim replied. "There's a huge fucking crowd of people out there!"

"Genius, why the hell do you think I brought you to my church? We know it's empty and we know it's unlocked. You said we had to be downtown—well, we're downtown. Isn't this close enough to the middle?"

"Yeah. Yeah, sure," Tim said. "It's just…" He looked at one of the stained-glass windows.

"What?"

"I'm not sure if Bat-with-ten-eyes can go *inside* the church. You know, *demon* and all." He dug his free hand into his jeans pocket and pulled out a small bundle of bloody paper towels. "Got a nice treat for him when he gets here, though." He wrangled the sticky parcel open with his thumb to show Connor the severed finger inside. Tears of fear streamed down Connor's cheeks. Who the hell's finger was it?

"Gross," Gwen said. "Well, let's figure that out when the time comes, huh? At least *we* can hide out inside until then." She motioned him toward the stairs. "Grab his arm and hold him tight. Keep that knife under his heart." Connor looked at her pleadingly. "Sorry, darling, but we both know this was going nowhere. I'd say it's not personal, but—it is. You fucked around on me. *You* fucked around on *me*." She laughed incredulously. "What do you think that does for my sense of self-worth to have my sex-predator teacher stick it in one of his *old* cumrags? Did you think I could just let that go? I mean, in other circumstances,

I don't think I'd take it *this* far, but as it's kind of a you or me situation, that's an easy choice to make."

They hauled him upright and each slipped an arm through his. He tried to kick his feet forward onto the steps and push off, but then crumpled with a yelp as the knifepoint slipped through his shirt and punctured the skin. Afraid, unsure what to do, he complied and let them guide him to the top. They bunched close around him, trying to block sight of the knife and gag, and led him to the front entrance.

Officer Bundy sometimes likened being a cop to playing football. Someone handed you a playbook. You studied it and you practiced executing the plays. Then the ball was snapped, and everything went to Hell. Adler as a sleepy little town might've already seemed like a distant memory, but this was some deep-fourth-quarter chaos happening now. Grant had never had to orchestrate an evacuation before, but the last thing he expected was for pedestrian traffic to flow in the wrong direction. All efforts to get the crowd to disperse had failed. Barkley and the county cops weren't having any better luck. Half of the people appeared dazed, and the other half were entranced by them. A few people waved him over to insist that the person they were standing next to was so-and-so, their dead relation/friend/coworker. Grant had only been in Adler for twelve years and didn't recognize anyone presented to him—until he saw Lorne Shepherd, his first "smell call." Lorne looked just like he did in the family photograph attached to his case file and nothing like the bloated, purple-gray log Grant found lying across a stain in the low-pile carpet. After his hand passed through Lorne, swallowed by unnatural cold as the figure before him rippled like a reflection in water, Grant stopped trying to shout instructions to the civilians. Who would listen? Who *could* listen?

He was glad he kept watching where some odd movement had drawn his attention in the direction of the Baptist church. It was almost a relief to see Tim Neuworth holding two hostages at knifepoint. He wasn't sure, but he thought the girl might be a friend of the chief's daughter. Here was a situation with a clear goal, requiring immediate action. Like Coach always said, when all else fails, just hit somebody.

He glanced back toward Officer Clay. Barkley was on the far side of the intersection, pumping air with his palms while the crowd grew denser around him. Grant didn't know the county cops, and they were similarly busy anyway. He broke from his cluster and charged through the crowd and across the church lawn, watching as the left side of the heavy double doors swung shut beneath the stone entry arch. He didn't think Tim saw him approach. Which just might mean Tim didn't worry about locking the doors behind him. He drew his service weapon and switched off the safety as he flattened against the right door. He pressed the thumb latch on the handle of the left-side door and pushed it open a crack. Leaning his ear to the opening, he heard footsteps moving away and a harsh whisper he couldn't make out. He pushed open the door, stepped inside, and promptly discovered he was wrong about what Tim had seen.

He was struck on the side of his head by something metal. He staggered sideways. He bent and raised one hand to the already throbbing spot near his temple and tried to blink back into focus. There was a blur of motion and he raised both hands across his face defensively. The weapon hit his favored hand. He heard a crack and his hand buzzed and fell limp. His gun clacked on the tile floor. He heard a clatter; the circular base of a display stand rolled into view.

Tim dove for the gun at Grant's feet. He didn't expect Grant would recover so quickly or move so fast. A giant paw snatched him up by the arm and swung him like a rag doll. Tim flew across the narthex and slammed into the interior doors.

Gwen gasped as Tim tumbled into the sanctuary. Connor howled into his gag and clumsily tried to headbutt Gwen. She hissed, "Fucker!" and thrust Tim's knife up under Connor's rib cage. He screamed and doubled over; Gwen buckled under his weight and toppled to the floor with him, her hand still on the knife hilt.

Grant teetered into the sanctuary. He saw Tim on the floor, stunned but stirring. The girl who might've been Britt's friend was on the floor cradling the man they came in with. He was slumped over. The girl drew away from the man and let his body drop back on the end of a pew. Her hands were covered in blood. A knife stuck out from the man's abdomen.

"He stabbed him!" Gwen cried, pointing at Tim.

Grant wasn't sure if that's what it looked like. His head was still foggy. "Miss…"

She backed away toward the altar. "I'll go get help!"

"Wait! No, miss, you have to—"

"Watch out!" she screeched and pointed emphatically behind him.

Grant wobbled as he spun. Tim leaped at him. Grant treasured a split second of amusement. The kid was half his weight and didn't even have a weapon. Grant's right hand wouldn't let him make a fist, but he didn't need it. He brought his forearm down like a club on Tim's shoulder and felt satisfaction as the boy crumpled.

He turned toward the altar. The girl was gone. The man looked dead, but if he had a chance, he needed prompt medical care.

Grant was still woozy. He started to reach for the radio clipped to his shoulder, but realized he was still holding his gun. Instead of radioing for assistance, he holstered his weapon and grabbed Tim's ankle. He dragged him out of the sanctuary, through the narthex, and onto the church's front lawn.

Tim laughed. "Now you're gonna get it," he said limply.

Grant looked at him and saw his gaze directed to the church's steeple. He looked up too, blinking under the assault of the bright sky. Then he saw it. Something big and black was holding onto the church steeple. It was something from a nightmare, and Grant was thankful long after that he couldn't quite make it out.

"Come and get it!" Tim shouted hoarsely, laying on the lawn.

Grant's breath shuddered in his chest. He drew his service weapon again and raised it up in his left hand, trying to steady the shaking with his wounded right.

Tim laughed with perverse glee. "You think that's gonna do anything?"

Grant continued to aim his gun at the steeple for several seconds and then slowly lowered it. "Don't have to," he said.

"What?" Tim propped himself up.

Grant saw him favoring one side. Maybe he dislocated the kid's shoulder. Good.

"It's gone," he said, and looked again at the naked steeple to confirm it. "It backed off and flew away."

"Bullshit!" Tim said. "It's about to swoop down and tear your fucking head off."

"Don't think so," Grant said. He searched the sky in case Tim was right, but the body language of the thing—whatever body, whatever thing it was—had seemed to indicate disinterest in attacking.

"What?" Tim asked again. Then, weakly, "But it *has* to."

By the time Grant raised his hand to his radio, Barkley was already running toward him, asking, "Grant! What the fuck?!"

CHAPTER 32

A LLAN STOPPED AT THE end of the short connector street. The fly on the steering wheel vaulted onto his left hand.

"Given what we've just seen, I know that shouldn't be so disconcerting. But it is." He turned left onto another sleepy residential avenue. "Not that you've got it any easier."

Allan's jacket sat in Eve's lap, plumped into a bundle by the two stiff, jagged clumps wrapped inside.

"It *is* easier, somehow," she replied. "Because it's preposterous for me to be cradling a man's resin-covered head and heart in my lap. It's too horrific to be believed." They both understood the part left unsaid: "like what that demon said about my husband."

After five hundred feet, the road took a sharp right. Just as Allan made the turn, the fly whirled frenetically in front of his face. "What the heck?" he said as he stopped abruptly. The fly darted out of the open driver's-side window and flew straight to a small house with wide, dingy, white siding. "This must be the place." He gripped the handle but stopped before opening the door. "What the double heck?"

Eve leaned forward to look past him toward the house. "What is… it…?" The last word dying on her lips as she saw the old woman, small but sturdy, laboring to drag an encumbered blanket down the gravel drive to the street.

Elba would never have been able to move Joe Underwood's body at his full weight. She had cried out when a propitiously effective strike of the poker split several seams in the encasement simultaneously, sending large chunks of orange rock tumbling and freeing Joe's corpse to topple forward on top of her. The fall to the carpet hurt worse than the avalanche, though, as both the glassy fragments and her dead friend's body were lighter than expected. She realized she shouldn't have been surprised given the state of his desiccated corpse. She had intended only to pry loose the body and leave it in the hall. Realizing it could be moved more easily than expected, she changed her plans and decided to bring Joe to the station. Maybe the chief would believe her *then*. She didn't feel she'd disturbed the crime scene—how would they be able to determine his cause of death if they couldn't get to the body? She was just speeding up the process. She felt bad about his foot, though. It had remained stuck in the rock, severed at the withered ankle, when the rest of the body fell away. Elba broke it out as well and put it on the blanket with everything else, but only that errant detail made her feel she'd done anything wrong—in the execution, not the act. Though perhaps the Lord blessed her with the mistake; otherwise, she might have dragged him feetfirst down the porch steps, and who knows what might then have happened with his head?

"That must be what the demon said about the sacrifice being removed," Allan said. "Maybe I should go help her."

Eve grabbed his arm as he tensed to go. "No! Definitely not!" she hissed. "We don't have time to get involved. Duck down so she doesn't see us."

Allan complied, sliding forward to slouch, but continued to watch through the window. "I don't think we have time *not* to help," he said. "I don't like her chances of maneuvering that body into the back seat of her car," which was what Elba now endeavored to do, looking back and forth between bench seat and body with her hands on her hips as she caught her breath. Allan went on, "We'll get out. I'll go over there. You wait a few seconds and go around back. I'll keep her concentrating on her task. If you can't get in back, by then she'll be crawling over the back seat, and you can try the front."

Eve didn't have confidence in the plan, but she wasn't sure a good plan was available. She nodded and opened her door immediately after he did. She slinked to the back of the truck, satchel in her arms, and then ducked down and squeezed tight against the back gate. She had to wait there briefly while the others conversed. Presumably, the old woman was explaining why she was dragging a corpse to her car. Her voice was loud and clear, but Eve's ears thrummed with anxious blood and she could only hear the nasal accent, not the words. Allan patted the old woman on the shoulder. Probably she was too flummoxed to realize he shouldn't have been so ready to accept her explanation and she shouldn't have been so ready to accept his help, but they soon reached an accord. Allan opened the back door on the street side and climbed across. The old woman bent over to grab the lead edge of the blanket and Eve scampered across the street.

She tip-toed up the drive in the shadow of the house. She hadn't looked back after she'd started and vowed to herself to continue on regardless, relying on Allan to distract the old woman or placate her if she had seen Eve. She went around back and up the steps of the small deck. The back door was open. One of the small glass panes was broken out, but the glass was all brushed aside. It seemed the dead man's house had been unusually busy of late. Eve went inside the kitchen and then on into the transition to the living room. She wondered briefly if it mattered at all where she put the heart and head. Then she saw the mess down at the end of the hall, the empty cocoon and the detritus strewn on the floor. She stepped delicately between the chunks and shards, unconsciously reluctant to displace them. She squatted before the crude, inverse and inverted relief of a man's form. There was a sort of shelf where his legs must have begun. Eve unfolded Allan's jacket. She picked up the heart and placed it in a crook to the side of the shelf. Next was the head. She winced and sucked in her breath at the sight of the dark crevasse of Lyle's mouth and the pits of his eyes. She placed her hands directly on the orange rock and tried to think—and tried *not* to think—of Zander's head encased in the same way. Horrified as she was, she placed the head gently, making sure it was securely balanced before she let go.

"No," she had said to him before backing away half a step. "*You* put it in there."

Her mother's ashes were in a pewter urn with a twist-on lid, shaped in classic Grecian style. Zander held it in two hands under the bulbous top half. The attendant's retreating footfalls clipped between marble tile and arched white ceiling in the columbarium until they faded, and then there was only the sound of the two of them breathing. "Okay," he said. He stepped forward and placed the urn into the niche.

When he was done, she grabbed his arm and rested her head on his shoulder, sniffling. "Thank you," she said. When he'd mentioned inurning her mother's ashes, Eve had balked initially. Her slow, then terribly sudden death had cost so much already. The funeral arrangements were as cheap as could be (they insisted there be no embalming and the public service was performed after cremation). Eve had planned to scatter the ashes somewhere. But she couldn't think of anywhere meaningful. Nowhere seemed right.

Zander saw how she wrestled with the decision and proposed the alternative. Eve didn't see the point. Watching her wilt under the strain of spending another cent somehow strengthened Zander's resolve. He decided, right or wrong, he was going to insist upon her doing this. He told her that this way, she could visit her mother, but more importantly, even if they never again entered the columbarium to gaze on the simple bronze plaque with stamped name and dates, at least they could end this travail with a positive note—that the only consideration should be what *they* wanted. Eve hadn't been sure that this was what she wanted at all. But she was suddenly relieved, seeing the brushed metal urn in the blank whiteness of the niche. It didn't matter if she wanted this or not, if it was convenient or not; there were no real considerations at all in that moment. It was the right way to end it.

"Well, at least she won't be lonely," Zander said, glancing around at the surrounding plaques.

Eve snuffled through a giggle. Her mother had never been especially sociable.

"Oof. I wonder if anyone asked Mrs. Leon Christopher if she wanted to spend eternity with Mr. Leon Christopher. The end date is the same. Wanna bet she was still hale and hearty, but they stuck her in there anyway when he kicked?"

"That's terrible," she said, referencing both his humor and the antiquated convention that prompted it.

"Marcus Washington," Zander read. "Oof. That had to drive down property values.."

Eve gasped in playful revulsion. "My God! Are you being racist in a cemetery?"

"*I'm* not being racist," he protested. "The institutionalized prejudice of prior generations is well-documented. You should read a history book sometime."

She slapped him on the shoulder. "Shut up."

"Holy shit! Stavros Castellanos! Your mother is gonna be sleeping with a James Bond villain!"

The attendant, drawn by their laughter, returned soon thereafter.

Eve retraced her steps down the hall. She yelped at seeing Allan's frame darkening the front doorway.

"Sorry," he said. "She's gone."

"Okay. Then we go back to the warehouse, I guess."

"And get your husband back."

"Sure," she said. "Because it's just that easy."

"You think it's lying?"

"The demon?" she chortled. "Yeah, I think the *demon* is lying."

"What if it's not?" Allan asked.

"We're wasting time," Eve replied. "Let's go."

CHAPTER 33

"**B**OBBI? HEY, BOBBI, IT's John. Has the chief checked in yet?" To Valeria: "Do you see it?"

"No," Valeria answered, scanning the skies through the Rover's windows.

"John! Thank God, I've been waiting all morning to hear from you. Chief Pearcey was on his way to find you out at the Dietz residence."

Valeria's phone rang. She answered excitedly, "Britt! Oh my God, you won't believe it!"

"The chief found me, but not at Darren's. He's at that crafts place on 219, the Funzone or whatever. He's there with Darren now. I had to leave him, Bobbi. There was a hostage and a… a bat…"

"I'm at your dad's place!" Britt shouted. There seemed to be a lot of noise on the other end. "He said you had a catering thing?"

"Say again, Officer Tuttle," Bobbi prompted. Did he say, "a bat"? But that didn't matter: "Did you say there was a hostage situation?"

"We're on our way there—to my house, I mean! Oh my God, Britt—Lita's dead!" Valeria cried. "S-she wanted to kill *me*, but then—this guy killed *her* and there was this—this *thing*—"

"Please!" John barked. "Miss—uh…"

"Valeria," she reminded him.

"What?!" Britt shouted. "Lita's dead?"

"Valeria, I need to coordinate with Bobbi... with dispatch." John hated to admit that he was still having a hard time concentrating, but the competing conversation wasn't helping his clouded brain to process the situation.

"Officer Tuttle, are you still there? Did you say there was a hostage situation?"

"Bobbi, no, t-there was, but I have her. She's safe. But the chief was still there with Darren." He remembered the pertinent fact that Valeria had mentioned. "Darren killed someone. I had to leave, Bobbi. Chief told me to." He knew he wasn't making any sense.

"What?" Valeria asked.

"What *kind* of 'thing'?" Britt repeated.

Valeria shuddered, thinking about it, and tears came. "It was awful, Britt. It was a nightmare. I can't—I can't describe it. It was like a giant bat or a spider or something."

"A demon," Britt said.

"It flew away," Valeria added.

"We lost track of it," John told Bobbi, then, failing to clarify, added, "This thing."

"There was this big crowd at the center of town, and we couldn't follow it anymore," Valeria said.

Which reminded John to ask a question he suspected could only have a negative answer. "Bobbi, can Bark or Grant get down to the Funzone? I'm worried about the chief."

"I know where it's going!" Britt shouted.

"John, Bark and Grant are tied up. There was a tanker that overturned on Market and Main. And then the ghosts—" It was her turn to stop, unsure of how to explain. "John, if Walt's in trouble, you have to go back. Please, John! Go and help him out!"

"I know where it's going!" Valeria shouted. "Or Britt knows. She told me. It's going to the abandoned factory across the field from my dad's farm, where Bill Wollert got killed last night!"

John's head swam. He wanted to turn around. He remembered his instructions. He pointed at Valeria. "First: Take you home." He pointed forward. "Second: Follow the thing."

"Same direction," she said. "We're on our way," Valeria told Britt.

"I'll be at the factory," Britt said, but only after Valeria'd hung up.

ELDON DIDN'T DRIVE off in any other direction like he'd promised. For a while, he didn't leave the station parking lot at all. He sat behind the wheel of his wrecker sipping from the emergency flask he'd liberated from the glove compartment. "Sorry 'bout that," he apologized to the dwindling, metal-tanged bourbon. "Shouldn't have left you alone so long."

As per usual, he'd been drinking bourbon the night he killed Christine Pearcey. He shouldn't have been driving; he knew that. He hadn't planned on going out that night, but he'd forgotten to take himself off of on-call status with one of the insurance companies he contracted with to provide roadside assistance. And anyway, he needed the money. That never changed. Hell, there was a worn tie rod on his right front wheel; he shouldn't have been driving on *that* even sober, but how was he going to fix it if he didn't have the available funds? All things considered, he thought he did just fine, though his customer was surely as happy as he was to have a friend come to pick them up while

Eldon hauled the dead car to a closed garage to be serviced the next day. On his way home, he didn't feel sharp, but he'd driven in worse condition. He had no problem keeping in his lane. He'd already passed a half dozen cars headed the other direction with no problem on that curvy road carved into the hills. The approaching headlights on the straightaway didn't merit a second thought.

He hurt his head in the accident. Immediately after, he legitimately didn't remember the seconds right before it. And when he did, he didn't tell the cops. Then they would have been sure he was drunk, if they didn't think he was crazy. Maybe he could have said it was a buzzard. Sometimes, he tried to convince himself that's what it was that swooped into the glow of his headlights. But he knew better. And somehow, he could never bring himself to lie about it to anybody else.

It wasn't just the size of the thing either. It *overtook* him from behind—no way in hell a buzzard moved that fast. Then it did a weird spiral loop-de-loop and flew back at him. The oncoming car's headlights shook side to side; she must have seen it too (he didn't know then it was *she*, didn't know the despair he'd feel when he found out who *she* was). Then he saw it in full, for a split second, heading right at him: huge, polished obsidian in the headlights, wings spread wide as the road, legs flared like a spider pouncing, a perverse gap of a mouth underneath. He screamed and he swerved.

He didn't *not* blame himself. If he hadn't been drinking, maybe he would have had the sense to react differently; maybe he would have swerved the other direction. But if that thing hadn't had been there at all, maybe everybody got home safe and sound, and that night would've faded into memory just like ten thousand others. But it *was* there. And now it was back.

He thought about the shotgun in the hall closet at his house.

"That ain't gonna do the job," he muttered, and took another long slug.

He got out of the wrecker. It was only a couple of blocks' walk; no need to drive. He put his flask in his jacket pocket. There was a loose stream of people walking slowly toward the center of town. He fell in step immediately. Bobbi stood behind the station door, watching the parade. She didn't see him. There were other people watching in wonder or fear or walking excitedly between the slower strollers. Eldon didn't understand the confusion. He knew what they were. And he knew she would be there, somewhere. Shortly after he got to Market and Main, where the throng stopped and waited, he saw her on the far side of the circle, beyond the married tanker trucks (the one at two angles up on the sidewalk, and the new one receiving the contents of its tank). He wouldn't have been able to pick her out of a crowd before the accident. He'd never known her at all when she looked right. But he knew her now. He'd heard long before he saw her standing outside his garage five days ago about how much work they'd done to make her presentable, though, seeing the results, Chief Pearcey had ultimately decided on a closed casket. She was crooked. Her shoulders were not level, and one side of her face was frozen in a grotesque wink—"see, I'm not dead after all!"—a perverse punchline incongruous with the evidence. She had on a scarf that didn't cover all the scars. Most of the ghosts seemed normal—lifelike, if dull. Not all wore their final formal wear; only some seemed damaged. If there were rules dictating how they should appear, Eldon couldn't guess them. None of that mattered anyway.

"You look how you look," he said, and helped himself to another swig.

Officer Clay suddenly rushed across the intersection. Eldon watched him. Clay ran up onto the lawn of the Baptist church one door down from the intersection. That other cop, the big one, was already there, with his gun out. There was a teenage boy on the ground, but Eldon couldn't see him well. He wasn't concerned about it. He took advantage of the depleted police force to cross the open space they struggled to maintain. As he walked past the second tanker truck, he asked the man watching the valves on the back, "Just about done?"

The man glanced at him, irritated, and grunted, "Yeah. Get away from the truck. It's not safe."

"Oh, I'm a hauler too," Eldon said, surprising himself with his ability to affect casual friendliness. He bounded up onto the side step and peered inside the cab.

"Hey! Get away from there!" the trucker shouted.

"She's a beaut!" Eldon called back, stepping back onto the pavement. He waved and wandered farther forward, past the front of the truck. He turned to survey the progress of the work, standing next to Christine's disfigured specter.

"I'll get it," he said to her. "Soon as they're done. I'll go and kill that thing that killed us."

Christine made no indication she heard.

CHAPTER 34

That bitch, Gwen thought.

She'd killed the man this woman slept with last night, and here the slut was following *another* man. Gwen had crossed a dreadful line, and the woman who had helped to shove her over seemed altogether unconcerned (though, sensing the ebbing ripples in a deep, dark pool in the recesses of her thoughts, Gwen had to admit after the fact that the act of murder seemed inevitable in the due course of her life, and that she felt some instinctive relief at having her first out of the way). She viewed her impulsive homicide as inspired. The original impetus—saving her own skin from her brother's would-be resurrectionist—was essentially null with the arrival of the police. But then she'd have to account for her role in Connor's abduction. Likely, she would have been able to talk her way out of it, given Connor's disinclination toward cooperating with the authorities, and with his reasons for doing so still in her hand to play. Of course, killing him meant that she needn't fear his boiling resentment overwhelming his discretion in the moment. It was also an opportunity to get rid of Tim entirely. Who would believe a word he said? He was the perfect patsy. And with him out of the way, she didn't have to worry about him coming after her ever again—*and* she had secured his treasured choice to take back to the demon. She *could* bring her brother back, and she might do just that, for lack of a better option. But she wondered if perhaps she could haggle for something else. After all, Keith was dead, and his return would bring a lot of questions. She might be able to rule her house with an iron fist, threatening to expose his existence if her parents didn't give her everything she wanted, but, really, other than peddling a bit of chicanery now and then, she already had that. So she luxuriated in drifting through a shopping list of favors she might procure from a demon in lieu of a recycled baby brother as she drove Tim's mom's shitty minivan to the location Tim had mentioned (no mean feat in itself, as she'd failed the driven portion of the license test twice before deciding she liked it better when other people drove her around anyway—her standing excuse that her parents didn't want her driving yet was believable pretense).

Of course, the best part of killing Connor was getting to do it. Getting to do it, knowing she would get away with it, and having him know it too, as he bled out on the carpet of *her* church. The best part of it was *satisfaction*, and that's why she went ahead with it. The fortuitous circumstance was just icing on the cake.

The delectable, heady glow of her personal evolution was swept away as she watched the two vehicles a quarter mile ahead of her turn off the main road toward her destination. The second car, lagging the delivery van (Gwen didn't know Hannah was just as confused as to why she was following a delivery van), had slowed when the leader turned off, and then pulled forward past the factory drive entrance before executing a quick U-turn on the unbusy two-lane road. Gwen mimicked the small blue car's movements when she got to the entrance, for the same reason, she realized: to keep far enough back to avoid detection. She had to wait for several seconds, stopped on the road, before the blue car disappeared around the back of the factory. Then she proceeded, creeping slowly down the drive. She parked at the corner of the factory before the turn. She regretted having to leave the knife behind, but she couldn't take the murder weapon with her and still maintain her innocence, now could she? The minivan was a shabby mess, but there was nothing usefully dangerous on the floor or in the glove compartment. She got out. Just before closing the door, she noticed the ball peen hammer in the door pocket. She smirked. "Afraid of drowning, Mrs. Neuworth? Here's a tip: Don't drive into lakes, you fat sack."

Gwen scurried near the factory wall, ducking down. She crept up to the passenger's-side window of the blue coupe (parked away from the entrance, she noted) and peered inside. She could see from a distance the delivery van was similarly empty. She had thought for a second someone ducked behind it, but she didn't see any feet when she bent to scan underneath. She saw the open dock door. She didn't see the woman and she couldn't see inside the factory. She crept up the ramp and along the narrow walk outside the bay doors. She stopped and listened. Not hearing anything, she leaned forward to peer inside.

A man grabbed a fistful of her blouse and swung her around. She squealed as she tumbled across the cement floor; the hammer flew from her hand to the shadows.

"It's turning into a goddamn party in here!" Darren bellowed. "My kinda party too!"

Gwen flinched as someone touched her shoulder. She turned to see the other woman, clearly as frightened as she was, trying to help her up. She slapped her hand away and leaped to her feet. "Get away from me, you fucking bitch!" she screamed.

"It's okay," Hannah said. "I'm not gonna hurt you."

Gwen snickered. "You? You couldn't hurt *me*."

Hannah frowned. "I'm sorry. Do I know you?"

Gwen gasped indignantly and slapped Hannah as hard as she could.

Hannah drove her fist into Gwen's nose; bright red blood erupted.

Darren howled with laughter. He felt energized. He felt liberated from a life half lived. He regretted nothing; regrets were for the weak and easily misled. Everything he'd done had been right. He had been right to live for himself and to live for the pleasures of the day. He had been right to be smart and cautious when it was palatable. He had been right to give in and indulge his baser instincts when they demanded it. But all that was prelude. His life had brought him here, now, and the future was not restricted by what had gone before, not limited by his meager understanding of the world. He'd tasted the deeper dark, and he liked it. He would bring Lyle back, sure. Why not? But not because he was tied to his brother, and not because he wanted to regain the paltry material loss that Lyle had hidden away. He would do it because he *could*, and for now on that would be his only guiding principle.

Darren pulled out the SIG Sauer tucked behind his belt buckle. He popped out the clip and then bent to slide the gun across the floor. It came to rest a few feet in front of the women, perfectly equidistant from each.

"There's one in the chamber," Darren said. And then he howled with laughter again, because they did exactly as he expected: Hannah glanced back at Darren to see if he could be believed, to gauge if he'd considered what she would do with the gun if she was first to retrieve it—which, of course, gave Gwen the advantage as she dove straight for it.

"**D**o you know the minivan?" Allan asked as he maneuvered around it.

"No," Eve replied, "I don't know anyone here."

"Two more," Allan observed, indicating the coupe and the van. "You sure you don't want to call for backup?"

"We can't trust the local PD," Eve said. "We already know the sheriff is corrupt."

"How do you feel about his daughter?"

Allan pulled to a stop at the base of the ramp leading to bay four. Hearing their approach, Britt paused at the top and looked back. A padding of gauze was wrapped tight underneath an ace bandage around her wounded hand (courtesy of Mr. Hernandez), though there was still a rose bloom to mark her missing finger. In the other hand she wielded (against his strong, but ultimately yielding objection) the axe Mr. Hernandez had left out after chopping the wood for his daughter's party the night before.

"I think she might be a bit of a badass," Eve assessed, "but she shouldn't go in there alone."

"Probably nobody should go in there," Allan said as he got out of the truck. "What's the play here anyway?" He grabbed his rifle from the back. She held the tranquilizer gun.

"I don't know yet," Eve said. "But we have to—"

She stopped short at Britt's sudden gesture for silence. Britt then pointed to the open bay door, indicating they were not alone. Eve and Allan hustled up the ramp and the three of them eased forward. A burst of laughter, somehow vile in its unrestrained joviality, rang from inside the factory, punctuated by a woman's shriek. Allan lunged forward with the intent of going around Britt and leading the charge, but Britt was already moving, the axe raised awkwardly in her off hand, and Eve did not wait behind. All three hurtled into the factory and tried to understand the sight before them: a young blonde woman reaching for a pistol on the cement floor in front of her, struggling against the wiry woman behind her who held her back by two handfuls of hair.

Though she had no concerns for her former friend's well-being, Britt reflexively shouted, "Gwen!", who looked up in surprise.

Eve shouted, "You!" recognizing the suspicious woman from Rosa's.

Seeing her, Hannah blurted, "I'm sorry!" Eve didn't know what she would be apologizing about, but her presence was unwelcome, and Eve's nerves were frayed, and so she squeezed her fists without considering that one fist held the tranquilizer gun. The *pop* puff of air surprised Eve, but the dart surprised Hannah even more—so much so that she didn't know how lucky she was when the dart struck her forehead at a shallow angle, and, other than nicking the skin, ricocheted away (almost) harmlessly. The shock caused her to release her grip on Gwen, however, who took advantage of her freedom, throwing herself forward to snatch up the pistol.

Allan recognized the unaccounted-for element of the situation. A man's laugh indicated another player. He pivoted to scan the farther recesses of the factory, scoping down the barrel of the rifle. Suddenly, the scope was obscured by a man's large hand. Allan tried to maintain his grip as he was swung downward. A sharp blow struck him on the side of the head, and he crumpled. Darren pulled the rifle away with his left hand; Chief Pearcey's service weapon, drawn from the back of his belt, he clutched in his right.

Hannah staggered. She felt like she'd just shot two double bourbons on an empty stomach and she prayed it didn't get worse. She saw the gun in Darren's hand, and he saw she saw. "You think I'm just giving guns away?" He laughed.

"I'm fine with just the one bullet," Gwen said as she stood. She pointed the gun at Hannah.

"No!" Eve screamed. Whoever the nosy girl was, and whatever she had to apologize for, Eve didn't want anyone to be shot.

"Who even are you?" Gwen asked caustically. Then she saw Britt and pointed the gun at her. "Choices, choices."

"Y'all go ahead and sort out your drama without me," Darren said. "As entertaining as this is, I'm gonna go ahead and talk to the main guy and get my brother back."

Gwen swung the gun around a third time. "You? You don't get your brother back. I get *my* brother back!"

"'Fraid not, sugar tits. You have to put the work in first." Darren tipped the rifle back and leaned it on his shoulder. "And you don't strike me as the killing type."

Gwen smiled and cocked her head. "Don't let the drop-dead looks fool you. I just left my boyfriend bleeding out in the sanctuary of a church."

"You did?" Hannah gasped. "You killed Connor? But I thought…"

"'Connor'?" Darren repeated. "The high school teacher? And here I thought he was gonna be a problem." He scowled at Hannah. "But why would you think I killed him?"

"Maybe she thought you're the jealous type," Gwen growled.

"Oh, my. I had no idea you were so free-spirited," Darren said to Hannah. "She was my brother's girl, not mine. So, you can go ahead and kill her, if it makes you happy," he told Gwen. "Don't mean no never mind to me. Like I said, I got other business. You might've killed someone, but there's more to it than that. If it was just about killing, then I would get two wishes."

Britt put it together. "You're Darren Dietz. And if you're here…"

He looked at her. "I'm Darren Dietz and I *am* here. And just who might you be?"

"I'm Britt," she said. "Britt Pearcey."

Darren paused. He felt something unwelcome, a chink in his bravado, a flaw in what was supposed to be an unassailable new attitude. Somewhere in the back of his mind, he felt the scales shift with a whisper of the word "comeuppance".

"That so?" he said tersely.

"Enough prattle. There is… work to be done."

There was a shuffling, dragging sound as the demon emerged from the gloom, trailing its tattered wings. As it moved into the stronger light near the open bay door, the foul idiot in its abdomen shut its eyes tight in anguish and uttered a strangled moan through its puckered mouth. Ixixiklis reared its broken-beaked, vermin-shrouded head as though sniffing the air.

Hannah would have screamed if she wasn't sure she was hallucinating. She commanded herself to keep it together and stay conscious. Gwen shrieked, but awe swiftly muted the instinctive reaction. Hundreds of Sunday mornings spent earnestly struggling with her sins, or grasping ineffectually toward belonging within the mystery of belief, or just bored and uncomfortable, suddenly fell away. Here, at last, was an avatar of God—a God who she now understood fit her unconscious expectations of both grandeur and decadence; a God who would fulfill her needs exactly. Something beautiful and horrible and real.

"The work's all done, boss," Darren said. "I completed the sixth point."

"Sixth point?" Gwen scoffed. "You're playing catch-up, hockey hair. I put the pin in the middle."

"What?" Darren asked.

"*Only… five points hold. Another altar… was compromised. The offering at… the north point was used… to restore it.*"

"The north point?" Darren wondered. "But that's… that's *here*. That's *Lyle*."

"Lyle?" Hannah asked, following Darren as he hurried deeper into the factory around the bulk of the first green machine.

"But what about my sacrifice?" Gwen asked. "I was the one who placed the seventh point!"

"*There is… no seventh point. There is only… the confluence.*"

"Then why did you command Tim to do it?" Gwen pressed. "What's so special about the center?"

"You wanted him there," Eve guessed. "You wanted him in the middle of town."

"Where everyone is gathering," Britt continued, "following the ghosts."

"Straight toward the overturned tanker," Eve concluded. "My God."

"*We are bound… to the one who summons us. We would… sever that bond.*"

Gwen huffed exasperatedly. "By killing him? So, I did nothing?"

"Not just him," Eve said. "You want to blow up the town! You said you eat the ghosts—"

"*The more the meatier.*" The demon did not have the features to smile, but its neck rolled as though uncoiling in a lazy stretch.

"Blow up Adler?" Gwen considered blandly. "Cool."

"That's insane!" Britt shouted. "We'll stop you!"

"*Do as you will. We… honor the compact.*"

"'Honor the compact,'" Eve quoted. It all fell into place. "It doesn't just need the symbol; it needs the wish!"

"To flip the switch," Gwen said, and she smiled.

Hannah's head was fuzzy and she felt distant from her hands and feet, but she was otherwise steady. She reasoned she couldn't have been hit with too heavy a dose of the tranquilizer. She could walk and function. She'd even spoken coherently. Unfortunately, that meant that the things she was seeing were real, which made her appreciate the dulling effect of the drug. Here now was her boyfriend—ex, she supposed, given his condition, and the events of the last two days notwithstanding—or most of him, at least. His head was gone and his body shriveled (this last meaning less than it might in someone not as gaunt to begin with). She recognized his clothes and the length of his limbs and even his posture, despite his body's odd, forced arrangement. And there was a large depression of shattered orange rock and dried, black viscera in the center of his torso.

"He's dead," she said. She felt useless for stating the obvious, but she had to say it for her own benefit. For her own belief. She understood now that the strangeness of his appearance the night before was caused by a deeper disconnect than diverging life paths. Yet realizing the chasm of death separated them made her feel no worse for rejecting him. She was horrified by what had happened to him; she lamented the pain he had suffered and grieved to see the grisly state of a body she once knew. But, in that moment, she felt unashamed relief that she could never go back to him. She had no choice but to find her own way forward.

"I knew already," Darren said. Hannah jumped, having forgotten he was beside her, squatting to touch a chunk of orange rock. "I'd seen him. But not like this. He was... intact. And Ixixiklis—the demon—said it could bring him back if I... if I did his bidding."

Hannah gestured at the wreck in front of them with her open palm. "The thing that did this… said it would undo it?"

Darren felt himself trying to be instantly sober. He felt the struggle of his reasoning mind taking up the plight of his lizard-brain's instinct for self-preservation, felt the race of measuring his current handicap and trying to push through it. Despite a lifetime of taking recreational drugs, he'd only ever felt that way a few times. Mostly because he was careful going in; he was unwilling to relinquish control, to become a slave, to stumble toward the spiral of addiction. But a few times when he was at least partially fucked up, the situation had turned bad, and he'd coordinated his reason and his unbending anger in a flash. The goal—get free until you can get clear—became a resolute focus. And if he felt that way now, that meant he *was* high. Not high on drugs, but still—under the influence. He felt *too good* and recognized the lie of it. He scowled, staring at the shattered mess of his brother's body.

She didn't want to be with him, didn't want to be there at all. But he seemed to know more about the situation than she did, so Hannah asked, "Darren?"

He continued looking at his brother as he stood. "Nothing's changed," he said.

"So we don't wish," Eve said. "We can't." A knot twisted in her stomach. She knew what not wishing might mean for Zander. But how many more would suffer if she did? Why did *she* have to be the savior of this damned town—when all she really wanted was to never have come here?

"But—but my dad," Britt said uncertainly. "And your husband… probably."

"My husband," she repeated, and admitted, "definitely." She wanted Zander to come marching into the factory to tell her he was alright, to grab her and kiss her. She wanted to see him. But she dreaded seeing him as he really was in that instant. Despair swelled to anger, thinking of her husband with his throat cut, frozen in a final scream, drained of blood and vitality and propped up—a museum piece awaiting exhibition in a house of horrors. "It's not fair!" she screamed at Ixixiklis. "It's not natural for him to die that way!"

"All death… is natural. Only fairness… is unnatural."

Eve punched away the tears gathering at the corners of her eyes with the heel of a palm. "You can't do this—it can't be real. Demons don't just set up shop somewhere and—and feed!"

"It happens… all the time."

Darren popped the clip from the chief's pistol to check the available ammo. Hannah flinched as he slammed it back into place. He scowled at her. "Much as I'm not too fond of you right this minute, if I can get Lyle back… well, I'll let him sort that out." He gestured with the barrel of the gun toward his brother's corpse. "You're his girl." He shrugged. "And I oughtta know better than to even consider keeping that crazy blonde around for myself. But I guess I got a type. And the chief's daughter… there's enough damage done."

He marched around the big, green machine, breathing hard in anticipation. He glanced at the mammoth, tattered demon resentfully. He raised the gun and aimed at Eve.

"Looks like it's gotta be you, legs!" he shouted.

"I s THAT IT?" THE county deputy asked.

"Yeah, all transferred," the trucker replied as he unfastened the feed line from the valve on the back of the newly filled tank. "Just got to stow this stuff and then I can clear out."

"Thank God," the deputy said. "Maybe then this crowd will disperse. Never saw so many goddamn idiots tryin' to get themselves blown up."

"On a Sunday too!" The trucker laughed. "Don't they know the Steelers are playing?"

"Alright, then," Eldon said. He looked at Christine's ghost's crooked face. "Guess it's only fitting for my shitshow life that you're the only person I got to say goodbye to." She turned toward him as though she might have heard, but her expression remained unchanged. Eldon shivered. "Huh. Yeah. 'Get on with it, then.'"

She raised her right hand to her face. She worked her fingers between stiffly yielding lips, then moved them around for several seconds, as though tugging at something. Then her jaw fell open and she exhaled with a hiss of escaping gas. She moved her hand away. Her jaw jerked back and forth, but she did not speak.

He shivered again and nodded apologetically. "Okay," he whispered.

He bounded to the truck, opened the door, and climbed inside like he'd owned it for a decade. The keys were in the ignition—as he knew they were from glancing inside the cab earlier. He locked the doors and started the engine.

"Eldon! Hey, Eldon, get outta there!"

Eldon turned at the sound of his name. Officer Clay, back from the incident in front of the church, ran up to the truck and banged on the door. "What the hell do you think you're doing?"

"Only two things I was ever good at!" Eldon yelled back. "Driving and killing." He put the truck in gear and began to pull away.

Barkley jogged alongside. "Stop right now!" He pulled his gun from its holster to emphasize his authority. "That's an order!"

"Are you crazy? Put that thing away!" the trucker shouted. "You want to get us all killed?"

The crowd half parted for Eldon. He drove through those that remained, hoping that the living had all had the sense to move aside. Christine appeared before him again, in the middle of the street. "This time I'll say it: I'm sorry." She flickered and went out when he drove through her.

Z ANDER USED TO CALL her "Legs." He wasn't the first; it was hardly an inventive nickname. But, perhaps realizing that, he would usually follow up it up with a few more remarks of play-fully offensive nonsense delivered in a Forties' gangster-movie rapid patter ("You're my moll, doll, see? Shimmy those pins over here for a minute.") If Darren hadn't called her Legs, she might have noticed him a second too late. If he hadn't used that ridiculous sobriquet, she might have froze at the sight of the gun.

Instead, instinct took over and she dove to the floor. She wasn't sure where the two shots hit, but they didn't hit her, and she rolled sideways toward the wall.

It was Hannah's conscience that sent the two shots off their mark. She caught up with Darren when he stopped to aim. She yelled, "No!" and swatted his right arm off target. Enraged, he swung around and knocked her to the floor with his forearm. He loomed over her threateningly. "I can still change my mind about you!"

His forehead exploded. Hannah shrieked as a spit of fine red droplets landed on her face. Darren crumpled to his knees. His mouth slacked open and he crossed his eyes as though trying to see the wound. Hannah shrieked again and rolled to avoid being caught underneath his body when he fell.

"No, you can't," Gwen said, smiling. She wiggled her eyebrows and blew across the muzzle of the small pistol in her hand. Then she tossed it aside.

Hannah backed away in a crab walk, too startled to guess what Gwen was doing as she stooped beside Darren's fallen bulk.

"Not just a pretty face," she said. "I was paying attention earlier when he said there was only one bullet in that one." She peeled the chief's weapon from Darren's limp grasp. "Not sure how many are left in here. Enough, I'd wager." She stood and turned. "Britt, be a darling and drop the axe. At this point, I think I've killed enough people, so I don't *have* to kill you if you don't make me."

Britt had forgotten she still had the weapon in her hand. She let it fall at her feet.

"Thanks, you're a good friend." Gwen smirked. She backed away from Darren's corpse and lifted her head to address Ixixiklis. "I know I've made a mess of him. But will he do for... for whatever sacrifice we're on at this point?"

Ixixiklis dropped its arms to the side and then raised them up. The spike-talon hands punctured purple flesh as the decrepit cloak of its wings spread behind the green scales and blue feathers. The idiot in its abdomen opened its bulbous eyes and yellow pus dripped from the cracks.

"We can work... with this offering."

A chorus of terrified cries greeted the sudden appearance of the black thing that dropped from the ceiling. Bat-with-ten-eyes bent to its task. Its legs clicked together rapidly as its feet worked to unzipper Darren's face from the wound in his forehead. Then it lurched forward, the terror of its mouth mercifully hidden beneath the jerking obsidian body undulating like a rutting beast.

"MY DAD MUST BE freaking out so bad right now," Valeria said.

He stood from the plank bench he'd set out the night before and raised his hand as they approached. Valeria didn't think Britt would have relayed to him all that she'd told her over the phone—there was too little time to explain, and half of it seemed impossible—but, whatever else he might not know, here his daughter was being brought home in a speeding cop car. When they drew close, she could see his forehead knotted with worry.

He reached to open the door for her as the Rover's skidding tires spat gravel sideways. "Valeria! What is happening?"

"Papi!" She leaped out of her seat and into his arms. She tried to explain, but her words caught behind a sob of relief.

"What is going on?" Mr. Hernandez asked Officer Tuttle.

"She's home," he replied. "She's safe. I have to—"

He was interrupted by a distorted burst from the radio. "John! John, you out there? It's Bark! You hear me?"

Valeria sniffled into her father's shoulder. "Where's Britt?"

"Bark, it's John. I'm here."

He turned her sideways and pointed across the fallow field. "She went there. I tried to get her to wait. Mija, she took my axe with her! Why would she do that?"

"That crazy fucker Eldon stole a butane tanker," Officer Clay reported. "He said he was gonna kill somebody!"

"That crowd at the center of town," Valeria said.

"I couldn't get after him," Barkley continued. "There's this big crowd—some of them are real. Goddammit," he scolded himself, knowing what he said made no sense. Then he added the salient part, "He's headed north on Wilburville!"

"I'm there!" John shouted into the radio mic. "There's only one place he could be going," he said to the others.

"Britt went to the factory!" Valeria cried.

"Get inside! If that thing blows—"

If he finished the thought, they didn't hear it. The tires spun and caught; the Rover fishtailed as John pointed back toward the road. He sped off, lights and siren blazing. The passenger door finally slammed shut as the Rover came down hard on the dirt four-wheeler path leading across the divide.

G WEN WATCHED BAT-WITH-TEN-EYES finish its work (sloppily, Tim would have observed if he'd been there to witness the rushed treatment of the sacrifice). She hadn't been able to determine if the amber sap flowing over Darren's corpse—bundled by the black creature into a fetal ball—had been regurgitated through its mouth or shat from some hidden orifice. She didn't mind not knowing. As unquestionably deadly and horrific as the beast before her was, with its of indeterminate number of legs and wings, all assiduously knitting and kneading, there was still something unimpressive about it. She was reminded of an afternoon in July when she was giving Bill Wollert a handjob as he drove down the highway. His excitement made him unmindful of the speed of the car and sent them left of center on several occasions as he failed to navigate even shallow curves. She was enjoying his recklessness. Neither was buckled in; if he crashed, they'd both be dead. She wasn't sure if he saw the buzzard at its meal before he'd made an asterisk out of it. But she saw. The thing was fully engaged in pulling tenders loose from the flattened meat in the middle of the lane. Blissfully, stupidly unaware of anything besides its hunt for scraps, it didn't even flinch.

"Awesome," Gwen said. "Now, can we discuss the details of this arrangement? Like, do I *have* to bring someone back from the dead? What I'm really asking is, what *else* can I get?"

"*A bargain… is a bargain.*"

"Seriously?" she asked. "You're a fucking *demon*. Are you sure there isn't any—" she pointed at his twitching, red cock— "wiggle room?"

"*A bargain…*"

"Oh, for shit's sake. Fine." She crossed her arms and sighed exasperatedly. "I mean, there's always Keith. Or, I could auction it off."

"You don't even *care*?" Britt asked. "My dad… is dead…" She started to speak the words to castigate Gwen for her apathy in the face of all the destruction that had led them there. But she finished it as though floating an idea. Eve's suspicion about the final part of the compact setting the town up for annihilation slowed her from suggesting aloud his resurrection was an option. She wasn't even sure it was what she wanted if there were *no* strings attached, thinking of what the evil of the deal had led her father to do—could he come back from that? And what might it mean for her to be a party to it?

"No, Britt—you can't!" Eve urged. She was still on the floor, instructed by Gwen to keep her seat. But she moved her hand, preparing to stand despite the command, and in doing so, felt a smooth, wooden handle.

"Ah! Ah!" Gwen reminded Eve to stay down, waving the gun at her. To Britt, she said, "What have you got to offer to bring back dear old Chief Dad?"

"Save your money," called a man's voice from the bay door. "Your wish would be premature."

"Dad!" Britt cried.

Walt lumbered forward, silhouetted against the brighter world outside. In his right hand was a shotgun he labored to keep steady, as it was unassisted by his left, which hung limply at his side; the sleeve of his uniform was slick with blood. "Drop the gun," he instructed.

Gwen laughed. "Stand up straight," she countered.

She whipped the gun to aim at Walt and fired. He leveled the shotgun and fired, but too slowly; the impact of the bullet on his chest threw off his aim and he buckled to a prone position with a groan. Nevertheless, Gwen screeched and ducked before realizing he'd missed. Britt cried out for her dad and sprang toward him. Gwen grinned maniacally and coiled to aim at Walt again, gleefully wondering whether she'd hit him or his daughter about to cross the bullet's path—just as Eve hurled the ball peen hammer across the room perfectly. The head struck Gwen on the wrist. She yelped in pain but kept her grip on the gun. Now she knew who to shoot.

"You bi—"

The word stopped short, cleaved in two in the middle of her brain.

Gwen staggered two steps in place, amazed. The axe handle stuck out from the side of her head, pointed back like an oversized snorkel. As she dropped to her knees, she cocked her head, as though her body made a belated effort to turn away from the pain. Blood flowed over her face like a caul being drawn, and she at last fell dead.

Hannah stood revealed, holding her shaking hands in front of her. Her eyes were wide with horror at what she'd done. She looked around at the faces of the others. "I'm sorry," she said, though she didn't mean her last act of violence. She said it again, to Eve, "I'm sorry for what I did to your husband. I'm sorry for all of it." She squeezed her hands into fists to stop them quavering and forced her arms down to her sides as she turned to face Ixixiklis.

"Bring her husband back," she said.

"No!" Eve hastened across the floor and grabbed Hannah by the shoulders. "You don't know what you're doing!" She spun back and faced the looming demon as his broken head lolled with satisfaction atop the willowy neck. "I refuse!"

"*A bargain… is a bargain.*"

Bat-with-ten-eyes surged from its perch atop the globe of golden tar. Its wings unfurled, two or four, its legs spread as it did on descent, and a dreadful, whistling cry erupted from its dripping maw. It swooped through the bay door, causing Britt and her father to throw themselves flat beneath its exit.

John saw it emerge from the factory and instinctively executed a 180-degree turn through a break slide. He had been tasked with following the foul creature. But, no—not now. He knew Britt was inside, and judging from the four other vehicles parked near the rear, she wasn't alone. He shuddered to think what carnage might await him. He ran across the lot directly at the open bay door and vaulted into the factory, nearly colliding with the injured man on the floor and his daughter helping him upright.

"Chief!" he shouted. "You're bleeding!"

"Took one in the shoulder," Walt said, wincing at the reminder. "And two in the chest." He winked and tapped the Kevlar vest beneath his uniform.

"Dietz?"

Walt nodded. He looked up at his officer. "I'm sorry, John. I know you were friends with him."

"A long time ago," John said resignedly.

Eve felt a strong urge to go kick the chief in the face as hard as she possibly could. She'd show him what long legs are good for. She didn't care much if he was a cop. He seemed to be getting his tearful reunion—for what? A late change of heart? She had no forgiveness for him.

A groan drew her attention. Allan stirred.

She knelt to help him up. "Careful," she said. "You missed a hell of a show."

He surveyed the scene, blinking it into focus. "Wow. Guess I did."

"Dad, we have to warn everyone!" Britt said. "That thing—we think that bat creature is gonna set off the tanker and blow up downtown!"

"No, it—it can't," John said. "That's why I came here, to tell you to get out. Bark said Eldon stole the tanker and said he was gonna kill somebody. I figured he must've meant that thing, which would mean he's on his way here now, and he probably isn't gonna ask who else is hanging around!"

"*No!*" Ixixiklis lurched forward out of the gloom. "*He seeks to rob me of my due?*"

"Holy fucking shit!" John screamed. He drew his service weapon and emptied it into the nightmare barreling toward him.

I T WAS SLOW GOING managing his way through the crowd. Eldon didn't want to kill anyone else. Just one hellspawn to burn. Whatever it was, nothing could hide inside the factory if there wasn't any inside to hide in. Fortunately, though the crowd might have slowed him, it stopped pursuit cold. And what the hell was Clay or the county boys going to do about it anyway? Nothing—nothing but clean up after.

He passed the old railway station and its historical marker. He stayed slow going through the next stretch, as it was all residential without much berm. No point in tempting fate. Once he got north of Union Cemetery, things opened up and he picked up speed, passing farms set back from the road bounded by stretches of woods and a few manufacturing ventures like the one he drove toward. He was about a mile out when he saw it.

Bat-with-ten-eyes stood out like a blasphemous mistake on the puff-white-and-blue child's bedroom sky, a mobile puncture wound bleeding shadow. It flew high above the placid Pennsylvania countryside, no longer hiding in the dark. From a distance, the rapid flutter of its wings produced a strange locomotion that seemed more like tumbling or oscillation or both. Far overhead as it was, Eldon almost believed it would not come for him. But then, as though in response to the thought or as in response to an unheard command, the creature abruptly ceased its forward motion. It paused to spread its wings, stamping its shape against the sky for no more than a second before plunging downward, swooping in an intercepting arc.

"Coming out to meet me, huh?" Eldon growled.

He pushed down on the accelerator. The truck groaned in protest, coughing exhaust as it tried to comply, dragging forward leadenly. "Come on, you son of a bitch," Eldon encouraged it.

Bat-with-ten-eyes descended in a corkscrew, the spiral tightening as it drew near. Its dive drooped flat in the rut of the roadway and it flew straight at Eldon. He didn't let up, pushing the truck for all it could give him. At the last moment, the foul beast flipped skyward, out of the truck's path.

"What'cha doin'?" howled Eldon. "Trying to keep me away from your den? You got babies, motherfucker? I'll kill *all* your babies!"

Bat-with-ten-eyes swooped downward to Eldon's right, parallel to the roadway. He lost sight of it behind a stand of trees up a short rise. He leaned forward, darting glances between the road ahead and up to his right and left. His mouth was suddenly dry and his heart throbbed in his head. He was acutely aware of his impending end. It had been his choice, without equivocation, but the possibility of being kept from his self-appointed task accentuated the tragedy of failure and waste that had been the whole of his legacy until then.

"No way!" he shouted. "Fucker! You ain't stoppin' me no matter—ah!"

The impact on the top of the cab caused the whole truck to wobble. Eldon looked up at the smooth, white ceiling and yelped again as the first black dagger punched through. A second followed, then a third, piercing the metal with the pop of a gunshot. Eldon looked forward, saw he was too close to the berm on the right, and swerved. Two of the shard-like feet withdrew from their holes and Eldon heard the scream of scraping feet above him.

"Ha!" he shouted. "Want some more?"

He threw the wheel back and forth, sending the truck in lurching zigzags, trying to dislodge his attacker.

"You like that?!"

The answer was two legs in tandem brought down on the front windshield like picks on thin ice.

"Y OU ARE SMALL… TRANSIENT *and weak!*"

Ixixiklis's roar held no pain; it seemed to make a statement of painlessness, to show the futility of the bullets and the pockmarks they left in its skin and the tufts between feathers and scales. The plague of whispers in its voice gave way to a roaring drone, a scouring tempest in the minds of the six men and women still alive in the warehouse.

"*You are… pitiful morsels… but we will feed!*"

The mouth in its belly opened wide with a viscous squelch; a belch of sulfur assailed their nostrils. A muculent, pearl-white, tubular tongue shot out from the awful gape. It whipped straight, too quickly to dodge. The open end smashed into Hannah's chest and caught her fast instantly. She screamed as it pulled her above the floor and twirled to coil her in.

"Take him!" Eve shouted and pushed a still-unsteady Allan into John's arms, his gun discarded.

"I have to help," Walt grunted as Britt helped him to his feet.

"You have to get her out of here!" John shouted at him, helping Allan toward the bay door.

Eve spied Allan's discarded rifle on the floor and decided against it. She leaped over Gwen's body to get to the axe handle pointing the other direction and nearly lost her footing sliding in the blood on the cement. She grabbed the handle and planted a foot on Gwen's forehead. Hannah's screams urged her on. Eve cried out, pushing down with her leg, trying to keep both feet steady in the muck on the floor and the slick in Gwen's plastered hair. She straightened her back, heaving up and away. At last, the axe came free; slop flew from the blade as Eve swung it back. She screamed and charged at the towering demon. Hannah struggled vainly against the constricting roll holding her fast, drawing her into the obscenely wide, waiting mouth. Eve raised the axe as she ran forward, but then had to slide to the floor to duck a swipe of one of Ixixiklis's long, talon-tipped arms. She had intended to hack the tongue, but no longer had the angle for a backswing and despaired she might not be able to cut the thick, sinewy cord. So, she took aim at the other tentacular appendage on display directly in front of her and struck with every last bit of her fear-fueled strength.

She was not able to see the result of her attack immediately, as the pain in her head blinded her, but she felt hot splatter on her arms, and she understood the pain in her head was *in* her head, a telepathic communication announcing success. She screamed back against the pain. She started to focus, not well, but enough to see the disconnected snake-like penis flopping angrily, thrashing around as though attempting to fend off another attack. Eve grabbed Hannah's legs, but Ixixiklis's tongue still held her tight. Then she heard a gunshot and the tongue slackened slightly. She pulled at the disgusting muscle, her hands slipping in the crevasses between coils, trying to find leverage to ply away the slithering constraint. She heard a strange roar, but she ignored it as she bent to her work, noting only that the sound was not in her head as before. She got both hands on a loosening coil of tongue and pulled. Just then the first flies buzzed in front of her face, causing her to flinch reflexively—which aided her in her effort, as she kept her hands locked. The tongue whipped outward and smacked her backward. She fell in a seated position, kept upright by the tacky, warm wart of Darren's globular tomb.

She saw now: An unending mass of flies erupted from the hole at the top of Ixixiklis's neck. Its ruptured head twitched on the floor as the pouch inside the broken beak pulsed frantically. The back of the head was hollow-eyed, exposed bone. Britt and John had a hold of Hannah's arms and dragged her away. Walt's shotgun went off again, and Ixixiklis lunged blindly at the offending instrument, swinging its arms and tattered wings in a flurry. As one arm swung past her, Eve shot up onto her feet and ran in an arc out of the reach of the next strike. She saw Allan at the door, gesturing emphatically to her—and everyone—to exit. She saw he was shouting ("Come on! Come on!" she guessed), and only then realized that the drone of the flies was smothering anything quieter than Walt's gunshots. John got Hannah over his shoulder in a fireman's carry, and Walt ushered them both, then his daughter, out the door. Eve jumped off the edge of the dock. Britt followed John with Hannah down the ramp. Walt ducked out the door and then Allan yanked the supporting broomstick from its spot in the track. The door fell halfway by itself; he grabbed the handle in the center and slammed it the rest of the way shut.

Eve heard her rushed, strained breathing. She heard the hellish drone locked away inside the factory, surprised that the tsunami of vermin had not followed them out.

"Come on!" Allan shouted, and this time she did hear him, spurring her to action. John and Britt loaded Hannah into the police Rover while Walt got behind the wheel. Eve followed Allan to his truck and leaped into the passenger's seat. Both vehicles peeled out, skidding over the cement, correcting, and then nearly tipping over as they rounded the corner of the factory, avoiding the minivan parked there.

As they sped down the drive to the highway, Eve saw the white tanker truck shakily approaching the turn. The black demon covered the front window and she wondered how the driver could see a thing.

"Should we try to stop him?" Allan asked.

The police vehicle in front of them kept its lights off and turned hard to the right when it got to the road, nearly sliding into the ditch on the far side.

"There's your answer!" Eve shouted. She reached for her seat belt to pull it across as Allan executed Walt's maneuver after him. She yelped as she swung sideways, clutching the vinyl belt in her fist. As Allan straightened the car to go north, she saw the tanker truck miraculously make the turn onto the factory drive. She thought she saw Eldon between the furiously stabbing legs, his face covered in blood, dead already, determined to reach his destination. "Go as fast as you possibly fucking can!" she screamed to Allan, and he obliged, throwing her against the seat back.

She didn't say anything more. No encouragement would make the truck go any faster. In the rearview mirror, she saw the tanker truck pass the hedge-wrapped power station. She looked forward;

the police Rover was a hundred yards ahead. She looked behind them again but couldn't see the truck.

There was a flash of orange-white light so beautiful that the world shuddered to see it.

And the shudder moved so, so fast.

Eve's scream was lost in the deafening blast. The truck shifted sideways. Allan braked and tried to control the slide, pulling almost parallel in the far lane, but not quite enough, and the truck pitched hard into the ditch. Eve felt like she was punched in the chest and was glad for it—her belt held. She struggled to get her breath. She wanted to ask Allan if he was okay—and then wanted to shout for help. He slumped against the wheel, bleeding from his forehead. She called his name and shook his shoulder. At last he moaned, and blinked, and reached out a hand, as though woozily trying to make sure *she* was alright. Still straining for breath, she took his hand to reassure him she was. Then she heard car doors slam and urgent voices approaching.

Valeria and her father stood from behind the couch in their living room, clutching each other. She held his hand as they walked over the broken glass of every window, only letting go to allow him to lead the way outside through the door, clinging on one hinge. They stood on the porch and looked at the terrible roiling flame across the field and roads, at the tower of darkening smoke billowing heavenward, at the little plumes like errant children in the tall grass between them.

And Mr. Hernandez vowed to move to Pittsburgh to keep close to her when his daughter went off to college—if not sooner.

CHAPTER 35

A LLAN RAISED HIS FOREARM from the gurney and tried to give a thumbs-up. The breathing mask kept him from offering any verbal encouragement. Eve suspected that, even if the paramedics hadn't been dragging the rattling cart over the asphalt, Allan's hand would still be shaky. He couldn't quite close the fingers into a fist. One of the paramedics held a compress over the wad of pinkening bandages on his forehead. Eve hoped it was nothing a few stitches and a few days' rest couldn't cure.

"He's married," she said to Officer Tuttle. "Someone should notify his wife."

"They will," he replied. "I'm sure."

Another ladder truck approached from the south, lights flashing. Someone was shouting to keep the northbound lane clear so emergency personnel could get through. The southbound lane was lined with county and state highway patrol cop cars and ambulances. Two stations' full complements of firefighters were already engaged in the fight, shooting arcs of water into the inferno behind the black shell.

"There won't be too much to burn in the empty factory," John said. "What there is of it left."

"Let it burn to ash," Eve spat. "They shouldn't even try to put it out."

Walt approached them, shooing off a paramedic. His left arm was in a sling; his uniform had been cut away. He wore a blood-stained tank top under a department bomber jacket draped over his shoulders. "John, why don't you go ahead and take Mrs. Nowlan back to the station? I'm sure she's anxious to be on her way."

"Missus!" Eve scoffed. A tear of anger spilled down her cheek. "Just like that, is it? Don't you need another statement? Set up the video recorder again?"

John looked at the chief skeptically. Eve's questions were legitimate, whatever her tone.

"We have your contact information if we need anything further," Walt said.

Eve's indignation was too strong for her to form the torrent of abuse she wanted to unleash, leaving her sputtering.

Walt drew nearer to her. "I've done wrong," he said. "But I've got my daughter to think of." He cocked his head backward to indicate Britt, waiting by the police Rover, which weathered the explosion far better than the Forestry Service vehicle.

"You *had* your daughter to think of," Eve seethed, "and you didn't!"

"I've done wrong," he repeated, "and now all I can do is try to do right. And the best way to do that is as a cop. I can never make up for it—"

Eve's dark laugh cut him off. "Jesus! 'Make up for it'? No, you'll just feel a little bit guilty now and again and drink through it when you need to, and, hey—there's your process, right, so maybe one day, redemption? And then you can just pat yourself on the back for persevering." She shook her head and locked her arms tightly to avoid taking a swing. She looked him in the eye and said, "Fuck you. *Fuck. You.*" It wasn't enough, but it was all she had.

Walt opened his mouth; the job had accustomed him to offer condolences automatically. But he knew saying "I'm sorry for your loss" would be the height of ignominy—and to simply say, "I'm sorry" would never be adequate. The only thing he could do was to let her be angry at him. So, he swallowed the sentiment, truer than it might ever have been before, and instead looked at John, and asked, "Officer Tuttle?" He turned and walked back toward his daughter.

John grabbed Eve's arms and held her fast to keep her from flying after him.

She shrugged him off and wheeled around. "You know there's no such thing as a good cop who covers for a bad cop, right?"

He winced. "We'll be sorting out what happened here—and what we can live with—for a long time." He sighed. "But there's no way to sort this out… *truthfully*. What we've seen… that had no place in nature."

Eve scoffed and shook her head. "Only fairness is unnatural."

B OBBI TURNED AWAY FROM the door and crossed the lobby. "It's weird," she said.

"Hmm? What's weird, Bobbi?" Grant looked up from his desk. The slight motion of his head sent a new wave of pain through his skull and he sucked air loudly through his teeth. He pushed away from his computer and leaned back as he put the cold pack to the side of his head.

"Now that… now all the *others* have disappeared, everyone's just walking on home. I thought for sure the station would be packed with people demanding answers."

Grant looked past the counter as Bobbi settled behind it. She was right: People straggled by the station; few of them conversed with each other, and any who happened to glance through the windows quickly looked away. "Embarrassment?" he guessed. "I don't know what they'd have to be embarrassed about, but sometimes people just feel that way. They look like both teams after a tie game, like they're not quite sure how to feel."

"Could be," Bobbi said. She crumpled a handful of sticky notes to throw in the trash, but instead dropped them on the counter and picked up the sheet of paper revealed beneath. "Oh! I almost forgot this came in yesterday."

"What's that?" Grant asked.

She turned, the document in question held before her. "The employees of the dollar store wrote in with a request to city council that Selby Run Park be named Dora Givens Memorial Park. That's very thoughtful." She looked up, surprised to see Grant's expression was a scowl of pain. "You should go to the hospital and get your head looked at."

"I'm fine," he assured her. "My pride's hurt worse than my giant nugget. Talk about embarrassing: getting clipped by that hundred-pound punk is gonna stick with me for a long time. And *you* shouldn't even be here on Sunday!"

Bing-bong!

They both stood at the sound of the bell. A teenage boy with short, sandy-blond hair entered the station. He wore black pants and a partially unbutton white shirt. Grant thought he must have come from church. Bobbi thought he looked familiar but couldn't come up with a name. "Can I help you?" she asked.

He swayed where he stood and his gaze seemed unfocused. When he didn't answer, Bobbi started to ask again, "Young man, can we—"

"Tim Neuworth is here," he said blankly.

Grant approached the counter. "Yeah, he's here, but he's not able to see any visitors. If you—"

"He's my friend."

Grant nodded, smiling. "Okay. I confess I'm a bit surprised he *has* any friends. Regardless, he can't see anyone. Not you, not nobody. Federal officers are—"

Bing-bong!

"What in the blue hell?" Bobbi asked.

Elba backed into the station, grunting and swearing, dragging a blanket through the door she struggled to prop open. When she got the bundle into the station, she paused to straighten her back and take in a deep breath. Then she shouted, "Joe Underwood!" She bent and grabbed two handfuls of blanket and snapped her arms. Joe's tar-crusted, shriveled cadaver spilled onto the low-pile, light gray carpet. The larger part cracked and one arm fell away at the elbow. The foot, already separated, bounced under one of the lobby chairs.

"Jesus!" Grant barked as he shuffled around the counter. "Elba, what—"

"Now maybe you'll listen to me!" Elba roared. "Where's the chief? I want him to see this!"

There was a disturbance at the front of the station, but the only words Tim caught were "see this" as the door to the holding area swung open. He got up from the cot. When he saw who his visitor was, he rushed to the door and grasped the bars.

"Keith!" he exclaimed. He laughed. "It worked! But I-I didn't get to make my wish."

"Tim," Keith said.

"Yeah! Yeah, man, it's me! And it's you, back from Hell to raise some hell, right, bud? We're gonna fuck this town up, you and me, just you watch! They can't hold me here, not with the power I got backing me up. Wait 'til you meet him. You're gonna flip the fuck out."

"Tim," Keith said.

Tim hesitated. "Yeah!" he laughed nervously. "Are you okay?"

"Can I tell you a secret?" One of Keith's eyes twitched as his cheek muscle rippled.

"A secret?" Tim was surprised. "Yeah, sure. What is it?"

Keith inched closed to the doors and leaned forward to whisper. Tim waited for him to say something, but he remained still. "Okay," he said, and pulled his ear up to the space between bars.

"Ixixiklis," Keith said, and white pills fell from his mouth and clicked on the tile with the last syllable. Then the pills writhed and a tumult of maggots spilled from his slack maw and splattered to the floor with the rest. His eyes bulged and rolled as something pushed from behind. Flies burst forth from the red rims and flew at Tim, into his ears, up his nose, stifling the scream from his mouth. Keith's deflating body collapsed, its loose skin sloughed by the squirming legion of glistening white worms departing the useless husk. They crawled in a stream through the bars, toward Tim's spasming legs, following the drone call of their elders who smothered the dead boy's crown.

E VE PACKED UP THEIR few belongings left at the hotel. There was nothing of Zander's to be sentimental about. Everything they'd brought was strictly utilitarian. Nothing smelled like him either, not even his dirty shirts. They smelled like camp and woods and exertion and bug spray. Not like Zander at all.

As she zipped up the last pack, Eve heard a timid knock at her door. Her weary brain briefly entertained the idea that it really was Zander, back from the dead as promised, but no—he never knocked on a door with a rhythm other than "shave and a haircut—two bits." She left the bags on the bed and went to answer. Hannah stood in the corridor, silently crying—thinking about what had happened after she'd knocked on this same door not twenty-four hours before.

Eve closed her eyes and clutched the doorframe, trying to collect herself. The two stood like that for several seconds before Hannah whispered, "I'm sorry."

Eve lifted her shoulders and then dropped them hard to release a sigh. "Why are you here?" she asked.

"I wanted to say I'm sorry," Hannah said.

"You've said that," Eve replied. "Is that all?"

"I didn't know what he was gonna do," Hannah said. "B–but I didn't *not* know either. I shouldn't have gone along with it. I should've told Darren no."

"Darren? Which one was he?"

"The one that crazy girl shot in the head."

Eve pursed her lips and looked at the floor. "There you go. All's well that ends well."

"I really thought—maybe if I wished for it, I could undo some of the wrong and get him back."

A door two rooms down opened and a round, middle-aged woman stepped into the hall.

"But demons lie, don't they? That's what they do," Eve said.

The woman screwed up her face and hurried the other direction.

Eve folded her arms and leaned her shoulder on the frame. "So, what now?" she asked.

Hannah didn't understand. "Excuse me?"

"Well, the chief seemed to have this grand plan of covering every goddamn thing up and going back to normal. So, I'm curious—not really, mind you. Mostly, I don't give a shit. But you at least said you're sorry, and you're still standing there. I'm guessing you want to tell me about the changes you're going to make. Unless you're planning on busting the whole thing wide open. Probably not, though, right?"

Hannah looked at her and bit her lip. "I want to run," she said. "Desperately. But if I did, I'd just end up 'here' somewhere else." She shook her head slowly. A laugh popped between sniffles and she wiped her eyes. "My father is an optometrist." She blinked and frowned and shrugged. She backed away, shook her head again, and then turned to leave.

Britt pulled the Rover into the drive and turned off the engine.

"Thanks for driving, hon," Walt said. His favored side still worked, but they'd given him a strong dose of painkillers at the hospital (stronger than they'd given her). "Wait," he said as she reached for the door handle. He tried to turn toward her but the pain in his shoulder and the obstruction of the monitor sticking up from the center console made it impossible. "I want you to know that—that this is over. I don't mean just all the bad stuff...

the demon. That's done with, obviously. I mean me. I'm sorry about the terrible things I said to you this morning. Not just that, but the way I've neglected you all these months. I get it now. Your mom is gone. And we're still here." He hunched his wounded shoulder and winced at the pain. "I guess it took getting shot to remind me of that."

Britt turned her head to look forward. "Scars are cool, Dad."

He chuckled. "Well, thanks, I—"

"No, Dad. *Scars* are cool." She held up her hand, finally stitched and bandaged correctly. "Being down half a finger for the rest of your life? Not so cool." Her severed digit could not be located. Tim had dropped it before they moved Connor into the church. Police had found the paper towel it had been wrapped in, but not the finger. They assumed an animal had made off with it.

Britt opened the door and got out of the car. Walt chased after her, saying, "I know, honey. You didn't deserve—"

She wheeled around and cut him off. "Christ, no one gets what they deserve, Dad. Did you even think of it? Kate and Charlie Belores have lost *both* their kids now. Maybe they were too damn strict, or, hell, maybe too damn nice—I really don't know—but they didn't deserve that, did they?"

Walt kicked at the ground, shaking his head. "It's a hell of a thing to lose... to lose that much," he said, and then asked, "Do you think I should get what I deserve?"

"God." Britt rubbed her forehead with the heel of her palm. Her hand dropped and she regarded her father. "You know what, Dad? For all that you paid into it, for all that you made other people suffer for it, I really wish that you would have gotten Mom back. I really do—for your sake. Because you needed each other and I... I didn't. I don't. And I'm okay. You get that?" She opened her arms and turned her palms up, one naked, one wrapped. She scanned the sky, shaking her head and laughing through tears. "I'm okay! Gwen thought I needed to rebel—she thought I *had* to be angry at authority and restrictions because of the house I grew up in. But I didn't, and I wasn't. And *I* thought there was something wrong with me because I didn't hurt enough when Mom died. But all that worrying whether it was enough or not was just me masking over the pain I *did* feel. Pain that was mine to suffer or dismiss or do whatever I wanted to do with it. Look, I'm sure I sound selfish. Just young and naive and selfish. That's probably right. And maybe that's what I'm supposed to be at my age. But I'm trying to be honest, and I hope we've both learned that honesty is essential, if we're gonna live together for ten more months, or if we're ever gonna talk again after I'm gone."

Walt looked at her, unsure of what to say. He thought he should be angry with her, or ashamed of himself at deserving every word she'd said. Or he could say something positive about honesty. But mostly he was struck by how she was right: They didn't affect each other the way the world had taught them they were supposed to. So, what did he do with that?

"It's late," he said, before remembering the sun had set only an hour ago. He corrected himself, "It's been a long day."

"Yes, it has," Britt agreed. She turned and looked at the facade of the only home she'd ever known. "And this is where I sleep."

The porch's wooden stairs creaked as they ascended. Britt moved aside to let her father unlock the door. He pushed it open and stepped back to let her in. She began up the stairs to her room wearily, then stopped and turned back. Walt waited.

"I think Bobbi likes you," Britt said.

"N o matter what: Sunday night, we're back home," Eve said to herself.

There was her house, with its timer-controlled porchlight on. There was a neighbor she didn't know walking his dog. She heard a car horn honk in the distance. What happened to her couldn't be real.

Her phone rang. The display advised her the Adler Police Department was calling. She felt violated that they could reach her here, in the waking world, from their picturesque nightmare town cradled by the Allegheny National Forest.

"Hello," she answered.

"Mrs. Nowlan, it's Officer Tuttle from the Adler Police Department. Uh, John. I'm calling you because we think we've located the scene where... where your husband was."

He left off "murdered," Eve thought.

"Mrs. Nowlan?"

"Yes, I'm here."

"We were informed he'd been taken to the field house at the park where the first victim was discovered."

Where the first sacrifice was disturbed, she thought. Where the man who got his brains blown out had to set up another one, not with just the head and the heart like she had done, but with the whole... the whole body. "Kit and kaboodle," Zander would have said.

"We've taken some blood samples to test to, um, verify the story the young woman told us. If they match up, then we should be able to issue a death certificate."

Eve blinked. Most of his words were more nightmare falsehoods, so she'd let them drift, only vaguely paying attention. But the last part stuck. "Wait, what?"

"We have the blood—"

"Yes, I heard that part. W-why wouldn't you be able to issue a death certificate?"

"Mrs. Nowlan, we have the statement from Miss Linscomb, but we haven't yet discovered your husband's body."

He started to say something else, but she cut him off. "I have to go."

She got out of the car and shut the door. She paused there, looking at her house, listening to the rustle of the neighborhood, to the jingle of a dog's name tags. She left everything in the car. Maybe if she left it all outside, it couldn't despoil her home.

A chill of apprehension overwhelmed her as she unlocked the door (un*locked* the door, she emphasized to herself). What was she scared of (admitting, at last, this was no dream)—that he had come back? She never *knew* he was dead to begin with. (Yes, she did, she told herself. She knew, because that's the sort of thing you're supposed to sense somehow, and she had sensed it.) But so what? If he was back… The words echoed again, spoken by that thing, repeated by her… *only fairness is unnatural.*

He sat upright on the sofa, facing the television, powered down. Copper brown stained his shirt front.

"Zander?" Eve asked tentatively.

He shook and gulped air, as though suddenly roused from sleep. He blinked and then turned his head to look at her. His gaze searched her face anxiously. She realized he was afraid. He chuckled nervously. "I'm sorry, did I fall asleep in the car?"

She eased closer, then answered, "Yes."

"Wow," he said. "I don't remember… I don't remember leaving the park." He grimaced, searching the blank spaces inside.

She swallowed and asked, "What *do* you remember?"

He rubbed his head, hoping to dislodge a memory. Orange crumbs dropped onto the carpet. He looked at them confusedly.

"We saw that ghost last night," he said. He looked at his leg. "My knee is better." He gave her a quizzical look. "Why did we leave a day early?"

"You weren't feeling well," she said. She crossed to him slowly and hesitantly extended her hand to touch his arm. It was warm. She raised her hand and rubbed her fingers together, feeling a slightly tacky residue. "You're a mess. Let's get you cleaned up, okay?"

"I wasn't feeling well? Should I go see the doctor?"

"I expect you'll sleep through the whole day tomorrow and be right as rain," Eve said, backing away as he stood.

"'Right as rain,'" he repeated. "What… what a strange thing to say."

"It's a funny saying," she agreed.

"Funny," he repeated.

He took a shower. She offered to make him something to eat and he agreed he was starving, though he only ate half of the grilled cheese and tomato that she prepared for him. They sat on the couch together and watched a series of prime-time game shows. She looked at him frequently (and she hoped, inconspicuously). Several times, he seemed about to ask something, but then stopped. She was afraid to ask him anything besides, "Are you okay?" a few times.

"Yeah," was all he said in reply, though never with conviction.

Finally, almost dreading to do so, she asked him, "Do you want to go to bed?"

He answered absently, "You go ahead. I'll be up in a few minutes."

Eve changed into a loose tank top and soft sweatpants. She brushed her teeth and wiped her face clean and went to the bathroom. She turned off the bedroom light and got in bed. But she couldn't get to sleep. She couldn't even imagine it, tired as she was. She stared at the open doorway. Half an hour later the television shut off, followed by one of the downstairs lights.

Then, after a minute more, she heard a familiar soft tread coming up the stairs.

THE END

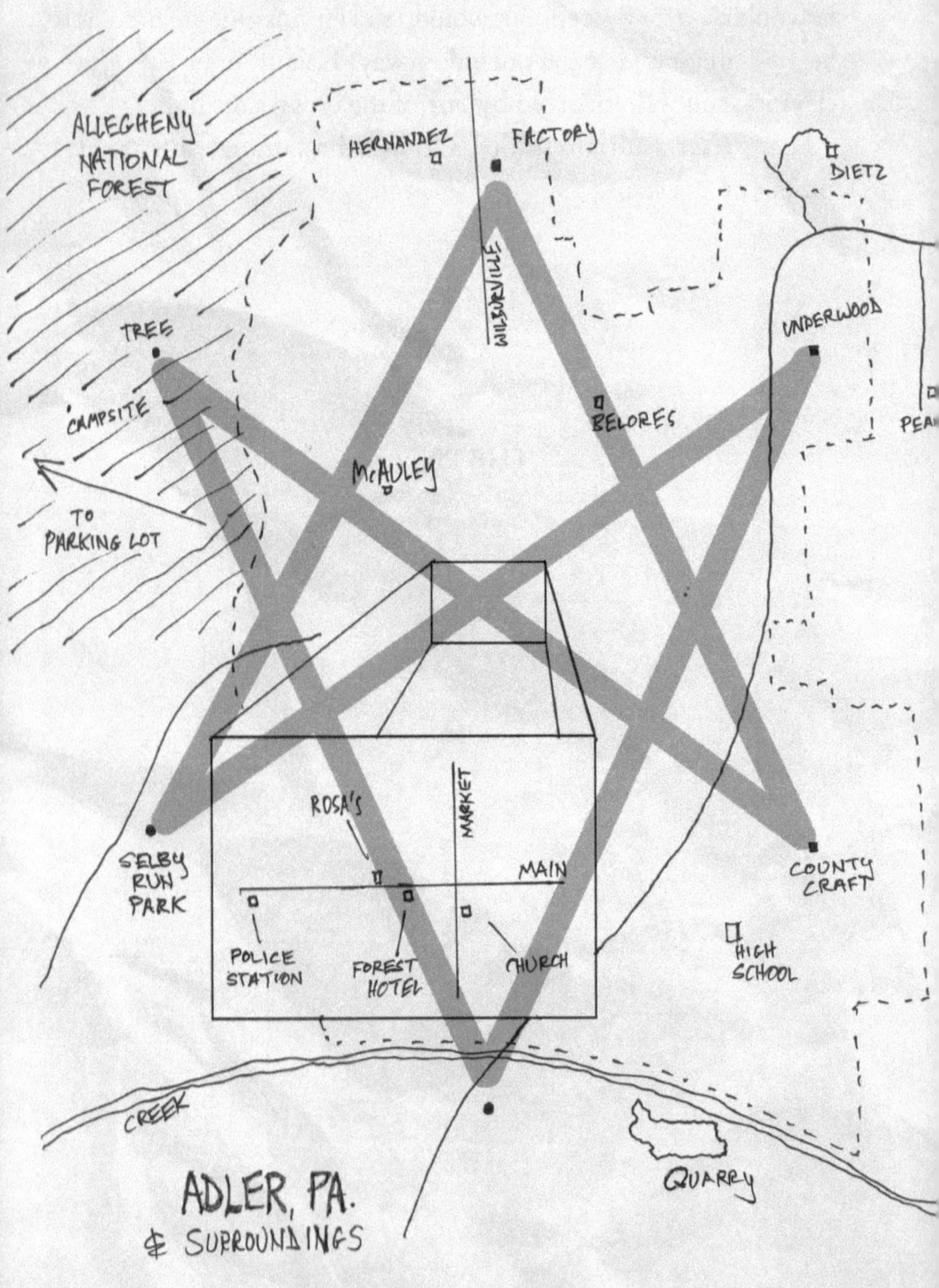

ALLEGHENY NATIONAL FOREST
HERNANDEZ
FACTORY
DIETZ
TREE
UNDERWOOD
CAMPSITE
BELORES
TO PARKING LOT
McAULEY
WILSONVILLE
PEA
ROSA'S
MARKET
SELBY RUN PARK
MAIN
COUNTY CRAFT
POLICE STATION
FOREST HOTEL
CHURCH
HIGH SCHOOL
CREEK
QUARRY
ADLER, PA.
& SURROUNDINGS

Jason A. Wyckoff is the author of two short story collections published by Tartarus Press, *Black Horse and other Strange Stories* (2012) and *The Hidden Back Room* (2016). His work has appeared in numerous anthologies and journals. He earned a Bachelor of Music degree in composition from Ohio State University, which is why he works in an office. He lives in Columbus, Ohio, USA. Married, with cats. IXIXIKLIS is his first published novel.

Special Thanks

I would like to thank Susan Russell and Kasey from Grendel Press
for helping to bring this book into being.

www.ingramcontent.com/pod-product-compliance
Lightning Source LLC
Chambersburg PA
CBHW031206310726
48969CB00001B/239